ELIZABETH WILSON, an independent researcher and writer best known for her commentaries on feminism and popular culture, is currently Visiting Professor at the London College of Fashion. She is the author of several non-fiction books, including *Adorned in Dreams: Fashion and Modernity*, and has written two other crime novels, *The Lost Time Café* and *Poisoned Hearts*.

The Twilight Hour

Elizabeth Wilson

A complete catalogue record for this book can be obtained
from the British Library on request

The right of Elizabeth Wilson to be identified as the
author of this work has been asserted by her in accordance
with the Copyright, Designs and Patents Act 1988

Copyright © 2006 by Elizabeth Wilson

First published in the UK in 2006 by
Serpent's Tail, 4 Blackstock Mews, London N4 2BT
Website: www.serpentstail.com

Designed and typeset by Sue Lamble
Printed by Mackays of Chatham, plc

10 9 8 7 6 5 4 3 2 1

Thanks for their help and support to the usual suspects, and especially Ellie.

prologue

◻◼◼◼◼◼◼◼◻

AFTERWARDS, YOU RETCHED WITH LAUGHTER. The sound ripped through the stagnant air. Then silence seeped back, stifling. Solitude; a moment before there'd been two of you, but now you were alone.

It had been more difficult than you'd expected. It had been so intimate. You'd had to *embrace* the unconscious body, as you leant over, touched and ministered, as if you were saving, not ending a life. You pressed and pressed until you thought your arms would give way and the breath would burst from your lungs. *You* were the one gasping for air. It was hand-to-hand combat with a primitive force, a blind, unthinking will to live, distinct from the shell that housed it, a force that fought and struggled and clung to that body as you crushed the life out of it.

At last it gave up the ghost and left its inert and cloddish house of flesh just lying there stupidly. You staggered back. Who was it, laughing and laughing? Who was it standing there, turned to stone?

But you had to get on. There was still so much to do. You shook yourself back into life. You rearranged the body so that it looked less peculiar, more *natural*. You found a half-empty bottle of brandy on the floor and poured it around in the hope of disguising the smell. All the while you hurried, because you had to find what you'd come for, the things you needed so desperately. You wished now you'd talked more beforehand. There was so much you didn't know.

Too late for talk now. You searched everywhere, in cupboards, in boxes and cases and drawers. You hadn't expected so much *stuff*, it took much longer than you'd thought. And you hadn't expected to be so clumsy, and as you dropped things and tripped on the rubbish you were terrified someone would hear. The place was empty, but you kept stopping to listen for the sound of a key in the lock, for voices, a footstep on the stair.

Finally, when you'd almost given up hope, you found what you were looking for – but one thing was missing, the most important thing of all. *It wasn't there.*

You dared not look any longer. You had to get away. You clicked the door shut, crept down the stairs and stepped out into the freezing afternoon. It would soon be getting dark. You pulled your hat down and hurried away, but not walking too quickly, trying to look casual and ordinary.

From now on you'd listen to the wireless and buy a paper every day. Of course, it might not make the national news. Not that it mattered; there was nothing to worry about, nothing to connect you to that room and its sightless body, nothing, that is, but the very thing that gave you perfect protection.

Then you had a huge piece of luck, your first real lucky break – after all those years of being the unlucky one. It was in the news all right, the very next morning, but for a very different reason. You laughed and laughed again as the irony of it sank in. It must have been *meant*; no need to worry any more that what you'd done would catch up with you. The past was wiped out and now there was only the future. Your new life, your *real* life, the one you'd so nearly been cheated of, could begin.

one

◻◼◻◼◼◼◼◻◻

THE DAY HIROSHIMA WAS BOMBED I WEPT. The war was over. There'd be crowds singing in the street, they'd be waving flags in Trafalgar Square and doing the conga down Whitehall and cheering the King and Queen in front of Buckingham Palace – while I was in despair because the end of the war meant the end of my independence. I'd have to go home and live with my parents – like young women had done in that prehistoric era: Before the War.

Of course I was glad we'd won the war! Of course I was! But – I'd never be able to live on my own in London now it was all over. In the year since I'd left my boarding school, life in London had propelled me dizzily into adult life. The Nazis' new rocket, the doodlebug, whizzed out of the air without warning; you had to live for the moment, but the strange thing was that the big threat of war made everything else seem safe. I had no fear as I trod the blacked-out streets, the light from my torch veiled with tissue paper. My feet scrunched on glass and I passed craters and gaping holes where buildings should have been, but hope and excitement bubbled up within me as I made for my latest rendezvous.

Now the war was over and with it my new life. I'd be

going back to Hampshire. The mushroom clouds of the atom bomb darkened the future as the truth of its devastation slowly leaked out. The blackout curtains had been down for nearly a year, but I contemplated my future prospects with deepening gloom.

Then I met Alan and the sun shone again. Marriage: it was the ideal solution.

. . . .

Cigarette smoke fogged the air, but at least it was warm in the pub, hot in fact. I loosened my musquash coat. Alan smiled down at me.

'What'll you have?'

'Cherry brandy please.' Huddled in with the crowd at the bar, I looked round, excited. Already I was drunk with the voices, the drifting smoke, the warm orange light and the familiar faces. There was the drunken old painter, smelling of pee, who muttered 'Got any mun?' – money – as she leered up at Alan, then swerved away. Maclaren-Ross at the far end of the bar held court as usual, his cigarette holder at an aggressive angle. Hair swept back, eyes bloodshot, coat shabby, his lordly manner negated it all, force of will trumping reality.

There was a blast of freezing air as the door opened and shut. Hugh waved. With Colin he surged towards us, slapped Alan on the back and then bent with parodied homage over my hand. 'Dinah! You look stunning this evening.' He turned to Alan. 'The usual for me.'

'They've run out. There's whisky, though.'

Colin, only recently demobbed, continued to wear his army greatcoat, which made him look larger than ever. He towered over me, with his horn-rimmed spectacles and shock of blond hair, savagely shaved up the nape of his neck, but erupting in massive waves above his forehead in a parody of an Eton crop. You could just imagine him striding about in the Spanish Civil War, he was so impressive, distinguished, commanding. Alan said he was tremendously clever; and a Communist. Cleverness and communism, which seemed mysteriously linked, surrounded him with an alarming aura, and I was afraid he thought I was stupid.

Now we were wedged round a table with our drinks. Hugh's face was alert with expectation. 'Enescu's promised to look in.'

'The Romanian?' Colin frowned. '*House of Shadows*? That Enescu?'

'The very same, old dear. As if there could be more than one.'

Colin looked from Hugh to Alan and back again. 'Why are we meeting *him*?'

Hugh's thin face broke into a smile. He tossed the long lock of hair foppishly back from his forehead. 'We're cultivating him,' he said. 'Good idea, eh? Working with the director of the moment?'

'Why haven't you told me about this?' Colin looked very put out.

'I met him by chance – I just took the initiative, that's all.'

Colin raised his eyebrows. 'You should have asked me – after all, I know Romania, I was there, remember? The most fascist nation on earth.'

Hugh smiled winningly. 'That's probably why he left.'

'Oh, really? Rather depends on when he left, doesn't it? When did he leave, by the way?'

Hugh didn't know.

'He just wants to make films,' said Alan mildly. 'Not much chance of that in Romania at the moment.' He put a hand on Colin's arm. 'You're right. We should have discussed it first, but Hugh just happened to meet him – it was too good an opportunity to miss. And they say he's brilliant at getting money, so ... we took the plunge.' He paused. 'Is Romania really the most fascist country? More than Germany?'

Colin didn't reply. He was still scowling. Alan and Hugh exchanged looks.

'It's just a drink, old man.' Alan patted his shoulder.

'We haven't been plotting behind your back.' But this remark of Hugh's seemed to irritate Colin even more.

I sympathised with Colin, because I felt excluded too. I did sometimes feel they treated me like a child. I was a married woman, after all, even if I was only twenty. But then again, they were so much older. Alan was thirty. That had worried my father. I know about these things, he'd said – he didn't do divorce work himself, but as a barrister he knew all about it. The war's caused havoc with marriage, he said and wanted us to wait, but I threatened to go off and live in sin or elope, so he more or less had to give his consent.

Well, anyway – I didn't care if the three of them ignored me. The prospect of meeting a film director was thrilling.

They were still arguing. 'Rossellini; *Rome, Open City*, now that's cinema! Enescu's film is just Transylvanian gothic rubbish.' Colin could be awfully pompous.

'Your ideological slip is showing, old man,' said Alan. 'You have to admit it was pretty atmospheric.'

The door opened and shut continually. The extremes of heat and cold made me feel feverish, desperately excited, I was unsure what about.

'I thought *House of Shadows* was beautiful,' I said. 'Chilling, actually.'

'*She's* coming,' said Hugh with a flirtatious glance sideways, as though that would win Colin round. 'Of course, she can't really act, but she does look wonderful.' But Colin frowned even more.

'She?' I looked from one to the other of my three musketeers. Alan smiled kindly.

'Gwendolen Grey.'

'The star!' I looked round at them. 'Why are you laughing? She was marvellous. How thrilling to meet her!'

'Darling,' said Alan, 'Miranda in *The Tempest*! "Oh brave new world" and all that. I wish I were young again.'

'You're only thirty! That's not old.'

More friendly laughter: 'Oh yes it is,' said Hugh, 'I feel terrible when I wake up in the morning. I bet you just leap out of bed, Dinah.'

'Not if I have anything to do with it,' said Alan.

I blushed. Anyway, we all knew it was a question of experience, rather than age itself. Alan and Hugh had been with the Crown Film Unit pretty much all through the war, so they hadn't seen active service as Colin had, but they'd been right through the Blitz, and risked their lives doing fire duty and all that sort of thing. Besides, before the war they'd already been adults: students at Cambridge and involved in all the politics of that time; Alan had *nearly* gone to Spain to fight Franco in the Spanish Civil War. And Colin really had!

And where had I been? At boarding school in the windswept wastes of East Anglia, where the war had meant merely boredom and a sense of thwarted rebellion. Even a year in the lowliest reaches of the War Office couldn't compare with what they'd been through, the V2 doodlebugs notwithstanding. Although I'd been thirteen when war broke out, I hardly remembered what life had been like before 1939. Everything had always been: For the Duration of the War.

Then, finally, the Duration ended. The war was over. Perhaps it was because I was older now, a grown-up married woman, but the strange thing was, quite soon, everything seemed almost worse than the war itself. The joy and relief of victory leaked away and – well, abroad it seemed so grim, with the concentration camps and refugees all over Europe, and starvation, and a sort of dark cloud all over eastern Europe that was Soviet Russia. Meanwhile at home, in a different way the Duration still carried on: the queues and the drabness, the shortages and the discomfort, but without beating the Germans to give it all meaning.

My new rackety life with Alan outweighed all that, though. Life in London was absolutely thrilling.

The men had stopped arguing. Colin was outlining his plan for a film about refugees in Europe. He'd been all over the place, seen what was going on. It angered him that Germans were actually fleeing the Russian-occupied eastern zone. His face darkened. 'They don't know what's good for them,' he muttered.

'Some of the Russian troops are pretty brutal, I heard,' said Hugh with a sly smile, hoping to provoke, but Colin had turned away.

'They're here,' he said in a completely different tone of voice.

A lull in the braying and chatter cleared a zone of quiet recognition around the film star. She was flanked by two men, positioned just behind her like a minor entourage, and was smaller than I'd expected. Nor was she beautiful exactly, and certainly not pretty; but the heavy-lidded eyes in her sad oval face suggested dark, tragic romance. And there was a brightness about her, setting her apart from the grey, postwar faces. Perhaps it was nothing more than good make-up, but because I'd seen her only in black and white on celluloid, her blue-black hair, blue eyes and white skin seemed vivid beneath her black astrakhan hat. With her red lips and spiky lashes she reminded me of the stepmother in *Snow White*.

It was only a moment; then the waves of talk rose as the

newcomers bore down on our table. There was confusion; chairs scraped back, Alan, Colin and Hugh stood up, drinks were obtained, the circle widened. Eventually we were all sitting rather uncomfortably, knees squashed together, chair legs entangled. I inhaled her scent. It was heavy, intoxicating.

'I love your scent,' I said, daring.

'*L'Heure Bleue*,' she murmured, as if letting me into a secret: the twilight hour. Then: 'Have you met Radu before?'

I shook my head and she and I both stared at the director, cornered by Alan and Hugh. My mother would have said he was a bit too good looking; in a bad mood my father might have used the word 'dago'.

Radu Enescu certainly looked a bit spivvy, but perhaps it was just his astrakhan coat and the thick wavy hair oiled back from his forehead. His chestnut brown eyes darted around as he listened, bent slightly towards Alan because of the noise. A half smile curved his full red lips and when he laughed he showed dazzling white teeth. For a moment his eyes met mine and I felt the electric shock of his attention. Looking into my soul – or just undressing me; I wasn't sure which.

Colin looked on in belligerent silence. I wondered if he was going to pick a quarrel. He simply could not resist a political argument. But he suddenly turned his back and spoke to the third member of their party, whose name I hadn't heard. He too looked out of place in his pin-striped suit, among the Wheatsheaf crowd with their tweed jackets, corduroy and mouldy polo necks. Perhaps Gwendolen Grey and her escorts had been to some grand restaurant for dinner.

Colin said: 'Not your usual watering hole? You're in films too?'

The stranger smiled. 'I'm in the property business.' His grey homburg hat sat on his knees.

Colin bristled – well, perhaps not visibly, but I knew it

would rile him. A real-life capitalist: Colin hated those. He held out his silver cigarette case. The man with the homburg hat shook his head. 'Thanks. I don't.'

I put out a hand. 'What about me? Please?'

'I'm so sorry, of course.'

The non-smoking stranger had a lighter all the same, and it flared swiftly as he held it towards me. As I bent to the flame I lightly touched my hand over his, a sophisticated gesture I'd only just acquired. 'I'm sorry, I didn't hear your name,' I said.

'Stanley Colman.'

'I'm Dinah Wentworth.' I nodded my head towards Alan. 'He's my husband.'

He looked me over, seemed to find something amusing. 'You often come here? Bit noisy, isn't it?'

'I don't mind. I like it.' I more than liked it; it was our social centre, *the* place to be. 'We come here all the time,' I said proudly, 'we're regulars.'

Gwendolen Grey suddenly spoke, addressing Colin. 'Stan has money to burn. He wants to invest in films. Talk to him. You'll find he's very generous.' She spoke with a kind of proprietorial contempt. Her diction was perfect, yet her voice had a metallic edge to it. I found myself thinking of a rusty blade, something harsh. It hadn't jarred like that in the film – or I hadn't noticed, anyway.

'Not so fast, Gwenny. I thought you wanted me to underwrite Radu's latest plan.'

'I'd rather you didn't call me Gwenny, sweetie.'

Colin unbent a little. 'Are you seriously interested in films?' Either he no longer cared that he was dealing with an evil capitalist, or else ambition had driven out doubt. Anyway, as he'd already told me more than once, for a Communist the end justifies the means.

'So which one is your husband?' the rusty voice

murmured. She made me feel terribly shy. 'Alan – Alan Wentworth.' I smiled bashfully sideways.

'Yes, but which one is he, angel? I can't tell them apart.'

'The one with black hair.'

'Lucky you – the handsome one.'

I felt myself blushing, which was ridiculous, but I couldn't help it. 'Oh … I don't know,' I stammered, but of course Alan *was* good looking with his beautiful straight nose, rosy skin and narrow eyes – something about those dark eyes signalled intelligence.

'And what do you do?'

'Do?' Now my voice sounded squeaky. Normally I was quite confident, but for some reason she made me feel shy. 'Well – nothing much – at the moment. We haven't been married long.' I hesitated. Did I dare say it or would I look idiotic? I had to take the chance: 'What I really want to do is act.'

It was as if she hadn't heard. I felt snubbed by her blank silence. Still, I had to keep my end up, so I tried flattery. 'I just loved your film. I thought you acted so beautifully.'

'Thank you,' she said, but she didn't seem especially pleased. 'Really, you know, it was all due to Radu. It's the director who makes a film, the actors are so very secondary.' She was watching the Romanian as she spoke. 'He has an extraordinary talent, you know.' She stared across the table at Enescu for a moment. Then her tragic gaze beamed itself at me. 'You should talk to him about acting. He might find you a part.'

This was so exciting I could hardly speak. 'Oh – ' and my voice came out all squeaky, 'that's … thank you! Thank you so much.'

The men were all still listening to Colin's pitch. Perhaps Gwendolen Grey didn't like not having the full attention of all the men in the vicinity, for as soon as Colin finished speaking, she murmured: 'Chuck me a cigarette, would you, angel?' And she smiled at him. 'Colin, is it?'

Colin sprang to attention, but I could tell she wasn't his type. Colin was a bit of a dark horse where women were concerned; or perhaps it was just that he was too serious to flirt.

Later we walked in a crowd up Charlotte Street to Tommy's basement café. It was a steamy, dirty, friendly place. Mother would have thought it dreadfully unhygienic, but the pub shut at ten, so if the conversations and projects and plans and gossip were to continue it was Tommy's or nothing.

Stanley Colman stared around with a look of amusement – you could tell he felt he was slumming – tipped the homburg hat back on his head, then removed it altogether. I hadn't noticed before, but he was good looking. He had masses of curly hair, a noble face, a Grecian profile and his greenish eyes with their long lashes tinged his expression with melancholy. He had broad shoulders too, but he wasn't as tall as you'd expect if you saw him sitting down; the lower half of his body dwindled away to short legs. Still, I liked the way he stood, planted firmly on his feet, what you might call a commanding presence.

We sat at two rickety tables. Tommy's minion, a weedy-looking boy of about fifteen, came over and wiped the shiny tablecloths. Soon he returned with thick, chipped white plates piled with bacon and eggs, fried cabbage and bread and fried potatoes. There was tea in mugs. Our new friends weren't eating. The two men ordered coffee, but when it came, Enescu nearly choked. 'You call this coffee? My God, you British. Never have I eaten such terrible food,' he said tactlessly. 'I tell you, in the war, and during my escape, and all through Europe, never, never did I eat food so terrible as what I eat since I come here. Your food is a crime!'

I felt a faint, resentful flicker of patriotic pride. Didn't he know we'd had rationing, shortages, fair shares? That's how we'd won the war. And I'd heard that the French had had to make coffee out of acorns. But before I could speak Colin cut in.

'Fighting the Nazis, were you?' he enquired in a dangerously neutral voice. I stared at Alan, willing him to head Colin off, but Enescu smiled dazzlingly. 'One day I hope to make a film on this subject. The time is not yet. What you and I – ' and with the hand holding his cigarette he gestured at their circle – 'what we should be doing is a different project. I am telling you, the success of my film, this is what should be pursued. People are wanting fantasy, escape, beauty. They are not yet ready to hear more about the war, about horrors. Later that will come. For now it is romance, excitement, yes, but in history – historical drama. Look at Olivier in *Henry the Fifth*.'

Alan said, rather ponderously: 'But that was about *this* war in a way. It was extremely patriotic.'

Radu smiled harder than ever. 'Your Gainsborough films then – *The Wicked Lady*! What a film. A tragedy Gwendolen has not starred in this film. Margaret Lockwood was okay, she was good fun, you might say, but with Gwendolen – ' and he kissed the tips of his fingers – 'it would have been unbelievable.'

I waited for the explosion. I knew they all despised the Gainsborough films, tosh for housewives, they thought those costume dramas. But there was merely a chilly silence.

'What subject exactly,' began Alan cautiously, 'had you in mind?'

Radu looked round at them. He must have caught the atmosphere, for he changed tack. 'Maybe it is possible – the refugee idea. But this has to be done in dramatic way, romance, passion. Otherwise, it is too much for audiences.'

All the while, Gwendolen Grey smoked languidly.

'How did you get into films?' I asked her.

Her long lips curved in a faint smile. 'Oh, it's a long story.'

A story she evidently wasn't going to tell me.

· · · · · · · · ·

Someone had heard about a party. We all squeezed into the back of Stanley Colman's Bentley. I was on Alan's knee. Gwendolen Grey sat in the front.

The party was in a lofty, battered stucco terrace overlooking Regent's Park. We passed under the scaffolding that seemed to be keeping the house from collapsing altogether, and trudged up magnificent flights of stairs. Bomb damage had torn the plaster away from the walls in places and the lower floors looked uninhabitable. A howling draught came through badly boarded up windows from which all the glass had long since been blown out. It was not completely dark, for candles had been perilously placed at intervals on the stairs and sent long shadows up the walls.

At the top of the house the windows had somehow remained intact, held together by criss-crossed strips of brown sticky paper. You could still feel the wind coming up through the floorboards, but that didn't matter. The rooms were jammed.

'We're drinking home-made mead,' said our host. I hadn't met him before, but he knew Hugh.

Enescu, Stanley Colman and Gwendolen Grey followed along behind. Heads turned when Gwendolen appeared in the doorway. It wasn't that everyone recognised her, so much as that her strange looks couldn't pass unnoticed. She slayed them, just as she'd slayed the crowd in the Wheatsheaf.

She and I left our coats in a little side room. 'Who are

these people?' said Gwendolen in a low voice.

'I don't know them! We're practically gate crashing.'

'Your friends – your husband – ' Gwen put a hand on my arm. Her voice was hoarse and low. 'Stanley's taking them for a ride, you know. He's only interested in films because of me.' I stared at her, surprised and discouraged. It was the very opposite of what she'd said earlier. 'Radu might get something out of him, but I doubt if he has as much as he claims. Men like him, they're all so boastful. That's how they make their money in the first place.' She put her hand – such long, dark red nails – on my arm. The hand looked so white against my dark blue velvet sleeve. 'Still, Enescu deserves the money,' she said. 'He's a genius. You know that.'

Her sudden change of mood startled me. But it was less a change of mood than a feeling that the different things she said didn't quite add up; there was something dislocated about her. Perhaps that was part of being an actress. Now, she changed again. She turned to the mirror and patted her hair. 'Are you in love with your husband?' She paused again. 'Oh – I'm sorry, I've shocked you. Of course you are!' She leaned against the wall. 'I suppose you'll be having babies.'

I felt myself blushing, thinking of the awkward, grown-up business of birth control, French letters, or the slippery dutch cap, and that other, more shocking method, causing first pain, but then a fiercer, darker thrill, a rush of sensation that left me shaken. 'Well, perhaps not quite yet, but … of course I expect … eventually …'

'Don't,' she said coldly. And moved away into the room where the party was in full swing. I followed her, but at a distance. Our little group had stuck together, the men still talking film business. Gwendolen sank onto a sofa. A couple of admirers bent towards her. The mead was very sweet. I stood near the door, drinking greedily.

A rotund man with wild carrot curls and a pink face reeled against the wall beside me. 'I say – haven't got a cigarette, have you?'

I silently passed him my packet. He lit up. 'Just had a bit of a shock. Saw my ex. She bloody cut me dead. That's a bit rich, don't you think? Didn't even *acknowledge my existence*.' He giggled. 'Who are you anyway?' He leaned close to me.

Close to, he smelled of drink and that ear-wax smell, the smell of a man who doesn't wash a lot. I glanced at my friends, but they'd forgotten about me. I didn't care; I could flirt with this rather unsavoury specimen of manhood. 'I'm Dinah. Who are you?'

'Who am I?' He giggled again. 'What a very existential question. Who – am – I! Name's Titus Mavor, dearie, ex-gentleman, ex-communist, ex-Surrealist, ex-painter, ex-hausted.' With that he planted a pudgy hand on my breast and made an attempt to kiss me.

Already things had gone too far. I didn't think I could cope in my present state. The mead was making me feel woozy, and, worse than woozy, queasy. I feared I might actually be going to be sick. 'Excuse me,' I muttered and tried to move away.

'Wassa matter?' He looked at me blearily. 'Cocktails too much for you? That silly ass Simon spiked the drinks with Benzedrine. Said it'd make the party go with a swing.'

Now I was feeling I really might be sick. I pushed past him and made for the passage, hoping there'd be a lavatory close by, but instead I found myself in the room with the coats, and lay down. The bed at once swooped up – up in the air and then sank down – down, then up – up and down again. I lay there with my eyes closed. Either I should soon be sick, or the feeling would pass off.

Dimly I heard voices in the corridor. I listened, to take my mind off the nausea.

'Mavor, isn't it? I'm Noel Valentine. I've been trying to get hold of you. I'm an art dealer – I believe you own some paintings that – '

'Of course I own some paintings – I'm a bloody painter, aren't I?'

'Naturally your own work would be of interest, but ... I heard ...'

The bed was still lurching up and down like a ship in a storm.

' ... major Surrealists ...'

'Wassa supposed to mean ... 'm a *major Surrealist* in m'own ... are you saying ...'

'I was just interested ... just a proposition – '

'Oh, push off, you ... wretched little ... uaargh – '

Someone invaded the room, my refuge. It was the redhead again. He fell heavily on the end of the bed. 'Oh – ' he reared up and looked blearily in my direction, 'didn't see you at first. Feeling rotten? Home-made alcohol is the devil, it really is. Got a fearful headache myself.' He began to stroke my foot. That was the last thing I needed.

I pulled my foot away, almost kicking him. 'Please don't do that!'

'Don't be such a frigid little bitch.' But then he keeled forward, and was sick. 'Need the lavatory ...' He rose, swaying, to his feet. 'If you'll excuse me ... feeling a little strange ... think I'll just ...'

He staggered towards the doorway and toppled through it. A moment later I heard more violent retching.

The next thing I knew Alan was standing over me. 'You all right? I couldn't think where you'd gone.' He looked at me sternly, and, as so often, I felt he was accusing me of something, that whatever it was must be my fault. 'They're leaving,' he said. 'Gwendolen's had enough. They'll give us a lift if we go with them. You don't want to stay, do you?'

I shook my head. I sat up slowly. I was feeling a little better. I stood up, staggering slightly.

Alan steered me downstairs. 'That mead was pretty lethal.'

Outside, the freezing air sobered me up. I took a great gulp of it, but then nearly slipped on the ice. It was so cold – colder than I ever remembered it.

We crushed ourselves into the car again. Stanley Colman dropped Gwendolen and the Romanian near Marble Arch. Hugh replaced Gwendolen in the front seat.

We drove on through the freezing wastes of London. It was one o'clock in the morning. And in spite of feeling sick, I was so happy. Life was so exciting; new things happening all the time.

I'd never have dreamed how quickly it was all going to get much too exciting – excitement toppling over into dark hysteria.

two

■□■■■■■■□

THAT WAS THE BEGINNING OF THE GREAT FREEZE. It was darkest winter, dark, endless winter. Every time you left the house you faced ice, blizzards, biting wind. Simply to keep going was an effort. Standing in the queue for rations was torture. By the end of February there'd been twenty-one straight days with no sunshine. Disaster and bankruptcy threatened as the nation ground to a standstill. Coal couldn't get to the power stations. The trains couldn't run. There were fuel cuts, no electricity. Street lighting returned to blackout levels. London became a black and grey world of frozen shadows.

Yet there was a thrill in these *extremes* and I wasn't going to be a prisoner in this undiscovered country, even if I risked slipping and breaking a leg the moment I set foot outside the front door (precipitous steps). Alan worried when I went out on my own, not because of fractures, but we lived in Murder Mile, near the Notting Hill hotel where Neville Heath had murdered his first victim the previous year. Gentlemanly Neville Heath had been hanged, but prostitutes lingered in the shadows of decayed stucco terraces along the Bayswater Road and in the last few months two had been stabbed and strangled. I shuddered when I thought of the mangled corpses of those women, and when I passed the few tarts desperate enough still to stand out in the freezing cold, in their platform shoes and bedraggled fox furs, I thought how brave they were. I'd never be able to do that: stand there exposed to all comers, putting my life on the line.

There was another murder trial on now, a woman who'd done away with her husband, with the help of her lover. How could love turn to sordid crime, I wondered. For love was so thrilling.

Every morning I opened my eyes to see Alan's dark hair so close on the pillow and his shoulders turned away from me as he slept. I could slide my hand under his pyjamas and stroke his back until he woke and rolled over to look at me with the serious, intense look I found so exciting. Still waters ran deep, they said. At times his passion almost scared me. Even at his gentlest, there was always a sense of withheld violence. I was not *quite* a virgin when I married him, but I hadn't dreamt sex could be like this. Dangerous; there were troubling depths to my need for him – or was it just for the dark sensations he aroused in me. I did things with him that would have made me die of shame a year ago, which still half shamed me when I recalled them in the light of day. He triumphed in wrenching cries and moans from far within me. He led me into areas I'd thought were forbidden territory. He gave me *Women in Love* to read and I saw that our love was Lawrentian: thrilling, yet disturbing too, when I sensed I was out of my depth, submerged in his domination, losing my grip on my ambitions, on my sense of an independent self.

· · · · · · · · ·

There were times when it really was just too cold to venture out, the streets swept with flurries driven by a Siberian wind. Then we stayed in bed all day. Not just to make love; it was the warmest place – the only warm place – especially during the power cuts, and hour after hour we put off the leap from the warmth of our marriage bed and the eiderdown out into the freezing cold. 'Nine months later there'll be a huge rise in the birthrate,' said Alan. 'That'll please the government – so worried about the declining population.'

We'd used up our coal ration weeks ago, but Alan found some packing cases and smashed them up for firewood. I sometimes wore my fur coat indoors now and in the street I felt I must look like a tramp with an old plaid blanket thrown over it and Alan's sweaters bulking it out underneath.

So for me the world was not dingy and drab even if London lay waste all around. Austerity couldn't dim my glorious excitement. Life was opening out in the most amazing way. It was an adventure to scavenge for firewood, to search round Soho for little treats, to sit in the loud, beery pub of an evening and then stagger home along the icy wastes of road, blackened snow banked up by the kerb, treacherous ice along the pavements.

We led a hand-to-mouth existence on hardly any money. Colin had a private income, Alan told me, but most of it went to the Party, the Communist Party, that is. Alan had had a few savings, but he'd blown them on a short-lived little film company he and Hugh had formed. It went bust after one brief documentary and now they subsisted on bits of freelance work. When push came to shove I could cadge a fiver off my parents, and Alan's occasional meagre little cheques for articles and short stories seemed like a windfall, a free gift, manna from heaven, so we always blew the lot at Fava's or Chez Victor, after which we'd go on a pub crawl, eventually fall into bed and wake up next morning to start all over again.

How happy we were! I lived in a bubble of happiness, seeing life through its iridescent glitter. But bubbles are transient, and after the murder everything changed.

· · · · · · · · ·

Hugh had inconveniently moved to digs in South London. One Saturday we set off on the lengthy journey to Lavender Hill, by way of Islington to pick up Colin. We got off the Circle Line at King's Cross and struggled up the Pentonville Road to the battered terraces of Islington. It was the first time I'd been in a district where everyone looked so poor. Colin was living in a slum! Perhaps he had to, because of the Communist Party. I was shocked. In spite of the war, I'd led a sheltered life: 'class privilege' Colin said, irritated by my naïve dismay at the poverty all around.

At the Angel station it was like going down a coal mine as a gaunt industrial lift jerked us down into the bowels of the earth. At the bottom a flight of steps ended in the horror of a single narrow platform between two live rails. I clung to the balustrade. Alan was impatient: 'There's nothing to be frightened of! What is the matter with you!'

I took a few paces out onto the tightrope, but: 'I'm sorry, I can't do it,' I cried, 'I know I'm a coward.'

A wind whirled hotly out of the tunnel as the train roared towards us with stupendous force.

Hours later, it seemed, we came out of a different station into another shabby slum. A winding road meandered without purpose into the distance, no end in sight, frozen in the arctic cold. The odd gap where a stray bomb had hit a house gaped, the houses like a row of rotting teeth, grey, discoloured, dreary. Some of the shops, more like hovels, were shut. Some still had boarded-up windows, where the glass had been knocked out by bomb blast.

At last we turned up a side road and came to the house. Inside, at least it was warm, and Hugh's bedsitter was quite comfortable. 'She charges me five shillings for lighting and hot water, and there's a meter for the gas. Rent's only fifteen bob a week.'

The flames of the gas fire made a little popping noise and roasted the front of my legs. The smell of gas – like Benzedrine or menthol, sharp, slightly sweet, intoxicating – tainted the room, yet made it feel even cosier.

Hugh handed me a toasting fork and some slices of bread while he made tea. I held the slices against the ceramic filigree that caged the flames of the gas fire, and the three of them plotted and planned.

Before the war they'd been so close, Alan said, thick as thieves. They were the Three Musketeers of documentary film. But now ...

My father said that when you're young you're all in an undefined lump with your friends, you're all unformed like molten toffee, but as you get older you harden out and separate. Peculiarities of character stiffen into incompatibility. It had sounded a bit lonely. I wondered, too, if it also applied to marriage – you might wake up one morning and find the person you'd married had gradually turned into somebody else. I hoped that wouldn't happen to Alan and me.

I was beginning to think it was happening to the three of them, though. Colin returned from the war a grimmer person, Alan said. What he'd seen had hardened his political views, but if only he didn't throw his weight about so pompously: 'You weren't there – I was'. He always fell back on that.

Hugh with his effete Noel Coward manner had changed in the opposite direction, Alan said, more of a gadfly, skating along on the surface of life. He said he was still a socialist, but he hadn't a good word for the government. He just seemed utterly disillusioned and did nothing but sneer and make cynical little jokes.

'You're incurably frivolous,' Colin glowered.

'You've no sense of fun, old dear.'

'Life isn't much fun.'

I wondered if Colin was hopelessly in love with some girl. That might explain a lot. I went out of my way to be nice to him, and he took more notice of me than Hugh ever did – or for that matter Alan at times.

Since the film company had folded they'd been plotting how to start another one, or at least get money for the film they were desperate to make. 'We *need* Enescu.' Hugh's hair flopped forward. 'His film has done so well – investors will be falling over themselves. That friend of theirs, Stanley Colman, for example.'

'But Enescu would be the director,' protested Colin. 'He'd be in charge.'

'Not if we played our cards right.'

'But what have we got to offer?' insisted Colin.

Alan and Hugh *did* have something to offer, because *Home Front*, their wartime documentary, had been a critical success, especially for Alan as the main scriptwriter. I hadn't seen it and didn't remember it at any cinema, but that's what they said, anyway; all the right people had taken notice. The little documentary they'd made about post-war reconstruction had got less attention, but they weren't letting that discourage them. It was Colin who'd been out of the picture. Colin needed them more than they needed him.

'We have to make important films, films that tell the world what is really happening. Enescu won't want that. He won't want anything with a message.' Colin stared at his friends defiantly.

Hugh attempted his most winning smile. 'We can work round this,' he murmured. He flicked ash delicately off the end of his cigarette. 'You're the brains, you can get the message into the story – and we're right behind you. An audience likes a story. They want to identify with the characters. They have enough austerity in their daily lives.'

'You mean the masses are stupid. They just want escapism.'

'That's not what I mean, not at all. Surely art has to inspire, to energise, to arouse our sympathies ...'

'To *entertain*. That great American word.'

'Hang on – I didn't say that. But people are tired. There's not a lot of sympathy around. We have to create it, we have to *show* what it's like in Europe today. There's a Little England mentality in this country at the moment. It's not anyone's fault, and it's not surprising people are fed up. We won the war, didn't we, but what have we got to show for it? That's what people are thinking. You can't blame them. They're not interested in how much worse things are in Poland or Germany – least of all Germany. But a story – a romance, I'm not afraid of that word – a love story will get them to *feel*, it'll arouse their pity, they'll stop thinking about the rations and the fuel shortage, and start to think how lucky we are by comparison and how we can *help*.'

'That isn't Enescu's agenda. He's just a little fascist toerag. His film's hit a reactionary chord and – '

'Don't be so bigoted,' interrupted Alan. It was the match to light the tinder, and with one impatient remark he'd ruined all Hugh's attempts at diplomacy.

'Bigoted! Me!' Colin leaned forward, menacing. And now the real problem began to emerge: the Party. 'I can't go along with capitalist lies!' shouted Colin. 'I'm already in trouble with London District for querying the line on post-war reconstruction.'

Alan leaned forward, genuinely interested. 'You've never said anything about that.'

Colin wouldn't look at them. He pushed his hair back,

staring downwards, possibly at his own feet. 'That's not relevant. It doesn't matter.' I knew he already regretted letting it slip out.

'You're in trouble with the Party?' Alan, of course, wouldn't let it go. 'Why didn't you tell us?'

Colin's twisted smile was closer to a grimace. 'You think friendship's all-important, don't you. But for me, you see – '

'No one wants you to say anything you don't want to,' soothed Hugh. 'And the Party doesn't even come into it.'

'The Party comes into everything.'

An awkward silence. Then Hugh tried again. 'I'm sure there's a way round this.'

'A way round *what*?' muttered Colin.

'Look,' said Alan, 'I know it won't be easy. You're right – Radu wants melodrama and a vehicle for Gwendolen Grey. It's not just you that wants something better than that. We do too. But we *can* get there with Radu. It'll be in the way we write it – get the right kind of hero into the plot – '

'He doesn't want a hero. He just wants *her*.'

'But Gwendolen will want a strong leading man. She'll be that much stronger with someone to match her.'

'For God's sake,' muttered Colin, 'we don't want a lot of romantic tosh – love scenes, sex, that's just bourgeois decadence.'

Alan and Hugh both shouted their derision, and I was puzzled. Why was Colin so down on passion? He *must* be unhappy in love. There was another angry silence.

'D'you want more toast?' I enquired brightly, to cover up the sticky silence. They ignored me.

After a while Hugh said cautiously: 'I know you think I shouldn't have been talking to Enescu off my own bat, but it really will be worth it. Working with him we'll get known – and then we won't need him any more. Besides which, he's in with Stanley Colman and Colman's the man with the money.'

This further enraged Colin. 'Stanley Colman! Why the hell do we want to have anything to do with him?'

Hugh smiled: 'He's got money, hasn't he? He's just someone who got lucky in the war. I quite liked him.'

'Black marketeer more likely. For heaven's sake, what are we doing with these people?'

'We're trying to get money for our film. We can't be too choosy,' said Alan. 'And you're the one who says the end justifies the means.'

That shut Colin up. He sat there sulking. I spread the toast thinly with marge. 'He won't give you any money, anyway,' I said, 'he'll give it to Gwendolen Grey.'

The three men stared at me.

'He's in love with her, didn't you notice?'

'Oh, darling!' said Alan with an indulgent smile. They thought love had nothing to do with it. They were so wrong! Love – or sex – had everything to do with what happened later ... or some twisted version of love.

'Giving it to Gwendolen Grey *will* be giving to us – if we get in there,' said Hugh. 'Enescu is a real original – he's taken something from the German expressionist films of the twenties and put a new slant on it – it *can* be used for social criticism, it heightens everything, it makes it all less drab. And he's had this wonderful idea of giving his next film a really artistic dimension.' He paused and looked sideways, enquiringly, at Alan, but Alan gave a shake of the head so minimal I don't think Colin noticed it.

'Artistic? What does that mean?' Colin was frowning.

'Oh – I don't know the details. Anyway, really it's up to us to develop the refugee idea in a way that'll interest Radu. If he takes the bait, well and good, if he doesn't then – ' and he shrugged, 'we try something else.'

three

ALAN AND I HAD OUR FIRST BIG QUARREL outside the Communist Party HQ. Covent Garden seemed an odd place for the Communist Party to have their headquarters, I thought, as we picked our way over the cobbles, trying not to slip on the packed snow or trip on potatoes and broken orange boxes. I'd passed through Covent Garden from time to time – after we'd been to the Charing Cross Road bookshops, once to the ballet – but I'd never guessed that Communists occupied the ordinary-looking building on the corner, across the street from Moss Bros, who hired out evening clothes. It was just another office block, and it seemed incredible that behind its façade lurked that secret, mysterious entity, that shadowy – shady – organisation: 'The Party' – as Colin referred to it, as though it were the *only* political party.

We waited for Colin outside. Alan stamped his feet and banged his gloved hands together. He'd wrapped his woollen scarf, which I'd knitted him, right round his mouth and jaw, and was wearing a wide-brimmed black hat. I huddled into my musquash. My toes had gone numb.

A man in a heavy overcoat and a homburg hat hurried out, followed by a woman in belted tweed. 'Are you waiting for someone?' She sounded suspicious, as though we were spying on 'The Party'. Her hair, permed into ringlets, sprang out stiffly, like iron filings, from a dark green beret.

'Colin Harris. He's expecting us.'

The woman looked us up and down in appraisal. 'Why don't you wait inside? It's unbearably cold out here.' There was a pile of *Daily Worker*s in a bin outside the door. She handed us one. 'You could read that while you're waiting.'

I smiled. 'Thanks. We often get it from Colin, actually.'

'Do you?' The woman hesitated. I thought she might be sizing us up as potential recruits. But her companion, who had walked on, called back.

'Come along, Doris. We'll be late.'

Alan watched them go: 'Doris Tarr,' he said, 'I remember her. It was her job to recruit intellectuals, the workers by brain. Thank God, she didn't recognise me. Ugh, so patronising and proselytising.'

'What does proselytising mean?'

He looked down at me with a kind smile. 'Always trying to convert you, get you to sign up to their beliefs.'

'Colin doesn't do that.'

'That might be because he's having problems,' said Alan, darkly.

'I don't think he thinks I'm worth arguing with. He thinks I'm stupid – or just some flighty deb you've unfortunately got mixed up with.' This actually wasn't what I thought at all, and the moment I'd said it, I couldn't think why. Perhaps I was *wanting* to quarrel.

'Don't be ridiculous. Communists believe in female equality.'

I'd been planning my next move for some time, and this seemed a good moment to grasp the nettle. 'I'm going to get a job. I'm sick of moping about the flat all day. And it doesn't make sense, we haven't any money, we're broke.'

I wasn't sure how it had happened in the first place. While I was still at the Ministry, I'd discovered an amateur theatre group in Notting Hill. They'd given me a small part – that was how I'd first met Alan. After I'd holidayed with Mother in Devon, I'd meant to start looking for a job, but by that time Alan and I were talking of marriage. Three months later I found myself married and a housewife and somehow in the meantime I'd dropped out of the theatre group, which folded anyway.

The government was desperate to get women back to work; their posters begged women to train as nurses or teachers or go into factories. Nursing and teaching didn't appeal to me at all. I really only wanted to be an actress, but my father completely squashed that idea. No daughter of his, etc. My headmistress, Miss Pennington-Harborough, had said I was Oxford and Cambridge material, but Dad wasn't having that either. No, it was secretarial college for me, but I didn't much care for the idea of a secretarial job either, now the war was over.

Alan and I had discussed it, in a desultory sort of way. When I first met him he'd even said he might be able to get me an acting part in a film, but now we were married I had a feeling he liked me being at home. The flat was small, but still took a lot of cleaning, rations had to be queued for, it all took such ages, or perhaps I noticed it more, now the cold meant we were going out less.

'What d'you intend to do?' enquired Alan in a neutral tone of voice.

For the moment it was just about money, not an acting career: 'I thought – something in publishing. Or possibly ... with a magazine.'

'You can't just walk into that sort of work. You need experience.'

'I have to start somewhere.'

'You could start by helping me. I need someone to type out my manuscripts.'

So that was it. 'You mean as your unpaid secretary.' I was surprised how angry I was.

It was one of those blazing rows that ignited from nothing. We were shouting at each other by the time Colin appeared.

'What's up?'

'He doesn't think I should get a job.'

'I didn't *say* that!'

We rowed furiously as we walked towards the Charing Cross Road. Finally when we reached the corner, it was Colin's turn to shout: 'Oh do *shut up*, both of you! Of course you should get a job. There's no place for ladies of leisure in the post-war world. That may be what your mother expected, Dinah, but things are different now.'

As if *I'd* been the one who wanted to stay at home! I was speechless with impotent fury.

Swiftly, though, my rage leaked out into bleak desolation and I was left as flat as a deflated barrage balloon. Who was this man I'd married? He was a stranger, I didn't know him, didn't understand him. And he didn't love me, he thought only of himself, his career. And all those promises of a film part – just a cheap seduction technique.

Leicester Square tube was nearby. 'I'm going home,' I said. I began to walk away, but he put his hand on my arm to pull me back.

'Dinah! Don't be ridiculous.' For a second I believed he was contrite, but all he said was: 'You're behaving like a spoilt child.'

I stood there, hanging my head, mulishly silent, fighting tears.

'Oh, do come on,' said Colin. 'We'll be late. We're meeting Hugh and the Enescu gang at some seedy little club Colman belongs to in Mayfair. For God's sake, let's get it over with, try and make Hugh see sense.'

'*Please*, Dinah.' Alan's voice was a little kinder now. I gave in, ungraciously. At that moment I'd honestly rather have been on my own, in the flat, having a good cry, not having to cope with the strain of keeping up with all these older people. They had such large, bulky plans, careers, obsessions – structures so large I couldn't get past them, couldn't get out into some space, some freedom, a place where I could have *my* plans, not fit in with them – with *him* all the time.

Alan hailed a taxi. That was another problem – we hadn't any money, but we took a taxi whenever we saw one, especially now it was so cold. Fortunately for our finances they weren't that frequent.

Now as we rattled along, Colin said: 'We need to know a lot more about Enescu. How did he get the money to make *House of Shadows*, for example?'

Alan shrugged. 'The fact that he got it is surely what matters.'

The taxi turned into a narrow street off Piccadilly. Colin muttered: 'I'm sure I saw him hanging around the Athénée Palace in Bucharest with all the bourgeois riff-raff.'

Alan stooped to climb out of the taxi: 'Are you saying you know more than you're letting on?'

Colin shrugged, but he looked at Alan very hard.

'Well, keep it to yourself for the time being. Don't mess up this meeting. I mean it. *Don't*.'

Hugh was waiting for us in the tiny foyer and led us upstairs. The rather odd trio – possibly a *ménage à trois*, I suddenly thought, how very sophisticated – were seated at the far end of the room in a warm twilight of soft beige carpeting and tapestry *fauteuils*, tinted mirrors and vellum-shaded wall lights. I'd expected a more masculine sort of place, with leather and wood panelling, not this boudoir.

'Like a tart's flat,' muttered Colin. That shocked me. How did he know?

The men stood up. Enescu actually kissed my hand! Stanley Colman clicked his fingers to bring the barman over to our table. There seemed to be a wide choice of drinks; no shortages here.

I sat and watched and listened – as Stanley Colman was doing. The Romanian seemed to like Hugh's idea for a feature film about refugees. Colin sat stonily silent as Enescu outlined his vision of a dark, romantic film, the tragedy of central Europe in the aftermath of war.

Finally Colin spoke: 'I still think a documentary would reveal the truth more clearly.'

Radu smiled winningly. 'But fiction *is* truth, really, it is just as true as *reportage*,' pronouncing the word in French. 'What do *you* think, Stan? Would you put your money on a documentary?' A sly move, I thought, bringing in the money man like that.

Stanley looked from one to another of them. 'I'll be frank with you,' he said. 'I haven't even dipped a toe in the water, and I don't know if I will. To begin with I was interested in the cinemas – the buildings themselves. I didn't understand the link between the distributors and the actual theatres at first. But J Arthur Rank has that all sewn up – he owns the Odeons *and* the Gaumonts. The next thing is – well, how is this country going to compete with Hollywood? Things don't look good financially. And documentaries – is that what people want? Radu's right. All very well in the war, kept people's spirits up, that sort of thing, but now – don't you think the audiences want a bit of colour in their lives? A bit of escapism?

Refugees – is that going to take people out of themselves? You know something? People don't *like* refugees. They don't want to hear about all the suffering in *mittel Europa*, they're too busy grumbling about the electricity cuts and the meat ration.'

Hugh was delighted; it was just what he'd said. '*Exactly*. We've been through all this, and I thought we'd agreed.'

Colin sipped his whisky in silence. Then, unexpectedly he turned to Enescu. 'How did you start in films? There's no film industry in Romania.'

Enescu smiled modestly. 'I have been very fortunate,' he said. 'I was able to work abroad, in France, and before that in Berlin. With UFA. This was before the Nazi time, of course.'

'You must have been very young.' Colin hardly bothered to hide his scepticism.

Radu smiled. 'Indeed,' he said modestly, 'I was very fortunate,' he repeated.

There was an awkward silence. Alan was looking apprehensive.

Colin was staring at him. 'When did you actually leave? How did you escape?'

Enescu's smile never wavered. 'Oh – this is a long story, very long. You don't want to hear the history of my life, I think.'

'On the contrary.'

'*Please*, Colin.' Alan frowned at his friend. Colin shrugged and looked away. I wondered what *really* was wrong. Colin so touchy; I couldn't believe it was just about what sort of film they were going to make.

Hugh turned to Radu. 'Perhaps we can flesh out the ideas a bit.' He was clever, making the storyline sound less exaggerated and at the same time selling himself, referring to his wartime experience at the Crown Film Unit. Radu liked it, I could see. Alan nodded approvingly, although Hugh wasn't giving him enough credit for the success of *Home Front*. Colin sat stonily silent.

I got the feeling that Gwendolen was just bored by the whole conversation. Soon she stood up. She wore a close-fitting black dress with coffee piping, and a black and coffee turban hat. Her leopardskin coat lay abandoned on an empty chair. She walked over to one of the mirrors, removed the turban and shook her pageboy hair over her face, before smoothing it back again and replacing the hat. Stanley watched her.

I stood up too. 'D'you know where the lavatory is?'

'I need the powder room myself.' Again that hoarse voice with a metallic edge to it, not an accent, nothing you could pin down, just a rusty edge to it, the way blood tastes of iron, the way iron smells of blood.

In the stuffy little dressing room I stared at Gwendolen staring at herself in the glass. She took out her compact and powdered her face.

'Nice to get away from the men for a few minutes, don't you think? They are so boring. Even your husband, dear, and he's quieter than the others. Don't you think? Talk, talk, talk, and all getting us nowhere.'

'I thought the story for the film sounded rather exciting.'

Gwendolen smiled her slow, world-weary smile. 'Oh ... so far as that goes. I can tell you already exactly what will happen. Radu will get money for his film, he's probably going to New York soon to talk to his distributors over there, but he won't get the money from Stanley. That boy isn't serious – he's too busy buying up bombed buildings, he's making a fortune, he won't want to risk it investing in some crazy film idea. He knows Radu's been successful so far, but the movies are far too risky for him. It's just that he likes hanging around with arty people, he thinks we're all frightfully bohemian, he loves all that.'

'I thought it was because he's in love with you,' I said boldly.

Gwen smiled. 'You don't miss a trick, do you, although you seem such an innocent. But in love ... that's a bit of an exaggeration,' and she gracefully shrugged away the idea of an admirer. 'He's trying to educate himself. Those East End Jews have a touching faith in learning and culture, you know.'

'I didn't know he was Jewish.'

'Oh darling, of course he's a yid! You *are* green, aren't you? Anyway, never mind about him, I'm just telling you – your husband and his friends, they shouldn't expect any shekels from that direction, they're wasting their time. They should get some money from the government and make documentaries about the welfare state, the new post-war Britain.'

Her dismissive tone hurt me. In spite of the quarrel I utterly believed in Alan, and rushed to his defence. 'Alan's really talented, you know. His wartime film was a huge success.'

Gwendolen smiled faintly: 'It's a difficult, difficult business, the movies. And the economy's in such a mess, you know. These awful Labourites dragging everything down.'

That startled me. Everyone I knew supported the Labour government – apart from my father, but that was different and to be expected.

'Don't you ... ' I began, but my own ideas were so unformed I didn't want an argument. I stared at my reflection. I looked like a scarecrow compared to her. My hair just grew and fell about my face in messy curls. Even my lipstick, so carefully applied (blot three times and press your lips together), looked amateurish. I wished I were twenty-five, an ideal age.

'Anyway,' said Gwendolen, 'who wants to talk about politics. Tell me what you're doing with yourself.'

'I want to get a job,' I said. 'Well – what I really want is to get into the theatre, but ... well, we haven't any money just at the moment, so anything really.'

She looked at me via the mirror – two reflections and a single gaze. 'I see. Yes.' She smoothed her glossy hair and replaced her hat for the second time. 'I remember you said you wanted to act. You should talk to Radu. He might be able to get you something. I'll mention it to him if you like.'

'Oh, would you? That would be marvellous!' She'd said it before, and nothing had happened, but this time surely she'd remember!

She continued to stare in the mirror, looking at herself now. Then: 'We'd better be getting back. They'll be wondering where we are. Might even send a search party.' And suddenly she laughed, a jarring laugh and rather coarse, out of keeping with her graceful, stilted movements. She paused with her hand on the doorknob. 'You know, you should visit me one afternoon. Radu and I are off to Paris soon, but after we get back ... come and have tea. I'm resting at present. I get quite bored – and if Radu goes to New York I'll be all on my own.'

New York – Paris – it all sounded so exciting. 'I'd love to.'

The men hardly looked up when we returned. Enescu was holding forth. Stanley sat a little back from the group – as he had when we'd met them before, but the other three were clenched round Enescu. His melting brown eyes would have charmed anyone – he really was persuasive. 'And then you see – I imagine this wonderful dream sequence. It will be this wonderful surrealist dream, when Gwendolen imagines what her new life might be – and then perhaps it will turn dark and she will remember the nightmare that was.' His hands were as voluble as his words as he sketched his ideas.

'Surrealism? What's that? I don't understand all that stuff,' interrupted Stanley. 'Sounds a bit phoney to me. But then I'm ignorant about these things.'

Only Hugh could have explained an artistic movement to a self-confessed philistine with such exquisite good manners; he didn't once sound patronising. The property developer listened doggedly. 'Not much money in experimental films, I should have thought,' was his only comment when Hugh had ended his exposition.

'And for this sequence I have found a wonderful artist – ' He paused. Alan stiffened. Hugh looked strained. 'You must know him – Titus Mavor.'

Colin exploded. 'Mavor! Are you insane?' He swivelled round towards his two friends. 'Did you know about this? The last person on earth I'd ever work with!'

Gwen looked on, expressionless. Hugh tried to calm Colin down.

'He did some scenery and stage sets for the leftwing theatre movement before the war – the Unity Theatre – it's not as though he doesn't have some experience.'

'I know *that*, you bloody fool!' Colin was in a towering rage.

Unexpectedly Gwendolen spoke. 'They say he's destroyed himself with drink, darling. He may not be capable ...'

'I'm afraid that is true, Radu,' said Hugh, placating. 'Drinks like a fish – hardly does any work these days.'

If he'd hoped to head Colin off, he failed. 'Surrealism is the absolute end. Bourgeois rubbish. But that's not the point. Mavor's a degenerate – '

Radu sprang to his feet. He was angry now. 'You're crazy, crazy, stupid anglo-saxon moralists.' He walked off angrily towards the bar.

Stanley Colman came to the rescue. 'What about going

for a spot to eat at the Café Royal – how about that? My treat.'

We all jumped at the idea with relief. Only afterwards, much later, did it occur to me that it might have been a plot – that Radu might have put Stanley up to it, knowing that Titus Mavor spent most of his time at the Café Royal, even when he was broke.

'Dinah and I will go on ahead to get a table.' Stanley Colman smiled at me in the friendliest possible way.

This was startling. Why me? Downstairs the porter rang for a taxi – another taxi! Such incredible extravagance, all these taxis! And for such a short distance! But then it was so cold. It was *so cold* and the pavements so slippery.

'Shouldn't we wait for the others? I mean – four of us at least could get in one taxi ...'

If I hadn't felt certain he was sweet on Gwendolen, I'd have wondered if he wanted to get me alone in order to try something on. If I'd imagined getting married would put a stop to that sort of thing, well, I couldn't have been more wrong. I was quite used to it now, and knew how to deal with it. But the way he smiled told me that while he found me an attractive young woman, I had nothing to fear. He was entirely respectful. 'I've had enough of their arguing, frankly. And I thought perhaps you had, too.'

It was nice of him to have noticed my discomfort. All the same, I hoped the others would join us before the taxi arrived, for I felt shy with this stranger, although I couldn't help quite liking him, even if he was a spiv. Anyway, the taxi came and the two of us were driven along Piccadilly. I remembered Mother's advice concerning men: get them to talk about themselves.

'How did you come to be in the property business?' It came out as both prim and intrusive, but he didn't seem to notice.

'I was wounded early on in the war, never saw active service. It happened during training, literally shot myself in the foot. Sounds like a bad joke, doesn't it? But in a business sense I have to admit it was a lucky break.' He smiled sideways at me. Shooting yourself in the foot was suspiciously like dodging the call-up, or rather, getting out of it. My companion seemed almost to read my thoughts, for he continued, 'On the other hand, doesn't look good, not to have seen action. It can give the impression you're a bit dodgy – that you wriggled out of it somehow.'

My face felt hot, I hoped I wasn't blushing.

'I don't think you and your friends have met many people like me, have you,' he remarked, as if reading my thoughts. 'I suppose you were just about old enough to be called up for war work, but ...?' His voice trailed off into a question.

'I worked at the War Office the last year of the war, I was a secretary. I saw life then,' I said.

As he talked I was trying to pin down his accent. It wasn't common, wasn't cockney, but it wasn't public school either. It was also difficult to guess his age, but it came as a shock when I found out he was only the same age as Alan and the others – he somehow seemed older, and even more grown up.

'The war shook everyone up, but now things'll revert to type, whatever the government does. It'll take a while, but when things have settled down ... mind you, it'll still be a *different* world, but not in the way your friend supposes. There ain't going to be no soviet utopia.'

'You mean Colin?'

'All of you – not much idea how most people live. Take me. I left school at fourteen, left school on the Friday and started work on the Monday. My first job was with a landlord. My boss – '

But we'd arrived. The cab drew into the kerb, Stanley paid,

and we slid across the frozen pavement and into the Café Royal. I'd been there before, of course, but I had a feeling it was Colman's first visit, although he appeared cool enough.

'I'm not really properly dressed,' I said, aware of my shabby old black jumper and tweed skirt, but Stanley brushed that aside. 'A fur coat is always good. And no one will notice once you've sat down.'

We were shown to the room at the back. I sat beside him on the red velvet banquette. Stanley looked round, taking in the Edwardian opulence of the place, the cloudy gilt mirrors, the mahogany, overripe, yet at the same time faded. I watched the drinkers and diners. Even if they weren't famous writers or artists, they acted and dressed as if they were. It was all so glamorous.

Stanley ordered me a sherry, and as I sat beside him waiting for the others, I was happy and excited, my row with Alan forgotten. I looked round. 'I say, look over there: there *is* Titus Mavor.' I recognised him at once.

Stanley looked across the room. 'How convenient,' he said with an enigmatic little smile. 'Well then, when the others arrive, they can ask him to join us, can't they? That'll please Radu – and ... well, depending on how he behaves it might settle the issue anyway.'

I wished I hadn't pointed him out. 'Oh no, don't let's tell the others,' I said quickly, 'Colin's so touchy about him – we don't want another row. Let's just hope they don't notice him.'

Stanley looked at me. 'Not much chance of that, is there?' He was right.

four

■□■■■■■□

I WAS ON MY SECOND SHERRY BY THE TIME Alan, Colin and Hugh arrived, having walked through the freezing streets from Green Park.

'Gwenny not with you?' Stanley tried to sound casual.

'They should have been here by now,' said Hugh, looking round as if expecting to find them behind a pillar. He caught sight of Mavor, stared sharply, but didn't say anything. 'They were taking a taxi – they'll be along any moment.'

The waiter came to our table with menus and a jug of water. By the time he returned some minutes later to take our order, Stanley was fidgety. 'Where *are* they?'

'Let's order anyway,' said Alan. 'What about roast beef followed by apple pie, Dinah?' He beamed at me, my childish behaviour was forgiven, but he didn't wait for me to reply. I agreed meekly, because although I'd wanted to choose for myself, I wasn't going to risk another quarrel.

When Radu and Gwendolen finally turned up it was with some story of their taxi running out of petrol. 'And me in these shoes!' Gwendolen gestured at her feet and we all stared at her elegant, silk-stockinged legs and high heels. She laughed, but I thought she was nervous, as she headed off to the ladies. We all laughed – a bit too loudly.

My eyes flickered to where Titus Mavor sat at the opposite side of the restaurant. He had his arm round a girl with black hair in a bob with a fringe. He looked up at the loud burst of laughter. He'd seen us. I looked quickly away.

The next thing I knew he was looming over our table, the girl dragged along with him, his arm still round her shoulders. 'Well, look who's here,' he said, swaying slightly. I concentrated on the girl. She was wearing a red bouclé sweater with large wooden buttons marching diagonally across the bosom. Mavor looked more than ever like a cherub gone to seed.

I realised that, drunk as Mavor was – as they both were, I think – they were waiting for me, the only woman present, to invite them to sit down, so of course I had to. Alan kicked my ankle under the table. Mavor slumped on the banquette next to me.

Gwendolen wove her way back from the ladies between the tables. Mavor stared at her as she sat down at the opposite end of the table, next to Colin. A strange, unpleasant smile twitched his rubbery lips and he half rose in what seemed a parody of good manners. 'Lovely to see you, Gwendolen.' She smiled back, a tight, tense smile. His fat fingers spread over his girlfriend's shoulder and stretched towards the highest button as if they were thinking of undoing it, but his eyes swivelled biliously towards me.

'So you're the little girl hitched up with Alan Wentworth. Finally settled down, has he?' I knew all about Alan's colourful past, and it didn't bother me, not at all. I ignored the leering innuendo. I took out a cigarette. His hand shook as he lit it. 'And still knocking round with Comrade Harris,' he continued, speaking to me, but of course it was meant for them. He was looking at them all the time. 'Wentworth never quite took the plunge, did he, just hung about on the edge of the pool, not quite daring to jump in. But Colin Harris – my God, it's *so true* what they say about converts. He's worse than St Paul. And the funny thing is, his road to Damascus was the Nazi Soviet Pact. My Party right or wrong. Just when anyone with any sense was getting out, he took it as the great test, the supreme test of loyalty. Since then, of course, I've become a *rotten element.*' He sagged against the red velvet bench and laughed, but the laugh turned into a bubbling, heaving cough. Spittle sprayed. His poached-egg eyes watered. 'What's *your* assessment of Comrade Stalin? Think he's the people's hero, eh?' As his voice rose I could feel the sweat under my arms. This was horrible. Mavor leant towards me, but the words were directed towards Colin. His thicket of red curls fell over his sweating forehead. He had bad breath and bad teeth. And then he spoke directly to Colin. 'How are the comrades these days, old chap?' And he smiled with insulting insistence.

'We're making advances,' said Colin, tight-lipped.

Titus snorted. '*Making advances*! Advances on what? You make it sound like a seduction; making advances on the great British people. Or is it a military campaign? Advancing over difficult terrain, what,' he said in a Blimpish accent.

Colin should have laughed it off, but of course he didn't. He scowled. 'Things are obviously more difficult than they were during the war. There's so much anti-Soviet propaganda now – everyone's forgotten who really won the war. The reason we're sitting here, y'know, is the battle of Stalingrad. The Yanks seem to think they won the war, but it was the Soviet Union that saved us.'

'I thought it was the Battle of Britain,' said Hugh rather sharply.

'If you take my advice, old man ...' Titus leaned forwards in a distinctly hostile way. I wondered if he was ever sober. 'If you take my advice, your lot should shut up about the Soviet bloody Union. There's a lot more going on in Russia than we get to hear about, and even if there wasn't, the Soviet Union is the Soviet Union and England is England, *it is a different animal,*' he said, with a drunken wiseacre nod, 'and old Comrade Stalin will do what he thinks is good for him and possibly them, like he did with the Nazi Soviet Pact. Or have we forgotten all about that?'

Hugh leaned forward. 'Let's leave politics out of it, Titus.'

But Titus wouldn't be shifted. 'That's precisely the problem. You can't separate art and politics. You'd agree with that I think, Colin. Art is always political. The comrades are very hot on that. Unfortunately, the result is the incredible idea that the highest form of painting is a huge canvas showing burly factory workers or alternatively what are actually the conquered inhabitants of Uzbekistan rejoicing in their slavery, in the most disgustingly sentimental Victorian style you can imagine. Now for a humble Surrealist, such as myself, that's just a little hard to take.'

'Look, hang on – ' began Hugh, and Colin had gone very red, but now the three men at the next table began to get involved. Two were dishevelled arty types, in the usual corduroy and dusty hair, cut long to touch the collar; the third, who looked younger than his companions, at the same time dressed older, in an uncared-for suit with a waistcoat, a conventional shirt and tie. He was going bald, wore glasses and had buck teeth that seemed too large for his pale, round, schoolboy's face. He leaned forward, holding a card towards Mavor.

'Remember – we met the other evening – I've opened a gallery – '

'He thinks the moment has come for a great revival of Surrealism,' said one of his companions, rather jeeringly. 'He's after those Dalí paintings you're always banging on about, Mavor.'

Mavor took the proffered card, and leered craftily at his fellow painter: 'Who says I own any Dalís?'

The man laughed. 'Well you, mostly, old boy.'

Colin couldn't hold back any longer. 'Revive Surrealism? People want something uplifting, not that sick Freudian fantasy stuff. It's degenerate, utterly degenerate.'

Weirdly, he was beginning to sound like my father.

'So my work's degenerate, is it? Salvador Dalí's degenerate, Max Ernst, André Breton. It's degenerate to paint the unconscious, to unleash the imagination, to explore the erotic. That's degenerate. But it's not degenerate to sell your soul to the Party, to lap up their propaganda, for all we know you were one of their double agents, one of their spies. What exactly *were* you up to in the Balkans, Harris? Doing the Russians' dirty work for them?'

There was a horrified silence. He'd gone too far. I looked round the table, seeing them for a split second frozen, as if caught in a flashbulb photograph: faces distorted with anger, or apprehension; only the onlookers, Radu and Stanley, detached and even amused, while Gwen's face was a blank white disc, expressionless as ever as she gazed at Mavor.

Colin leaned forward, his face even bonier in rage. 'You *are* degenerate, you absurd, drunken aesthete, with your effete, ephemeral paintings and your ... look at you, if you weren't so drunk I'd knock you down, I'd kick you all the way to – '

'Colin! *Shut up!*' Alan laid a hand on his friend's arm. Titus was smiling and smiling. He was enjoying himself. Colin had responded exactly as he'd hoped.

'Oh dear, I must have touched a raw nerve there, hit a chord. We have a spy in our midst. Spying was heroic, of course, during the war. We should be grateful to you, Colin, just as we should be grateful to the glorious Soviet Union.'

Seeing the look on Colin's face, the girlfriend was agitated now. '*Titus*,' she whined.

'Shut up, Fiona.'

Colin stood up, lurching slightly. Perhaps he was a bit drunk too. 'Shall I tell you something – I hate people like you. You're the scum of the earth and after the revolution, there won't be a place for people like you.'

'I'll be liquidated, I suppose.'

'That would be a very good idea.' Colin stepped dramatically backwards and his chair fell over. He left it where it was and strode out of the Café. The two artists at the next table clapped. Not the little bald man – he seemed appalled.

Titus stared stupidly, his mouth open. Then he started to laugh and splutter. I felt a pinpoint of spittle on my cheek.

'What the hell were you thinking of?' muttered Alan.

Titus blustered, but he was looking a bit shaken. 'It was only a joke – no need to go off the deep end like that. You heard! He threatened to kill me!'

The food arrived. What a relief. Now we could all eat. It covered the thick, awkward silence.

Stanley said calmly: 'You know, I think we were all in a state of chronic hysteria during the war. Everything was mad and crazy. Extraordinary things could happen. The street I was living in then, there was a bomb and a woman in her bath was lifted right out of her house by the blast – still in the bath, stark naked – and landed on the pavement. She was completely unhurt. How could that happen? But things like that happened all the time. We were permanently on this hysterical plane where everything was exaggerated. Now we've come down and we can't cope with it. And nothing really *is* back to normal anyway.'

Titus said: 'I like the woman in the bath – that's pure surrealism.'

I watched him, repelled. His flaccid lips, his mouth gaping open; the whole of him was incomplete, soft at the edges, a monstrous mollusc without its shell. His appetite amazed me. We'd hardly started and he'd cleared his plate and started to grab bits from his girlfriend's. He was appetite incarnate, a giant baby, a mouth, an orifice. Now the mouth was nuzzling Fiona's cheek and neck, grazing snail-like, slimy. I squirmed inwardly, felt suddenly very prim, but at the same time unpleasantly fascinated. He was a kind of life force, something rising from the primeval slime, in a primitive way more alive than any of us with his viscous, oozing extremities and the malice gleaming from his eyes.

Yet within a few weeks he was dead.

five

■□■■■■■□■□

I USED TO HAVE A RECURRING DREAM. I would walk through the frozen square, up the steps and into the house. Or sometimes the dream would begin when I was already inside. I would peer up the stairwell to where the landing was lost in darkness. I would climb the stairs through the silence and push open the door to the room at the front of the house. He would always be lying on the sofa. Sometimes he would sit up and speak to me, and I would realise that he was drunk, but also dead. Sometimes it was as if we were back at the party and there would seem to be people laughing in the next room; sometimes he would simply lie there in the moonlight. I was always so cold, paralysed with cold.

It wasn't exactly a nightmare. I only ever had one nightmare: the first time, after it happened.

. . . .

We were broke. Alan got a job. He sat in an office off the Haymarket working on scripts for an American producer. He read masses of frightful novels and tried to turn them into film scenarios. At first he'd thought it would be a lifeline to Hollywood, but he was already disillusioned. In fact, he hated it. 'Anything even faintly decent they chuck straight into the wastepaper basket.' The pay was terrible too. So when Stanley Colman rang up and offered me a job as his secretary, Alan was hardly in a position to veto it, although I knew he'd have liked to. We needed the money. I wasn't keen to be anyone's secretary, and I had grave doubts about Gwendolen's spivvy admirer, but I supposed it was better than nothing. I had heard nothing from Radu about film work; perhaps this was a kind of consolation prize.

Stanley's office in a building off Regent Street consisted of two first floor rooms – actually one room partitioned into two, so that the ceilings seemed much too high for their size – and a windowless lobby containing a sofa and some filing cabinets. We each had a substantial oak desk, unnecessary really, but: 'They were going cheap – government sale,' said Stanley.

Stanley did almost all his work on the telephone. I typed a few letters and contracts, but it wasn't strictly speaking a full-time job. He had hardly any visitors either. Nevertheless, my role was to give his enterprise a bit of class. Even if he took most calls himself, I was the cut-glass voice of bona fide property development, and even if no one turned up to be impressed, I was the ladylike secretary to offset the ramshackle office. I was also there to keep him company.

Post-war reconstruction was a golden opportunity for Stanley, however much he complained about all the red tape and government restrictions, and I understood – if only dimly – how much he could benefit from this strange time when empty buildings lay around bombed cities and the govern-ment needed offices. He relished the challenge presented by the tortuous government controls and his labyrinthine journeys through them. He was a master of all the ways in which deals could be struck, and the grey areas where officials and developers could come to arrangements that were mutually beneficial: a place on the board for a district surveyor in return for favourable assessments of war-damaged buildings, for example. And then, now that he had his own property company he could purchase the very properties for which he was acting as agent and then re-auction them at a much higher price.

'And the great thing is, Dinah,' he said, 'it's all quite legal and it's all pure profit. Untaxed gains. If this was really a socialist government, they'd worry less about the mines and the railways and pay more attention to the ownership of land ... Of course they have to nationalise the coal industry, the way it's been run. That's doing no more than making capitalism work more efficiently. But they don't understand the property issues. Either that or they're too nervous of all the vested interests ... you know who owns most of Mayfair? Some blooming duke or the other. You can't have socialism with that sort of situation – that and the public schools.' He stared out of the window. 'Now, don't get me wrong. I'm not a socialist, I didn't vote for this lot – tell you the truth, I didn't vote at all – but I'd have more time for them if they had the courage of their convictions.'

'They're doing as much as they can,' I said, hopefully. 'The country's practically bankrupt.'

'You're right about that. And the Yanks are dragging their feet. But they'll have to bail us out in the end. And in the long run ... ' He paused. A grin spread across his handsome face. 'In the long run things'll be hunky-dory. You'll see.' And he went back to his telephone.

'Go and get some lunch,' he'd say. 'Have a look round the shops. Buy yourself a hat.'

I went to the nearest Lyons tea shop for a poached egg on toast, and read *Sons and Lovers* as I ate. I had so much reading to catch up on. Alan had planned a whole reading programme to make up for the shortcomings of what he referred to as 'that ridiculous boarding school'. In fact it was a perfectly good school. Alan simply didn't realise that being so much older than me he'd just had more *time* to read everything.

Stanley was a talkative chap and I was a captive audience. He was fond of telling me how he'd come up the hard way – I soon knew the story of his life off by heart. Not that I minded.

'I left school at fourteen, left school on the Friday and started work on the Monday,' he would say. So many times he said it! It was his litany. 'My first boss was a landlord. He sent me off round the East End. There were a lot of private rented houses then, owned by this or that small-time landlord. He was a bigger landlord – my boss, that is. My job was to get the little minnows to sell – the miserable rents they were getting weren't worth the effort, so in a way they were getting a bargain, an unexpected little windfall, see, we were doing them a favour. Afterwards we'd auction them off at a much higher price, that's true, but they weren't in a position to make those sort of profits.

'Next I got a job as a clerk in an estate agent's. There'd been tailors' shops off Regent Street, going down towards Hanover Square, but then along came the multiple men's wear chains, Burtons in particular, and that hit them hard. It was all changing along Maddox Street – estate agents' offices springing up where the tailors used to be. Us clerks from the different offices'd go to a Lyons tea shop and talk property. Shops – that was the thing then, there was a lot of money to be made from shops.' He paused. 'Look – I hope I'm not boring you.'

'Oh no, not at all.' I'd heard it all before, but I wasn't bored. This unknown world of clerks and small business intrigued me. I was so green I'd thought that either you – well men, at least – went to public school and Oxbridge, or else you'd be a docker or a miner or something like that. I'd never imagined the lives of all the millions of men who, both before the war and now coming back from it, were something in between.

'1939 – I got called up – went off for training, then there was my accident. After I got discharged I was back in civvy street, back with my old boss again. Things were just ticking over for a while, but around the time of the D-Day landings the property market began to recover – everyone feeling a bit more optimistic, when at last it seemed we were going to win. I went into partnership with a friend, Arnold Franks, and we began to buy property. He's older than me, had a bit of capital. That's how it started. And now – well, the way I see it property's an essential part of post-war reconstruction. Absolutely vital. Look at London, look at the way it is. Something's got to be done. The bomb sites! You been down the East End? I thought not. Something chronic. Well, all this council house building, and new towns – it's all very well, but it'll take years. The red tape – murder! What needs to be done is unleash the power of the money markets. Investment – we can put the money to work. There's masses of money no one can spend at the moment; if we can liberate it, we'll be doing the nation a service. We can rebuild the bombed cities, we can make life a better place after the war. It's creative. People tend to think property development's all about greed. That's a very wrong view.'

· · · · · · · · ·

One cold, frozen afternoon I went with Stan to visit a bomb site in the City. Broken heaps of rubble, walls and sightless gaps where once windows had been, pushed starkly up out of the filthy snow, with the skeleton of an old church standing bleakly behind it. The site was cheerlessness itself, but it thrilled Stan. It was to be his latest acquisition.

He stared over the low wall that remained. 'Deserters hid out in the bomb sites, you know – some of them still there, I shouldn't wonder, except it's too cold for them now. Get frostbite or something.' He laughed.

We took a taxi back to the office. Stanley was circumspect in his use of the Bentley. Only the previous week he'd been stopped by a policeman and quizzed about his source of petrol. He'd got away with it that time, 'But it's put the wind up me, I can tell you,' he said with a laugh.

In the impersonal confessional of the cab he began to talk about Gwendolen. I'd heard their telephone calls. He was polite, but persistent. Not that he wooed her exactly. He was more the helpful benefactor: anything she wanted, every little whim, he would obtain. I couldn't see the point. He was getting nowhere. It seemed he might finally have admitted this to himself, for he grumbled: 'I can't make Gwendolen out. What is it with you females, always falling for these ...' He groped for an adequate word.

'Cads and bounders?' I suggested helpfully – or fascists, in her case, if Colin was to be believed.

'You're all the same, you women. Well, not you, you've got a head on your shoulders, Di. But take my sister now – she fell for some swanky con man who ran off with her savings. Then there's my wife – mind you I'm divorcing *her*.' Then, as if he remembered something, 'But that's turning out to be a nightmare too. Turns out getting a divorce is more difficult than closing a property deal. A *lot* more difficult. It's worse than abortion,' he said, warming to his theme. 'All you need's the right contacts and the cash for *that*.' He stopped abruptly, looked at me. 'Sorry, excuse me for mentioning that.'

'It's all right,' I said airily. 'I know all about these things.'

He looked at me quizzically. 'Yes, I daresay you do. In

theory at any rate. Anyway, the divorce laws are bloody archaic, absurd. It was only a quickie wartime marriage, and now we've gone our separate ways, but my lawyer's saying I have to fix up a dirty weekend in Brighton, so it looks as though we're not – what's the word – "colluding". I couldn't believe it at first. I said to Joe, that's my lawyer, I said, "You mean to say we can only get a divorce if one of us doesn't want to? That's barmy, completely barmy." "It's the law, Stanley, old son," he said.'

Stanley looked at me. 'Don't suppose your old man could help out there?' he said.

'*Alan*?'

'Don't be daft. Your dad.' He spoke in an almost wheedling tone. 'He's a lawyer, isn't he?'

I had to tell him my father didn't do divorce. He was a criminal lawyer – and a pretty important one now, after his success at the Nuremberg trials.

'Not to worry. It wouldn't matter if …' He let the sentence trail off into a shrug and stared out of the window at the murky streets where bent, cowed figures scuttled through the Stygian gloom.

By the time we got back to the office it was completely dark. It was the time I normally went home, but Stanley asked me to make him some coffee. He insisted on coffee, even at tea time. That was another scarce good he could always get hold of. He said I made a good cup of coffee, which pleased me inordinately, and I usually made enough for myself as well, for I enjoyed the chats we had together then, savouring our coffee with evaporated milk, and sometimes delving into the broken biscuits I bought from Woolworth's.

On this particular afternoon he still seemed preoccupied. Then, abruptly: 'It's late, after six. Are you wanting to get off home? Doing anything this evening?'

I shook my head. 'This weather's so awful, once you get indoors, you don't want to go out again.'

I thought he was going to invite me out for a drink, or even a meal. He hedged around a bit and then produced a letter, which he pushed across his desk towards me. A name was written on the envelope, but there was no address. The name was Titus Mavor.

Stanley didn't know the address, he said. He thought I could find out, and post the letter, or even take it round.

'This evening? *Now?*' I was taken aback.

He looked a bit guilty: 'Would you mind, Di? It's quite important. Take a taxi. At least it's not snowing. I wouldn't have asked if it'd been like last night. That was a *blizzard*.' And he pressed a ten shilling note into my hand.

His furtive behaviour intrigued me, but it was disturbing too. I took the blue envelope – and the rusty brown banknote.

'Hugh might know,' I said doubtfully, 'we don't have it, I know that much.'

'No, don't ask Hugh,' he said hurriedly. 'What about that pub your lot go to? Someone in there might know.'

I had such an easy time as Stan's secretary that I didn't like to refuse. Actually, I didn't *want* to refuse. It was a challenge. It was even an adventure.

I crossed Regent Street and walked on until I reached Rathbone Place and the Wheatsheaf. Inside the bar I glanced swiftly round, hoping I wouldn't see anyone I knew, but in this weather the place was almost empty. I walked straight up to the bar and asked for a sherry.

'All on your own, then? Where's that husband of yours? Letting you out on your own like Little Red Riding Hood? You never know when you might meet a wolf. Specially now Britain's turned into Siberia.' Gully the barman roared with laughter at this feeble joke.

'Get caught in a blizzard, more likely. Frozen to death in the snow.' I took a gulp of the sherry. 'Look, Gully, I wonder – the thing is, I'm looking for Titus Mavor ... actually I need his address.' I blushed as I spoke, and hoped Gully wouldn't get the wrong idea. He raised his eyebrows and I was sure some risqué remark was on the tip of his tongue, but he restrained himself.

'This is his only fixed abode these days. He's moving around at the moment – trouble with the bailiffs.'

I must have looked disappointed, for he fetched a bit of paper from behind a row of bottles. 'I'm not supposed to give this out, but he wouldn't mind for a good-looking girl.'

Mecklenburgh Square lay at the far side of Bloomsbury. I swallowed the rest of the Amontillado and set off eastwards. At least it wasn't snowing, but a wind had got up, and blew the ragged clouds aside to unveil a bleak full moon. It took me nearly half an hour to reach the square. Its imposing terraces seemed both menacing and tragic, part bombed, the railings long gone, only their sockets remaining, privets growing wild, curtains shrouding the once grand windows. How gaunt and black the surviving houses looked. There were no lights in any ground floor rooms along the terrace, a few gleams here and there from an upstairs room. I walked along, peering at the numbers until I found the right door. I mounted the shallow, cracked black and white checked steps.

The door was not quite shut. How strange. I pushed it. It was very stiff and scraped against the lintel. The wood must have swollen in the cold. It would be easy for someone to think they'd shut it when they hadn't. I hesitated, then stepped into the soft-as-cobwebs darkness. I felt along the wall for a light switch. The little metal fitting felt cold and hard. I pressed it down and a faint orange twilight gleamed from the unshaded twenty-watt bulb that swung eerily in the wind from a cord far up in the ceiling over the stairwell.

The stairs stretched upwards into shadows.

I called Mavor's name. My voice sounded hollow – and weak at the same time. I hesitated, then tried the first door on the right. It was locked.

I moved forwards towards the long flight of stairs and peered upwards. The slender banister curved round at the top, and more flights above that wound away into endless gloom.

A sudden sound – my heart thumped. Soot tumbling down inside the chimney stack; crumbling plaster; a cat jumping from a chair. Yet I was not seriously frightened. It was the sort of building that would attract squatters, yet I felt almost certain the place was empty, abandoned. I walked along the corridor to the back of the house, but those doors were also locked, so there was nothing for it: I began to climb upwards, stepping gingerly on each creaking tread, hoping the stairs wouldn't actually give way, and trying for some reason not to make any noise, as though I were a thief, an intruder.

I *was* an intruder.

As I adjusted to the semi-darkness I made out odd shapes in the gloom; on the landing a suitcase and a broken chair. Here were more doors, another set of rooms. I tried the door of the room at the front. It opened.

The first thing I noticed was the smell. Alcohol? I looked around. There were no curtains and the moonlight was quite lurid. Bottles clustered by the grate. Paintings were stacked against the walls. Others had been thrown over anyhow onto the floor as if someone had been turning them over. I walked round the end of the sofa near the door.

Someone lay on the sofa, with splayed legs and moon face, eyes closed, mouth open, gleaming in the livid light.

The silence thickened. I stared. He lay so still. It gradually dawned on me that he was dead.

For a long time – how long? A minute? An hour? A hundred years? I didn't move. At last I bent slowly over him and my hand, with a life of its own, stretched out to touch his face. He was *cold*. Yet I jumped back as if I'd been burnt.

The room was cold too. I came to, as if from a dream. I was perfectly calm. I'd seen a dead body before – once; at the end of the war, after a V2 attack. It had looked a lot worse than this one: blood, wounds, half a face, one eye staring upwards. Mavor's eyes were closed. He looked peaceful.

There was no other living person in the house; I was certain of that. I was alone with a dead man. But I was not afraid. I was eerily alert, abnormally aware of my own reactions, noting as I pulled my coat more tightly around me that there was an exhilaration, an illicit excitement in my grim discovery, almost as if his lifelessness made me that much more alive.

I looked carefully round the room, noting the mess he'd lived in, and wondered how long he'd been here. He must have been far gone – perhaps despairing. Even his paintings were in a state, almost as if he'd attacked his own work.

I walked back round the sofa, out of the room, down the lofty stairs and out of the house. The door scraped on the stone lintel, and I couldn't get it shut. A lone pedestrian was approaching me, and glanced at me as we passed. I looked back, and it seemed to me that she was turning into the house I'd just left. I walked more quickly, hurried down Lamb's Conduit Street, suddenly needing the brighter lights of Holborn and Southampton Row, hurrying towards the underground, the Central Line to Notting Hill and the flat where Alan could hear the tale of my adventure.

Then I remembered my errand, Stan's letter still crushed into my bag. I slowed down. In fact, I sobered up. Why had Stan written to him? I walked along until I found a phone box.

I clanged my pennies into the slit and waited. But it was long after six now, and I doubted Stan would still be at the office. I didn't have his home number.

He answered. Thank God! I pressed button A and the pennies clattered down.

'Hullo! Hullo!' I shouted. 'It's me, Dinah. Something's happened. I found him, but – he's dead.'

Silence; then: '*Dead*? Can you meet me somewhere? Meet me at the milk bar round the corner from the office.'

'I'd better dial 999,' I said. 'Report it to the police; or get an ambulance.'

There was another silence, then he said slowly: 'No, don't do that. Not yet. We'll sort that out later. You've still got the letter, haven't you? You didn't leave that behind?'

My money ran out. I hung up. I stood there, and the letter was burning a hole in my bag. I honestly didn't mean to do it, but I drew it out and examined it. Why wasn't it sealed? Had Stanley just forgotten to lick it down? Carefully I pulled out the flap and drew out what was inside. There was no letter, simply a cheque for £150.

I left the sour-cold fug of the kiosk for the frozen street. I walked along, thinking. I didn't see a taxi, so I walked. It wasn't that far, even in this weather, and I needed time to think. £150. That was a staggeringly huge sum of money. Maybe it was for a painting. Stanley had said something about investing in art, although I doubted Mavor's style would have appealed to him.

Perhaps he'd simply been doing Mavor a good turn. Perhaps saving Mavor from destitution was his good deed for the week. Mavor was a notorious cadger, never paid for his drinks, someone always treated him, he was Fitzrovia's mascot ...

All the while the memory of his congealed body in the

cold empty house sank deeper and deeper into me. Cold in death. Death in this dark, endless winter. The inert, indigestible *fact* of it grew larger in my mind, heavy, morbid, menacing.

He'd died of drink. Must have. He was an alcoholic: sad but hardly sinister.

His eyes had been closed. Had someone closed them? Or had he simply slipped into a coma, floated peacefully away on an ebb tide of whisky?

· · · · · · · · ·

Stanley was waiting for me in the milk bar. It was pretty empty – it was a place for a lunchtime clientele, not really an evening place, tucked in as it was behind a big, impersonal department store, but maybe it stayed open for the cinema crowd later on. I'd have preferred to meet in a pub. I needed a drink. But Stanley never drank.

'Are you all right?' He looked at me. 'I'm so sorry – what can I say – I'd no idea ... ' He shook his head. 'Bloody hell – excuse the language – it's not the Blitz any more, you don't expect to find –' and in the nick of time he lowered his voice, 'dead bodies.' He bought me a coffee – pretty weak – and I handed him his envelope. He took it with an odd, crooked smile. 'Sure you're all right? Okay to tell me what happened?'

All the while he fingered the envelope, turned it over, laid it down, then picked it up again. He had a habit of chewing his nails when he was on edge – closing a deal, say, or ruminating on Gwendolen – and he was biting them now.

The woman behind the counter wiped its Perspex top. She eyed us sullenly.

'He was just – *there*. The place reeked of drink.' I paused. 'No. The smell was ... different.' What was that smell? It reminded me of ... 'I suppose he must have died of drink,' I said doubtfully.

Died of drink: it was a fate my father mentioned from time to time in connection with some school or college friend, gone to the dogs in the colonies or the army. It sounded plausible. I said it with confidence. And yet ...

'There was no sign of violence,' I added, 'but ... there was something ... I mean, the room wasn't just untidy. It was more than just alcoholic squalor. It had been turned upside down.'

The more I thought about it, the more suspicious it became. That could be how he'd lived, yet ... would he have hurled his own paintings around like that?

'Perhaps he was in such bad financial trouble that he killed himself,' I said. Mavor hadn't seemed the suicidal type, but – another of my father's insights drawn from the experience of years at the Bar – 'you never could tell.' My father's firm belief was that the least likely individuals were the most liable to end it all.

'What made you say that?' said Stanley.

'Say what?'

'No sign of violence. Why should there have been?'

Why had I said that? There was no reason to think ... but Stanley was disturbed by the suggestion. 'What made you say that?' he persisted.

'I don't know. Nothing. It was the shock, I suppose,' I added, as though in need of some excuse.

He leaned towards me, contrite. 'Yes – I'm sorry. Must have knocked you sideways.' He looked at me, consideringly. 'You've got pluck. You're bearing up well.'

'I'm okay. Really.'

'*Are* you?'

I nodded. And I was. But the unassimilable fact – Mavor dead – was congealing inside me like cold porridge, indigestible, inedible, impossible.

After a while Stanley muttered: 'He was a nasty bit of work, you know. Look how he insulted your commie friend that night at the restaurant.'

'Yes.'

Another silence. Stanley was biting his nails. He glanced sideways at me. 'There were rumours, you know ... he knew too much about people and ... ' he was almost whispering now, but seemed to have second thoughts and didn't finish his sentence.

As we sat there, our coffee growing cold, a suspicion trickled through my mind, like icy water. Could Mavor have been a blackmailer? Was that the explanation of the £150? Had he been blackmailing Stanley? Demanding money with menaces? I was anxious about being late home. Alan would worry and that would make him cross. Yet I sat on, held by a strange sense of camaraderie with Stanley. There's nothing like sharing a secret to bring you closer to another human being.

A secret: but was it a secret? Why was it a secret? Why did I think of it in that way? But of course: I'd found Mavor's body while delivering a letter for my boss. That would be just unusual enough to arouse curiosity if not suspicion in the minds of the police. Or did I just think that because I knew what the letter contained?

The police would have to be informed. We discussed this for some time. Everything about my upbringing had trained me into truthfulness; and truthfulness was not simply not telling a lie, it was telling the truth, the whole truth and nothing but the truth: above all the *whole* truth – but if I reported Mavor's death, I'd have to explain what I was doing in Mecklenburgh Square, why I'd been looking for Mavor.

'The thing is, Di,' said Stanley, man to man, 'I don't want my name brought into this. You understand that, don't you?

You know me, you know what I do, you know it's all perfectly above board. But in my line of business everything depends on trust, trust and reputation. I can't afford to have my name dragged into some sordid little ... scandal, mystery, whatever it is. Not that it probably is anything – just another arty-farty has-been who thought he was a genius and drank himself to death.'

'Alan said he confused self-indulgence with inspiration.'

Stanley liked that. 'Sums it up pretty accurately.'

But there was still the problem of what to do about it. I continued to urge informing the police as the only moral course of action. Stanley listened, not unsympathetically.

'Look,' he said finally, 'I agree. You are right. But let's just wait until tomorrow. With any luck someone else will find him. He is well known, after all, he won't just lie there to rot indefinitely. It's not as if he hasn't got any friends. Let's wait until tomorrow,' he repeated almost pleadingly, 'see if it makes the news.'

'And if it doesn't?'

'I'll see you in the office.'

I reminded him it would be Saturday. He said to come round anyway, and then we'd decide what to do.

I couldn't help feeling it would be even more difficult to go to the police tomorrow, but Stanley was persuasive, and anyway I wanted to go home. Sitting in the milk bar with its few stale sandwiches and buns had reminded me I was tired and hungry.

He walked me to the underground and patted my arm as we parted in the station ticket office. 'It'll be okay,' he said. 'Don't worry. It'll all be hunky-dory.'

Maybe optimism was what you needed more than anything else if you were to become a successful property developer. That and making other people believe you. And the thing about Stanley was you *did* believe him. For the time being, anyway.

s i x

❑❚❚❚❚❚❚❚❑

IT WAS THE MIDDLE OF THE EVENING and only a few tired passengers were scattered along the underground carriage. No one even glanced at me. I must look quite normal, when in fact I was radioactive with the shock of finding Titus Mavor's dead body in Mecklenburgh Square. I could hardly sit still, but my agitation was all in my body; I fidgeted and wriggled as if my clothes were filled with itching powder, while my mind was blank. There was no emotion, simply this epileptic feeling of having been wired up to the mains. Of course my weary fellow travellers sagging dejectedly along the seats were probably used to dead bodies. Perhaps everyone was still in shock after the war. There'd been so many dead bodies then. And this grey time was less Peacetime than the Aftermath of War. We were living in an Aftermath of dulled and deadened feelings.

My promise to Stanley: keep quiet until tomorrow – how could I? My loyalty to Alan, to my husband, clashed with this new loyalty. Stanley *must* be wrong; it must be one's duty to report the discovery of a body.

At Notting Hill Gate I made for one of the row of call boxes in the station. Again the metallic smell of the kiosk as I waited for 999 to answer.

'Ambulance!' I shouted, when I finally got through, and then, 'There's someone very ill in Mecklenburgh Square.' The man at the other end was asking questions. 'Where are you? Is he breathing?'

My heart thumped. What on earth could I say?

'Is the person breathing? Are you there?'

I panicked, hung up, and bolted from the phone booth, pulling my scarf round my face for fear someone would notice me, and remember me later.

I tried to hurry, but the ice and snow slowed me down as I stumbled along. My boots squeaked along the dark street towards the flat. The body of another tart had been discovered the previous week, but I was too worried about Mavor to be scared. Could they trace my call? I'd left fingerprints at the kiosk too – I'd taken off my gloves to put my pennies in the slot. I hadn't even disguised my voice. The police were sure to discover I lived in Notting Hill, because they would, in the end, in fact probably quite soon, discover the body, identify Mavor and find out all about his friends and acquaintances. They'd find out I'd failed to report his death. They'd arrest me. They might even suspect I'd murdered him.

Murder? He'd died from drink, from artistic excess.

I dreaded facing Alan. What was I going to tell him? Stanley had sworn me to secrecy, but I had to tell my husband. According to the Christian marriage ceremony we were one flesh anyway: one flesh, one person, so telling Alan wasn't like telling another person at all, not really – only would Stanley understand that? I didn't think so. To him it would be mere quibbling, which it was.

I wasn't sure, actually, that we were one flesh, since we'd only been married in a register office (my mother mortified, cheated of even an austerity white wedding, my father secretly relieved to avoid the fuss and expense).

I reached the house and looked upwards. The flat was in darkness: a surge of relief; Alan was out. I ran up the stairs to get out of the cold, lit the gas oven and left the door open to warm up the kitchen while I made hot Bovril and toast. I turned on the radio, hoping for a news bulletin, but there wasn't one due.

Time ticked idly by. Now I was agitated because I had no one to talk to. I wondered where Alan was and what he was doing. I wandered into the sitting room, to see if he'd left a note. There wasn't one, and anyway, he'd have left it on the kitchen table. We lived in the kitchen, to save electricity. Since we'd burnt the wood we'd collected we hardly used the chilly sitting room and it smelled musty and stale.

It was ten o'clock before I heard voices on the stairs – huge relief. Alan wasn't alone; Hugh and Colin must be with him. My confession could be postponed – though at the same time I was bursting with the need to tell all.

Alan surged into the kitchen followed by Hugh. Colin wasn't with them after all, but the cramped room felt overcrowded even with just two great big men. They were triumphant and euphoric, like commandos after a successful mission.

'Darling! Hugh thinks he's winning Radu round.' Alan, usually undemonstrative in public, hugged me. He was rosy from the cold and he smelled of the frost and smoke of the streets.

He produced a half bottle of gin from his capacious coat pocket and set it on the table. They'd obviously already had a few. And was there something odd about their mood? A tinge of schoolboy guilt as if they'd pulled off some prank? Alan searched around and found some Rose's lime juice to have with the gin and we gathered at the table to celebrate. He sat leaning back majestically, the monarch of all he surveyed. Hugh was sparkling with glee.

'Where's Colin?' I asked.

They exchanged looks. Hugh went a bit pink.

'Had something better to do,' mumbled Alan.

I listened to them for a while as they mapped out the plot. With each shot of gin their script grew more elaborate. They were totally absorbed. I sat there with a lump of concrete in my stomach. Mavor. I hadn't forgotten. Of course I hadn't. Why couldn't I tell them? I simply couldn't, not with Hugh there. I needed to get Alan alone.

'Alan ...?'

'Yes, darling?' He looked up distractedly.

'I'm a bit sleepy. Would you mind if I ...'

He completely misunderstood. Sweet – he thought I was trying to entice him to bed. But how would he have guessed what I had to tell him? He wouldn't have in a hundred years. He grinned. 'Okay, I'll be along in a tick.'

· · · · · · · · · ·

As I groped my way forward the shadows pressed round me. The house was icy cold. Moonlight gleamed on his glistening face; the body lay on the sagging sofa. Terror rose from the pit of my stomach and became a scream as I surged up towards consciousness and surfaced in darkness.

Alan's arms were round me. 'Darling – darling. You had a nightmare. You must have been cold – the eiderdown's slid off.'

The feeling of horror, so overwhelming in the dream, faded, but of course I told him everything.

We were still talking three hours later as it got light. What Alan called my pluck astonished him. To take it so calmly, to report back to Stanley – actually he was annoyed I hadn't gone straight to him (only I couldn't have, because he was out). I could see that the more he discussed it, the more sceptical he became. 'Are you *sure* he was dead?' he kept saying. 'You couldn't have imagined it?'

'Imagined it? Don't be such a clot!'

'Stanley should never have sent you round like that.' He was outraged that *his wife* had been used as messenger on some shady errand. It must have been some crooked deal, he said. But if Stanley was crooked, didn't that mean that Titus was too? I asked, but Alan endearingly resisted the idea that Titus – an old Etonian, after all, like him – could have been implicated in anything underhand. Yes, he was a cad, but vulgar criminal activity, never.

'Then what was the cheque for, darling? *A hundred and fifty pounds!*'

'Are you sure you read it properly? It wasn't fifty? Fifteen?'

'It wasn't fifty, or fifteen, Alan.' I paused. 'You don't think it could have been blackmail, do you?'

Blackmailers hounded their victims, hounded them even to death. Blackmail was a private crime, to do with secrets and sins, with adultery, poisoning, incest. It was a spiteful, twisted thing, a form of persecution – and the painter had certainly struck me as spiteful. At the very least, he liked needling people, although that wasn't quite the same thing. Anyway, what could he have blackmailed Stanley *about*? If my boss dabbled in the black market it was on a very small scale; and even with his property deals he was only doing what everyone was doing all over the country: getting around rationing, restrictions and red tape. Even my father, who deplored the mounting crime wave in the strongest possible terms, even he had accepted a goose from a client – a farmer – he'd successfully defended. That wasn't under the counter or black market; that was gratitude.

It was true, too, that Stanley was trying to get divorced, but no women ever called the office, he didn't seem to have a girlfriend: unless – and the thought struck me forcibly – he was actually having an affair with Gwendolen. But I didn't believe that either.

Alan scoffed at the idea of blackmail. 'Titus! Don't be ridiculous. Even if he wanted to he's simply not organised enough; chaotic, his life's in a state of advanced decomposition.' (He spoke as though Titus were still alive.) 'It might have been Colman's idea to pay him to keep quiet about something, I suppose ...'

I was afraid Alan would want me to stop being Stanley's secretary now. To avoid, or at least postpone that argument I set him off on what was after all the greater puzzle: why was Titus dead? Drink – yes – yet many forty-year-olds drank as much as he, with no apparent ill effects. Everyone we knew drank – everyone except Stanley, anyway, and that didn't count, because he wasn't one of the Wheatsheaf crowd.

It was getting light now. Alan sprang out of bed: 'We're going round there.'

'What on earth for?'

He pulled on his trousers: 'We were going to Charing Cross Road anyway, remember? It's more or less on our way – well, sort of.'

'The bookshops won't be open yet!'

'By the time we've had breakfast – and I'm having a bath. If there's any hot water.'

An hour or so later as we walked to the bus stop he said: 'You are sure it wasn't *all* in the dream? Only in the dream. You don't think – '

That *was* it! He thought I'd imagined the whole thing, the pig. That's why he wanted to go round to Mecklenburgh Square. He was expecting to find Titus Mavor alive and well –

alive at least.

The square was deserted. The door of 119 was still not quite shut. We stepped inside. 'Wait here,' said Alan in a low voice. 'I'll go on up.'

When he came down again he looked very pale. 'We'll have to report it,' he said. He walked a few steps away from the house, stopped and, for once, seemed at a loss. 'We *have* to report it, can't just let it go ... Oh God, I wish I hadn't dragged you round here now ... Let's just say we called round to see him – no need to mention last night. Yes, that's it. We'll just say we called round this morning and found him like that.'

We walked across to the police station in Tottenham Court Road in almost total silence. The officer on duty was deferential, and promised to send someone round right away. 'Must have been a bit of a shock for you, sir. A friend, you said he was?'

'Yes – well, not a close friend, but ... known him a long time, you see.'

The policeman took down our names and address. 'I daresay this statement will be sufficient, but we may need to see you again.'

We came out into the grey street. Some shop windows were still boarded up, but articles for sale were beginning to reappear in the others. We walked towards the Charing Cross Road, passing Heal's, where a beautiful blue sofa in the window caught my attention. Export only, of course, and anyway we had no money to buy a sofa, nor anywhere to put it either, for that matter; but it took my mind off Mavor – briefly.

We wandered down to the Charing Cross Road and browsed round the bookshops, but our hearts weren't in it. 'D'you think the police will get in touch with us again?'

Alan shrugged. 'Don't expect so. We gave a statement, after all.'

'You did.'

'It's not as if there was anything suspicious.'

Alan had taken charge in the police station, but I could see that underneath the air of authority he was shaken. Titus Mavor sprawled on the sofa in broad daylight must have been an unpleasant sight. The house was arctic but he'd been dead for nearly twenty-four hours now: at least. And it was odd, but Alan had come through the war without seeing any dead bodies. With death all around he'd floated through, only to come up against a corpse, now, in peacetime. It was ironic, but I was almost – not glad, but ... relieved to see him vulnerable. Somehow it vindicated me.

On a normal Saturday we queued for food in the Portobello Road market, and got our meat ration from the butcher we were registered with over there. This was not a normal Saturday, but food had to be obtained, so we abandoned the bookshops for Soho, where we scraped together some vegetables. They were terribly expensive – carrots at a shilling and sixpence, when normally they'd be about twopence, but we bought them anyway, and they all went into my string bag, which I took, rolled up in my pocket, wherever I went, because you never knew when you might chance upon something worth getting, a jar of Bovril, for example, or something off points like Ovaltine (which I didn't like, but Alan ate it neat, the granules straight out of the tin).

As we went from shop to shop and then passed up and down the vegetable stalls we spoke only to consult about the food. We walked back through the gritty streets without a word. I stopped outside the French pub and said: 'Why don't we go in here?' but Alan shook his head.

'Might see someone we know – what are we going to say?'

Until that moment it hadn't occurred to me that we were the bearers of bad news. He was right. How could we sit among friends and not say what we knew? Yet we couldn't tell them either; it'd open up such a Pandora's box of lies. We found a café with steamy windows in a side street and sat down. Alan removed his hat – the broad-brimmed black effort, which made him look very artistic and *fin de siècle*. He was frowning and worried. 'How do we explain why we found him, how we happened to be there?'

We sat over our coffees in a cloud of cigarette smoke. There was something nauseating about having this secret to ourselves. It was shock, it was gossip, there was an unpleasant thrill about knowing something before anyone else knew. It was frightening too; someone who'd been a disreputable but minor character in our social world, had turned the tables on us. He'd become tragic and now we couldn't laugh at him or despise him any more.

'Why do we have to tell anyone?' I asked, but even as I spoke I imagined the gossip there'd be in the pubs and clubs and how could we just sit there and pretend to know nothing about it? There'd be news items saying he was found by a friend. It was all looking awfully awkward. 'Talk to the others,' I said, meaning Hugh and Colin, and lit a cigarette. (I'd switched to Craven A, because I liked the packet, red with a picture of a black cat, or rather its head, in the centre.)

'Good idea. I will. D'you mind?'

'I'll go home with the stuff. I'm exhausted anyway, we had so little sleep.'

I was secretly pleased, because I didn't intend to go straight home. I had to confess to Stanley that I'd told Alan everything and he needed to know we'd reported the death. I felt terrible – it felt like a betrayal and I dreaded facing him. At the same time I wanted to get it over with as soon as possible, and I hadn't forgotten he'd said he'd be in the office.

As I walked down Maddox Street I saw a man and a

woman coming towards me. They were walking slowly, heads bent, close together, like conspirators: Stanley and Gwendolen. As I drew near I saw that Stanley was holding her arm. I almost turned into a doorway to try to avoid them seeing me – I don't know why. Anyway, it was too late. Was it my imagination, or were they for a split second trying to avoid me too?

We drew close in the narrow stony gorge off busy Regent Street.

'Dinah! Darling!' Detaching herself from Stanley, Gwendolen stretched out her gloved hand to me and caught me in a rigid embrace. The stiff veil attached to her hat scratched my cheek.

Stanley watched us, slightly apart, his homburg hat slightly back on his head, how he always wore it. 'On your way to the office?'

'I wanted to tell you – ' I stopped; I didn't really want to say it in front of Gwendolen. But that was ridiculous. 'We went to the police.' I smiled hopefully. 'We just felt we had to ...' Why was I being so pathetically ingratiating? It was obviously the right thing to do.

They stared at me. Stanley patted my arm. 'Probably for the best.'

'I'm sorry. Alan insisted.' It was cowardly of me to blame Alan. I'd been all for going to the police myself. As it was, I'd failed to report the death immediately and I'd broken my word to Stanley; the worst of all worlds. My words congealed in the frozen air. Why didn't Gwen say anything?

'We're going to lunch at the Hungaria. Why don't you join us?'

'No, no ... I can't. Thank you all the same.' I was dying to talk to Stan, to 'chew the fat' as he'd have put it, but I couldn't with Gwendolen there.

In her bold leopardskin coat she looked frozen: 'It's such a shock. I can't believe it.' The words came slowly as though she were dragging them up from the bottom of a well.

We walked on, out into the main street and towards Piccadilly. Suddenly more words came, staccato: 'I knew him when I first came to London, you know, when I worked as an artist's model. He drank so much, even then. Such a waste.' She pulled her fur more tightly round her. 'Radu will be upset. He was so keen to have Titus work on the film.'

. . . .

When I reached home, Alan, Hugh and Colin were already in conference in the kitchen. It wasn't just the smoke and the fug – chilly and stuffy at the same time – there was a feeling of tension in the air. I put the kettle on and stood by the stove.

Alan looked up at me. 'We were just talking about Titus. You know how Radu was hoping his name would help get financial backing for the film.'

I'd forgotten. 'But will it really affect the film? He hadn't got involved, had he? Not really?'

'At the very least, Radu *liked* the idea that Mavor might be involved. He loved the whole idea of Surrealism.'

'It was more than that,' insisted Hugh. 'Mavor may have pissed all his money away and drunk himself to death, but he's a pretty big name in the art world, you know. Well he *was*. And Surrealism went beyond the art world, anyway, they were so good at publicity. Dali especially, of course – and Titus was a sort of disciple of his.'

'That's such rot.' Colin always seemed to be in a foul mood these days, and now he was scowling and disagreeing as usual. 'Before the war, maybe, but Titus was a busted flush, everyone's forgotten about him now. Him dying's just the logical conclusion.'

'That's a bit heartless. What was it he said – he was a rotten element – I suppose that's the *line*, is it, just as well we're rid of him?' Perhaps Hugh really did fear that without the name of Titus Mavor they wouldn't get any money. He too seemed in a very bad mood.

'I didn't say that,' said Colin, 'but you'd hardly expect me to pretend to be upset.'

'Revolutionary honesty, I suppose.'

'Oh, come on, Hugh,' said Alan, 'none of us liked the man.'

'Well, everyone knows you hated him, Colin, since that very public row in the Café Royal.'

Colin now looked so angry I quickly changed the subject: 'I ran into Stanley and Gwen on the way home.'

'Oh really? Had he told her?'

'Yes. She seemed stunned.'

seven

■■■■■■■■□

AROUND FITZROVIA INDIVIDUALS CAME AND WENT. They faded in and out of the raffish throng that eddied around the shabby streets, floating along from pub to pub on waves of unfulfilled hope and indecision. Mavor's death had caused ripples, but failed artists and alcoholic has-beens were two a penny and the habitués soon forgot about the pallid corpse as it was borne away downstream.

Or would have done had rumours not started to circulate. And the most awful thing was they were swirling around *us*.

The weather briefly eased. We returned to our usual haunts – the Wheatsheaf, the Caves de France, Chez Victor, the Barcelona – to find ourselves the centre of attention. They all knew we'd found Mavor. I don't know how, but they did. A miasma of notoriety followed us, almost as if we'd murdered him ourselves.

Rumours were flying around like confetti, thanks largely to Gerald Blackstone. Blackstone was the local paper's crime reporter, and as such he cultivated the police. At first the story was that 'the cause of death has not yet been established', but soon Gerry began to drop massive hints in his reports for the *St Pancras Chronicle* that the police suspected foul play, and in the various watering holes he frequented he went considerably further.

He said the police had bungled the case from the start. You'd find him after a few beers leaning forward in a conspiratorial manner, with a little cluster of gossips hanging on his every word. There wasn't a proper forensic examination at first, he claimed. 'But now there has been. Seems there were burn marks round the mouth and nose that they think were caused by chloroform.'

I remembered the smell in that room again; the smell that was not quite like alcohol.

According to Gerry, someone had first drugged, then suffocated the artist. The post mortem had shown that Mavor's liver and heart were seriously damaged, but – amazingly – he hadn't been drinking the night he died.

'The cops are playing it down for the moment – embarrassing for them. Haven't you noticed, there's been hardly a squeak from them since the original news he was dead? But now the family's started to create a stink, so they're going to have to smarten up.'

A frisson rippled round the bars as the thwarted geniuses contemplated murder. Insidiously, an atmosphere of conspiracy and paranoia developed. To have actually known a murder victim swelled the hangers-on with a sense of sinister importance. Detectives were seen in the Wheatsheaf and the Barcelona. Compulsively the talk went to and fro. Had he *really* been murdered? Who could have done it? Couldn't he have sniffed the chloroform himself?

Always the big question was: why should anyone have wanted to murder Titus Mavor? What could have been the motive? Hardly burglary! He hadn't a penny.

'What about his paintings?' Noel Valentine was most aggrieved as if Titus had died on purpose to thwart him. 'He said I could represent him, but then he slid out of it again.'

'Broken promises! Verbal diarrhoea, he'd promise anything,' sneered Marius Smith, who was one of the painters who'd witnessed the Café Royal brawl. 'But that gives you a motive, eh,Valentine?'

Noel laughed. 'Stuff that! I wanted him *alive*, didn't I. I needed his signature. And his bloody canvases.'

'He'd have got a big spread in the *Statesman*, the *Spectator*,' said Hugh, 'not to mention the art journals; there'd have been huge obituaries all over the show. Bad luck, to die at a time like this, when they've all been suspended because of the fuel crisis. But the *Daily Worker* did their bit, at least.' That was Hugh needling Colin again, because never mind about speaking no ill of the dead, the Communists proclaimed in no uncertain terms their disdain for the renegade painter. Whoever had written it (and we all thought it was Colin) almost implied that Mavor, having preferred the seduction of reactionary bourgeois art to the truths of socialist painting, deserved to come to a sticky end.

And now the ugly truth was slowly sinking in: Titus Mavor *had* come to a sticky end. And lurking underneath the gossip was always the frisson of fear and doubt and mutual suspicion. For the answer to the question, who would have wanted to murder Mavor, was: almost everyone we knew.

· · · · · · · · ·

When I answered the door, out of breath as I'd run down three flights of stairs, I found myself face to face with a stranger in a crombie and a trilby hat: the police. He raised his hat. Eerily, he reminded me of Neville Heath; the same neat face, the same dapper toothbrush moustache. 'Detective Inspector Bannister,' he said. He stamped his feet to get the snow off, and I led him up to the flat.

'Shocking weather,' he said, 'Can't believe this freeze can go on much longer – and then again, it seems as if it don't want ever to end.'

Alan was standing tousled in the kitchen, in pyjama trousers and two sweaters. 'Who was it?' he shouted when he heard my footsteps.

'It's the police to see us,' I said brightly. I wasn't apprehensive; why should I be? I offered him tea or coffee, which he refused. The kitchen was such a mess that I showed him into the stale-smelling, chilly sitting room.

'I'm sorry to trouble you,' said the inspector, 'I'm making enquiries about the death of the artist, Titus Mavor. I believe it was you, sir, who found him and reported the death.'

Alan pushed back his tousled hair. 'That's right.'

'I wonder if you could just go into a little more detail as to exactly what you found. There wasn't a lot of information in the original report.'

The constable at Tottenham Court Road police station had, I remembered, been a bit casual about it all. The experience of the war, when the finding of corpses was a routine event, must have blunted his sense of urgency; it was the Aftermath effect again.

Alan described Mavor lying on his sofa and the debris surrounding him. He, like me, had noticed the way canvases had been roughly treated. Inspector Bannister ignored that information; he was more interested in Mavor's appearance, the bottles, the smell.

He also wanted to know why we'd visited Mavor on that Saturday morning. Perhaps it was naïve of me, but this did come as a surprise. I hadn't expected him to be interested in us. Alan looked blank. He'd probably forgotten what we'd told the other policeman. I certainly had. Finally Alan said hesitantly: 'He and I – there was some talk of our working together on a film.'

A look of almost salacious interest appeared on Detective Inspector Bannister's face, as if film making were some dubious activity, somehow not quite nice. 'A film, sir?' He put his head on one side.

Alan was happy to enlighten someone he'd all too obviously cast as a philistine. He spattered names and information about, and told Inspector Bannister rather too much, I thought, about Radu, Hugh and Colin. At the name of Gwendolen Grey the policeman smiled. 'Ah,' he said, '*House of Shadows*; a very ... unusual film. My wife greatly enjoyed it.' He paused. Then: 'So the deceased was a friend of yours. Would you know, did he have enemies? Anyone who had a grudge against him? Professional rivalries, anything like that? We've heard he was a somewhat ... controversial character. Colourful, but controversial. As his friend, you might be able to help us there.'

'He wasn't a close friend, but I suppose you could say we moved in the same social circles, before the war, but then I lost sight of him again. He wanted to be a war artist, but there was never any chance of that and he rather went to the dogs, I gathered. I've – well, we've seen him a few times recently again, that's all. Isn't that right, Dinah?'

I nodded. I'd been brought up to look on the police as 'on our side'. My father regarded them as civilian NCOs and other ranks, subordinates, good chaps, if a bit thick. Alan was the same; so far as he was concerned policemen were a kind of public version of the servant class (although of course everything was changing now and the servant class had disappeared, to my mother's dismay). Yet something about this conversation disturbed me. I had a strong suspicion the detective knew something he wasn't telling us.

'He had a bit of a reputation with women, I gather, sir,' he said. 'You must have known if he had a lady friend, a fiancée, anything like that – someone who might feel resentful if his behaviour wasn't up to the mark.'

'There was a girl called … Fiona, I think,' I said. 'We didn't really know her.'

'Ah.' The inspector looked at us. 'You see, a young woman was seen leaving the house in Mecklenburgh Square the evening before your visit.'

He was looking at me. My face felt hot. Oh God, was I blushing? I didn't look at Alan, and I knew he was looking anywhere but at me. I managed to shake my head, miming bafflement, swallowing hard.

Alan put in coolly: 'You said yourself – he had a reputation.'

'As a bit of a ladies' man, yes,' confirmed the inspector. 'So, it might have been this – Fiona, did you say? Any idea where I'd find her?'

'We just met her once. We didn't know her at all,' said Alan firmly. 'And I think you're barking up the wrong tree there, if you don't mind my saying so. I'm sure she's perfectly harmless – just one of his models, probably.'

'I see.' He stood up. 'Well, thank you. You've been very helpful.'

After he'd gone Alan and I looked at each other. 'Someone saw you.'

We needed something stronger than coffee. Alan found the remains of a bottle of Algerian wine.

I remembered the shadowy figure who'd passed me in the street. I'd looked back. She – he – was it she? – had looked back too. I'd thought at the time that whoever it was had gone into the house I'd just left, but that seemed unlikely; because that person would have found Titus dead and would – surely – have reported it.

'We lied to Bannister,' said Alan. 'We didn't say it was you who found Mavor.'

I knew that all too well. 'If it comes out, it's going to look suspicious.'

'Why should it come out?' Alan spoke belligerently. 'It's ridiculous – no one could think you were involved! Anyway, we can't change our story now.' That was the problem. We were stuck with a version that was not quite the truth, and certainly not the whole truth and nothing but the truth.

'Was it okay to tell him about Fiona? Was that the right thing to do? I hope he isn't going to think ...' More guilty feelings!

'Colman got us into this,' said Alan savagely.

Stanley was the only other person who knew I'd found Titus. So the one good thing out of all this was that Alan could hardly stop me working for him now. Our secret had bound us together.

eight

■□■■■■■□□

IT WASN'T ENOUGH FOR GERRY BLACKSTONE just to spread rumours based on what he'd gleaned from the police. He actually managed to get down to the Mavor family's country house in Suffolk on his motorbike, in spite of the blizzards. When he returned from what was by his account a journey comparable to Scott's to the South Pole, the whole of Fitzrovia once more hung on his every word.

Mavor's mother, the family matriarch, was a terrifying woman, he said. 'Old as the hills, but got a girl who couldn't be more than ten. Imagine a woman of that age having had sexual intercourse as recently as 1937! And the house!' he went on. 'Victorian gothic, absolutely ghastly, worse than Balmoral.' At this point in the soon-familiar story he would pause for effect and light a Woodbine. 'They don't want any of Mavor's Fitzrovia friends at the funeral, I can tell you that much. I managed to convince them I was from the *Daily Telegraph*, or I don't think I'd have got past the door. They blame us, you know – all our fault – we drove him to drink. *And one of us murdered him.*'

The funeral was delayed by the blizzards, and few of the Charlotte Street hangers on would have made it in any weather. It would have been quite beyond their planning capabilities or stamina to cross the freezing wastes of Essex and Suffolk to get to a funeral – even if the thought of free drinks at the end might have been an incentive.

But Hugh was determined to get there. 'Someone has to represent us.' But it was his curiosity that drove him rather than any sense of camaraderie or group loyalty. 'And you never know, I might pick up some useful information.'

A couple of days after he got back he came round to tell us about it. The funeral had been a macabre affair: the family formed a small procession in black, like beetles scratching along the snow. 'It was a bit like that scene in *Ivan the Terrible*. There was a kind of Utility service in the unheated church (nineteenth century, most undistinguished) with no music or flowers, apart from "Abide with Me" at the end, accompanied by a wheezing harmonium. Don't you *hate* "Abide with Me" – it is so abysmally maudlin.' He paused for dramatic effect. 'And you know who was there – the policeman: Bannister.'

Afterwards, he said, the dozen or so mourners all stood shiftily round the graveside in the little churchyard, staring down into the gaping black wound in the snow, not knowing quite what to do after the vicar had retreated and the gravedigger tried hopelessly to pile the frozen earth onto the coffin. 'But then,' said Hugh, 'just as we were about to wander away among the gravestones, with that sense of anti-climax and incompletion one always gets at the end of a funeral, you know – and I can tell you, they *didn't* invite me back to the house – guess who turned up! His floozie! That girl ... Fiona! God knows how she got there. Anyway, she created an appalling scene. You should have seen the consternation on their faces, they clearly thought she was a tart, they backed away as if she was contagious, while she was screaming and sobbing hysterically, and shouting abuse at the assembled throng. Embarrassing enough that Titus was murdered, without the added *faux pas* of a hysterical mistress. Bloody good thing I was there,' said Hugh. 'I led her away – took her to the local pub. All they had was ginger wine. We got drunk on that. Which was damn difficult, I can tell you. Good move though,' he went on. 'The publican was a garrulous old chap – place was deserted, probably hadn't seen a customer for weeks, they were completely cut off, he told me, until a snow plough got through weekend before last. Anyway – I've no idea how he knew, but apparently the family's kicking up no end about the bungled investigation. And he insisted Titus had a *child*. Did you know that – she's down there, living with them, they're bringing her up it appears. Some ex-mistress or other … that upset Fiona. And the other thing he told me was the family had some fantasy that Titus was fleeced – by all of us, I suppose. Something about his paintings; it all got rather garbled at that point, or perhaps the ginger wine was taking its toll. Fearfully sickly. A bit rich, don't you think? They can't stand him or his art while he's alive and won't give him a penny, although they're incredibly rich, and then before he's cold in his grave they're fighting over the spoils.'

'I'm not sure how much his stuff is worth these days,' said Alan. 'English Surrealism was never that big, and it's all gone rather out of fashion. I know Valentine is trying to revive it, but …'

'I left Fiona at Liverpool Street. She said she'd be all right, but … I felt a bit rotten, but I was so tired and it was so late … look – why don't you go and see her, Dinah. She's in a terrible state.'

'We probably should talk to her anyway,' said Alan, 'she may be a suspect.'

'I'm sure she is,' said Hugh, and now he seemed deadly serious. 'That policeman came round to Lavender Hill the next day, you know. He'd noticed me go off with her after the upset. He was quite unpleasant, actually.'

'Why didn't you tell us sooner?'

'Oh ...' and Hugh shook back his flop of hair, 'it was nothing, nothing really. I mean, I've got nothing to hide.' At all costs he had to preserve his sangfroid. 'But he was awfully interested in Fiona.'

. . . .

We didn't know Fiona's surname or where she lived, but it wasn't hard to find her. Our first port of call was the Wheatsheaf, naturally. Gully the barman said she didn't drink there any more, not since she'd broken up with Mavor. He thought she might be found at the Caves de France. 'Poor old Titus,' he said. 'Terrible! It really knocked me for six. I mean, he was a bad lot, wasn't he, but talk about hitting a man when he's down ... owed me money, too. I'll never see that now.'

The Caves de France was a dingy tunnel of a basement. Fiona was sitting by herself in a line with other solitaries drowning their sorrows in weak tea. She seemed not to recognise us at first. At least, she knew she'd seen us somewhere, but didn't recall the occasion. When it dawned who we were, she seemed pathetically pleased.

'Let's go somewhere more cheerful,' suggested Alan.

The difficulty was: where. Reluctantly we followed him out of the fug of the basement into the frozen air of the street. I'd learned something this winter: you *never* get used to the cold. If you lived all your life in Siberia, there'd still be that shrinking into the shell each time you were exposed, that chill of its slow, relentless penetration of your whole body, its fingers sliding beneath your clothing, nipping, pinching, piercing your very soul as it slowed you down and brought you to a standstill of frozen endurance. Just grit your teeth and survive.

We stumbled along uncertainly in the re-imposed blackout until Alan said: 'I know – we'll go to the Strand Palace. That should cheer us up.'

In fact, it did, although we looked rather out of place in the flashy mirrored grandeur of the lounge, and dishevelled by comparison with the nouveaux riches types who made up the clientele. I was quite thankful we weren't asked to leave, but Alan's commanding manner managed to neutralise his black fedora hat, my moth-eaten musquash and Fiona's threadbare coat.

Beer didn't seem quite the right drink in this glass palace, so it was spirits all round, and owing to the awkwardness of the situation – we hadn't actually known Titus well, I certainly didn't; and Fiona didn't know us – the three of us got rather drunk.

Fiona was definitely one of those young women my parents had warned me against. (If you're not careful, Dinah, you'll end up one of those bohemian women who hang around the arty crowd. Semi-professional, they'd added darkly, in some dingy bedsitter in Chelsea. Or worse.) Yet she seemed vulnerable and a bit stupid rather than evil or sinister.

It was just as well we sought her out, because Bannister had got there first. She was rattled and fearful as she told us about his visit.

When she heard about Titus she'd been so shattered she'd left town for a few days, she said. 'We hadn't separated, not really. We had a row, that's all. I couldn't tell you what it was about,' she said, close to tears again. 'It was just – you know – a *row*. He drank so much and he never had any lolly. We might have got back together again,' she added, and at that began to sob uncontrollably. 'I don't know what I'll do now,' she choked.

'For God's sake, control yourself.' And Alan looked round uneasily, hoping the waiter hadn't noticed. I put my arm round her. It felt awkward and stiff and didn't seem to help, but after a while she calmed down, sniffed and wiped her eyes.

Alan must have realised he'd been brusque, for now he was gentle as he asked her about the night Mavor had died. 'It was a Friday,' he prompted her, 'it was the night after that snowstorm.'

But how would she remember that! We'd had more blizzards than Siberia! She shook her head drearily. Her hair drooped over her face. She began to irritate me. She was attractive in an obvious sort of way, and could have made something of herself if she hadn't been so spineless. I wished she would stop snivelling. It was late and I was tired and I'd had too much to drink.

And I was worried. Mavor's family were cutting up rough and the police had stepped up their investigation. They were taking it very seriously now. It was turning into a major newspaper story.

Worst of all, nagging away in my mind was always the fear they were going to find out I'd been round to Mecklenburgh Square that night, that fatal night. *I* could be a suspect. At the very least, I'd concealed the truth. I'd failed to report a dead body.

To make matters worse I had, without meaning to, exposed Fiona by mentioning her to Inspector Bannister. He'd acted fast. He must be seriously interested in her. He was seriously interested in all of us.

I sat in the showy glitter of the hotel lounge and wondered how soon I'd be caught. I didn't really believe, deep down, that they'd think I'd murdered Titus, but there were other crimes: accessory after the fact, concealing evidence, well – just lying to the police was bad enough.

'But who could have ... done it?' whimpered Fiona, and in a low voice: 'That policeman asked me about everyone I knew; all his friends – the Barcelona crowd, but I told him Titus had quarrelled with all of them – and your lot; the detective was interested in your friend and the row in that restaurant, you remember?'

'Colin?'

'That's right. The political one. Titus couldn't stand him.'

Alan's face darkened. 'Who told him about the row? Did you tell him?'

She shook her head. 'He knew already. He brought it up.'

We hadn't any more money for more expensive drinks at the Strand Palace, so we braved the cold again, and parted company with Fiona at Leicester Square. At least we knew where she lived now, and I still felt so worried and guilty about her that a couple of days later I called on her in Charlotte Street. I'd left work early – three in the afternoon – but Fiona was still in bed. She got up, frowsty and groggy in a soiled satin dressing gown, but seemed quite pleased to see me.

Her bedsitter was dismal. The curtains were grubby. There was a gas ring by the fireplace, and a little sink in a corner behind a screen, over which various garments were flung. The unmade bed took up a good deal of the room.

She apologised as she pulled up the blankets and eiderdown. I sat squashily on the mauve artificial silk counterpane. She offered me cocoa, but there wasn't any milk. Anyway, I'd brought some cheap wine I'd picked up on the way, so we opened that instead.

The room wasn't too warm. She put a thick cardigan on over her robe and I huddled into my fur. I was wondering how to launch my interrogation, when there was a knock on Fiona's door, and before she even had time to say 'Come in,'

Inspector Bannister stood in the doorway. He looked very alert when he saw me.

'I hope this isn't an inconvenient time, miss,' he said to Fiona in a not very respectful way. 'Would it be better,' he said, casting a dubious look round her chaotic room, 'if you got dressed and we had a talk down at the station?'

Fiona pushed back her tumbled hair and shook her head. With more presence of mind than me, she said: 'I'm not under arrest, am I.' It was a statement, not a question. She cleared a heap of clothes off the only chair in the room. 'Excuse me a moment.' She disappeared behind the screen.

'So you know Miss Johnson quite well, do you?' Bannister gave me a straight look, as though I'd been deceiving him before.

'No; but with all that's happened, she's upset, we've tried to help,' I said righteously. I felt righteous too, although the real reason for my visit was to help us, not her. 'Would you like some wine?'

He shook his head disapprovingly. 'Not the sort of friend I'd have thought a young lady like yourself would have,' he said prissily.

I ignored this rude remark. Fiona was only behind the screen and must have heard it. When she emerged she was wearing slacks with the cardigan and had combed her hair and put on a bit of lipstick. She bent over the gas ring to boil the kettle.

'Please don't bother, miss,' fussed Bannister, but she insisted on making him a cup of tea. I wished we'd stuck to tea too, for the wine was making me feel somewhat befuddled.

Fiona handed him the cup and saucer. 'There isn't any milk.'

When Bannister looked crafty he reminded me more than ever of Neville Heath. 'Perhaps, Mrs Wentworth might like to get some milk while we have a chat.'

The cheek of the man! I wasn't running errands for him. Fiona wasn't having it either. 'If this is just an informal chat, I'd rather she stayed. I've nothing to hide, but I know the tricks you lot get up to.'

'I hope you're not suggesting I'd falsify a statement,' he said with his Cheshire-cat smile. He began to ask questions about Titus, especially the evening Titus died. It was obviously to see if Fiona had an alibi. She said she'd spent the evening with a friend. The more he pestered her to be more specific, the more uneasy she became.

Perhaps, I thought, she hadn't been with anyone at all. Perhaps she'd just sat in this dreary bedsit and cried – and got drunk, and smoked and possibly taken drugs. Perhaps she'd sniffed ether or chloroform, which I hadn't even realised you could use as a drug until all this had happened. Perhaps she'd set out for Mecklenburgh Square with the bottle – even in this weather it wasn't that far – found her ex-lover in a drunken stupor and simply finished him off; except that it appeared that he hadn't been in a drunken stupor. And anyway, it would have had to be in the afternoon, because he was already cold when I'd ... but I had to forget about that. Although the room was chilly, I was sweating now.

'I was seeing a friend,' she finally admitted sulkily. 'I can't tell you their name.'

'Was that a gentleman friend?' said Bannister, nastily. Fiona nodded reluctantly.

I was shocked. So she was a tart, after all, or at least a kind of good-time girl. I'd been too naïve to believe that at first, or rather, I couldn't believe that *I* could ever come into contact with a prostitute. Then I was shocked at this thought too; what a miserable little middle-class prig I was, after all, beneath my veneer of sophistication. Colin was quite right when he criticised me for my 'bourgeois consciousness'.

'You mean you don't know his name, or you don't want to tell me his name because it'll damage your business?' persisted Bannister.

Fiona began to look a bit scared, but she said defiantly: 'I don't know what you mean by business. I hope you're not suggesting anything.'

The detective looked at her speculatively. 'Suggesting what? I've spoken to the people downstairs. Men in and out. You'd better think carefully,' he said. She flushed up. He let the humiliation sink in.

'What else d'you want me to say? I've nothing more *to* say. So if you wouldn't mind, I'd like you to leave now.'

'Certainly.' He turned to me. 'I'm glad to have seen you, Mrs Wentworth. There were one or two more points I wanted to take up with you and your husband. Perhaps a convenient time – tomorrow evening?'

'I don't know if my husband'll be in.'

He smiled. 'I might just look in on the off chance. I'll see myself out.' And he was gone.

Fiona became tearful again. 'I suppose you think I'm a tart too,' she sniffed. 'But it's only … when I was with Titus I was ever so pure, I never went with anyone except him. And now – what's he been saying to Giorgio? Stirring up trouble … ' She pressed her lips together, trying not to cry.

'Giorgio?'

'My landlord – he owns the restaurant downstairs.'

We're in this together, I thought. I hadn't liked her to begin with, but she'd dealt with Bannister pretty well, all things considered: better than I had.

'I *couldn't* have murdered him, I *was* with a friend, I was here,' she said miserably. 'You believe me, don't you?'

'Of course I do,' I murmured. 'But what I believe doesn't

matter. It's what the police believe that matters. Isn't there someone else in the house who could back up your story?'

'Yes … maybe Giorgio, possibly, but he's never liked me much, and now that policeman … but thanks, it's an idea anyway. Oh God, I hope they don't give me notice. What'll I do then?' And now she began to cry in earnest.

I felt both chilly and sweaty in the stale room. I looked at my watch. Stan might still be in the office. I somehow wanted to talk to him. I wanted to get away. But I had to stay to try and cheer her up. 'I expect it'll be all right,' I said feebly. 'Here, have some more wine.'

She wiped her eyes and swigged wine from the bottle. 'Was he really murdered? Do you really believe that?' She looked at me.

'I suppose so. It must be true, it's a murder inquiry.' Why did we all find it so hard to believe? But deep down I still didn't believe it, remembering his sprawled, peaceful body – like that painting of Chatterton the poet, only in black and white in the livid light from the moon.

When Fiona was calmer, I left with a promise to come and see her again soon, and hurried back to the office. Stanley was still there, doing deals on the phone. 'I didn't expect you back, Di. How did the visit to Mavor's shiksa work out?'

'I didn't have time to ask her much. The detective came while I was there. She's upset. We had some wine. I've got a headache.'

He shook his head. 'All this drinking, Di … ' Then as the penny dropped: 'The *police*?' His fingers crept to his lips and he began to gnaw. A bad habit – it made him look furtive. 'That's awkward. But they're bound to go round asking everyone questions, aren't they?'

'The inspector wants to talk to us again – me and Alan. Someone saw me leave the house in Mecklenburgh Square.'

'I got you in trouble, Di. That's bad, that's really bad.'

'It's not *that* bad. They don't know it was me. It was dark. I had a scarf round my head.'

'Just in case, though, we need an explanation. What were you doing there? What time was it? You'll have to say he was still alive – or you thought he was still alive – asleep, you didn't like to disturb him. But why were you *there* in the first place?'

'A message from you,' I said stupidly.

'I told you before, my name can't be brought into this. Don't get me wrong. If I'd known this was going to happen I'd never have asked you to go round.'

'I'm sure you wouldn't, Stan.'

'But that's why I did it; I didn't want to seem to be involved.'

'Could I say it was something to do with Radu – the film – something like that?'

'No, no, that won't do, girl. It'll have to be your hubby or one of his chums.' He paused, watching me, and I made a decision.

'Stan – tell me the truth. He wasn't blackmailing you, was he?'

His gaze didn't waver, yet there was a blankness in his eyes. 'Blackmail? What gives you that idea? If he was a blackmailer, why was he so hard up?'

'Maybe he wasn't very good at it. Something Colin said about the sort of person he was made me think … '

'Your friend Colin should be careful what he says.'

I'd said the wrong thing. The conversation stalled. After a while Stanley said: 'You'll stick to your story, won't you. Say nothing about the Friday evening. Remember: it didn't happen. You were never there.'

nine

YOU WERE NEVER THERE.

Inspector Bannister came to see us again the next day. Of course I should have taken Stan's advice, but by the time I realised, it was too late. I'd made the fatal mistake.

Why had Bannister come back so soon? It scared me. He asked us again about finding the body on the Saturday morning, which was all right – to be expected. He then started asking all sorts of questions about our friends and acquaintances. Finding me *chez* Fiona had obviously convinced him I knew her better than I was letting on. He asked all sorts of questions about her to which I didn't know the answers, but the more I insisted I didn't really know her the more I sounded as if I was just stonewalling.

He said suddenly: 'The woman seen near the house in Mecklenburgh Square that evening – it wouldn't have been you, would it, Mrs Wentworth?'

My heart pounded. I felt it must be visible, jumping like a fish, and I was a fish out of water, gasping for air with my mouth open. How had he *guessed*? 'I – '

Alan swiftly stepped in. 'What are you implying? Why should it have been my wife? You don't know who it was.'

'I'm not implying anything.' The inspector looked at me attentively. 'No need to rush to her defence like that is there, though, Mrs Wentworth, especially since you say you hardly know her.'

I could feel I'd blushed scarlet. I looked away.

'It's just that she was consorting with the late Mr Mavor and then it seems he ended the relationship.'

That wasn't what she'd told me. 'How d'you know that?' I asked rather too sharply.

He looked at me. 'Do you know different then?'

His knowing look annoyed me. I felt quite angry. His case against Fiona was a house of cards. Yet why should I care? Fiona was nothing to me, just a miserable, silly girl leading a silly rackety life. Yet – I felt so guilty. I couldn't get an innocent person into trouble. It would be so dishonourable not to tell him the truth. I was no good at concealing the truth.

'What's the matter, Mrs Wentworth?' The inspector was gazing at me sparrow-like, his head slightly on one side. He knew something was up.

I swallowed. 'The thing is – ' I saw Alan's horrified expression and stopped. He knew I was about to go too far, to advance from the honourable to the mad.

'What is it, Mrs Wentworth? You've something more to tell me?'

'The thing is – it *was* me. I was there that night. The Friday.'

The inspector stared. 'You *were* there?' He hadn't expected this. His question had just been a shot in the dark. 'Why didn't you tell me this before?'

Alan burst in: 'The fact that my wife saw Mavor the previous evening is completely irrelevant to his death.'

'Not necessarily. And what is or isn't relevant to a murder

investigation is for me to judge.' After a moment's rather horrid silence, he continued. 'What were you doing in Mecklenburgh Square, Mrs Wentworth?'

I swallowed. But at least I'd thought of a reason for the fatal visit. 'I went round to see Titus Mavor after work, because I wanted to buy one of his paintings. I mean, I couldn't really afford to – well, I wasn't sure how much they cost, but ... anyway, I wanted one as a present for Alan, for my husband. And I thought, perhaps my parents could lend me some money towards it.' I stopped. The memory of the moonlit room was choking me.

'So – ?' he prompted me.

I pulled myself together. 'I – I went round. I knocked – there was no answer. But the door wasn't properly shut, it was jammed, and I went in and ... found him. He was asleep,' I said firmly. That would make it all right – no reason to report to the police; it was just a friend, an acquaintance, rather, asleep. That was all. 'I didn't like to wake him up,' I rushed on, astonished at my inventiveness. 'So I just tiptoed away.'

Inspector Bannister looked sceptical. 'What time was this?' he said.

I had to tell the truth about that, because I'd been seen.

'So he was still alive at seven in the evening,' said the inspector.

Then I saw the chasm I'd dug for myself. At that moment I'd have given anything to stuff the words back in my mouth, to swallow them, never to have said them. I'd blindly walked to the edge of a precipice: *because my lie inexorably pointed in the wrong direction*. He must have already been dead for *hours* when I'd found him. Now they believed the opposite. I'd hindered the police in the course of their investigation. I was frightened. I was out of my depth.

'You're *sure* he was still alive?' The inspector was watching me closely.

I nodded frantically. Silence. Alan uncrossed and re-crossed his legs. I reached for the Craven As, and offered the packet to the inspector. He shook his head but reached forward to light the cigarette I placed between my lips. I inhaled, exhaled. It steadied my nerves. Perhaps the story didn't sound so crazy after all. In fact, it was very plausible. The more I considered it, the truer it seemed.

'You may have been the last person to see him alive,' said Bannister in a pleasant tone of voice. 'Now – don't get me wrong – but the last person to admit to seeing a murder victim alive is always a very crucial witness, a very crucial *figure* shall we say.'

Alan sprang to his feet. 'Now look here,' he thundered, 'I won't have you making insinuations of that kind. How dare you suggest that my wife might have had anything to do with this.'

I was speechless.

'I'm not insinuating anything,' said the detective, as pleasant as ever. 'I just want you both to understand that this piece of information is more important than you seem to have realised. You will have to make another statement, but we'll leave that for the moment, shall we?'

I misunderstood, and thought that meant he was leaving; but he was far from finished with us yet. He wanted to know about all our friends: how long Radu had been in Britain, whether he was or had been a displaced person, what his film plans were and how they were to be funded. The nature of his connection with Titus Mavor came almost as an afterthought. Then the inspector was keen to know more about Alan's relationship with Titus before the war, whether Hugh had also known the artist at that time, what Mavor had done during the war and all about his relationships with women. Then there was Hugh.

Finally he came to Colin. Was it true that Colin had threatened Mavor?

Stiffly, Alan questioned the need for all this.

'Just trying to build up a picture of the circles he moved in,' the policeman replied with his neat little smile.

It was difficult to object. Already in trouble, we didn't want to appear even more unhelpful, but the questions ranged so widely, even extending to Colin's politics: 'Mr Harris writes a column for the *Daily Worker* I understand?'

'I'm not sure he's doing that any more.' Alan was cagey about Colin in a way he hadn't been about the others.

'But he didn't want Mr Mavor working on the film?'

I sneaked a glance at Alan. He looked very disconcerted. 'Why do you say that?'

Bannister didn't reply.

Alan made an attempt to change the focus. 'Have you spoken to any of the Surrealist group – the painters he used to know? They were at daggers drawn with Mavor.'

'We have interviewed a number of artistic gentlemen, yes.'

Marius Smith and someone I didn't recognise had been with the art dealer Noel Valentine in the Café Royal on the night of the quarrel, I remembered. They'd witnessed the quarrel, so they might be the source of Bannister's information. But why should they wish to cast suspicion on Colin?

'I'm making enquiries in a number of directions. But why do you mention them especially?' Bannister paused, his bright eyes alert with interest.

'Mavor was unpopular, he became a drunkard, he alienated all his friends, he was a pain in the neck, he provoked. It's not them in particular – it's everyone.'

'I see. So you didn't like him either.' Bannister let that sink in. Then: 'And now, let's return to when you last saw Mr Mavor, Mrs Wentworth.'

Just when I'd thought he was about to leave! He made me go through the whole thing again. I had to concentrate very hard indeed to make sure I hadn't changed my story in any way.

At last he left us in peace. Well, not in peace; Alan was extremely agitated by the questions concerning Colin. 'Bet it's that Surrealist group,' he said. 'They've got it in for Colin – he was rude about them in the *Daily Worker*.' He paced up and down. 'But there's so much loose talk, all those idlers and layabouts sitting around drinking, with nothing to do but gossip. Poisonous lot. I'm going to boycott the Wheatsheaf in future.'

I'd thought he might be angry with me for blurting out a new version of the truth that was actually just a different lie, but he was very sweet to me, protective. I sat on his knee with his arms round me and my arms round his neck. He stroked my hair. 'You know what Gerry Blackstone said about the police having botched up the post mortem. He thought to begin with they might even hope to get away without doing one at all, which sounds pretty far-fetched, but apparently there's such a shortage of pathologists ... So you see if it was delayed, if the death had been treated too casually to begin with, then they're uncertain about the time of death, or at least the parameters are very elastic. And anyway, it was so cold. I suppose that would delay decomposition.' If he thought that would cheer me up, he couldn't have been more wrong. It just made my lie more important. In trying to edge closer to the truth, I'd moved fatally further away from it.

. . . .

I told Stanley the following day. He glanced at me sideways from under his lashes – a disarming, little boy look. 'Why did you do that?' He seemed genuinely puzzled. 'You don't really know her.'

'It seemed unfair, that's all. Why should she get into trouble? It was me the neighbour – or whoever it was – saw.'

He shrugged, and pretended to read a letter, but after a minute or two he started again. 'You're a caution, Dinah, you know that? I can't make you out at all. I thought you were a nice ladylike young woman. Now I'm not so sure. More like one of those tomboy types in the movies. All scouts honour and stiff upper lips.'

'What tomboy types?'

He spread his hands. 'Well, you know … *The Thirty Nine Steps* … *Bulldog Drummond* – you know what I mean, Girl Friday types, getting into trouble.'

'It was *you* got *me* into trouble, if you remember.' I couldn't resist adding: 'That was a lot of money, that cheque.'

'If I was paying him money, I wasn't going to bump him off, was I.'

That was an odd remark. 'But no one suspects you, Stanley.'

'Good. I'm glad to hear it.' Was he joking or not? I couldn't tell. He added: 'I tell you one thing, Dinah, we alibi each other, don't we. If the stiff was cold when you found him, that means he'd been dead since the afternoon, and we were together in this office until you went round there.'

I thought about it. 'That isn't quite true. You went out for a late lunch, remember?'

He looked at me oddly. 'Why, so I did.'

'Whatever's the matter with you, Stan? You're being so peculiar. Are you joking, or what, because if you are, it isn't funny.'

'Feeling a bit rundown, that's all. And – well I'm worried about this film business. Wish I'd never got involved, if you want to know. The British film industry's going under, the government's not closing the dollar gap, the country's going bankrupt and the movies'll go down with it. J Arthur Rank'll be okay with all his cinemas, he'll just show Yankee films, but Radu and your friends – *nada*. Not a word to Gwenny or Enescu, mind, I'm in it now, the die's cast and all that, but – was I crazy, or something? You tell me.'

I was stunned. So he was financing the film after all. I was sure he hadn't meant to blurt it out like that. A moment later he said: 'Mum's the word, eh? I don't want it getting around.'

Later Gwendolen rang, and it seemed to cheer him up. He put the handset down briskly and said: 'I'm finished here for the day, Mrs Wentworth. What say you and I go to the movies?'

That seemed like a rather jolly idea. It was quite cosy in the cinema in the late afternoon, though the film we saw was perfectly dismal: *It Always Rains on Sunday*. Colin would have liked it: neo-realism, ordinary people, working-class lives. But what an understatement the title was! It didn't just rain on Sundays, it rained for the *whole of the film*! And Googie Withers, although she was in love with a robber on the run, settled for her dreary husband in the end, which wasn't very romantic.

Stanley didn't like it either. In the frozen darkness of the street, he said: 'That's not my idea of the East End, not at all. And as for that gangster type, what a liberty making him Jewish. Jews have got where they are through hard work, not crime. What a nerve, after all that's happened.' Yet in the days that followed I noticed he'd picked up a phrase from the character to whom he'd objected. 'I gotta blow,' he'd say, when leaving the office at lunchtime. It sounded very American, especially when he pushed his homburg back in that wide-boy way of his.

As I rode home in the underground I couldn't help thinking about his odd remark about having an alibi. But I reasoned that if he'd had anything to do with Mavor's death, he'd hardly have sent me round there to discover the body. And why had he given me the envelope unsealed? Could he possibly have *wanted* me to see the cheque? The more I pondered the more puzzled I grew. And I didn't have any answers.

t e n

■□■■■■□□

ENDLESS WINTER: IT WASN'T JUST THE AIR, the streets that froze; human beings froze. Body, mind and feelings slowed to a halt. Moods were locked in ice, were as leaden as the skies, the skies darker than the stucco streets under snow. And the horror of Mavor's death was ice-locked into my mind.

. . . .

Alan said: 'Radu and Gwendolen are back from Paris. They've moved to Kensington. He's invited us over to discuss the film. The thing is – he doesn't want Colin along. What d'you think I should do?'

He stood in the kitchen, looking at me, half puzzled, half guilty, but longing for me to say it was all right.

'Oh, Alan – '

'I thought, you see, if we get a firm deal, I could sort of wangle Colin back in later.' But he had that small-boy, hangdog expression.

'I can't say, Alan. You have to decide.'

We went, of course. I arrived first, straight from work. Ormiston Court was a newish apartment block behind Derry and Toms department store. There was an air of hushed somnolence in the carpeted foyer. A porter rang for the lift for me.

Gwendolen was wearing a violet-coloured dress that day. It draped across her bosom and diagonally over her hips, drawing attention to her sinuous body. She met me in the dark but wonderfully warm hall of the flat and led me into a large drawing room.

'Ignore the Utility furniture,' she said, 'we're renting it furnished, you see. It's quite nice otherwise – there's a decent restaurant and a swimming pool. And central heating; though of course with all these power cuts you can't rely on it – it keeps going off.'

She sat me down by the window, which, veiled in netting, looked onto a courtyard garden, cold and still.

'It's a service flat – no kitchen, I'll get Pauline to send down to the restaurant for tea. It won't take long – they're quite efficient.'

She sat near me and looked me over. What a strange, insistent smile she had. It seemed to hold some meaning that escaped me. 'This cold weather's terrible, isn't it,' she said. 'Do you think it will ever end?'

I felt myself blushing – purely from awkwardness. I couldn't think what to say. 'I suppose it will sometime,' I stammered out idiotically, uncomfortable in the beam of her blank gaze. I wished Pauline, whoever she was – the maid, I assumed – would hurry with the tea. I was hungry, as usual.

'Do you manage to keep warm enough?' she enquired. 'It's so difficult with clothes, don't you think? I could let you have one or two things of mine, you know. We're about the same size.'

I felt more embarrassed than ever. 'But you're taller than me,' I stammered.

She sprang to her feet with uncharacteristic animation. 'Talking of clothes – I have to show you what I bought while I was in Paris. There's this new designer, Dior, a friend got me into the show, and the dresses were out of this world – full skirts, tight waists, a completely different line! Come into the bedroom, I'll show you.'

The bedroom was curtained in deep rose damask to match the counterpane. The furniture was less spartan than in the drawing room and the dressing table was littered with cosmetics and big glass scent bottles. Gwendolen opened the wardrobe and pulled out a stiffly rustling evening gown. It was the most extravagant thing I'd ever seen: airforce blue, stiff ribbed silk with a corset-like strapless top and layers and layers of skirts, the silk belled out with tulle or organza in an incredible excess of luxury. She showed me the inside of the bodice, which was shaped with whalebone ribs and canvas lining, a structure unlike anything I'd ever worn.

She held the gown against herself. The subtle colour was marvellous with her dark hair, white skin and almost violet eyes.

'And the new length for day is to the calf or even the ankle,' she said. 'A completely new look, it's revolutionary.'

She handed the garment to me to hold. It was so stiff it was almost like holding a person, a doll, at least. I held it at arms' length. It seemed to have a life of its own, as though it might whirl me into a waltz. The silk was cool to the touch as I grazed my fingertips over the bodice. Luxury – the thing life was so drained of – spoke from its every curve and drape. It was love at first sight.

She snatched it back from me. 'Look, I'll show you, I'll try it on.' For once she was animated. She dropped it on the bed and slid out of her dress. Underneath she was wearing only peach cami-knickers; she pulled apart the poppers that fastened them between her legs and raised her arms to lift the flimsy garment over her head, so that the whole of her smooth, perfect ivory body was revealed.

I was hideously embarrassed. I wasn't prudish, but there was no need for her to flaunt her nudity like that! And now she stepped into the magnificent ball gown and I had to help her by doing all the hooks and eyes up at the back. It was all too personal and intimate. She did look stunning in the dress, though.

When she'd got dressed again and returned the gown to the wardrobe I felt it was like a fairy story doll. I imagined it coming alive at night, pushing open the cupboard door and emerging to perform a mechanical dance, like a figure from the *Nutcracker* ballet.

Gwendolen drew out some boxes from a drawer and sat beside me on the bed to show me her lovely lingerie. I still felt uneasy, for there was a lingering, oppressive hint of physical intimacy as insistent as the aura of artificiality faintly cast by her scent, *L'Heure Bleue*.

'Why don't you have this? I've got more than enough.' And Gwendolen held up a ravishing slip of eau-de-nil silk trimmed with black lace.

'It's awfully kind of you, but I really couldn't.' It was acutely embarrassing; one couldn't accept presents of that sort, it was not done, would be bad form.

She hurled the garment onto the floor. She looked really angry. 'All right then. If that's how you feel.'

I couldn't think why it had annoyed her so much. Her sudden burst of rage was quite upsetting.

'I'm sorry – please don't take offence, it's lovely, but ...'

She stood up, paced up and down for a moment, then, as if the flare of anger hadn't happened: 'I think that's Pauline with the tea.'

When we returned to the drawing room a dark, sallow woman, dressed in a badly bagged tweed skirt and a grey twinset, was setting out plates and cups and sandwiches. She hardly acknowledged us as she poured tea and sat down and Gwen didn't introduce us, which was awkward, but I felt more at ease now I had something to do with my hands, and, after all, it was thrilling to be having tea with a film star. Perhaps Pauline was Gwendolen's companion; I had an idea that actresses had companions – rather as the Queen would have a lady-in-waiting. She sat by impassively, with us but not of us. There was an awkward silence. Finally Gwendolen said: 'You're Stan's secretary now! Are you enjoying it? I hope he doesn't work you too hard.'

'Oh no, quite the opposite,' I said, 'I'm enjoying it. Of course it isn't – I mean I didn't originally want to be a secretary.'

'Yes – you said. You told me you wanted to be an actress.'

'Of course.' I felt myself blushing again. 'I'm so sorry, how boring of me.' But because I was nervous, I found myself rushing on. 'I'd have liked to go to university too, but of course Daddy wouldn't hear of that. He says it doesn't matter for a girl. He thinks men hate bluestockings. My brother went up last year, after he was demobbed. He's at Magdalen College. I try not to feel too envious,' I said with a merry laugh. 'There are acting opportunities there, you see. He's in OUDS – the Oxford University Dramatic Society. Not that he wants to *be* an actor, later on, he's reading law and then he says he wants to go into politics.'

'Acting isn't so wonderful,' she said flatly.

'How can you say that! You're so lucky!' I blurted it out without thinking. 'You must have wanted to act, otherwise how did it happen?'

'By accident really.'

'A lucky accident,' said Pauline. Her pale, thin mouth twitched in a little smile. 'Fortuitous. Meeting Radu like that.'

'I was working as an extra at a little film studio in North London.'

I wondered how Gwendolen had managed to avoid the call-up. Surely being a film extra hardly counted as part of the war effort, but I didn't like to ask.

Another stilted silence; I wondered why Gwen so often made me feel uncomfortable, and suddenly I knew: she was shy. She didn't know how to make conversation, wasn't socially polished at all. It was a strange thought; you'd expect a film star, well, any actress, really, to be good at that sort of thing.

Luckily, the front door banged. Radu was home, bringing a hitherto missing vitality to our awkward trio. 'Darling!' He bent to kiss his star and then: 'Wonderful to see you, Dinah.' He kissed my hand. 'But where is your husband?'

'They should be here by now. They said five o'clock.'

And soon they did arrive. Radu was in a tremendously good mood. 'We celebrate this evening, I think. I have good news about the film.' He sprang to his feet again and went over to a drinks cabinet.

'Hang on,' said Alan, 'I think we should have the discussion first.'

'For sure – as you wish. Yes, this is better.'

Hugh had a title for the film: *Be Still, My Heart.* Alan made a face; he didn't like it, but he kept quiet.

Hugh had also written a new 'treatment', which he outlined to them. The story was of a young woman – to be played by Gwendolen, of course – who'd escaped from a displaced persons camp by stealing the papers of a dead fellow inmate and assuming her identity. As she made her way to England she was exposed to many dangers and threatened by enemies, ranging from Nazis on the run to secret service agents, one of whom – Radu was hoping to get James Mason to play the part – fell in love with her and she with him.

I'd read Alan's original version, which had had subplots and much more on the situation of displaced persons in Europe, in camps and so on. As revised by Hugh, the script seemed focused on romance rather than on the plight of refugees, and I could tell Alan wasn't too happy with the way it had shaped up, but we needed the money badly and – more important – this was his big chance to get properly into films. I could see, too, that he thought Hugh was giving himself too much credit.

But Radu was delighted. When Hugh finished his outline of the narrative, the Romanian looked across at Gwendolen. 'What do you think of this, darling? This is a wonderful part for you, I think.'

'Yes – yes, it is.' She didn't even smile.

Pauline piped up unexpectedly, her coarse voice sounding out of place. 'I think it's the perfect part for you, Gwen.'

Gwendolen looked towards her. 'Would someone do that? Steal another person's identity?'

'I think they would, dear, in those circumstances.'

'It seems far-fetched to me.'

But Radu brushed this aside. 'You do not understand, darling, how these people are desperate. Our film will show the world their suffering, what they have endured.' He turned towards Alan. 'And the good news I have is, I think we have secured the financial backing that we need. I *hope*. It was difficult, but I have done it; the last piece of the puzzle in place. Or very nearly. When I'm in Paris.' He didn't explain any further, but simply chuckled, delighted with himself. And I knew then that he thought he could do anything. He believed in his luck. He would make his own luck. He was a chancer, a gambler. 'Only I am superstitious, unlucky to talk too much about it before all the details are settled. Don't count your chickens! Isn't that what you English say? I think soon we have a contract, a formal arrangement.'

Alan stood up. 'Hugh and I need to think this over,' he said. Hugh looked startled, but he stood up beside his friend. 'I'm sure we can come to an arrangement, Enescu – but you understand, we need to think it through a little further. We'll talk tomorrow.'

I was scrambling to my feet as well, in disarray, it was all so sudden, but Radu said: 'Oh, you at least can stay for a little while? *N'est-ce pas*, Gwendolen? We have hardly spoken.'

Alan said carelessly: 'Yes, why don't you stay, darling? Hugh and I need to talk things over.'

I was happy enough to stay in the warm, softly lit room. Radu saw them out and when he returned: 'Dinah – you will have a cocktail? Allow me to mix you a Manhattan. And then you must tell us about yourself.'

The cocktail was strong and soon I felt a little tipsy. By the time Pauline cleared the tea things away I'd embarked on the story of my life, prompted by Radu, who displayed a flattering interest in my secluded middle-class existence.

'So your father is a lawyer? He has a dramatic role, I think. He speaks in court, he makes a dramatic speech, he is almost like an actor in a way?'

I thought of my father's pronouncements at the dinner table. It was true. There'd been times – over Alan, say – when I'd felt I was jury and accused in one, being harangued across the exiguous Sunday joint, as if, like me, it had been reduced and shrivelled by the force of my father's arguments, when in fact its size simply bore witness to food rationing. Yes – he was an actor. 'In a way,' I said, and couldn't help smiling.

'This is interesting. Gwendolen tells me your wish is also to act, so this is perhaps why.' He laughed.

'My father was part of the prosecution team at the

Nuremberg trials,' I said proudly – and perhaps also a little bit to test him, to see how he reacted.

Radu looked grave. 'Ah, yes,' he said quietly, 'it is good these evil men have their reward, that they are punished.' He leaned back, crossed his legs, lit a cigarette. Surely he wasn't a Nazi! Colin must have been wrong about that.

'But now is more important we talk about you. I can get you screen test, you know – I am sure the camera will love you – such cheekbones.' His glance lingered on me. I felt embarrassed, yet at the same time there was a little surge of hope. 'We make a part for you in our film.'

This was wonderful. I could hardly believe it. I stole a look at Gwendolen, wondering if she'd be jealous, but she was leafing through a copy of *Vogue*.

'I am sorry Alan does not seem so pleased with the new treatment. I have been hoping we can all work together. Hugh and I have been talking things over. We think exactly along same lines. Your husband – I'm not so sure, perhaps you can tell me. He seemed he was the one in the middle, between his two friends. Unfortunately, Mr Harris is not right for this project, but I hope your husband will not find that an … obstacle, because now I have seen your husband's film I should be sorry not to collaborate with him.'

'You've seen *Home Front*?' I hadn't even seen it myself.

'But yes, of course. I have arranged a special showing. It is very good.'

I felt myself blushing scarlet as I stammered: 'Alan is very keen to work on another film. He'd do anything to get a script-writing job.' Well – almost anything, I thought guiltily. I wasn't sure if 'anything' would include completely ditching Colin. I hoped it wouldn't. Then I realised I hadn't said quite the right thing. 'Of course he'd really love to work with you – he admired your film so much. He's awfully talented,' I went on rather desperately. 'But he won't compromise with commercialism.'

Radu laughed. 'But my films are artistic – you know that. If they are also a box-office success that is an ... an unintended consequence. But anyway, I'm sure we can make a collaboration, Alan and I, with Hugh as well, of course.' His smile was dazzling. 'It is my dearest wish.'

I was glowing inside from the cocktail, which I'd drunk rather quickly, and I didn't refuse when Radu refilled my glass. He matched me, and became even more expansive, outlining his plans for a film about central Europe that would astonish with its passion and tragedy. One might have expected this to engage Gwendolen's interest, but the strange thing was she seemed bored, seemed even to be becoming restless. I caught her looking at her watch, and I knew it was time to go home, to go toiling up the snowy wastes of Church Street to Notting Hill and murder mile, but I put off the moment of braving the cold, until Gwendolen smiled in that melancholy way of hers and said apologetically: 'Darling – we have to go out soon.'

It was more than a hint. I knew I had to leave the warmth and face the elements.

'Come and see us again soon, Dinah darling,' said Gwendolen and kissed me on the cheek. Another little frisson of awkwardness. It was odd, all this kissing. My mother and aunts kissed one another in greeting and Mother also kissed one or two of her closest women friends, but I hardly knew Gwendolen. Perhaps film stars, actresses, were more demonstrative. 'Oh – and I forgot to tell you, there's a dinner dance here next month, at Ormiston Court. You will come, won't you? We're making up a party.'

Radu insisted on walking me down to the street. He wanted to wait with me for a taxi, but I insisted I'd take the bus. 'There probably won't be a taxi anyway,' I said.

'They are rare birds,' he agreed, 'but then so are the buses.' He put an arm round my shoulder and marched me along the road to the bus stop. This made me feel most uncomfortable. While we waited he stamped his feet, folded his arms and beat himself with his hands to keep warm in his beautiful overcoat. 'You are very lovely, Dinah,' he said. 'I should love you to be in my film.'

His dancing smile mocked me and yet it held a promise. I didn't know how much to believe him. I peered anxiously along the High Street, wishing the bus would come. Radu's whole manner was so flirtatious.

'You would make perfect ingénue,' he said.

I shook my head and tried to head him off. I had the feeling he was about to pounce – out here in the freezing cold, by the bus stop. And he did. His arms were like bands of iron round me. I felt his lips pressed against mine, his whole body too, through all our layers of clothing. He was trying to force my lips apart. I was trying just as hard to turn my face away, but I felt myself weakening. 'You are so beautiful,' he muttered. We were struggling. Any minute we'd fall on the slippery pavement.

'Oh really, Radu!' I managed to push him away and extricate myself. I laughed it off, it was so ridiculous, the two of us scuffling on the ice, but at the same time ...

Just then, thank God, the bus came. Radu kissed my hand again and looked into my eyes. 'We will meet again very soon, beautiful Dinah.' And he waved me on to the bus as if it was entirely due to his goodwill that it had appeared at all.

I sat on the bus, and after all it wasn't just absurd and ridiculous. I was shaking. It wasn't so much that my dignity was in shreds. I wasn't even feeling – how dared he be so cheeky. I'd *responded*. A great shaft of lust – and now a wave of shame and embarrassment flooded through me. I was obviously a nymphomaniac of some kind.

It was only when I got off at Notting Hill Gate that I thought how strange it was that no one had mentioned Titus all afternoon. It was as if it had never happened; as if he had never existed.

In the arctic cold the streets were empty. I walked along on the impacted ice, my fingers and toes aching, my face skinned with the cold. I heard steps creaking behind me. I looked back. A man in an overcoat trudged along behind me. He was walking faster than me, gaining on me with every step he took. I was nearly home. I tried to walk faster, but it was impossible on the icy pavements. I huddled on, head down. I reached our house. The moment passed. I despised myself for being so cowardly. I wasn't an hysterical girl, after all. I was a married woman.

Upstairs in the flat Alan was at the stove, while Hugh watched from the kitchen table. A bottle of Algerian red stood open between them.

'You stayed on quite a while. I'm making spaghetti with that tin of anchovies I got hold of on my way home through Soho yesterday.' Then he looked at me more closely. 'What's the matter, Dinah? You look as if you'd seen a ghost.'

I couldn't tell him about the man, because it was nothing. It would just make Alan fuss and not want me to go out alone. I unwrapped myself from the layers of outer clothing. 'I'm tired,' I said and poured myself a glass of wine. 'This cold is killing me.'

Hugh said: 'Anything interesting after we left?'

'Not really. But he's awfully keen to work with you both. Dead keen.'

Alan was stirring the spaghetti sauce. 'It was Colin's idea,' he said in a low voice.

'It was *our* idea,' said Hugh firmly.

'It was his idea first,' said Alan, slowly. 'And now he'll hate the way it's going to turn out. As far as he's concerned it'll be a travesty.'

'Well, you don't have to work with Radu if you don't want to,' said Hugh. 'Anyway – it's no good having an idea if it can't be turned into a reality.' Hugh smiled. 'Rather like communism, really.'

Alan laughed, but he didn't seem amused. 'You're right, of course. Of course I'll do it – and it is Colin's fault in a way for being so bloody-minded.'

So that was Colin – ditched.

I stole away to the bedroom without their noticing. I lay under the eiderdown in the dark, but I couldn't stop shivering. I thought about the man who'd walked behind me in the street. I thought about Radu's kiss. That was something else I couldn't tell Alan about. Why did I feel so alone, when I was married? I cried, silently, for a little while, but then I must have fallen asleep.

eleven

A FEW EVENINGS LATER I'D JUST GOT IN when there was a
ring at the doorbell three flights down. I inched open the
front window, leaned out and saw Colin standing on the steps
below and looking upwards. I chucked him down the keys.

'Alan not about? I was just passing – I've had a grilling at
King Street. Just had to have some human company before the
final assault on the north face of Paddington.'

'King Street?'

'You know, Party HQ, you met me there that time.'

Notting Hill was hardly on a straight line between Covent
Garden and Paddington. It was proof of how quickly their
friendship had waned that Colin had to make such a feeble
excuse to drop in.

We sat at the kitchen table with our tea and cigarettes.

'A grilling? That sounds a bit grim.'

'The Party seems so different now. Perhaps I'm seeing too
much of the grey men in charge. D'you know the reason the
London District Secretary hauled me in? It was actually to ask
why I wasn't married! The Party has no time for bohemian
behaviour, I gather. Communists are family men and women
and having children is a communist duty. More socialists are

needed in the world. In France the Catholic Church and the Parti Communiste Français unite to condemn birth control!' He spoke with immense bitterness.

'But I thought you said they believe in equality for women.'

'Perhaps it was partly an excuse,' he muttered, more to himself than me. 'During the war there were none of these problems.' He took off his glasses and rubbed his eyes. 'There was a good side to the war. I know that sounds strange, but the comradeship of the ordinary soldiers was wonderful, you know, they had such simplicity and bravery. It was inspiring. Glad I refused a commission. And being in the Party was almost a plus; the chaps were ready to hear the message – no, that's wrong, they knew it already, knew Britain had to change. I mean, I didn't ram it down their throats, didn't even talk about the Party as such ... ' He sighed. 'It's just that things were black and white then, I suppose, but now it's all gone grey again.'

He lit a cigarette, then struck a second precious match, for no good reason. It was the only box we had. He frowned, knocked non-existent ash off the end of his cigarette, played with a teaspoon. 'I actually feel I *did* something in the war, struck a blow for socialism.' He was jabbing the teaspoon handle into the soft wood of the kitchen table. 'You know I thought I'd seen Enescu in Bucharest?' he said abruptly. 'I'm pretty sure. There was a crowd of people like him at the Athénée Palace. Out in the countryside peasants were starving all over the show, but in Bucharest there was this brittle bourgeois culture ... corrupt, cynical ... black marketeers, contact men, everyone on the make. I suppose he bribed his way out of the country.' He paused. 'I bet he was in Berlin, making movies for the Nazis – or under the Nazis, anyway. He's too young to have been there in the twenties, before they came to power.'

'You don't know that!' I exclaimed, too sharply. 'You haven't any proof.'

He looked at me grimly, misunderstanding my insistence. 'So Hugh and Alan are going ahead, are they.' It wasn't a question.

That was what this visit was about, then. He'd hoped to find Alan, to have it out with him. 'You should talk to Alan. I'm sure it isn't like that.' I knew I was blushing. We both knew it was a lie.

'But Alan seems to be avoiding me.'

The silence was awkward. Finally with an effort, Colin spoke. 'That's not really what I came about. It's this whole Titus Mavor thing. I had a very unpleasant session with that shifty little copper, and he wants to see me again. Some fool told him about the row in the Café Royal – y'know, that time? He came on pretty strong. He made it fairly plain I'm a suspect.'

'A suspect? *You*? How can you be a suspect? That's just absurd!'

'It's true I couldn't stand Mavor, but ... why did he taunt me about the Party?' He ran his hand through his thickly springing hair, then made a face. 'Oh, why do I ask, that was Mavor all over. He just likes making mischief, always has – well, *did* – playing people off against each other, picking up gossip, spreading scandal and rumour. Poisonous character.' Colin frowned at his empty cup. I poured him some more tea. 'Saying what he did! That was malicious.' He looked at me. 'Do you believe all the anti-communist propaganda that's flooding out these days? I suppose you do – everyone does. Even Alan's fallen for it.'

'No he hasn't,' I said stoutly. 'Nor me. I have an open mind. I'm trying to understand it all.'

'Everything was different in the war. The Soviets were our allies. In Bucharest ... the Red Army had arrived. I was only there a short time, but it was – ' He broke off, then started again. 'I'm a *Communist*, Dinah. I don't believe in petty national interests. I believe in the revolution. But I'm not sure the Party does believe in revolution any more. And our allies have changed now, of course.' His smile was bitter. 'One ought to have known it was too good to last.'

I didn't know what to say. After a bit he looked up as if he'd forgotten I was sitting there. He shook his head. 'That shifty little inspector. He near as anything *accused* me.'

'Honestly, Colin, you must be reading too much into it. It's so utterly far-fetched.'

'You're so young, you're so innocent, Dinah,' he said, rather sadly, 'you couldn't possibly understand how difficult it's all become.'

Oh, *why* did they all insist on treating me like a child? 'You could try me.'

He smiled then. 'You're lovely, do you know that.'

I felt uncomfortable. His gaze was a little too intimate.

'You're so sweet. You really are.'

My face was hot. 'I'm not.' I hoped he wasn't going to make a pass. That would be awful. 'I'm sure you're worrying unnecessarily.'

He shook his head. 'I even wondered if someone was trying to frame me.'

'Frame you!' I thought he'd taken leave of his senses.

'There's something else. So much I can't talk about.' He smoked ferociously. 'Oh well, it'll pass. Everything happening at once, I suppose that's what's got me down.'

'What do you mean, things you can't talk about? You can talk to us – to me. You'd feel better if you got it off your chest. Everything's worse if you bottle it up and hug it to yourself.'

He looked at me, seemed suddenly to make a decision. His mood seemed to change. Now he spoke calmly, but it was the calm of resignation. 'You see, I'm in love with someone I shouldn't be in love with.' He looked at me very hard. And then of course I understood. I didn't know what to say. It was a declaration – well, not quite, but as near as. It was awful, not because he didn't attract me at all, but because even to broach the subject as obliquely as he had seemed like disloyalty to Alan. Yet I couldn't help feeling flattered; and even that flicker of delight was a kind of disloyalty to Alan too.

'Oh, Colin ... I'm so sorry ...'

His attempt at a smile managed only to be a grimace. 'Not your fault, is it.'

Silence again. After a while he shook his head violently, as if his ears were air-blocked, managed a more normal smile, came back to earth. 'It's awfully good of you to have listened to all this rot. It must be the weather getting me down.'

His parting shot as he stood poised at the top of the precipitous flights of stairs was: 'You know, I don't think Alan quite realises how lucky he is to have you. You're so – so *clear*, Dinah, and so lovely.'

After he'd gone I sat at the kitchen table for quite a while. I lit a cigarette. Alan said the Party substituted for relationships in Colin's life. I'd thought it was heroic to devote yourself to a cause, even if, as everyone was saying these days, the cause was a misguided, or more likely, a sinister one. But now I knew Colin had hidden depths. My thoughts melted into a sort of daydream. It was flattering to think that Colin was sweet on me. Carrying a torch for me – '*I just want to start/A little flame in your heart.*' Of course I didn't want Colin to be in love with me, and would never give him any encouragement, that would be cruel, but ... the thought of having a hopelessly languishing admirer *was* romantic. I supposed that was how Gwendolen felt about Stan.

Alan came home and I told him Colin had been round. Alan frowned. 'Oh, God. How was he?'

I knew Alan felt guilty, but now I thought about it I was quite surprised that Colin had said so little about the film and Radu. 'He's worried about the inspector,' I said. 'He thinks he's a suspect.'

'That's absurd.'

'I know. I told him.'

In a way I think Alan was relieved that Colin seemed not to be bearing too much of a grudge. 'I'll talk to him,' he said, 'I daresay we can pull a few chestnuts out of the fire. After all, nothing's decided.'

But there he deceived himself.

twelve

■□■■■■■□

FOR THE DINNER DANCE AT ORMISTON COURT I wore my black parachute silk evening dress. My mother had got hold of the stuff from some surplus store and dyed it. Her little local dressmaker ran it up. Alan loved me in black. When I was all made up and ready to go I did a twirl in the bedroom for him to admire me and he caught me by the waist and began to fumble with the buttons at the back. The frustration made him even more excited. I was afraid he'd tear the delicate fabric as he pulled at the bodice, feeling for my breasts, his fingers on my nipples. They hardened and of course I felt excited as he pushed me back on the bed. He plunged his hands under the skirts, finding my thighs and the suspenders he liked so much, and somehow his being so rough and laughing so aggressively made me half not want it. I began to tighten up, I was afraid my dress would be ruined, but he was determined, his erection would brook no refusal and he pushed hard into me, again and again, and his eyes were blind with something fiercer than pleasure.

I had to do my hair and my make-up all over again, and that made us late.

· · · · · · · · · ·

The dance was in full swing. I looked about the ballroom as the swing band played a mechanical version of *Blue Moon* and saw Gwendolen and Radu at a table at the far end of the dance floor. We threaded our way through the tables to the lazy crooning brass and the brush-brush of the percussion.

It was the opposite of the Chelsea Arts Ball, my first ball ever with Alan. That had been chaotic, spontaneous and hilarious; the atmosphere at Ormiston Court was stilted. The faces of men and women alike looked bored and blasé or strained with desperate smiles designed to show the guests' determination to enjoy themselves in spite of the post-war blues. Some of the dinner jackets and the svelte dresses, narrow columns in sombre colours, looked jaded too, as if they'd spent the war in mothballs. I could almost smell the camphor.

Radu bent his lustrous head over my hand and as he pulled out my chair his hand rested on my waist for a moment. 'So lovely to see you,' he murmured. Ever optimistic, I'd hoped the other members of their party might be exciting individuals from the film world. There was a stick-thin blonde in red who was trying to look like Veronica Lake with a waterfall of hair over one eye, but I didn't think she was even a J Arthur Rank starlet, and if they'd invited her for Stanley I could have told them she wasn't, would never be, his type. But perhaps he'd brought her along himself, to put Gwen's nose out of joint – or to cut off his own nose to spite his face, as it were. The only other guests were Daphne and Reggie Constable, acquaintances of Gwen's from Ormiston Court, a hard-faced couple who drank whisky and reminisced about their gay life before the war, along the Riviera and in Nice and 'Monte', varying the theme with grumbles about the government. 'It's worse this year than last,' said Daphne. 'Everyone's spent their war gratuities and there's more rationing now than there was in the war. You could understand it then, but now it's just an insult. Nothing nice in the shops. And the crime wave!'

'It's not just the black market and men from the forces going AWOL. Crimes of violence are on the up,' said Reggie grimly, as we ate our roast chicken (to be followed by trifle or scotch woodcock).

'You live near where Neville Heath murdered that poor woman? I'd be terrified to leave the house!' cried Veronica Lake.

'And now those tarts – ' said Reggie.

I didn't want to think about Neville Heath. I'd tried not to read about it in the papers at the time, tried not to think about the gruesome details of stabbed women and the rituals of capital punishment. An unwholesome atmosphere had surrounded the trial, the public drinking in the shocking facts and taking a macabre interest in the dapper murderer's final hours; and all those black banner headlines about the hanging, and the crowd waiting outside the prison. Sleazy crimes in seedy hotels; it seemed to fit with the post-war mood. Still less did I want to think about the murdered prostitutes.

Alan looked fed up and I knew he too wanted to get away from all this talk of crime, because at any moment someone was going to mention Titus Mavor. And sure enough: 'Have you heard? That artist chap – said in the papers the police are close to making an arrest.' Reggie looked round at us all. Did he know we were all involved?

Radu stood up and took my hand. 'Let's dance.'

He danced well – much better than Alan. When Alan danced he clasped me to his chest and jogged from foot to foot, more or less on the spot. It was by far the least amorous feature of our marriage and I never felt swoony at all when I was dancing with my husband; it felt manly and comforting and comfortable. On the dance floor we were just good pals.

With Radu there was instant fluid harmony, our limbs in unison, and as he swung me round he pressed me close with his palm in the small of my back. It was a slow foxtrot, my favourite, and I rocked to and fro in his arms in a dream.

When he whispered in my ear, I almost lost my footing. I thought my heart would jump out of my parachute silk bodice. I swallowed. He held me a little closer. 'You are not scared.' It hovered between a question and a statement.

Scared of what? Of the erotic feeling that was melting me away? Or of the rumour of an imminent arrest?

I pulled myself together and chose the second. 'He's talking rubbish. There's been nothing in the papers. I haven't heard anything, have you?' But I couldn't help remembering how worried Colin had been just a few evenings ago. Alan had dismissed those fears as paranoia, but I wasn't so sure.

'No...' But he didn't sound too certain. His little half smile disturbed me and when he muttered: 'But I wasn't talking about that. I meant you are not scared of me.' Just then the foxtrot ended with a plangent wail from the saxophone. I started to walk back to our table, but his hand was round my waist. 'No, no, I can't let you go yet.' And as if at his will the first chord of a tango drew a long breath, paused, then marched out its strutting syncopations.

'I can't dance the tango.'

'With me you can dance anything.' He pressed his body against me and bent me backwards and I felt his erection. It was excruciating – too much – unnerving – what would the other couples think to see us locked together so tightly – and yet I'd inwardly wholly surrendered. Towards the end he gradually relaxed his hold, but I only came to my senses when the music finally stopped. Thankfully there was an intermission and we returned to the table. Radu pulled my chair back for me, but said not another word.

Alan could be jealous and possessive, but he hadn't noticed anything – he seemed to be deep in conversation with Stanley. Gwendolen was looking away, across to the other side of the restaurant. She stood up: 'I need the powder room, what about you?'

As she walked away a man approached her. He was tallish and untidy-looking in spite of his dinner jacket, one of those men who would always look crumpled, his black tie askew, his grey hair rough, hardly brushed, let alone Brylcreemed, his glasses not quite straight. He stood in Gwendolen's path and I heard him say: 'Excuse me, but is it – are you ...?' And there was a look on his face I couldn't pin down, but it must just be that he'd recognised her from the film. I thought it was rather bad form of him to accost her like that, but Gwendolen stopped on the edge of the dance floor, and now they seemed to be having a conversation. As I watched them they made for the bar. No one else had noticed. Alan, Radu and Stan were in a little huddle and the Monte Carlo couple and Veronica Lake were having another moan about rationing. I stood up and strolled over to the bar myself and stood near Gwen and the stranger. I was trying to overhear them – I don't know why, but I felt very curious – and if they noticed me I'd be able simply to join them, but in the meantime I preferred to eavesdrop. Perhaps the tall stranger was an old flame of Gwendolen's. That would be interesting; her life before Radu was so mysterious.

'You look just the same, but ...' The band struck up again and I lost the next bit. Then I caught another fragment of the conversation. ' ... you see we heard – or thought, anyway, it must have ...' Gwendolen was nodding, her expression was still, serious, sad perhaps and yet blank in a way. I heard her say something about the Blitz, but then the barman asked for my order, and at the same moment Stanley appeared at my side: 'Who's the geezer with Gwenny?'

So he had noticed after all. I shrugged. 'No idea.'

'Let's join them,' he said.

Gwendolen must have become aware of us because, rather abruptly it seemed, she held out her hand to the stranger and turned away from him. 'Stanley, angel,' she said, 'I'm feeling a little unwell, I think I should probably go upstairs to the flat for a while.' They walked off and I was left on my own with the stranger.

'You're a friend of hers?'

'Yes. Well, sort of.'

'She's Gwendolen Grey, a film actress, she said?'

'That's right. You haven't seen *House of Shadows*?'

He shook his head. 'Incredible. I'd never have thought it. You know, when I saw her ...' He shook his head, bewildered. 'Well, a lot of things happened in the war, I suppose. I'm glad she's doing so well. Have you known her long?' He fumbled in an inside pocket and drew out a cigarette case, took out a cigarette and tapped it on the lid. He forgot to offer me one. He seemed quite distracted.

'No, not long.'

'You see ...' I could tell he wanted to ask more, but as he drew in a lungful of smoke he shook his head. 'I'm sorry – never mind – best to let sleeping dogs lie.'

· · · · · · · · · ·

There was an odd follow-up to this encounter. We visited Ormiston Court again the following weekend. Gwendolen again led me away to her bedroom: 'Let's leave the men to do their talking.'

It was so warm and rosy and soft in there with the wall

lighting and the satin. I sat on a tapestry boudoir sofa. She smiled nervously. 'Well – so – I met someone I used to know at that dinner dance. You saw him, didn't you?'

I nodded.

'The thing is, he'd like to see me again, but I really don't want to, well, now that Radu and I ... I mean, it's quite impossible.'

I wasn't sure I wanted to be in her confidence. These woman-to-woman conversations were very sophisticated and grown up, but Gwen always made me feel just a little uneasy.

'I've written him a letter.' And she drew it from under the cushion. 'I wonder – would you mind posting it on your way home? I – I think I may be coming down with flu or something. I don't want to venture out into the cold. And the sooner he gets it, the better.'

I wondered why I was everyone's little postman, but I meekly took the envelope and put it in the pocket of my tweed jacket. 'Was that what you wanted to show me?'

She smiled. 'Radu got me some lovely boxes of soap when he was in New York. I thought you might like one.'

This time I accepted without a protest. I didn't want to upset her, didn't want her to lose her temper again. And soap was different from lingerie, anyway.

thirteen

ALAN KNEW HE HAD TO TELL COLIN he'd finally teamed up with Hugh and Radu: 'No getting round it. Got to bite the bullet. I'll go round first thing Monday before going in to work. It's out of my way, but he's sure to still be at home if I get there early enough. No point in putting it off.'

He telephoned almost as soon as I got to the office. 'Dinah.' His voice sounded odd.

'What is it?' He never rang me at the office.

'Colin's been arrested.'

I stared at Stanley across the room. I must have looked strange, for he half rose. 'Something up, Di?'

Alan was barking hoarsely down the wires. 'His landlady answered the door and said he'd been "taken away by the police". On *Saturday*,' he shouted. 'The stupid woman has no idea where he is.'

'Can they arrest you for being a Communist?' I said stupidly.

'*No!*' Alan shouted down the phone. 'It's to do with Titus, must be.'

'How do you know?' I was too shocked to react, mentally or emotionally, but Stan was there, looking alarmed. I knew he'd help. 'I'll talk to Stan. He'll know what to do.'

It took all day to find out what had happened. Stan's lawyer sorted it out, tracked Colin down to the police station where he was being held and telephoned Stan quite late in the afternoon with the news. Stan was looking at me grimly as he listened. The call ended, he said: 'They've charged him with Mavor's murder.'

The next day Colin was moved to prison on remand and the day after that Alan visited him. Later, Hugh came round to the flat. He'd brought some corned beef as a twisted sort of guilt offering. It was obvious they both felt so guilty about Colin. In theory, of course, cutting him out of the deal with Radu had nothing to do with the arrest, but I could see why they felt guilty. They'd cheated him. I felt guilty too. Somehow it seemed to me that if we'd all been nicer to Colin, he might not have got so angry and bitter. The row in the Café Royal might never have happened –

I made corned beef fritters, but they tasted horrible.

'Colin's bearing up fine,' said Alan, 'as we knew he would. He says he can't see what evidence they could possibly have – they asked him about the row at the Café Royal ... that seemed to be about it, they were playing it close to the chest. Asked him where he was on the evening in question.'

'There isn't *any* evidence, how can there be?' said Hugh, furious. 'Bannister's heard all about how Titus and Colin couldn't stand each other, how Titus accused Colin of being a spy. No doubt all those spiteful little Soho tittle-tattlers told him about their row – and there was another quarrel, you know, we didn't know about, almost a fight, in Tommy's one evening. Gerry Blackstone told me. But all the same – I don't see how they can hold on to him. They haven't got a leg to stand on. Just because they quarrelled doesn't mean Colin *murdered* him!'

Alan said slowly: 'I suppose the spy stuff is a motive ... of sorts. It blackens his character, anyway. He's a Communist, therefore he must be a devious person, he must be some kind of ... well, he must be *twisted* in some way. Communism's become a kind of moral defect. A perversion.'

Hugh smiled, but he was sceptical. 'The love that dare not speak its name, eh?' They exchanged looks. Something was left unsaid. Did they really think he might be a spy, after all? 'You're being a bit paranoid, aren't you?'

'Hugh – that's how it's getting to be these days.'

'Britain isn't a totalitarian state, you know.'

'He must have been framed,' I said.

Alan looked at me pityingly. 'Don't be absurd. Who would do that?'

But there seemed to be hardly any evidence, and what real motive could there possibly be? We talked and talked late into the night, but got absolutely nowhere. By three in the morning we'd reached a state of exhaustion. Hugh dossed down on the sitting-room sofa.

· · · · · · · · ·

'Colin gave me the name of some CP contact he wants me to get hold of; the secretary of his cell, or whatever they call it. He's hoping the Party will find him a lawyer, he hasn't got one.'

'What about Stan's lawyer?'

'He's a property lawyer. He just helped out in an emergency, as a favour to Stan, I imagine. We need someone who does crime.'

'Wouldn't it be more sensible to ask Daddy?' But then I pictured my father's reaction. He'd have a fit. So Alan phoned the man whose name Colin had given him: Jock Bunnage, who was what Colin called a branch secretary. Apparently he was a foreman at an engineering works in North London.

The next evening we trudged up Liverpool Road past the terraces of battered old houses until we came to River Buildings, which reared up like a prison from the joyless street. I still couldn't understand why Colin had chosen to live in this dismal district.

By contrast the flat itself was warm and cosy. Upright chairs were set at a round, modern table. A utility sofa with wooden arms, upholstered in sage green, and a matching chair were arranged behind it, so that the room was crowded with furniture. A framed picture of a man in a cap hung on the wall. Alan later told me it was Lenin.

Jock Bunnage was about forty-five. He resembled his own living room: neat, contained, buttoned up. He was spick and span in a pullover and flannels, no jacket, but a tie. His swept-back hair had been savagely Brylcreemed, his red face had a bare, almost raw look, as if it had been scrubbed to within an inch of its life, his blue eyes in startling contrast, his movements slightly military, his handshake crushing.

'This is a grim business,' he said as he handed us cups of tea. 'Comrade Harris has been framed, in my opinion. There's those in power want rid of people like him, plus it brings the Party into disrepute.'

I glanced at Alan, who nodded sagely. Jock Bunnage looked at us with undisguised appraisal. 'I don't know if you're sympathisers, although as you're friends of Comrade Harris ... ' He paused for confirmation. Alan nodded emphatically. 'Now, how do you think the Party can assist in the present circumstances?'

'Colin needs a lawyer. He thought you – the Party – could help. In the sense of recommending one, that is.'

Jock Bunnage nodded. 'We had thought of that. And from our point of view ... well, anyway, I expect that can be arranged. At the same time I can't believe it'll ever get to court.' The doorbell rang. 'Excuse me.'

Bunnage returned with a woman who was vaguely familiar. As she looked us over, I remembered we'd seen her outside the CP headquarters in Covent Garden, the evening I'd quarrelled with Alan.

To begin with she addressed the branch secretary as if we weren't present, or were children, or deaf: 'Are these Comrade Harris's friends?'

'Yes, that's right.' Bunnage looked uncomfortable. 'Alan and Dinah Wentworth. This is Comrade Doris Tarr.'

'Good evening,' she said. She neither smiled nor shook hands, just a frosty nod, that was all.

'Comrade Tarr has recently been to the Soviet Union with the Women's International League for Peace and Freedom.'

The older woman removed her woolly beret and her belted tweed coat and finally granted us a wintry smile. 'But you're here about Comrade Harris. Jock asked me to meet you, because of course in this very unfortunate situation the Party also has an interest.'

'Colin needs a lawyer,' said Alan. He was impatient already. I hoped he wouldn't antagonise her.

Doris Tarr sat down at the table. 'We've thought of that. From our point of view, it's better to have someone who'll understand the politics of the situation. I recommend Julius Abrahams. I'll give you his address and phone number.' And she took a small notebook from her bag. 'It's very disturbing. Sinister, don't you think? To have picked on a progressive activist?' she went on, leafing through the pages. 'Ah, here it is.' She watched as Alan wrote. 'I'd be obliged if you'd convey to Comrade Harris – I assume you'll be visiting him – that the situation creates difficulties for the Party. I'm sure he'll understand. Julius Abrahams will, of course, do all he can to help. With any luck the case won't come to court. In the meantime there's no sense in making a big issue of it, that will only make matters worse. So I hope Comrade Colin will understand if the *Daily Worker* doesn't make a song and dance about the allegations. These are very difficult times for the progressive movement. We're putting all our energy into pulling together to make a success of the export drive. We're a parliamentary party, we must act responsibly. And in any case with the paper shortage we have to prioritise. You understand what I'm saying.'

Alan frowned. 'But supposing Colin isn't released. Supposing it does come to trial?'

She stared at him. 'We'll cross that bridge when we come to it. But you know, Communists always think positively. Optimism. That's the key to the advance of the socialist movement.'

Alan got to his feet. That meant we were leaving. I felt we'd only just begun, there was so much unspoken in the air, and I liked her idea of optimism; but I stood up obediently too.

Bunnage saw us out. 'Colin has been engaged in some sharp debates with the London District Committee, but of course we'll all stand by him. I hope you'll convey our good wishes.'

As if Colin were ill; I expected the words 'for a speedy recovery' any minute.

Alan paused in the doorway. 'Will you be visiting him? You know remand prisoners get visits every day.'

Bunnage looked uncomfortable. 'That might be difficult. Don't see how I could get time off work. Perhaps one or two of the women comrades ... but most of them are working too, or else they have small children; campaigning too – we're very active in the community.' But in the passage he shook hands. 'We are behind him, you know.'

'What was all that about difficulties?' I asked as we walked back to the Angel. 'I don't understand the Communist Party at all.'

Alan was scowling. 'They're embarrassed; all they care about is how the blasted Party looks. They see everything entirely from the perspective of the Party. Nothing else matters to them. It's bad enough to have a party member up on a murder charge. That's disgraceful and humiliating in itself. But I bet the real problem is they've heard something about the spy stuff – rumours fly around, you know, Gerry's got a mate at the *Daily Worker* – whispers about spying is the last thing they want. You can understand that, really. Respectability. That's what it's about. And now we're all supposed to hate the Russians again, they don't want a whiff of treason, do they. As if going around preaching about the glories of the Soviet Union doesn't give precisely that idea, not to mention *completely* putting every potential voter off before they've even started.' He sighed. 'You can understand it in a way,' he repeated wearily, 'but they could be a bit braver about Colin. It wouldn't hurt them to run something in the *Daily Worker* about a frame-up.'

'You don't think he's been framed, do you?'

'There must be some reason he's been charged.'

· · · · · · · · ·

We met Julius Abrahams in his dim, shabby, comfortable rooms off Chancery Lane. Abrahams wasn't how I'd expected a Communist to be. He was more like us than like Doris Tarr or Jock Bunnage, only older, with a sardonic manner and an urbane smile. He wore a dark three-piece suit and what I guessed was actually a regimental tie. His dark hair was cut rather long, and as he wrote the light from the desk lamp caught his signet ring.

'Colin didn't do it.' Alan leaned forward and spoke the words with intensity. I knew Alan would stand by Colin to the bitter end, and all the more so because of the betrayal over Radu.

The lawyer's narrow lips twitched in a little smile. 'Naturally I'm operating on that assumption,' he said. 'Were you to suggest otherwise it would put a very different complexion on things.' His air of detached irony shocked me. He seemed so blasé, as though nothing would surprise him. 'Perhaps you can tell me what you know – I take it you've visited him?'

Alan wriggled around in his chair. 'They haven't told him a lot, but he did say they claim he was seen at the Mecklenburgh Square house, or leaving it, on the Friday evening, which is when they believe Titus Mavor was murdered. Colin told me he has an alibi – but that's a bit of a problem too.' He hesitated. 'It was – he met someone. Well, it was an – assignation.'

Abrahams watched us, still ironic, almost mocking: worldly, that was it. 'An *assignation*?' You could hear the invisible quotation marks round the pompous word.

'Of a particular kind.'

It must be a prostitute then. I flinched away from the thought of Colin with one of those raddled-looking women who stood on the corner of the Bayswater Road, or even with a sluttish girl like Fiona. And to think I'd secretly been hoping – without fully confronting it, but ever since that afternoon when we'd had our heart-to-heart – that he was secretly nurturing a *tendresse* for me. Nothing too tragic, of course ...

'If you're suggesting something illegal,' said the lawyer, 'that could make things *extremely* difficult. On the one hand: he's up against a murder charge, although it wouldn't *wholly* surprise me if they have to drop it, I'm not sure it'll stand up.

On the *other* hand, there are all sorts of practical problems with the alibi: can this person be traced; if they *are* traced will they be prepared to take the witness stand – inherently unlikely – but then if they *do*, Mr Harris's character is blackened even as he's exonerated and he's effectively pleaded guilty to another crime, which, to be frank, members of the jury might think was worse than murder.'

'What d'you mean?' I cried. 'What are you talking about?'

Alan groaned impatiently. 'Darling, for heaven's sake, Colin's queer. Don't tell me you hadn't noticed.'

I felt my face turn crimson. I shut up. After the first few moments of shock, a wave of revulsion left the taste of bile in my mouth. I felt physically sick. Of course in theory I had nothing against pansies. The effete young men you saw at parties from time to time were rather sweet. I was a modern young woman, wasn't I, things like that didn't shock me in the slightest. I just felt so sorry for them.

But – *Colin*! He didn't *look* queer. He was masculine, manly, he'd done dangerous things in the war.

I sat there, feeling as if I'd been punched in the stomach. The lawyer and Alan must have gone on with the discussion, but I didn't hear a word. I was sunk in my own embarrassment and – well – *shame*: shame for Colin, shame at my own reaction, and shame at being so green. How stupid of me to suppose he'd been in love with *me*! Stupid, stupid, stupid. And as if that wasn't bad enough, I was now so obviously shocked. How humiliating! What an idiot I was! I was afraid I was going to cry. But I pulled myself together. It was selfish and childish to be thinking of myself when it was Colin who was in danger – and in danger partly thanks to me. I swallowed the lump in my throat and tried to listen to what they were saying.

'I'll do my best to find this friend of Colin's,' said Alan, 'but I'm not that hopeful.'

The lawyer smiled. 'Nor am I.'

'He doesn't even want me to, actually.'

'He may well be right. You'll have to find out if it was a casual meeting in a public place – a pub or ... club. This sort of thing is very difficult, as I'm sure you realise. Homosexual activity is illegal. Even if a witness were prepared to say they were somewhere known to be a meeting place for men with those inclinations, they'd risk everything – and the prosecution would cast doubt on every aspect of their evidence. It would have to be passed off as a different kind of meeting – just a drink in some ordinary pub where there are no such connotations.' He paused, then said in a different voice: 'It is desperately embarrassing all round. I probably shouldn't say this, but you're Colin's friend and he's going to need all the support he can get, so I'll be frank. You probably realise anyway, more or less, how awkward this is for the Party. Some of the comrades are ... rather puritanical, shall we say. There was a certain ... reserve in some quarters about my taking on the case. On the other hand, I have heard rumours about Colin – things the dead man accused him of, and there is a view that I'd be better able to handle the case from that point of view.'

'What do you mean, exactly?'

'What I mean is that I'm representing Mr Harris as a solicitor who specialises in crime among other things, not as a fellow Party member,' said Abrahams. 'On the other hand, my particular position, my political angle on it may benefit the Party as well as Mr Harris. But my aim is to help him.'

I didn't understand any of this. But as I'd been listening I'd decided I had to come clean. 'There is something you have to know.'

I could tell my confession surprised the blasé Julius Abrahams because he raised his eyebrows ever so slightly.

'That certainly fits in with my suspicions about the post mortem. Incompetent forensic procedures, if the *St Pancras Chronicle* is to be believed. That would mean that Titus Mavor was killed much earlier than the police have assumed.' He paused. 'Give me a day or two to think about how best to handle it. From your point of view, it's a bit of a minefield, isn't it.' He looked at me, obviously puzzled. 'Didn't you realise you should have gone to the police at once?'

'Yes … I suppose I did, really, but … at the time … It was late and so cold and … it seemed all right to leave it till the morning. We – well, I never thought of murder.' It sounded awfully lame; and the truth was I didn't even understand myself. Stanley didn't want his name brought into it. That had seemed an adequate explanation at the time, but now I saw it explained nothing. It didn't explain my collusion with his need for secrecy. It didn't explain why he'd wanted his part in events kept quiet. It just raised more questions. 'I just thought he'd *died*,' I said feebly. And I wasn't even sure *that* was true now. I could no longer remember exactly what I'd thought or felt at the time. Hadn't I had some sense of things being wrong even from the beginning? I couldn't remember. It was all overlaid with what had happened since.

'Even so … ' Abrahams continued to look at me. He tapped his pen on the blotting pad. Then, as if dismissing some train of thought: 'Well … anyway, we'll find out what Colin was doing earlier in the day. That will become important if we can get the police to accept that the time of death was earlier.'

'If I tell them the truth they'll have to, won't they?'

He smiled. 'Not necessarily.' He paused, and then used exactly the same phrase as Doris Tarr. 'We'll cross that bridge when we come to it.'

But it was not this languid older man who would have to cross that bridge. It was me.

fourteen

□■■■■■■■□

'I'LL COME WITH YOU IF YOU LIKE,' said Stanley. 'I've nothing to hide. I didn't want my name brought into it, but in the circs ... and there could have been a legit reason I sent you round there. I'm sure we can think one up.' It was generous of him, given that he was so keen to have his name kept out of the whole business; but at best it would only prop up my morale, and it might well raise new questions in the mind of Inspector Bannister.

'That's sweet of you, but honestly, you'd better keep out of it. And I gave them a reason, anyway. I said I was going to look at Mavor's paintings.'

'That won't do,' said Stanley, patiently. 'You have to explain why you didn't report the death immediately. *That's* the problem, and that was my fault. I asked you not to. You lied to protect me.'

'I lied to protect myself. I told a second lie to cover the first.' I'd lied to protect Fiona. Which did seem pretty eccentric now.

'You have to spin a convincing yarn.'

'I can't tell more lies! I've perjured myself already!'

'Oh, Di! Grow up. People lie all the time!'

'Not in court. Not to the police.'

Stan snorted. 'Were you born yesterday or something? You toffs, you're living in a fool's paradise. Except most of you aren't, of course – just little Miss Innocence here. You've got a lot to learn, Di.'

'You're such a cynic.'

'I'm a realist, that's what. The situation is your friend Harris is on a murder charge. You think he's innocent.'

'He *is*! Of course he is!'

'Okay, okay. He's innocent. I mean, I agree with you. Just because they had a barney – it's a bit far-fetched. What it amounts to is what his lawyer says: the police have bungled things, but by an unlucky coincidence what you told them fits in with what they think, or want to think. You have to have a convincing story why that isn't so. On the other hand, who is this witness who saw Harris later on that evening? If we find out who it is we could go and have a word with them. Nobble them.'

He had shocked me again. This was a whole new world of murky motives and behaviour – perjury; interfering with witnesses – I'd always been taught that was completely beyond the pale.

He smiled – the look on my face must have amused him. 'I'm joking, Di! But it never hurts to find out more about people and what's going on. I have to have another look at that site in the City. Why don't you come with me and we'll have a dekko at Mecklenburgh Square on the way back. Talk to the neighbours.'

. . . .

Mecklenburgh Square looked more neglected than ever in daylight. Weeds pushed up between the paving stones; façades were streaked with soot, window panes broken and boarded up, still criss-crossed with sticky paper from the war or shaded with tattered, dingy curtains. The house – *the* house – looked utterly derelict. The front door was shut now, secured with a padlock and boarded up.

Stanley marched boldly up to the house next door. It looked more lived-in than the adjacent building, was even in better shape than most of the others. Stanley pressed the single bell. We waited. Just as we were on the point of giving up, we heard footsteps.

The woman who opened the door was thin as a scarecrow. Her grey hair fell in straight strands on either side of her papery white face. She wore a shapeless grey sweater and what looked like men's trousers. A cigarette dangled from her mouth.

'Yes?'

Stanley lifted his hat. 'We're friends of – the late Mr Mavor. I understand he rented a room next door.'

That was bold. I wasn't sure it was a good idea. She seemed to be sizing us up. There was a shrewd and at the same time enigmatic expression on her face as she looked us over. 'Owed you money, did he?'

'No, no, nothing like that. But – would you mind if we came in for a moment? It's freezing cold. You'll catch a chill if we keep you on the doorstep.'

She scrutinised us more closely. 'You were friends of Titus?' she repeated doubtfully.

'You don't know how we could get in touch with his family? There were one or two things …' Stanley stood there, legs apart. He was such a wide boy, it was rather endearing, with his big smile and dark eyes.

He looked a bit of a shady character, I thought, but he must have won her round, for she said: 'Oh, come in for a moment, don't stand there, it's unbearable with the door open.' She stood aside and we stepped into the dark, dank corridor. The house was the mirror image of the one next door. A once elegant staircase stretched up into the gloom. I looked up the dim stairwell and thought of Titus sprawled on his sofa. I wished I were anywhere but here.

Stanley had removed his homburg. 'Thank you.' What was it about Stanley that rubbed people up the right way? I almost thought the woman was going to smile, but she managed to suppress the impulse.

She led us into the front ground floor room. I suppose she'd have called it her drawing room, but it was a drawing room in ruins, little short of a bomb-site; everything in it was falling apart. Even the pictures on the walls hung askew. The double doors that partitioned the room were folded back to reveal a brass bedstead in the back half. There was a round table by the front window covered with papers and books, a sagging armchair by the grate, a broken-down sofa, a battered antique chest of drawers in the recess by the window and a glass-fronted bookcase opposite the marble chimneypiece. The general impression was of collapsing sofa springs, thread-bare upholstery, curtains weighed down with the dust of ages and newspapers, books, overflowing ashtrays and used cups and plates all over the floor and every surface. The slovenliness was positively bohemian; far worse than our flat, worse even than Fiona's room; so much more chaos in a far larger space.

She made a gesture that seemed to suggest we should sit down on one of the clapped-out chairs. Then, inexplicably, she laughed again, but this time the laugh turned into a hacking cough: 'Friends of Titus,' she said when she'd recovered. 'Titus didn't have any *friends*, not respectable looking ones like you, anyway. But I'll take your word for it that you aren't a couple of snoopers – or confidence tricksters trying to do me out of my savings or the family jewels.' She seemed to find that amusing too.

She lit another cigarette off the stub of the previous one. 'If you *are* trying to get me for breaking some tenancy law, he didn't rent anything. He *stayed* next door. He had nowhere else to go. With the housing shortage ... of course it's a dangerous structure, but then so was he.' More cackling. 'And he hadn't any money. But I expect you know that.' Her laughter was like a saw going through wood and again turned into a cough. Still, she seemed to have warmed towards us. 'Sit down. I'll make you a cup of tea,' she said and disappeared into the back regions of the house.

While she was out of the room I looked more closely at the paintings. I didn't know much about art, but I recognised a small portrait of a young woman that might have been by Augustus John, and an ugly surrealist effort: a Titus Mavor, perhaps.

She returned with three cups on a tin tray, and carried on talking as though there'd been no interruption. 'Titus was my – oh, second cousin once removed or something. Member of the family, anyway. Complete sponger! His poor mother, bringing up the kid, never got a penny for it out of him, not that she needs it, but that's not the point.' She was seated on the sofa, legs apart, and seemed to have forgotten she didn't know us. She was talking avidly, like someone who didn't have much opportunity to talk, living on her own, a lonely recluse. 'Next door belongs to me too, y'know. Derelict – shouldn't be lived in at all. I thought you might have come about that. Government inspectors or something. Found out I let him stay there. What could I do, though? Titus comes round, he's on his uppers again, desperate for somewhere to stay ... I told him it was only temporary, but ...' She shrugged. 'They'll requisition it soon. I hear they give you *nothing* for it, a mere pittance, but it's worth nothing anyway. Useless. Better to pull it down and build council flats.'

'On the contrary,' interposed Stanley, looking extremely sharp. 'In a few years this area'll be worth a fortune.'

'You really think so? Good heavens. Wonders never cease.' His interruption had brought her down to earth. 'I apologise – you don't want to be hearing about my cousin's sordid end. What's one more corpse, anyway. Corpses under the rubble all over London, I expect.'

Horrific thought. 'Oh no,' I cried. 'Unexploded bombs perhaps, but surely not ...'

'You didn't get on with him then, Miss ... Mavor.' Stanley was watching her, his curiosity obvious.

'Joan Mainwaring's the name.' Her cigarette-laden laugh rasped out again. 'Titus deserved everything he got. If someone else hadn't kindly done it for me, I'd have bumped him off myself sooner or later.' Her eyes, sharp and dark as two pieces of flint in her papery face, scrutinised us. 'Were you really friends of cousin Titus? Or are you journalists or something? Or perhaps you *are* snoopers? All these rules and regulations now. Trying to get me for renting a room in a condemned building? Well, I didn't charge him rent, I can tell you. Why bother? I knew I'd never see a penny of it.'

'No, no,' said Stanley, 'that's not it at all.' Again he smiled at her in that way that was so reassuring, so pleasant.

'You're not the detective. I've seen *him*. Common little man. Wouldn't be surprised if he informed on me to the authorities. Some of Titus's arty friends, then? Well, why not, I'm arty myself. Or used to be. Knew Augustus John, y'know, oh, years ago now. And when I say knew – ' She broke off and cackled cadaverously. 'I was quite a looker in my time, though you may find that hard to believe. Anyway – you've come nosing round here. What are you after? I'll lay odds you're after something.'

I decided on a direct attack. 'We just wondered what happened. It was so dreadful. Such a shock. Poor Titus.'

She snorted. 'Poor Titus! Don't be so wet. Treated women like dirt – one of them came to see him, I saw her leaving the house as I came home that evening, saw some woman, anyway. Wouldn't recognise her, mind ... must have been besotted to be out in weather like that.'

I felt sick – it was *me* she was talking about. But the weather hadn't been *that* bad! I almost blurted it out. It had let up a bit – there'd been a storm the night before, hadn't there, but that night – I remembered again the full moon – the wind – the wasted square.

Joan Mainwaring seemed quite pleased with herself about it, but then, just as I thought she was getting into her stride, she stopped and a different, thoughtful, wary look replaced the half smile. 'Why are you so interested? You *are* the press, aren't you? I've already had one unpleasant little whippersnapper prowling round. Just morbid curiosity, eh? You're not the only ones. Some of his painter pals came round too. I've had more visitors since he kicked the bucket than I had in the last six months. But I ain't going to start showing people round the scene of the crime. Sorry if that disappoints you.' She cast us a cynical look. The ash fell off the end of her cigarette and scattered over her bosom. She looked and looked at us. 'Ah – got it! Friends of the blighter who's been arrested. Colin Harris.'

I must have looked surprised, for she cackled again. 'I do read the papers. And I've got plenty of time to put two and two together. I'm just an old woman with too little to do now the war's over. The war was different, wasn't it. Everyone had a job to do in the war. It was all hands to the pump then.' She took a packet of Players out of her cardigan pocket, offered them to us, then lit up herself. 'I know a lot about your friend.' She looked at us, pleased with herself, an old woman of no significance, enjoying an unexpected feeling of importance. She sucked smoke deep into her lungs, blew it out in a long stream: 'Your friend Colin Harris and Titus were old enemies, weren't they, since pre-war days. You're too young, but the crowd you run around with, I should think you'd have heard plenty of gossip from them.'

She seemed to know an awful lot about us. But how could she? 'Did Titus talk about us?'

'Oh! Titus talked, all right. When he was coherent, which wasn't often. All the gossip, all his grievances, all his enemies, all the insults and injuries the world had done him. Still,' she added vaguely, 'he was family.' Ash had fallen onto her chest from the fag stuck permanently in her mouth. 'He was living in the country with his family for a while, then when he managed to go on the wagon for a bit, he felt better, came back to town. Met an old flame, he said. That seemed to unsettle him. Apparently she's become a *film star.*' This set off another volley of hacking. 'I met her – once – in the old days. Very fey, not quite all there, actually. But astonishingly beautiful – *d'un beauté*! You wouldn't believe. I must say I was *very* surprised to hear she has a successful career now. I never thought of her as a career girl. Seemed to have no drive, no gumption. But Titus said it was just that she'd found another man to batten on to. Abandoned her child, you know! Extraordinary! Usually it's the other way round, isn't it. They abandon you – that's what's happened with my lot, anyway. They've flown the coop. Haven't heard from the eldest in months, believe he's still in the Far East somewhere.' She didn't sound unduly put out, but the information triggered a further explosion of coughing.

Gwen and Titus: a child! I heard myself gasp as she said it. It must have knocked Stanley for six, but when I looked sideways at him his face was impassive. I couldn't let it go, though. 'They had a *child*?'

The old woman looked at me. 'Kept quiet about it, has she?'

'Where is the child?' Stanley spoke very quietly.

'Oh, living with Titus's people. In the country.'

Then I remembered. Hugh'd said something about a child, when he came back from the funeral. Titus's child – not that it was Gwendolen's.

'Anyway,' said Joan Mainwaring, 'that's all ancient history. In the meantime someone will have to sort out the mess he left behind.' Then, out of the blue, she added, more sharply: 'Your friend Colin Harris is in a lot of trouble.'

'He's innocent,' I said stoutly. 'We're determined to get him freed.'

A smile twitched her lips. 'That's the spirit,' she said. 'I admire your guts. Good luck to you.' There was something mocking about the way she said it and I suddenly decided I didn't like her.

'He *is* innocent,' I repeated.

'Oh really? I daresay he is.' But now she seemed bored with us all of a sudden. 'So – if that's all …' She made no attempt to get up from the sofa. 'Can you find your own way out?'

I pulled the front door shut with a bang. Stanley and I walked away through the dusk. 'What did you make of that then?' I asked him, for he was looking rather grim. He didn't speak.

'The way she talked about Colin! She seemed to know so much about him.'

Then I remembered what he must be thinking about. 'Did you know about Gwen and Titus? That they had a child?'

'No,' he said, 'I didn't know.' After which he never said

another word as we walked towards Tottenham Court Road. At the underground station we parted, I for the Central Line to Notting Hill, he on the Northern Line – he lived far out in Edgware or Barnet, somewhere in the suburbs, anyway.

· · · · · · · · · ·

Having considered it, Julius Abrahams thought I should contact Inspector Bannister with my changed account. He told me how to present my 'confession', and sent me away still feeling apprehensive, but convinced I could handle the situation.

It was odd to telephone a detective from one of the rank-smelling call boxes at Notting Hill underground station, and I hadn't expected him to be so difficult to get hold of. When at last I did, his response was rather cagey, but he agreed to see me at the police station the following afternoon.

I waited in the foyer. Seated on an old bench, its American cloth upholstery frayed and splitting, I watched the humdrum traffic of petty crime: a drunk, a spotty youth on bail reporting in, a prostitute in a garish fake leopard coat. There was less an air of villainy than of ineffectual lethargy. WE WORK OR WANT said the poster on the opposite wall, but perhaps criminals were as reluctant to do a decent day's work as the rest of the population was said – by the right-wing press at least – to be.

'Come this way, miss.'

Bannister was waiting for me in the interview room where I'd signed my statement on the previous occasion; the same dirty windows, table carved with initials and stained with ink, battered chairs, ancient paint. He stood up. Before, he'd shaken my hand, pulled out my chair, all politeness. This time he just stood there until I'd sat down.

'Now, what's all this about, Mrs Wentworth?'

Julian Abrahams had suggested the words I now carefully

recited: 'I believe I made a mistake in my previous statement.' It sounded stilted and false.

He raised his narrow black eyebrows, which looked almost as pencilled-in as his toothbrush moustache. 'In what aspect of your statement?'

'I have come to realise I was mistaken in supposing that Titus Mavor was still alive when I visited the house. That is, I think he must have already been dead when I called on him on the Friday evening.'

He looked hard at me. This was clearly an unwelcome surprise. 'What makes you think that now? You said before – ' And he read out that part of my statement, which he had in front of him. 'You said he was asleep.'

'Yes, but – '

'He must have been breathing, must he not, if you thought that.'

'I didn't actually hear him breathing. I was uncertain, there wasn't much light, it was strange being there ... awkward, I wanted to get away. I – I touched him. He was rather cold, so ...'

'Was there much noise? In the street outside? In the house next door?'

I shook my head. 'It was deathly quiet.' *Deathly* quiet: an unfortunate word.

'So, in a dimly lit room you find a man apparently asleep. You touch him. Was that to wake him?'

'Yes – no. It was more to see if he was ... all right.'

'Surely, Mrs Wentworth, if you hadn't been certain in your own mind that he was, as you put it, all right, you would have made some effort to get help at the time.'

'Well, it was only afterwards that I began to think that something was wrong.'

'Only afterwards? After what?' He stared at me very hard.

'After your husband's friend was arrested and you wanted to get him off the hook?'

I hadn't expected this. 'No! That's not what I mean.'

Inspector Bannister stared at me. My gaze faltered; I looked down. There was a long silence. Then: 'Isn't that what this is all about?'

'No!' I was scared.

'I think it is, Mrs Wentworth. Now, your motives may be well meaning, or perhaps your husband has put you up to this, persuaded you to help a friend. But I can assure you it will only make matters far, far worse, as if they were not serious enough already. For the suspect and potentially for you.'

I wavered. But I couldn't change my story a third time; besides which I was now telling the truth. Mavor had been dead. The lie was in explaining why I might not have realised at the time. 'It was eerie, and dark,' I said. 'And it was very cold. I thought perhaps he was cold because of that, because it was so freezing cold in the room. I wasn't sure, and I didn't know what to do.'

'I don't find this account credible. Do you honestly expect me to believe that you found what was clearly a dead body in a virtually derelict house and you did nothing about it until the following day?'

I tried not to panic. I swallowed, took a deep breath and looked him in the eye. 'I know it was wrong of me, Inspector, completely wrong. I can only explain my behaviour by saying that I was – I was scared. I wanted to get away from the house. I didn't really think. I didn't *expect* him to be dead, so I sort of assumed he was alive ... at the time ... I'm not even sure what happened next – I mean, I just wanted to get away ... and I ... I did ring 999 on my way home, at Notting Hill Gate, but then I ... panicked again and I rang off, I don't know. But perhaps they made a note of the call.'

Bannister looked at me. I couldn't meet his gaze. My story was true, or very nearly true. Unfortunately it was not believable. I didn't blame him for not believing it.

'Wasting police time is a serious offence. Even more serious is seeking to pervert the course of justice, concealing evidence or acting as an accessory after the fact.'

'I am truly sorry, but I am telling the truth.'

Another long silence. Then: 'Very well. You can make a formal statement now. I'll call someone in.'

fifteen

■□■■■■■■□■

'HE DIDN'T BELIEVE YOU! BUT IT'S *TRUE*! As if you'd lie about a thing like that.' Alan plunged his head in his hands.

'It might help if I could think of a better reason for having lied before.'

'You can't have been convincing enough.'

'What do you mean? What else could I say?' I cried. 'It was true. I was telling him the truth.'

'Look – all I said was you didn't convince him.'

'Why do you always blame me? As if I was stupid or something.'

'How like a woman to take everything so personally!'

'You *beast*!' I was so angry. Then I looked at his handsome, frowning face and took pity on him. How stupid and insensitive I'd been. He was frightened too. Alan, always so sure of himself, always in charge, always in the right – he didn't know what to do, he was terrified for Colin and he felt impotent. That was why he went charging about like a bull in a china shop.

'God – this is all so hellish.' Then, looking sideways at me he must have seen I was close to tears. 'Sorry – I'm not blaming you. I'm so worried about Colin, that's all.' He stared ahead grimly. 'Hell! Hell! *Hell*!'

In the silence I knew we were both thinking of the awful, dark dread, the mushroom cloud that hung on the horizon. Colin faced an ordeal at the end of which, if the worst came to the worst, was the condemned cell: the condemned cell where they never turned the lights off; the hangman to measure him; the last walk; the body dropping like a sack. After Neville Heath's the press had lingered on the ritual of the last meal, the final walk to death, the scientific skill of the hangman, the crowd outside the prison. There was a pornographic pleasure to it all. And now we were being drawn forward towards that obscene moment, powerless to halt the course of events. But we had to find a way out.

'It's more important than ever to find this … *chap* Colin was with that evening,' said Alan. 'I'm visiting the prison today, I'll talk to him, I'll try to get him to be a bit more specific.'

· · · · · · · · ·

Colin had told Abrahams about his companion, but then, maddeningly – with some kind of mistaken chivalry, if you could call it that – had refused to say who it was. When Alan came back from the prison, however, he said, almost triumphant: 'I got him to tell me, I know where we can find this boy. Colin wants him kept out of it, but if the police persist in saying it happened in the evening he *has* to have an alibi. Turns out Colin got him a job in one of the cutting rooms in Wardour Street – seems he hangs out in some café after work. Colin said it'd be better to try to see him there than at work. You'll have to go and find him.'

'Me? Shouldn't we both go? I'd feel more confident if – '

Alan looked at me as though I were mad. 'I can't possibly go to some queer hangout. What on earth would people think!'

'Nobody'll know! And anyway, what'll they think if I start slumming around all on my own.'

'Well, for one thing they won't think you're a homo, will they. Look – why don't you get Fiona to go along with you.'

I was far from sure that Fiona would welcome someone – me – who was trying to get the man accused of murdering her lover off the hook, but I did as I was told. For one thing, I quite liked the idea of seeing her again. I seemed to have lost touch with all my girlfriends since my marriage, and Gwendolen hardly made up for them.

I arrived at tea time, but Fiona was still in bed, frowsty and pale. Her room smelled intimately of stale face powder and stale tea with an overlay of gas.

She didn't seem to mind me watching as she slid out from between the grimy sheets in her *slip*. I was shocked! She slept in her underwear! But I wasn't as shocked as I would have been a year ago. I was learning fast that the behaviour I'd been brought up to think of as not merely normal but absolutely *de rigueur* was certainly not universal; and – amazingly! – the heavens didn't actually fall in if you sometimes forgot to clean your teeth or went to bed without taking off your make-up, or didn't use embossed writing paper.

Fiona padded over to the washbasin in the corner of the room. 'I've hardly any soap,' she wailed. 'Look!' She held up a tiny morsel.

'Ah!' I said, 'but I've got a present for you.' And I held out a round deliciously smelling cake of very expensive Roger et Gallet soap, wrapped in tissue paper, one of the three in the beautiful box Radu had brought back from New York and Gwendolen had given me. Fiona was thrilled.

She moved about the room very slowly. I couldn't believe how long it took her to get dressed, and I was wriggling impatiently about on her slidey counterpane long before she'd finished. She pulled on a pair of tweed slacks and the jumper with the wooden buttons she'd been wearing the first time I met her. 'Perhaps they'll think we're lesbians,' she said with a giggle. My face went hot.

'Oh! I hope not!' I cried.

She gave me a funny look in the glass at which she was applying her make-up. 'I thought that Gwendolen Grey was a bit sweet on you.'

'Fiona! What nonsense. That's ridiculous.'

We bundled up as usual to brave the cold. Now that we were ready to go I felt nervous. We stumbled down the rickety stairs past the restaurant and out into the street.

'I simply have no idea how we're going to find this boy.'

'We probably won't. He won't want to get involved, will he,' said Fiona shrewdly. 'If word goes out we're looking for him, he'll simply disappear. What's his name, you said?'

'Johnny.'

'There's a lot of Johnnys between here and the Thames.' And she sniggered.

But we were in luck. The first place we went was the Swiss Café off Charing Cross Road.

'We'd better have a cup of tea – wait for a bit,' said Fiona.

I thought the people there were rather awful, not only shabbily dressed and not very clean, but even a little mad-looking. One young man at least was muttering to himself and making strange gestures.

'They all think they're geniuses,' whispered Fiona. 'They think they're going to be actors or painters or poets. But actually they're just unemployed.'

At a corner table, two thin young men with extravagant gestures and shrill laughter were, I was sure, wearing rouge. 'Come on,' said Fiona, 'we'll have to go and ask them if they know your friend's friend.'

Just then the door swung open and they looked up. So did we.

This boy was different. For a start he wasn't a boy; he was in his early twenties I guessed, a bit older than me. He was short, but the opposite of willowy; stocky and muscular, with a very short haircut and a military look about him: quite unlike the rest of the café clientele, and obviously not a pansy. Yet he went and sat with the other two.

I plucked up my courage and walked over to their table. The two who'd been there all along stared and tittered in an intimidating way. 'He*lo*!' They looked me up and down. The recent arrival pushed his chair violently backwards as he stood up. He looked as if he wanted to get away. He had gone rather red. He swallowed. He wanted to speak, but couldn't get the words out. Finally he said, his cockney voice hoarse: 'It's about Colin.'

I gaped. *This* manly young man couldn't surely be ... I pulled myself together. 'I'm looking for Colin's friend, Johnny, but how did you know?'

'I'm Johnny. I saw Colin with you once – in a pub somewhere, Wardour Street probably, the Intrepid Fox?'

I'd never seen *him* before and my puzzlement must have showed, for he added: 'Colin wouldn't have introduced us. And I scarpered when I saw you together – he'd have been so embarrassed.' Whether it was irony, amusement or bitterness in his voice I wasn't sure.

'I need to talk to you.'

'Not here.'

Fiona followed us into the Charing Cross Road. There wasn't another café in sight. We could have gone back into Soho and found one, but Johnny strode off in the direction of Leicester Square. It was too early for the pubs to be open, and we ended up in the Westminster reference library just north of

St Martin-in-the-Fields. It seemed a funny place to go, but there was an echoing marble and wood-panelled hallway with a bench on which we sat down.

'Colin's in trouble – you know that? You know what's happened?' Silly question – of course he knew!

Johnny nodded. He was looking down at his feet.

'He needs your help.'

'There's nothing I can do,' he said huskily.

'There is – really, there is. Colin didn't want you involved. He wanted to protect you, but ... ' I hesitated. 'Have you been to see him at the prison?'

Johnny jumped in his seat. 'Oh, God no!' He looked appalled. 'More'n my life's worth.' He paused. 'I mean, I'd like to, but it's just too difficult.'

'He seemed to think you knew him quite well,' I said in a hard voice. I wasn't even sure that was true, but I didn't care. I was determined to push him, to get a reaction. 'If you're really his friend, you'll help him, now he's in such terrible trouble.'

He risked a sideways glance in my direction. His eyes were very blue, with long lashes, his cheekbones knobbly, his skin rough and badly shaved.

'There's nothing I can do.'

I was being too hard on him. My head girl demeanour just frightened him. He wasn't going to talk. It was all leading nowhere – as I'd always known it would, deep down.

Unexpectedly Fiona stretched a hand out and patted his knee. 'You mustn't be frightened. Dinah's only trying to help Colin.'

'I'm not frightened. Well, I am, but it isn't that. It's just ... I could get into trouble and it wouldn't do him any good.'

'He needs an alibi,' I said, still stern. 'Colin says you were with him on the evening it happened.'

The very word 'alibi' upset him. 'It wouldn't do any good.

It'd make things worse.' He stood up. 'Look,' he said, 'you don't understand ... '

'Please – can't you at least visit him?'

The boy shook his head, with a smile of utter contempt for my lack of understanding. 'That's the last thing I should do.'

He stood up. I took hold of his arm. 'Look – the case against him is really weak. The lawyer says so. It'll probably be dropped. This is just in case the worst comes to the worst, don't you see.' He shook off my restraining hand. 'At least leave me a number, an address, *somewhere* – '

Reluctantly: 'You can leave messages with the barman at the Fitzroy Tavern.'

And he was gone.

. . . .

Alan and I felt so desperate that we finally decided to see if my father could help. It wasn't that we didn't trust Abrahams, but Colin needed all the help he could get.

At Waterloo, all the trains were disrupted. We waited for nearly three hours. A grimy fog blurred the vaulted vistas of the terminus, and the atmosphere was thick with the resentful pessimism of would-be passengers. There was an air of endlessly, terminally putting up with things. Occasionally an engine in a siding trumpeted, mooed or bellowed like an elephant marooned in some distant holding pen.

Finally a train slithered, exhausted, alongside the platform. The interminable wait had drained our anger, reducing it to apathy, but now we felt a sudden surge of optimism, almost gratitude at our luck in there being a train at all. It was unheated, but it was surprisingly empty; we had a carriage to ourselves. In fits and starts we travelled past miles of suburban wasteland, bomb-sites and shabby buildings, a formless disorder that stretched on forever. Each time the train stopped at some deserted station I wondered if it would ever start again, but finally it got up speed as we came into open country.

Then unaccountably it stopped again, this time not even at a platform, but in the middle of a field. Silence fell. I went into the corridor, rubbed the window clear, and looked out. Snowfields stretched away in all directions, latticed with black lines of hedgerows, a white polar waste beneath a sulphur sky, a world slowly expiring in eerie silence. I wondered if we were now the only people on the train until I heard a high-pitched, bird-like twitter of human speech from the next carriage, in a language I neither understood, nor recognised, perhaps Chinese. I giggled rather hysterically, wondering if we actually were on the trans-Siberian express en route for Manchuria – marooned at the end of the world.

At length the train dragged itself forward again, and when we finally arrived at Alton we were not just relieved, but astonished. My father had heroically come to meet us. Somehow he'd got some petrol and he drove us at a snail's pace over the frozen roads.

My mother had prepared a feast of duck given to them by a friend; for pudding there was treacle tart. It was the best meal we'd had in ages. It was so nice of her to have taken such trouble, and I gave her a big hug.

Afterwards we sat in the freezing drawing room, huddled round a tiny wood fire, and listened to my father's view of the government, developed at great length. The government's failure to resolve the question of Germany, the government's failure to deal with Jewish terrorists in Palestine, with the chaos in Greece and the riots in the Punjab – 'What the hell is going on?' my father railed. 'We're going to hell in a handcart!' he cried, while my mother bewailed the fact that prisoners of war were still lurking – or, according to her, *larking* – about in the countryside, being ferried around in lorries using the petrol she and my father needed so badly.

The poor old government got it in the neck until Alan could no longer contain himself: 'What are they supposed to do? The Americans are slowly strangling us to death.'

'Are you mad! We'd be bankrupt if it wasn't for the Americans! Europe would be finished!'

'Then why did they end Lend Lease so abruptly? Whatever happens, it's Europe on American terms for the foreseeable future. The film industry, for example – all right, so there was the Anglo–US loan, but Senator Fulbright actually demanded restrictions in order to stop Britain building up a film industry that might seriously compete with Hollywood – ' And Alan was off on his (and Colin's) hobby horse, indeed as he denounced Hollywood and its films for promoting the flashy materialistic 'American way of life', his argument was Colin's, in other words it was the CP argument, an attack on the evils of capitalism.

Of course I agreed with him – of *course* I did. And yet – if I had to choose between a Hollywood musical and, say, *It Always Rains on Sunday*, I jolly well knew which I'd choose.

The only effect of Alan's harangue on the film industry was to convince my father more firmly than ever that my husband was a Red, while my mother now knew for certain that there was no prospect whatsoever that he was going to be able to support me in the manner to which I'd been accustomed, or of her ever having a grandchild. She took me aside at one point and asked me if anything was 'the matter'. 'I thought you'd have started a family by now,' and she looked puzzled, as if she'd never heard of birth control.

To mollify my father Alan said he'd had a script accepted, and told them about Radu and the success of *House of Shadows*.

'Has this chap got any money? Are you actually going to

get paid?' These days my father treated everything with a kind of enraged scepticism. Since he'd returned from Germany he'd seemed so much older, crustier, angrier. The sickening evidence he'd had to deal with at Nuremberg seemed to have eaten into him. He just was a different person.

We finally plucked up courage to broach the real reason for our visit. It was a disaster. The *Daily Telegraph* had reported the case, naturally, but my parents weren't that interested and had had no idea we were intimate with the leading characters in a sordid murder scandal.

My father raged impotently. This was the result of associating with artists and bohemians! How dare Alan lead *his* daughter into such depraved social circles!

'Colin's innocent,' I cried, fighting back tears of rage and frustration. My father took no notice. He grudgingly admitted that Julius Abrahams was the best in the business, even if he was a Red. He'd get Colin a decent barrister, another Red most likely. That was all he had to say on the matter.

After all this, we had to stay the night – impossible to get back to London the same day.

'For God's sake, stay out of it,' was my father's parting shot, when we left the next morning. 'I don't want my daughter's name in the papers, and certainly not in connection with this.'

But my name *would* be in the papers. Unless we could get Colin released and the charges dropped.

sixteen

■□■■■■■■□

WHEN THE THAW FINALLY CAME it was like being let out of prison, but that was London. Beyond our little Soho world was a countryside flooded with melted snowdrifts, sheep and cattle drowned in their hundreds of thousands and the nation plunged literally from one disaster to the next, like a sort of collective Jonah in his whale. What had the country done to deserve this, when Britain after all had won the war!

Alan took time off work to visit Colin almost every day. I was afraid he'd get the sack, but he didn't care. Apart from the film, all his energy was focused on Colin.

'I can't help feeling rotten about the film,' he said, one evening when we got home from the pub. 'If it hadn't been for the film, that row in the Café Royal wouldn't have happened. So much seems to hang on that; but it's so stupid. They've just got this fixed idea of a motive.' He sat beside me at the kitchen table and put his arm round me. 'You don't really know Colin very well, do you, but he is a really good person. I know he's difficult – a rough diamond in a way – but he's an idealist. He's been upset ever since he got back here, that things are going badly – the Iron Curtain, the Labour Party's problems, and he's disillusioned with the Party, although he can't quite admit it.'

He sat up late reading the hated scripts and novels he'd neglected during the day. At regular intervals he sank his head in his hands and groaned: 'But who did murder Titus, Dinah? If only we knew that. How can we find out?'

'Even if we knew, how could we prove it?'

'We'll cross that bridge when we come to it.' Everyone took refuge in that phrase; but it was just a way of saying 'I haven't the faintest idea'.

One wet evening we sat huddled rather miserably in the French, waiting for Hugh, when the little art dealer, Noel Valentine, walked in. Pint in hand, he pushed his way over to where we were sitting.

'Mind if I join you?'

Alan merely shrugged ungraciously, but I made room for Valentine with a smile because when Alan was in one of his moods almost anything was better than sitting beside him in doomy silence. I was just as worried about Colin as Alan was, so why did he have to take it out on me?

'Any news on the Mavor case?'

We hadn't seen Noel since Colin's arrest. 'What sort of news?' glowered Alan.

'Well, I know about the arrest.'

'Yes. My oldest friend's been arrested.'

'I know … I'm sorry.' Noel looked sheepish. Perhaps he hadn't known how close we were to Colin – yet everyone knew everything about everyone else in our little world. 'The thing is, I wondered if you knew what's happened to the paintings.'

'Mavor's stuff? How the hell should I know? Probably where they always were.'

'I could go round to the house … I suppose it belongs to his family now – did he leave a will?'

'For God's sake! How should I know? What are you on about?'

'It's not so much his own stuff,' said Noel, who seemed oblivious to Alan's barely suppressed rage, 'though I suppose that's worth something. But the thing is he owned some very valuable paintings, Dalí, Max Ernst – well, rumour has it, anyway.'

'And you're hoping to cash in!'

'Of course I'd love them for my gallery.' Noel was quite shameless about it. He added: 'But don't you think the paintings could be a motive?'

'Are you putting yourself forward as a suspect?'

Noel smiled, unruffled. '*No*! But it's very frustrating. I'd have persuaded him to part with them in the end – he was totally on his uppers. But perhaps there was someone who preferred a quicker route.'

'The problem with that,' I said, 'is, they wouldn't be able to sell the paintings, would they?'

'Oh, they would. Difficult over here because of the murder. But they could be smuggled abroad. The continent's awash with stolen paintings, stuff taken from the Jews, stuff looted after the war. Once you got them out of the country there'd be no problem at all.'

'Who knew about the paintings?'

Noel shrugged. 'The Barcelona lot, I suppose, Marius Smith and his Surrealist friends, the ones Titus quarrelled with. He really didn't want to let the paintings go. Not because of filthy lucre; it was the sentimental value. He was Dalí's disciple, you know, worked with him in the thirties.' He looked at us, smiled rather smugly.

. . . .

Radu had gone to Paris again and taken Stanley with him.

When Stan returned, his former partner, Arnold Franks, paid him a visit. They shut themselves up in Stanley's office and talked for a long time. I strained my ears, but although I could hear the tantalising murmur of their voices, I couldn't distinguish the words.

After Franks left Stanley looked a bit shaken, but he managed a grin and said: 'Come on, Mrs Wentworth, we're going to tea at the Ritz.'

Stan was good at treats. I loved the Ritz. Everyone looked sleek, well fed and smart. And I could have taken up residence in the ladies' lavatory, it was so luxurious; almost as big as our flat, with a wonderful sofa and yards of marble and mirrors.

'How was Paris? Did you have a good time?' I poured the strong tea.

'That's what I wanted to talk to you about.' He hunched forward over the delicate cups and miniature sandwiches. 'Dinah,' he said, in a quiet, solemn tone, 'I'm worried about what's going on. I've been a fool. Dazzled by the glamour of the film industry, Arnie said. He tore me off a strip. I wasn't going to say anything, to you, I mean, keep my worries to myself, but Arnie said it wouldn't be right.'

'So what happened in Paris?'

'The reason Radu wanted me along was to meet a few of his Romanian friends. You couldn't call them refugees – political exiles, more like, frightened of the Communists, had to get away for political reasons – or thought they'd be better off out of it anyway. No one wants to be the wrong side of the Iron Curtain, after all. The idea was he'd introduce me, it was a question of more investment in the film, or that's what he said.'

Stan paused as I poured him more tea. 'Aren't you having a cake?' I said. 'They're lovely.' I hadn't seen cakes like that for months.

He shook his head. 'I haven't got a sweet tooth like you, Di. Anyway – I didn't take to these geezers, didn't like them at all. Had a feeling they were anti-Jew, though naturally they didn't say so. There were three of them he was friendly with, plus a Frenchman, Jean-Paul Mercier, and a couple of women hanging around. They took us out a few places, there's a lot less austerity there, I can tell you. Mind you, they lived in an absolute slum, never seen anything like it, off the Faubourg St Antoine, a terrible hole, up a rickety staircase, more like a ladder, thought I'd break my neck – awful place.' Stanley shook his head. 'Chronic. Anyway, first thing was I had to keep paying them cheques so they could give me French money. That's not legal, but what was I to do? Had to pay my share. They said it would all be charged as professional services, but Arnie had a fit when I told him. The Romanians only really talked French – apart from Radu, of course. I made out I didn't understand, but I went to night school, I know a bit, it gives you a bit of class, knowing a foreign language. They jabbered away, half the time they lost me, but I did get the gist of some of it. It seemed to be about various dodgy business deals, at least it sounded dodgy to me. I think they'd been smuggling artworks out of Romania.'

'Are you saying Radu was involved?'

'Well – I'm not *sure*, not a hundred per cent – but why are you looking like that?'

I shook my head. 'Nothing. But what was the point of your being there?'

'I got a feeling Radu was hoping – I'm not sure, but maybe the idea was to get me involved in some way. But nothing was said directly and it all passed off, more or less. Just my suspicion, that's all. Then, one evening they started to talk about Titus Mavor. I couldn't follow it all. But it was obvious the French bloke, Mercier, had known Mavor in Paris before the war. Seems he'd got in touch with him again quite recently. But when I asked Radu what it was about he went all cagey on me.'

'Titus was supposed to have had some valuable paintings.'

'Was he?' Stan drew his mouth down dubiously. 'Bit fishy … it was all a bit fishy, but nothing you could put your finger on. Not really. And I honestly don't know how much Radu was involved.' He stared glumly at his plate. 'Makes me feel the film thing could be a bit dodgy too … too late now. And the figures for his other film were hunky-dory all right.' Then he cheered up slightly. 'Mightn't it be worth looking into though, from the Colin angle? You're seeing the lawyer bloke again tomorrow, aren't you, Di? Couldn't you tell him about all this? Don't they employ inquiry agents, can't his clerk do a bit of nosing about? Isn't it important to find an alternative suspect, even if it's only to muddy the waters?' He looked worried. 'Just so long as Enescu doesn't turn out to be involved.'

. . . .

I was indeed due to see Julius Abrahams again the next day, to discuss my interview with Inspector Bannister. The lawyer was the same as before: calm and dry as dust. He gave a brief resumé of the case. 'One of the strong points from our point of view is the delay at the police end. The whole post mortem business. The trouble is getting them to admit any of this. I can't get hold of the records that would prove the dates. They're dragging their feet. I'm determined to get it out of them eventually, but … it's all very frustrating.'

'And all that would make the time of death less exact?'

'It's not exact in any case, but yes – that would cast further doubt on the time. But they'll stick to their story if they possibly can, unless we can get proof. They won't want egg on their faces.'

'Surely they don't want a miscarriage of justice!'

'They want a conviction, Dinah. There's a lot of alarmist talk about the crime wave being out of control, they haven't nailed anyone for the women who were murdered around Notting Hill – near where you live in fact, isn't it. They tried to say it was Neville Heath, but it obviously wasn't because he's been hanged and the murders haven't stopped. Now there's a woman missing in South Kensington, Mrs Durand Deacon. It's beginning to look like another case of murder. Not to mention the black market, so-called cosh boys, spivs, prostitution rackets – the gutter press blows all this up into a major crisis. And we're trying to spoil their fun, by casting doubt on what they seem to think is an open-and-shut case.'

'But *why* do they think that? It isn't. Not really.'

Abrahams looked off inscrutably into a corner of the room as if it were some vista that led into the far distance. 'I suppose they want to think it. It's convenient; opportunism ... or perhaps there's something underlying it all. I don't know.'

'What sort of thing?'

Abrahams shrugged. 'I'm probably reading too much into it all. But I'm leaving no stone unturned in that direction too. And now you see they claim they've got a witness who saw Harris in Mecklenburgh Square that night. And that really is rather worrying.' He looked at me intently. 'That's why your second statement is so vital.'

I told him what Bannister had said to me. Abrahams didn't like it. 'It'll be worse than that in court. You'll just have to stand up to the cross-examination. You'll have to prepare yourself when the time comes. It would be better by far if we could get a really good alibi. What happened about the young man?' He looked at me.

I shook my head. 'We did get hold of him, but he was

dead scared. And I've left messages for him at a pub – he said that would reach him, but we haven't heard a thing.'

'Well – carry on trying.'

'There's something else you should know.' And I repeated Stan's account of the Paris visit.

When I'd finished Abrahams was silent. He played with a pencil, rolling it back and forwards between his fingertips. 'It's not my job,' he said finally, 'to find an alternative suspect. That's the job of the police. You've no evidence for any of this, but that's not the point. All these alleged – possible – illegalities ...' He shrugged. 'It's irrelevant, I'm afraid. I'm not sure exactly what you're implying. Is your friend – your employer – suggesting that a group of Romanians may actually be criminals who *might* know about some valuable paintings someone else says it's *rumoured* Mavor owned? Is he suggesting this film director is involved? Look, Dinah, it's all too ... nebulous. If we produced this information, all that would happen is your employer might be done for currency fraud. Even if there were any paintings – even if there *are* any – why would anyone murder him to get their hands on them? That would be a certain way of *not* getting them, wouldn't it? It's just unfounded speculation, I'm afraid.'

'Has Colin told you he met – or saw – or thought he saw Radu Enescu in Bucharest during the war? He seemed to feel he might be ... a bit dubious. Politically.'

Abrahams looked at me sharply. 'No. No, he hadn't told me that. But we don't want to get the case involved in anything political. That would more likely work against Colin than in his favour, can't you see that?'

We were interrupted by a knock on the door, and without waiting for an answer, a young woman launched herself into the room.

'Naomi! I'm in a meeting! I apologise – my sister, Naomi

Abrahams. Dinah Wentworth – a friend of Colin Harris.'

'I didn't know you were in a meeting! I do apologise.' Her mischievous smile contradicted her words, as if she were mocking her older brother. She was tall and dark like Julius, with the same thin nose and Modigliani face. They were like two elegant birds – cranes, I thought.

Abrahams smiled. 'Naomi's working on Harris's case with me. We're doing everything we can for him. In the meantime, do please make every effort to find the young man again, won't you.'

But Johnny had disappeared.

s e v e n t e e n

■□■■■■■□

OUR LIVELY SOCIAL GROUP HAD DISINTEGRATED THAT
spring. Hugh worked all hours with Radu on the film; Colin
was in prison and Alan's energy was divided between these
two claims on his attention. There was little time for raucous
evenings in pubs and restaurants or at parties in someone's
digs where everyone drank cheap wine. We found ourselves
thrown back on each other and we began to quarrel. Alan still
felt uneasy about the whole film project. He knew he'd let
Colin down, and took his guilt out on me, shouting and
losing his temper over the least little thing. Things weren't
going smoothly with Hugh and Radu either. Hugh loved the
film, he was full of enthusiasm, but they argued incessantly
over the script as Alan tried to smuggle back the politics Hugh
and Radu apparently wanted to exclude. Then there were
endless phone calls – Alan almost took up residence in the
station phone kiosks at Notting Hill Gate – and bad-tempered
meetings at the weekend. Alan began to think he was going to
hate *Be Still My Heart* when it came out. 'Going to be ghastly,
the kiss of death,' he said. 'I'll never be offered another script
after this.' 'I'm sure that's not true,' I'd cry, but that only
annoyed him. 'You don't understand, you know nothing

about it.' He started work on a novel.

Alan accused Hugh of not doing enough to help Colin, but, as Hugh pointed out, it was all very awkward. He visited Colin once or twice, but it went badly. Colin was still angry about *Be Still My Heart*. 'Not sure what else I can do,' said Hugh. 'You could give him an alibi,' was Alan's suggestion. To be fair, Hugh did consider it, but he'd been out of London all that day, talking to a prominent Jewish academic who'd survived the camps, and who was now ensconced at an Oxford college.

There were no more visits to Ormiston Court. That was a relief; I hadn't enjoyed those stifling *tête-à-têtes* with Gwendolen. She might have wanted to be friends, but she had no talent for it. She couldn't open up, didn't share confidences or perhaps had none to share. The word Alan used to describe her was 'inhibited'. It was odd, he said, when she wasn't inhibited on screen. 'Some actors and actresses are like that,' he said, 'empty vessels being filled by the characters they play, they have no personalities of their own.' *I* didn't feel like that; it wasn't what acting meant to me, but perhaps it was true of Gwen. Perhaps it came from her striking looks. She was a Sleeping Beauty, as imprisoned in her strange beauty that was not quite beauty as if she'd been surrounded by a thicket of thorns. She lived in the airless vacuum of her appearance and it sucked all the vitality out of the atmosphere.

Fiona was my new friend. We had a world in common, after all: Charlotte Street, Old Compton Street, the parties, the pubs and above all the idea that art and love and self-expression were the most important things in the world. I thought of Fiona and myself as 'sophisticates', by contrast with, say, my former school friends, now leading dull lives in the Midlands, the suburbs, or, in one case, the colonies.

Now we knew where Johnnie worked, at one of the studio buildings in Wardour Street, Fiona and I went there and asked for him, but the porter said he wasn't there. We left a message and returned the next day, but the porter still said he was out, or away, and wouldn't let us in. We were reduced to combing Soho in the hope we'd run across him. We sat in the Intrepid Fox at lunchtime – I'd rush down from the office to meet her there – hovered around Wardour Street at the end of the day in hopes of catching him as he left work and then moved on to the Fitzroy Tavern. We seemed to spend a lot of time having coffee too; soon we'd discussed the case in every café in Soho. Poor Fiona! She talked and talked about Titus Mavor. I couldn't understand it, but I realised she'd been devoted to the painter – and she was as desperate as we were to solve the mystery of his death.

Like us, she didn't believe Colin had murdered him: 'It doesn't make sense,' she said, one early evening as we sat in Bertaux's patisserie eating austerity éclairs. 'It was too late to stop Titus talking. Even if he thought Titus knew something, murdering him just drew attention to it all, just made it worse – well, it has done, hasn't it? And Titus told me afterwards, it was just a joke. He was just needling him because he doesn't like the Communists.'

'Yes, but Colin did over-react, didn't he?' The more I thought about the way Colin had gone off the deep end, the odder I found it. I hadn't dared mention this to Alan, of course; but while I never for a moment suspected Colin of murdering Titus, I had begun to wonder what he had been up to at the end of the war. 'You have to admit, Colin reacted as though it were true.'

'Nonsense,' said Fiona. '*I* didn't mind Titus's jokes, but he did get under people's skin. He could be really annoying. Anyway, it doesn't matter what Colin did in the war. The point is, lots of other people had it in for Titus. We ought to draw up a list of suspects. What about Noel Valentine, for instance, he was after Titus's valuable paintings. If they exist. I never saw any, but then I wouldn't know a masterpiece if I saw one. I couldn't make head or tail of all that stuff. Or not Noel – he's such a harmless little man! But someone else might have wanted to get hold of them.' She lit a cigarette. 'His painter friends – not that they were his friends any more. He fell out with them and they'd have known if he had any loot. They could be suspects, you know. And then – he owed so many people money. Marius Smith – he owed Marius a lot of money.'

So in the space of five minutes the whole of Fitzrovia was on the suspect list. That was almost as bad as having no suspects. 'The police must have followed up all those sort of leads,' I said uncertainly.

'There's his aunt,' said Fiona. 'She was a vicious old thing.'

'His *aunt*? Who lived next door?'

Fiona nodded. 'She was always going in there, nagging and bullying. She didn't like me, I can tell you. And she was always telling him things that made him feel paranoid.'

'What sort of things?'

Fiona shrugged. 'Dunno ... this and that. Stuff about his friends, people he knew ... she'd been in that world, before the war, you know, artists and that. And then during the war I think she had some hush-hush job. She used to tell him things about his left-wing friends.'

'She'd hardly murder her own nephew, though. What possible motive could she have had?'

'She was fed up with him, wanted him out. She was persecuting him. She said as much. Maybe they had one row too many and she decided she'd had enough. And then,' she went on, 'what about Enescu and Gwendolen Grey. You knew

Titus had an affair with her. She actually had a *child*. Can you believe that? Abandoned the kid, it's been brought up by the Mavor family.'

Until now, I hadn't fully considered how truly extraordinary this was. 'They behaved as if they hardly knew each other.'

Fiona nodded. 'It was weird. Titus was very cagey about it. There was that talk about him working on the film – that was peculiar too. Didn't Enescu know his mistress had a past? Didn't he see how awkward it'd be? Or didn't he care? Anyway, Titus had no intention of having anything to do with it. He didn't like her. She sort of treated him as though he didn't exist. Just sat there like the Mona Lisa, always with a half smile on her face and never saying anything.'

'She's very passive, isn't she. You never really know what she's thinking.'

Fiona opened her eyes wide. 'You don't think *she* could have wanted him out of the way?'

That was a new thought. I considered it. 'If she did, she'd have got some man to do it for her. She hasn't the will-power to do it herself.'

'Enescu?' Fiona looked at me.

'I had thought of that,' I said slowly, reluctantly – the man had me so fascinated and confused. 'But he wanted Titus for the film.'

And then there was Stan – whom Titus was blackmailing, or so I suspected. But I said nothing about Stan. It was the same as with Colin; I just didn't believe it.

'I wouldn't rule out Radu Enescu,' said Fiona, worldly-wise, 'he's a dreamboat, isn't he. Why are foreigners so good looking! But nobody knows where he comes from and Titus thought he was pretty shady, you know.'

'I think Radu might have been in Paris when Titus died,

you know. They went once ... but I think they might have gone again, for a weekend ... but I'm not sure.'

'Couldn't he have come back somehow, without anyone knowing?'

'They'd have stamped his passport.'

'If the police knew he was in France, he wouldn't be a suspect and they wouldn't check that up. I'll go and see Marius Smith,' said Fiona. 'He might know something and then again – he's quite a likely suspect, you know. He's got a raging temper and if he thought Titus had some valuable paintings ... or if Titus had just annoyed him somehow, he could easily have gone round – they had a row – it all went too far – I'll talk to him.'

'Be careful. Don't let him think you're suspicious.'

Her theory had one very big flaw. Titus had been chloroformed and suffocated. It was premeditated murder.

· · · · · · · · · ·

Radu was due to start shooting the film in two weeks' time, and Hugh arranged a social evening for us all as a sort of celebration. We met at Hugh's favourite Soho drinking club, the Harlequin, a dingy little place, I thought. Stan looked the place over with a tolerant smile, but Alan with his usual tact said: 'My God, this is tawdry,' as we sat round a bottle of over-priced champagne.

Hugh looked displeased. 'All right. We'll move on, then, when we've finished this. Where would you like to go?'

Alan said: 'Let's go to the Caribbean.'

'The Caribbean? What is this?' Radu looked very alert.

'You'll love the Caribbean – much more energy.'

Afterwards I wondered if Alan had done it on purpose, just to annoy. The Caribbean was a magnet for negroes from all over the world, one of the few places in London where they were welcome and felt at home. I was sure Alan knew that Radu would find it disconcerting; after all, he came from a fascist country where no one ever saw a non-European anyway and where everyone hated gypsies.

The place was jammed. The bars were crowded with guardee types and debs mingling with spivs and good-time girls. A couple of black US army sergeants lolled against the counter, chewing cigars, near a negro in a pinstripe three-piece suit – surely a doctor or a lawyer. I noticed a well-known actor escorting an exquisite blonde, but really every conceivable type was represented, and every conceivable colour as well.

We moved into the dimly lit dance room, where check-clothed tables surrounded the tiny floor. Coloured men stood around watching the dancers, smiling mysteriously, perhaps waiting their turn, for they outnumbered the women. We were lucky to find somewhere to sit, a vantage point in the corner from which to watch the three-piece band. I loved the music – its syncopated rhythm was so uninhibited. The pianist rolled from side to side as his elegant long fingers slipped along the keys and the bass player swayed to and fro, eyes half closed, in thrall to his music. The guitarist was wearing a chestnut zoot suit, blue trilby pushed back and yellow shoes that stamped in time to the rhythm.

Radu stared at the dancers, an expression I couldn't decipher on his face. There were many mixed couples on the floor. And it was as if there was something in the music that loosened them up, it was so much more abandoned than anything I'd seen – the Chelsea Arts Ball possibly excepted – freer and more pulsating even than dancing the tango with Radu; completely different in fact, for the tension in that had been as of a tightly coiled spring. This was loose, spontaneous.

Radu turned and invited me onto the floor. But on this

occasion he was very restrained; our bodies didn't even touch.

'Dinah – I am so busy with the film, but I haven't forgotten my promise.' He had to speak rather loudly over the noise.

'Your promise?'

'I promise you a screen test, remember?'

I'd forgotten! The tension of the weeks since Colin's arrest had driven everything else from my mind. 'It's all been so difficult,' I said.

'I know, this is terrible, with Colin.' His voice was warm, silky smooth. 'But if you would still like to do it? I will make an arrangement. I have time now, just before we start shooting. After that – no time.' He laughed. His white teeth glittered. 'Next week. I will call you at work,' he said.

No sooner had the dance ended than a lissom young man in a polo-neck sweater asked me to dance. It was a jitterbug! I hadn't thought I could dance like this; it was amazing. But when I went back to our table everyone except Alan had gone.

'Radu seemed annoyed about something,' he said in a clipped voice. 'He certainly didn't seem to appreciate you dancing with a man of colour. Let's go.'

It was a bad end to the evening.

For the next few days I tried not to think about Radu, but his promise of a screen test had stirred up all my old ambitions. It had rekindled all my conflicting feelings towards the man as well. Alan had implied Radu was anti-negro, that he was prejudiced. It was a hateful idea. Perhaps it was more that he'd been jealous of *me* – that he hadn't liked me dancing with the negro – not because he was a man of colour, but simply because he was a man.

The thought flattered me; more than that, it *excited* me. And that was wrong; already I'd been unfaithful to Alan in my mind, and not only my mind, my body had thrilled to Radu. I was ashamed and confused.

My feelings disturbed me so much that I borrowed a book on sexual psychology from the local library, to the consternation of the librarian until I managed to persuade her I was a married woman and nearly twenty-one! I'd begun to think I must be some kind of nymphomaniac, to have such feelings for a man who was not my husband. The book reassured me that they were natural, although of course they had to be mastered.

Later I decided that perhaps it wasn't me, but rather that Radu had irresistible 'animal magnetism' – a concept I'd got hold of from a romantic novel I'd been reading, to Alan's disgust. 'Animal magnetism' appeared to be some kind of irresistible force; which made it all the more essential to avoid the man. If he did arrange a screen test, I promised myself I'd turn it down.

eighteen

■□■■■■■□■□

I DIDN'T ACTUALLY EXPECT TO HEAR FROM RADU, BUT
when he rang and told me he'd arranged for my screen test to
be done in Wardour Street, I couldn't refuse. The office was
the very one where Johnny worked!

We met in the Intrepid Fox. 'It's so kind of you to do this,'
I said as we crossed the road to the big office building, pushed
through the swing doors, past the porter who'd refused me
entry, and walked along a corridor that smelled of – stone,
earth, something familiar yet elusive. Later, Hugh told me it
was film cement, to join the film after cutting. Radu took me
to a little studio, where it took ages to set up all the lights, the
angles and everything. Tedious, but interesting; I had to sit
very still, worrying about my hair. I'd made myself up quite
elaborately, but my hair was a riot of chaotic curls as usual –
I'd expected they'd do my hair and make-up for me, but Radu
explained he wanted me to look as natural as possible, and
insisted I wiped some of my make-up off. He gave me some
lines to read, and when I'd studied them, he said: 'If you're
ready, we shoot.'

It was all over very quickly. I hadn't been nervous at all. In
fact, it all felt quite unreal.

'You would like to see the cutting room? I show you – come.'

He led me to a room where a dishevelled technician was poring over a machine, red pencil poised. The film, running back and forth, made a clattering noise against the muted turbulence of martial music, the spatter of distant gunfire, voices from adjacent rooms.

'This is the cutting room, Dinah.'

He bent over the monitor, peering at the frames and talking to the other man. He became quite absorbed and I was longing to go and look for Johnny – of course he probably wouldn't be there ... 'Mind if I go to the lavatory while you're doing that, Radu?'

He barely looked up. 'At the end of the corridor,' he said.
I began my exploration. In the second room I looked in, three men were sitting talking. I asked them where I could find Johnny. The next room on the left, they said. It was all so easy! I pushed open the door and there he was, holding a can of film. He placed the can on a workbench, turned and saw me. He looked dumbstruck, rooted to the spot.

'I need to talk to you.'

He shook his head.

'I'll buy you a drink,' I said.

'Don't be stupid. I'm working.'

'Come outside for a minute then.'

We walked along the corridor. Multiple soundtracks muttered and droned in quiet cacophony beyond closed doors. The chemical smell reminded me of the science lab at school.

I glanced sideways at Johnny. With his chunky bullet head, high cheekbones and protruding teeth he looked excessively masculine. Had Colin – did Colin – *really* love him? Could that be real love? I couldn't imagine them ... did men *kiss*? I knew, theoretically, what men did with each other, but I could only imagine some kind of muscular wrestling.

'I left you several messages at the Fitzroy,' I said reproachfully. 'And I came here. Several times. But the porter always said you were out or away.'

'I told him to say that if anyone came nosing round.'

'That wasn't very nice of you.'

'Look – just keep away from me. Drop it. I can't help Colin. I had a visit from a bloke – he might have been plain clothes, but I don't think so. Don't know what he was. I asked for his card, warrant, but he just laughed. How did he know where I live? He was asking questions about Colin. Did you give him my address? I know Colin wouldn't.'

'Of course not.' I tried to sound bracing. 'You mustn't let them intimidate you.'

'Easy for you to say, isn't it! But that's not the point. The point is it wouldn't help. If I got up in court they'd *have* me. It would all come out – everything.'

'What d'you mean – everything?' I tried to be patient. 'You don't have to spell out what kind of relationship ... I mean, all you have to say is you spent the evening with Colin. Drinking. Perfectly innocent. A drink and a chat – you knew him in the war, in the film business, any old thing. It's not beyond the wit of man to embellish things in the right direction, is it.'

'You just don't get it, do you,' he hissed. 'They *know*. I wouldn't have to spell it out. *They* would. Some clever lawyer tying me up in knots. All that'd happen is I'd end up inside too. Lose my job; everything.'

'No!' I cried, desperate. 'Our lawyer will help you put it so they can't trip you up. You have to do it for Colin. Nothing as bad can happen to you as what might happen to him. You can't let them intimidate you! Hitler tried to intimidate us, and we stood up to him!'

He looked at me with utter contempt. 'Where have you come from! You don't know you're born. And don't bring the bloody war into it.' He leaned against the wall and let out a great sigh of exhaustion. I waited. After a long silence: 'I'll think about it. But I'm scared.'

'Don't you think Colin's scared?'

'You think I don't know that?'

'He could be hanged.'

'Don't say that! Don't say that!' He stared ahead. 'Look – I have to go now.'

'Please – *please* – say you'll do it.'

He looked away along the corridor with its queasy pale green painted walls. 'All right, yes, I'll do it. *All right*! Okay?'

'Speak to his lawyer – here's the phone number. And the address.' I pulled out an old envelope from my bag and wrote it all down for him. Johnny crushed it into his pocket without even a glance. We walked towards the swing doors and the room where he'd been working. Outside it he stopped. He was longing to escape, I could tell, but something kept him within my orbit.

'I did visit him, if you want to know. You think I'm a coward, don't you, but I did go to the prison. He got me this job; gave me a name, someone I could talk to. But maybe that was my mistake, maybe that's how they got on to me.'

I squared my shoulders. I hadn't been head girl for nothing. 'I know how difficult it is, but it's your *duty*,' I said, with a sudden vision of my headmistress, Miss Pennington-Harborough.

'You don't know what you're talking about.' He looked at me with naked dislike and resentment. I wasn't used to people disliking me. It annoyed me. I didn't even try to see his point of view; I couldn't afford to admit he might actually be in danger. Only afterwards did I feel ashamed of having persecuted him; of having lectured him from a moral high ground I had no right to occupy.

'You lot, you just don't understand.' He spoke with concentrated bitterness. 'I'll do it, okay? I'll *do* it. Now please just get out of here.'

He went back into his work room and slammed the door.

A week later they fished his body out of the Thames.

. . . .

The inquest was held in an unfamiliar part of South London. I got off the bus and headed along the dusty main road for a while before realising I was walking in the wrong direction. This part of London was a lot drabber than Notting Hill, more like Lavender Hill, where Hugh was living, but further east: Peckham, Camberwell. The plane trees had survived the war and the bombing and brightened the long, winding road, but there was an air of exhaustion about the whole district. Indeed, the whole of London seemed exhausted: a great tired beast, like one of the pale, dispirited lions you saw at the Zoo, reclining in listless resignation in a dusty cage.

Eventually I found the coroner's court, a battered neo-Georgian building. Due to losing my way I was late and slipped in at the back. I was the only spectator.

A young woman in a checked jacket and hair on top of her head like Betty Grable was in the witness box – at least I suppose that's what it was. She had a look of Johnny; the same cheekbones and round head. It was quickly obvious from the questions and answers that she was his sister.

Nor was there any doubt that he'd committed suicide. He'd left a note. The coroner read it out: 'I'm sorry I've let you down. I just couldn't go through with it.'

'Have you any idea what he was referring to?'

His sister shook her head and started to cry. Through her

tears she croaked: 'He'd had a lot of worries, had a friend what was in a lot of trouble, but I don't know much about it.'

It didn't take long for the coroner to reach a verdict.

When it was over I followed his sister out of the court building. She was wearing a floral dress under the checked jacket and instead of stockings she wore socks with her high-heeled shoes. There was something poignant about it, like a little girl dressed in her mother's clothes – but lots of young working-class women dressed like that – well, so many women, and men, had simply run out of clothes by the end of the war. One felt so shabby all the time. I minded clothes still being rationed even more than food.

I hurried to catch up with her. 'Are you Johnny's sister? He was a friend of mine – well, not really a friend, but I knew him. If you've time I'd like to talk to you about him. May I buy you a cup of tea somewhere?'

She wouldn't stop. She flinched away from me and frowned, wouldn't look me in the eye. 'I have to get back to work.'

She walked on, lighting a cigarette as she went. She didn't offer me one, and anyway I never smoked in the street. 'Please,' I begged.

'Nothing to talk about, is there?'

'You must be dreadfully upset, and I'm upset too – '

She quickened her pace. 'Dunno what you got to be upset about. You're one of that lot, aren't you, that arty lot he got in with. This is all about that Colin. Well, I suppose you got him to be upset about, now he's bumped someone off. That's who the note was for, right? Well, you tell your friend Colin he *ruined* Johnny. Johnny was never the same after he got in with him. And now he's bloody killed him.'

'That's not fair! They only met recently, they didn't know each other all that well.'

'Are you kidding! They was in the war together.' She was holding back tears.

'What? I didn't know that.'

'You don't know nothing.'

I flinched, but maybe it was all my fault, I'd made her angry, I'd been tactless and insensitive. 'I'm sorry, I didn't mean to upset you.'

'You couldn't care less if you upset me or not. Just like Colin. Doesn't matter now though, does it. Johnny come home. Demobbed. That was it. But then they met up again. P'raps they never stopped meeting. I hadn't seen much of Johnny, he had a bedsit up Paddington way. I should've made more of an effort, but he didn't seem to want to see me anyway. He had such queer moods.' She screwed her hankie up into a grimy little ball and dabbed her eyes with it. 'Too late now. But he was worried, I do know that.'

'D'you know what he was worried about?'

'Not really – seemed to go back to the war, but I dunno. There's more things went on in the war than we'll ever know about. We ain't ever going to know ... and it don't really matter now, does it.'

'Of course it matters! Colin – '

'I couldn't care less what happens to your friend Colin. He can hang for all I care.'

'Don't say that!'

She stopped on the corner. 'Look – I'm going that way. Got to get back to work. I took time off. I work at the Peek Freans biscuit factory, I'll get into trouble, I'll get my pay docked – but you wouldn't know about things like that, would you.'

'Can't you really tell me anything else about Johnny and Colin in the war?'

'They was in the Balkans together, that's all I know. Don't

even know where the Balkans is, to be honest. Johnny did used to boast about Colin sometimes, about how important he was, but ...' She shrugged. 'I thought that's all it was; boasting.'

'Didn't he say how he was important?'

She glanced at me scornfully. 'No! He's your friend, isn't he. I should've thought you'd be the one to know about that.'

· · · · · · · · ·

Alan raged with frustration. 'All that work, all that trouble you went to to get him to testify, and now he can't because he topped himself, the stupid fool.'

'He must have been desperate. I feel it's partly my fault.'

'Oh God, Dinah, it isn't. Don't blame yourself. But what a bloody awful mess.'

'All the things that were meant to end in 1945 just seem to be carrying on after all.'

'Peacetime's an undiscovered country, Dinah – I don't understand any of this.'

nineteen

COLIN'S TRIAL WAS SCHEDULED FOR THE AUTUMN. Life went on from day to day, but there was always that Iron Curtain, as decisive as the political one, dividing our lives not geographically, but in time.

We dared not tell Colin about Johnny. It was another bridge we'd have to cross, but Alan kept putting it off: 'He's bearing up at the moment, but it'd be such a terrible blow.'

'Aren't we being cowards? We'll have to tell him in the end. And we need to know why Johnny got a visit from the policeman or whoever it was. Colin must know something about that.'

'You're right. I'll tell him.'

But at each visit, he put it off again. The visits were so short; there was so little time; there was the case to discuss. Weeks later Colin still had no idea his lover had killed himself.

We went over and over our list of suspects. Fiona had drawn a blank with Marius Smith; he'd moved to Spain.

'D'you think he's done a runner?'

'Imagine – choosing to go and live in a fascist country!' That alone made the painter a suspect in Alan's eyes. But there was absolutely nothing we could do.

Because Titus had been murdered in such a calculated way, we'd discarded possibilities such as that some bohemian acquaintance to whom he owed money had gone round to the house and killed him in the course of a quarrel. Noel Valentine was still convinced it had something to do with the paintings he believed Titus owned. And there was also Stan's visit to France with Radu. But could Radu *really* have had something to do with it all, something to do with international art smuggling? We couldn't really believe it, but it made it very difficult for Alan to work with the director.

· · · · · · · · · ·

The shooting of *Be Still My Heart* was in full swing at Shepperton. Because of this, and the visits to Colin, Alan had chucked in his script-reading job, and we were living on the rapidly diminishing money from the film script; and my salary from Stan, of course.

One chilly spring day we visited the set. It wasn't how I'd expected. They were shooting a countryside scene. The actors sat around for hours while cameramen and electricians, continuity girls and a whole army of technicians fussed over the lighting and arranged a stile in front of the crude backdrop of a painted landscape against which the scene was to take place. They fiddled about with the fake grass and with the branches of a fake tree to the side.

When Gwendolen was finally called, she had to stand for about half an hour while they posed her and moved the lighting again. The leading man (not James Mason) joined her and after more fuss, largely to do with which profile he wanted in view, the moment finally arrived for the actors to speak. Radu made them do it several times before he was satisfied. And it all took place in one cheaply lit corner of a dark, bare hangar. Film was supposed to be the most realistic kind of art there was, but it turned out to be the most artificial medium of all!

At lunchtime we drank stewed coffee from thermos flasks and ate some damp cheese sandwiches. It was hardly film star luxury! I didn't mind that, but the whole day was awkward. I kept glancing surreptitiously at Radu and wondering if he was mixed up in Titus's death – and hoping perhaps to find him glancing at me. He didn't. He barely spoke to me all day – and said nothing about my screen test.

Everyone behaved as if nothing was wrong. No one mentioned Colin, let alone Titus, yet the atmosphere was poisoned. Everything was horrible.

Alan and Hugh were barely speaking. Alan had told Hugh about Stan's visit to Paris with Radu, but Hugh had just laughed it all off. 'Stan's a fantasist,' he said, 'or paranoid. He's smitten with Gwen, so he's jealous of Radu. And I don't suppose he understood a word of what they were talking about in Paris. He learnt French at night school! For God's sake, get a grip. As if Radu could have had anything to do with it! He wanted Titus to do some sets for him! That was the basis on which he got some of the backing!'

Relations even with Stan were poisoned as we brooded on why he'd needed to pay Titus £150. All he would say when I asked him was that he'd owed him the money. We couldn't afford for me to stop working for him, but it was becoming uncomfortable. Not that Stan was less kind and friendly; and truthfully, I still liked him. But the murder tainted everything.

Alan had taken to drinking at the Stag's Head, near the BBC, with Noel and some of Noel's friends, who mostly worked in radio or ran obscure little art magazines. Noel was busy setting up his art gallery. Alan thought he might have a job for me when it opened.

Things slowed down in the summer. Gerry Blackstone

lent us his mother's cottage in Cornwall for a week's holiday.

I was going through my winter clothes to be cleaned for the autumn when I found a letter in the pocket of my tweed jacket. I stared at it puzzled. Oh! – but it was the letter Gwendolen had given me to post months ago. I'd forgotten all about it. I stared at it in horror. How could I have forgotten? She'd never mentioned it again. What on earth should I do? Was it too late to post it now? Wouldn't that look odd? It was addressed to: Dr M Carstairs, Department of Psychiatry, West London Hospital.

I thought back to the night of the dinner dance – how long ago that was – and the genial man with Gwendolen at the bar. Had he been another lover from her mysterious past? Why had she seemed so secretive? Was she just naturally so, or did she have some real secret to hide? Was it something to do with the child she'd had by Titus? But why should that be?

I held the envelope in my hand, paralysed by the taunting enigma of her life. Perhaps this Dr Carstairs held the key to her reticence, her crippling inhibition. I toyed with the idea of delivering the letter in person. Then I could explain why it was so late – too late, months too late.

I was tempted to steam the letter open. I longed to know what secret it contained. That was the trouble with secretive people; they aroused the very curiosity they sought to deflect.

The sensible thing would be simply to post it. That's what I would do. I had to go to the post office anyway, I'd post it there.

Stanley had given me yet another day off. I set out with my bag of winter clothes, taking the letter with me. The cleaners dealt with, I moved on to the post office, where there was a long queue at every window. I waited for about ten minutes, but I'd chosen the wrong queue. The woman at the head of it seemed confused and was having an argument with the clerk. I was too impatient to wait any longer. I left without posting the letter. I stood outside and stared up Kensington Church Street. Should I walk up to Notting Hill Gate or wait for a bus?

The weather was beautiful. I started walking, but not up the hill. At first I think I thought I was walking to Ormiston Court. The best thing was to give the letter back to Gwendolen. To confess. But I didn't turn off Kensington High Street, I walked west past all the department stores: Barkers, Derry and Toms, Pontings and Pettits, with Daniel Neal, which sold school uniforms, on the opposite side. I walked past the Odeon and past the pretty rows of old houses, past the bomb-site, past Olympia and the Lyons grocery store, past the bombed church, past the red gothic pile that was St Paul's Boys' School, past the huge Guinness poster with its toucan and comic fat zoo keepers in green uniforms ('just think what toucan do') and past the modern flats. Everything seemed very clear and glittery in the sunlight, and yet slightly unreal as I walked mechanically on. I was as if in a trance. I didn't really know what I was doing. I just felt like walking on forever, walking away from it all.

Yet I must have known where I was going, for there, suddenly, was the West London Hospital on the right-hand side of the road. I never liked hospitals. I stood and stared at it.

A man walking past looked at me. 'Are you all right?'

I stared at him.

'Know where you're going? Needing directions?'

I stared at him blankly and crossed the road, unmindful of the traffic. I stood irresolute in the entrance hall and looked round at the vaulted ceiling, the mosaic floor and the infinite regress of corridors vanishing in different directions. What on earth was I doing here? This was stupid – crazy. I turned to leave, but the porter in his lodge was idling by the door; he was watching me.

'Can I help you, miss?'

'I'm looking for Dr Carstairs.'

'Come for an appointment, have you?'

'Not exactly ...'

'Along that corridor. Psychiatric outpatients, first floor, turn left, second on the right. Stairs at the end of the corridor.'

'I'm not a patient. I just – '

'If you're a relative, you can talk to Sister. She'll sort something out for you.'

I marched forward. I couldn't believe I was doing this.

The stairs wound round a lift encased in wrought iron. Men and women passed up and down. It was like a dream.

On the first floor I followed the signs to a waiting area where about a dozen people were seated. 'Psychiatry' to me meant loonies, mad people talking to themselves, dangerous perhaps; but these looked just like any normal people waiting to see a doctor.

A woman in a white coat sat at a reception desk behind a wooden counter. By now my mission had its own momentum. I walked boldly across to her.

'Yes? Name? You've come for the two o'clock clinic?'

'I haven't got an appointment. I wondered if I could just see Dr Carstairs for a moment.'

'You have to have an appointment, dear.'

'I've a message – a letter for the doctor.'

'That'll be the referral letter – they should have sent it to us, not given it to you.'

'No, it's not. It's a personal letter. I'd just like to give it to the doctor.'

The woman looked at me more thoughtfully. Her expression, kindly enough, was somehow at odds with her hard,

Hollywood style of make-up; a slash of scarlet lipstick, thick panstick foundation, bleached blonde hair, hard, pencilled eyebrows and heavy mascara, far too much powder and paint for a hospital employee, quite lurid in fact. I could hear my mother saying, 'She wouldn't have got away with that before the war.'

'Are you feeling all right, dear?'

What an odd question! I couldn't help laughing. 'I'm perfectly all right,' I said.

'You're looking rather flushed. Why don't you sit down and I'll get you a glass of water.'

'No, really. I'll just wait here for Dr Carstairs.'

'No – I'm afraid you have to have an appointment. If you give me the letter, we'll get in touch with you.' She held out her hand.

I backed away. 'No, I'd rather give it to him in person.'

She looked at me, an odd look. Then she stood up. 'Just wait here – I'll see if he's back from lunch yet. Or perhaps Sister can help you.'

I stayed where I was, standing by her counter. To sit down would have confused me with the patients. Standing up wasn't good either, for it made me self-conscious, I'd drawn attention to myself, I'd aroused a listless interest in the waiting throng on the benches. The old woman nearest me smiled and patted the seat next to her. 'You come and sit down here, dear, you'll feel better then.' My face went hot. I pretended I hadn't heard. 'Don't be nervous. He's ever so good, is Dr Carstairs. Helped me with my nerves. They was all shot to pieces after I was bombed out.'

To my relief, the receptionist reappeared. Behind her came the tall untidy man from the Ormiston Court dance, struggling into his white coat.

'This is the young lady.'

'I've seen you before somewhere,' he said, uncertainly. His face cleared as he remembered. 'It was a social occasion, wasn't it, that dance ... look, come into my consulting room for a moment.'

It was a bare room, not much better, although cleaner, than Inspector Bannister's interviewing room, with a linoleum floor, metal filing cabinets, a desk scored and stained with ink circles. He gestured towards a battered upright chair. The whole place seemed to have had a bad war.

'What's this all about?' he enquired, briskly, but kindly. 'You seem a bit distressed. My secretary thought you – ' he broke off, then continued, 'We don't normally see anyone who just comes in off the street.' He paused again. 'I'm sorry, that's not the right way of putting it. Look – I can only give you a few minutes. Then if you need to see me on a proper professional basis, we'll fix things up with your own doctor.'

I laughed merrily. 'Oh, that's not it at all. I'm perfectly well. The reason I came was – it's a bit silly, really. Actually it is about the dance where we met. Gwendolen Grey – you know, she was there, you recognised her – well, she gave me a letter to post to you, but I forgot all about it. It's months ago, I know, but today I found it again. I was going to post it, only then I thought – I'd have to write a covering letter explaining the delay and it seemed easier just to come and see you. To explain.'

He looked completely baffled. 'You came here just for that?' He was observing me closely. I felt uncomfortable. I was very thirsty. The glass of water hadn't materialised. He said quietly: 'Perhaps you'd like to give me the letter?'

I took it from my bag and handed it to him. He looked at it, turned it over. 'Would you excuse me while I open it?' He took a paper knife from his drawer and slit the envelope, drew out the single sheet of paper and glanced over what was written in Gwendolen's rather common handwriting, then refolded it and replaced it in its envelope.

'Did you know her well?' I asked. Again he looked at me. He seemed to weigh everything I said in terms of hidden meanings. Did he really think I was mad? Suppose he got in touch with my GP. That would be dreadfully awkward.

'Why do you ask?'

'I don't know.' I thought of Colin, of Stan's suspicion of Radu, but I couldn't possibly go into all that. 'My husband has been working on a film with her ... fiancé, he co-wrote the screenplay so we've seen quite a bit of her, but ...' I ground feebly to a halt, then began again. 'I just feel ... so much has happened, and you seem to have known her before she went into films, so ...'

He kept on looking at me in that thoughtful way of his. 'I'm afraid I don't understand. Can you tell me a little more?' His expression was so kindly, so concerned, that unexpectedly I began to cry, great awful sobs shuddering through my body. It all came out then: Colin, Johnny's suicide, the looming trial, my evidence, Alan's career, Radu and Hugh and the film. Dr Carstairs handed me a clean white hankie from his own pocket and I mopped up my face.

'You're under a lot of strain, aren't you. And it's easier to wonder about your mysterious film star acquaintance than all your other worries. Is that it?' He paused.

He was patronising me, but perhaps there was some truth in what he said. The trouble was, I couldn't understand myself just why I'd come to see him. It was all so mixed up with the trial. There was so much unexplained. Gwendolen was a mystery too. Perhaps if I understood her – her past life with Titus, I could begin to unravel it all.

'I can understand your curiosity. But there's not much I can tell you about Gwendolen Grey – or could tell you even if

I did know. We had a mutual acquaintance in the past. A rather sad story, as a matter of fact, but she was able to tell me – she was able to tie up one or two loose ends.' He was silent, looking at me still with that kind but somehow worrying look, as if he was sure I was unhinged. At length he said: 'Look – it's more important to face up to your real worries, isn't it? I'm sure you'll come through with flying colours, but you're in for a difficult time. For one thing, you are going to have to tell your friend about this suicide. He'll find out sooner or later, but the longer you leave it the worse it will be. The trial will be hard for you too; there'll be a lot of publicity. And perhaps your husband – I'm sure he's devoted to a lovely girl like you – but perhaps he doesn't quite understand how all this worry is affecting you. You should try to explain to him just how you're feeling. Don't you think so? And I also advise you to go to your doctor. He'll see you're run down and he'll give you a tonic. You're probably a bit anaemic. And now – my clinic's beginning in a few minutes. So if you're sure you're all right – '

As I left I heard him say to the receptionist: 'You did the right thing, Miss Fanshawe.'

I waited by the bus stop in a daze. I felt as if I'd woken up to find I'd been sleep walking and was in a strange and alien place. I couldn't imagine what had made me walk all the way from Kensington to Hammersmith to see the psychiatrist. I had been crazy after all.

Much later – months later – it seemed like a kind of intuition. But by that time it was too late, at least to save Gwendolen.

'Have you gone completely mad!' exploded Alan, when I told him. Then, seeing that wasn't very tactful, he grinned and hugged me. 'Sorry, old girl, I didn't mean it, but – you're a mystery to me sometimes. It's your Unconscious playing up again; you must have been feeling guilty, or something, about the letter, or – no – more like an unconscious search for help. God, I'm sorry, I'm useless, the head shrinker was right, I haven't looked after you as well as I should.' He hugged me tightly, poured me a glass of wine and insisted that he would do the cooking. Later, when he was peeling the potatoes, he said: 'But why the hell did she give you the letter in the first place?'

twenty

□■■■■■■■□

THERE WAS A BRIEF HEATWAVE IN JULY. Gwendolen came
to the office. She was closeted with Stanley for some time
(with me desperately trying and failing to catch even a snatch
of their conversation). When they emerged Stan said: 'I'm
taking Gwen for lunch, if anyone rings I'll be back by three.'

'Oh, sweetie, can't she come too? Don't let's leave her
here on her own.'

Stan was obviously put out and I wondered why she
wanted me along, but I gladly accepted. Instead of some grand
restaurant, we ate at a little place in Wigmore Street. Perhaps
Stan chose it because they'd put chairs and tables out on the
pavement, with coloured sun umbrellas. I happened to be
wearing my favourite frock; it was made of artificial silk and
patterned with red, blue and purple pansies against a black
background, and I had grey sheer silk stockings I'd had
invisibly mended, but as usual I was completely outclassed by
Gwendolen. She bloomed theatrically in one of her Paris
dresses, made from magnificently bold black and white cotton
satin with a hugely full skirt. Passers-by turned to look at her;
some even recognised her, I'm sure. But she seemed oblivious
to the attention. She wore sunglasses, very Hollywood, so

perhaps she didn't notice.

Stan coaxed a little animation from her by telling us about a house he'd seen in Suffolk.

'I didn't know you'd been to Suffolk, Stan,' I cried.

He winked at me. 'Property, Dinah! It opens so many doors. Friend of mine, interested in old houses. Goes about the countryside looking for them. He says, what with the Depression and the war, they're being allowed to decay and crumble into ruin. Criminal – now the war's over, someone needs to do something about it.'

Perhaps that someone was going to be Stan.

'I'd like to see this house of yours, Stan,' said Gwen. 'Why don't we drive out tomorrow – all three of us?'

'What, with petrol rationing the way it is?' said Stanley. And then, 'Well – maybe I can wangle some. This weather won't last long.'

. . . .

Stan's great grey cat of a Bentley purred along the empty roads through the endless edges of London and unfamiliar suburbs and out towards Colchester. It almost rocked me to sleep as I lolled in the back of the car, but the further we went the more uneasy Gwendolen seemed to become. She fidgeted with her hair and her dress, started up stilted conversations that quickly lapsed, and after a while suggested we stop for coffee at a roadhouse.

Stanley shook his head. 'We'd better get on, it's quite a long way, beyond Lavenham.'

Lavenham looked incredibly ancient as it slumbered in the sun. I felt we'd travelled back in time to the eighteenth century, at least. Certainly, in the pub where we stopped in the hope of getting something to eat, the few locals propping up the bar looked at us as if we'd just stepped out of a time machine. And there was nothing to eat but some dried-up pork pies.

Stanley consulted a map, and then we drove on until the road opened out to skirt the edge of a field. At the far end we turned left and were now driving alongside a broken-down grey stone wall. We saw a lodge on the right, standing sentinel by two stone pillars, surmounted by stone urns. The pillars must once have supported iron gates, for you could still see the sockets from which they'd been removed.

'This is it,' said Stanley, drove between the gateless pillars and brought the Bentley to a halt. 'I think we'll walk,' he said, and got out of the car. I thought Gwen was about to protest, but after a moment's hesitation she got out too. I followed.

A vast park stretched away into the distance. The parched lawns had changed to meadow and the horizon wavered in the intense heat. Elm trees stood motionless. The place seemed not so much neglected as bewitched.

The three of us walked into this silent territory, unsuitably dressed urban aliens in the sleeping landscape. Stanley took out his handkerchief and mopped his brow. Gwendolen almost turned her ankle. Rabbits skittered away as we approached. We walked on and on in the unnerving emptiness, the overgrown drive leading us forward with no end in sight through the bleached heat.

At last the drive curved, then opened out and a house rose silently before us. The windows stared out blankly. Grass and weeds covered the shallow steps up to the astonishing portico with its Doric columns and triangular pediment. I was reminded of the house in *House of Shadows*, although this was so different in style.

Even Gwendolen seemed impressed. 'Who owns it?' she murmured.

'I do.' Stanley, suddenly confident again, strode forward,

his energy miraculously renewed. The front door was wide open. We stepped inside, blinded by the sudden shade and then as we became accustomed to the dim light, we found ourselves in a circular hall, the marble floor of which was covered with sacks and sacks of potatoes.

We picked our way between the lumpy sacks towards a crumbling vast reception room, its parquet battered and scored, probably by the agricultural machinery left in one corner. Further on we found the kitchen and pantries, still with the old range and terracotta tiles, and a wheelbarrow propped in one corner. We returned to the circular hall and Stanley climbed the staircase, which curved upwards. The banisters had gone, but the delicate stucco panels on the pale blue walls were intact.

'Is it safe?' I cried. It looked as if it might collapse, but I followed him anyway. Gwendolen was looking out of the window at the empty park.

Upstairs, ancient wallpaper peeled away from the walls. There were stucco chimneypieces and even some oddments of broken furniture.

Stanley was beaming now, no longer broody and discouraged. He poked around, looked out of the windows, opened cupboard doors.

'Are you ... can you ... ?' I didn't know how to put it. Had he seen some new investment scheme? I somehow didn't think ruined country houses offered quite the same opportunities as all his London properties.

'I'm buying it. I'm going to live here one day.'

The idea of Stanley the country squire startled me. 'It will need a lot of work,' I said.

'You can see from the outside the roof's gone in places. Requisitioned in the war, that's the problem, probably used by the army and now some local farmer's decided he can use it as an outhouse. A wonderful Palladian house – and now it's a storage dump.'

We emerged into the blinding glare of heat and silence. It hit you with such force, yet I felt it as a surge of energy, an electric charge of ecstasy. You could feel the panic of the midday silence, the presence of the god Pan.

Gwendolen and Stanley walked on, oblivious to my euphoria. She stumbled; he took her arm, then released it. It was a long walk back to the Bentley. I turned for a last glance back at the house, but it was hidden now by the bend in the drive and the cluster of trees. You could imagine Sleeping Beauty locked in that house. And I knew that the sleeping beauty Stan had in mind was Gwendolen.

As we drove back towards Lavenham, Stan said: 'You know the Mavor family's place is quite near here. I thought we might look in on them.'

'Are you mad?' hissed Gwendolen.

'It makes sense, Gwenny. Titus is dead, you're going to have to do something.'

We rounded a bend and Gwendolen was suddenly shouting and grabbing at Stanley, trying to shift the wheel in a different direction. It was terrifying.

Stanley managed to bring the car to a halt at the edge of a field. He pushed Gwendolen away. 'You mustn't do that, Gwendolen, that's dangerous,' he said with astonishing calm, as though speaking to a child.

She responded by slapping him about the head. She was shouting and swearing incoherently – using the most terrible language. I'd never heard a woman talk like that before.

Stanley managed to grab her wrists. 'Calm down, Gwendolen, calm down. It's all right.' She subsided, started to sob, and very gently Stanley patted and soothed her. Eventually she muttered an apology.

I thought they'd forgotten about me, transfixed in the back of the car, but when Gwendolen had quietened Stan looked round. 'Gwenny's had a bit of a hard time, you know. You mustn't mind her.'

Gwendolen, slumped in the front seat, said nothing. Stanley got out of the car and brought out some bottles of lemonade from the boot. He leaned against the bonnet and drank. What *sangfroid*! I'd have been shaking if someone had attacked me like that. I drank too. I'd have preferred beer, the lemonade was too sweet to quench my thirst properly and it was warm from being in the car, but it was better than nothing. I walked up and down the road, smoking a cigarette to calm my nerves. I was more shaken than Stan! It hadn't occurred to me before, but now I saw it: Titus's death had upset Gwendolen too. She must have loved him once ...

At last Gwen climbed out of the car, looking as pale and cool as ever. She lit up and walked towards me. 'I'm sorry, Dinah.' She frowned, as if puzzled. 'I – I don't know what got into me.' She spoke very softly, in her usual blank way.

I knew it must be about the child – her child by Titus. But I was too afraid of starting another scene to ask her directly.

'I'm so sorry,' I said feebly.

That shocking volley of swear words! The words seemed to have come from some other woman – as if a stranger had spoken through her, some fishwife, a woman from the slums.

For the rest of the journey I sat very still in the back of the Bentley. Stanley and Gwendolen were silent too in the front.

twenty-one

□■■■■■■■□

HOW COULD TIME PASS SO SLOWLY and so fast together? It felt as if Colin had been in prison on remand for years rather than months, yet the weeks until the trial flashed by quicker and quicker. We hardly saw Gwendolen and Radu now the film was 'in the can', and there was a coolness between Alan and Hugh. In September Alan's new friends at the Stag's Head told him about a job on the new BBC Third Programme; he applied, and suddenly found himself with a career in radio! This was marvellous news and brought us into a different social circle. The future was still blocked by the coming trial, but making new friends at least took our minds off it to some extent.

I hadn't seen much of Fiona over the summer either, but one day I bumped into her in Oxford Street. 'Oh, I'm so glad to see you! I've been trying to get in touch, but I lost your address, and you never come to the Wheatsheaf any more.'

We sat ourselves down in the very same café where Alan and I had tried to recover after we'd been to Mecklenburgh Square and the police station that fateful Saturday morning: so long ago, so recent.

'I'm in a bit of trouble,' said Fiona. She certainly didn't

look well.

'I'm sorry, I wanted to see you too, but with Colin and everything ...'

'It's okay, the Colin business – must be awful. But now you're here there's something I was going to ask you ... but I don't know if you'd understand.' She smiled wanly. 'You've led such a sheltered life, Di.'

'Sheltered! I don't think so. I'm married, after all.'

'Exactly. *You're* married,' she said, and looked at me meaningfully.

I guessed immediately. 'Is it ... are you ...?'

She nodded miserably.

That was about the worst thing that could happen to a woman; to have an illegitimate baby. 'Who's the father? Can't he – can't you get married?'

'Oh God, Di! I'm not even sure who it is!'

I blushed. 'Sorry,' I muttered. At least she was honest about it.

'Thing is ... I haven't any money and even if I had – well, I thought I had a contact, but he's disappeared, I really don't know what to do.'

'I could lend you some,' I offered rashly, seeing she was close to tears.

'Oh, *would* you? I can't ask my parents. They used to be in service, but now Dad works in a hotel in Eastbourne and Mum looks after old people. And anyway, how could I explain it? I dunno what they'd do. They'd die of shame – probably turn me out of the house. They're so respectable. But it has to be soon, I'm nine weeks already.'

Abortion was illegal; and terribly dangerous. Of course if you had money and could go to Switzerland it might be all right. Otherwise ...

She lit a second cigarette off the first and looked at me

intently. 'You still see Gwendolen Grey and that lot?'

'Not much these days.'

'You see ... I remembered something Titus said. About some woman who lived with them.'

'*Pauline*?'

'I don't know her name, but he kind of hinted she'd been a nurse or something in the war, and was prepared, you know, to do a girl a favour.'

'Good grief!' Stupidly, the first thing I thought of was, where would she do it? 'In their flat?'

'Oh, not *now*. But I just thought she might ... just possibly ... out of goodwill, you know ...'

Goodwill was not something I associated with Pauline. 'If you like, I'll get in touch with her,' I said doubtfully. Anything to take my mind off the trial.

. . . .

I was relieved it was Pauline who answered the phone. How could I have explained it to Gwen, let alone Radu? I took a deep breath. I had to let her know what I wanted without mentioning the word.

'Gwen's out, I'm afraid.' Pauline's voice was frosty.

'Actually it was you I wanted to talk to. I have a friend who's in trouble.'

I thought she might stonewall or even put down the phone, but she said guardedly: 'I'm not sure what you mean by trouble – or why you think I could help. It depends on what sort of trouble.'

'It's difficult to discuss on the phone.'

'You'd better come round and see me,' she said. 'Come tomorrow lunchtime if you can. They'll be out then, we'll have the place to ourselves.'

I took the bus to Ormiston Court in my lunch hour.

When Pauline opened the front door she looked me over in an insolent way. 'I'll send down for some coffee.' She gestured me towards the drawing room and walked down the hall.

She'd been sorting through some old photographs. Inquisitively I looked at the snapshot on top of the pile. It was faded and one corner was bent. Four young men and women, grouped in front of a tennis court, smiled squinting into the camera. There was a large mansion in the background.

Gwendolen did look different, but you could see it was her, in the middle. Her hair had been curlier then, tied back with a ribbon round her head, but she was just as striking.

One of the young men was the psychiatrist, Dr Carstairs. I was sure of it.

I stared and stared at the photograph, convinced it held a secret, if only it would yield it up. I turned it over, and saw, pencilled on the back: Broadstairs, May, 1940. What funny things old photographs were, I thought. This one was a little piece of Gwendolen's past. It was an archaeological find, like a piece of bone or a shard of pottery, a fragment of an inscription; a hieroglyph with a hidden meaning, if only I could decipher it.

'Just some old photos.' I hadn't heard Pauline re-enter the room. She gathered them up and put them back in their box. 'So what about this trouble your *friend* finds herself in,' she said – quite neutral, no nasty innuendo. 'I thought it might be you, as a matter of fact. That's why I suggested you came round. But it's not, is it. I'm not working now, it was just – as I know you and you're a friend of Gwen's ... though I suppose you could give your friend this number. I might be able to suggest something.'

She passed me a cup of coffee. 'They've finished the film then,' she said.

'Apparently.'

'Any plans for another one?'

'I don't think so.' Why was she asking me? 'Alan's got a job at the BBC now.'

'Radu won't want to sit twiddling his thumbs. He's getting restless already.' She looked at me. I felt myself blushing. I had a feeling she knew something – knew that Radu had made a pass at me. 'He wants to get out of England – shake the dust of Blighty off his feet.'

'Really? Why should he want to do that?'

'You tell me, dear. Too hot for him here, I daresay. His Romanian friends pestering him, you know.'

'What Romanian friends?'

She looked at me slyly. 'I don't really know much about it, dear. All I know is, he's restless.'

. . . .

I gave Fiona Pauline's number and lent her £20 I borrowed from Stan. But if Fiona ever went to see Pauline, she didn't tell me. I didn't hear from her, and when I went round to her room above the restaurant, they told me she'd moved out. No forwarding address. Another unsolved mystery. It bothered me, but with the impending trial I had no time to worry about anything else.

One afternoon in October I came back to the office after lunch to find a note from Stanley: 'Gone to Ormiston Court. Come round at once.'

Pauline answered the door. Grim-faced, she gestured towards the drawing room.

'I'll tell Mr Colman you're here.'

While I waited I looked at an old copy of *Vogue*. It was a while before Stanley joined me.

He sat down on the deep sofa. 'Radu's gone to America.'

'America?'

'Hollywood. Left. Just like that. Gwen's taken it badly. Seems to think he's ditched her.' He sighed and wiped his face with his handkerchief. 'Don't tell a soul, but she took a small overdose – nothing serious, just a gesture, Pauline says she doesn't need to go to hospital, she's looking after her.'

'He's *left* her?'

Stanley shrugged. 'Looks like it.' Perhaps he wasn't entirely displeased. This might be his opportunity. 'The reason I called you round is about my appointments. I need to dictate a couple of letters. Well – that's not the real reason. I wanted you to know about Gwenny, but don't tell anyone else.'

He told me whom to telephone, but when I got back to the office the first person I rang was Alan. Alan got hold of Hugh and it all came out. Hugh was leaving too, on the Queen Mary, the following week. Radu had some deal with one of the studios, but they wanted one of their own big stars in Radu's next film; Gwendolen Grey wasn't a big enough name, apparently.

'Pretty ruthless,' said Alan. 'Trust Hugh – he didn't even bother to let me know. He sort of hinted that Enescu might still try to get Gwendolen into another film. Apparently it all depends how well *Be Still My Heart* does out there.'

I'd got over my troubling attraction towards the Romanian, or I thought I had, but now came a surge of bitter disappointment. Selfishly I thought only of myself; so after all the screen test had been meaningless.

'Why did he go now? Do you think it's because of the trial?' Radu had jumped ship for Hollywood. All our suspicions surged back. I repeated Pauline's enigmatic remark. 'But Hugh would never have gone with him if he'd thought ...'

'Also he's safe now, isn't he. Once they charged Colin – '

'But if Colin gets off – '

'Radu's never been a suspect.'

'*Why not!*'

We talked and talked, but got absolutely nowhere.

· · · · · · · · ·

Even more shocking was the speed with which Gwendolen found herself a new protector. Only a few weeks later: 'Gwenny and I are getting married, special licence,' Stanley said bashfully: 'I've found a place for her in Brighton – moved her down there last week. Sea air. Do her good.' It was almost as if he was moving her out of London in an attempt to hide her away. 'It'll be very quiet – just us and the witnesses. You understand, don't you, she's still a bit fragile.'

Later that day he sent me to Hatton Garden to collect a special present for her. Diamonds weren't rationed. You didn't need coupons for them, only money.

A week after that there was a photograph of their wedding on an inside page of the *Evening News*. There they were, standing outside Westminster Register Office. She wore a long mink coat and a hat with a veil. He looked pleased as punch. As if every self-made man doesn't want to marry a film star, I thought, meanly.

They honeymooned in Torquay, and when he returned he was in a buoyant, almost cocky mood. But that put me on the alert at once. I knew him well enough to recognise that when Stanley sounded that particular cheery note he was at his most insecure, his most anxious.

'You gotta come down to Brighton. Whaddya say? Gwen won't take no for an answer. I've a proposition for your hubby.'

· · · · · · · · ·

I had actually never been to Brighton. We followed a trickle of day trippers out of the wrought-iron station and plunged down a steep street at the end of which you could just see the sea. As soon as I heard the gulls shrieking, I knew I was at the seaside. It reminded me of childhood. Even in late autumn there was an air of holiday about the place. The salty wind bowled us down past the clock tower and past shabby little shops and houses until we reached the Front.

Embassy Court was a menacing modern building, a brutal block of concrete, but the geometric entrance was quite grand and a porter directed us from the softly lit lobby to the lift. 'Mr and Mrs Colman are on the top floor, they have the penthouse. I'll tell them you're on your way up.'

The penthouse; how grand and film-starry that sounded! When I emerged from the mahogany lift I saw a panelled and carpeted corridor. Stanley stood by the open front door.

'Gwen's in the lounge.' It was a great, light room looking out over the sea. Gwendolen lay with her feet up on a gold brocade Knole sofa. A bolster at each end dripped tassels to the floor. It was very hot.

'I'm taking you for lunch at English's. First-rate new fish restaurant. My treat of course.' (It was always Stan's treat.) Gwendolen seemed unimpressed by the plan, but after a round of gin and It from their cocktail cabinet we set off again along the windy Front.

English's might be new, but it had the air of a traditional oyster bar with a mirrored interior like a cosy Edwardian railway carriage with red walls and red velvet banquettes. I looked round the crowded little room. Brighton people were subtly different from London people, from the London people we knew, anyway. Everyone looked well off; people who'd had a good war and were doing well out of the peace. Next to us sat a middle-aged couple, she in a full New Look outfit and lots of make-up, he in a blazer, flannels and a paisley cravat, with Brylcreemed wavy grey hair and an RAF moustache, the sort of couple, I thought snobbishly, you'd expect to see at a roadhouse on the A1. But everyone down here was a little more theatrical, a bit more flamboyant than in London – and Stan was boasting that lots of 'showbiz' names had made Brighton their home: Anna Neagle and Herbert Wilcox, Tommy Trinder, Angela Baddeley, it was a glittering list, if that sort of thing impressed you.

Gwendolen frowned. 'Keep your voice down, *please*, Stanley.'

There was barely time to scan the menu before Stan was telling us his latest plan – and the reason for our summons. He was negotiating to buy up the Brighton film studios! His old dream of becoming a producer had taken on a new lease of life. It was all for Gwendolen, of course. Perhaps she wanted, after all, to continue her film career, and Stan had come up with the goods. 'I know you're working for radio now,' said Stan, 'but with all your expertise ... we thought you might be interested in my little venture.'

Alan said bluntly: 'Impossible I'm afraid – I'm only just getting into my stride.'

'It's frightfully kind of you to think of Alan,' I put in hastily, to take the edge off his rudeness. It was sickening really – a year ago, he'd have jumped at the chance.

Stan wouldn't take no for an answer. He talked up the venture, told Alan to think about it. And all the while he watched Gwendolen. Adoration glowed out of him. Poor Stan, I thought – for Gwendolen merely accepted his attentions. She was like a cat, not the friendly sort that rubs itself against your legs, but the taciturn, walking-by-itself kind of cat, that lets itself be stroked while remaining aloof in a feline universe all of its own.

Stan was obviously also in love with Brighton; or perhaps with the development opportunities he described to us as we ate our smoked salmon (not much sign of rationing here, although they kept within the rules). Great plans, he told us. Pull down the old terraces. 'Those stucco monsters! The whole of the Front needs redevelopment – some of these stuck-up architecture geezers don't like Embassy Court, think it's a monstrosity. Why can't they see that's the future! All that fuss about the Pavilion – the Regency Society's a pain in the neck – backward-looking, stuck in the mud – they want to get off their backsides, if you'll excuse the expression.'

Alan smiled. 'I thought they *had*! They *saved* the Pavilion, didn't they?'

'God knows why! It's hideous!'

I couldn't square Stan's futuristic vision with his Palladian mansion, that architectural sleeping beauty in its becalmed Suffolk park. 'But your house in the country. That's period, that's eighteenth century.'

Stan was unabashed by his contradictions. 'Brighton's different,' he said, 'Brighton's modern. Brighton's gotta be part of the new Britain.'

'You're beginning to sound like the Labour Party, Stan.'

'I've always supported a lot of what they're trying to do. "Work or Want" – that's a damn good slogan. All these spivs and layabouts – the country's bankrupt – they need to get their ideas in order. What I can't stand is all these planning restrictions.'

Gwen looked utterly uninterested.

After the meal Stan insisted on taking Alan to see the studios. 'The girls can take in a flick,' he said.

For the first time Gwendolen showed some animation. 'You know what's on? *House of Shadows*. What about it, for old times' sake.'

We climbed up a steep side street to a shabby cinema that showed second-run films. We sat in the half-empty auditorium with its balding red seats and giggling pockets of an audience that had probably come in just to get out of the wind, not to see a cinematic masterpiece.

At last the lights went down, the curtain scrolled back and the Pathé news came on, followed by amateurish advertisements for local shops and restaurants. Then at last *House of Shadows*.

The title drifted in a smoky trail across the static backdrop: an inky lake, a house in shadow. The sombre music turned on a discord, modulating to the dominant, an eerie minor key. Credits scrolled across in flowing script, culminating in: directed by Radu Enescu.

I glanced sideways at Gwendolen, but she was staring straight ahead. The first scene: I remembered it so well; the camera moving with sinister swiftness along a street through desolate suburbs towards a Victorian gothic mansion looming up, a driveway between gloomy shrubs, trees clustered at the edge of a lake like mourners at a funeral, with clouds gathering behind.

The camera passed magically into the house, pulling us along a corridor and into a panelled room. The rhythm changed, became static. And there, suddenly, was Gwendolen, seated on a sofa in an embrasured window. She was gazing up at an imposing older man, played by Eric Portman, who greeted her, the heiress, on her arrival at the family home. The manners and language were stately and almost Victorian, but the man and the woman were in formal modern dress.

In the next scene Gwendolen accidentally encountered the man who was to become her lover, the handsome, cadaverous Guy Rolfe. As they met, he smiled at her and his smile was both wrenchingly melancholic and sinister, almost vampiric. I felt the throbbing pull of romantic pessimism; doomed lovers, he poor, she an heiress, the one fatal step that led them to crime and catastrophe, the heartbreaking close-ups, the rainy vistas – this was the beauty of the movie, and I remembered something Hugh had said: *House of Shadows* had a tart's beauty, the beauty of the hackneyed, of stale, familiar, false emotions.

I thought of Radu and how we'd been locked together so briefly in the betrayal of a forbidden passion that could never be. It brought a lump to my throat. Yet as the film wound on, I became restless, and aware that actually I was slightly bored. A blasphemous thought; could it possibly be that this film, to which we'd all been addicted, all thought was wonderful, was not quite the brilliant work everyone believed? Alan always maintained you had to see any film, read any book at least twice before you could judge it, and films seen a second time did tend to disappoint, but I suppressed the thought, and soon the achingly mournful ending stifled my scepticism.

Gwendolen stood up. 'We don't want to stay for the second feature, do we?' I certainly didn't, after Guy Rolfe had killed himself and Gwendolen was walking away forever down the endless road. As we came out into the chilly light of Brighton, she said: 'That was very Radu, wasn't it.'

And I knew exactly what she meant.

twenty-two

SEASON OF MISTS AND MELLOW FRUITFULNESS! Lines from Keats' 'Ode to Autumn' were running through my head as I hurried along High Holborn, but today the poem I used to love seemed smug and sentimental. 'Close bosom friend of the maturing sun ...' The dusk tasted acrid; no maturing sun in London's damp streets. A drab civilian army of office workers marched, heads down, feet moving mechanically towards the jammed buses and packed trains. 'Conspiring with him how to load and bless/With fruit the vines that round the thatch-eaves run ...' What rot it all was; a cheap, picture postcard vision of a non-existent England. It began to rain. I was tired. And somehow I felt that all this was because I'd enjoyed that last year of the war and the first year of my marriage too much. I hadn't suffered as so many had. I was having my war now. The trial was to begin the following Monday.

Julius Abrahams had called us to an urgent meeting. At least his office was warm. Alan was already there.

'I was just explaining to your husband' – Abrahams looked at me over his spectacles – 'as you know, we were hoping Colin's friend on the *Daily Worker*, Charlie Porter, would give him an alibi for at least the early part of the evening. It didn't cover the whole evening by any means, but the time of death is so vague and at least it covers Colin up to about seven pm. He had a drink with Porter before he met Johnny. You know all this – but now there's a problem.'

'It's outrageous, Dinah. The Party doesn't want Porter to testify.' Alan looked at Abrahams. 'Can't he be subpoenaed?'

Abrahams shook his head. 'They're worried about the so-called spy angle. The prosecution case will dwell on that. Their case will be that Colin murdered Mavor because Mavor knew too much about his wartime activities.'

'But that's all lies!' I cried hotly.

Abrahams frowned. He seemed to be searching for words. Finally he said: 'Yes ... but how will it look if there are even hints he worked for the Russians rather than the British.'

'For God's sake, we were all together in the war!' Alan was almost shouting.

'We're not any more though.'

'Why can't you *make* him give evidence? Is it because it won't help Colin, or because it might upset the Party?'

'It won't help much,' said Abrahams patiently, 'it was always pretty marginal to the case. And frankly, the Party simply can't afford to be mixed up in this.'

'They are mixed up! Colin's a Communist!'

'All the more reason to steer clear of anything that underlines that.' Abrahams looked at me: 'This makes your evidence even more important, Dinah. You do realise that? Colin's alibi for the afternoon isn't really in question.'

· · · · · · · · ·

On the second day of the trial Stanley and I looked at the headlines in the *Daily Telegraph* and *The Times*. 'A bit lurid,' murmured Stanley, and chewed his nails. 'We should buy the

Graphic and the *Mirror* as well, see what they're saying.'

'It'll all be the same only more so.' In the end we bought the lot. The reports didn't stint on Mavor's lifestyle, his background or his work, which was treated in true philistine fashion as little more than a bad joke. One of the papers reproduced a grimy little photo of one of his paintings, *A Muse in Arcadia*. When you looked closely, you could see it was a portrait of Gwendolen; Gwendolen seated in an empty courtyard filled with exaggerated light and shadow, more like de Chirico than Dalí.

'She won't like that,' muttered Stanley.

'Don't show her then.'

'I won't,' he said grimly. 'But Pauline will.'

Alan couldn't take time off to be at the trial, but every evening we read the papers and listened to the wireless. 'How d'you think it's going?' We looked at each other.

'I'm not sure.' Alan spoke slowly, puzzled. 'Nothing about his politics yet. Perhaps Abrahams was too worried about that. Being a CP member himself, he may have exaggerated its importance. Perhaps they won't bring it up.' And we began to feel hopeful.

At the beginning of the second week, Alan did manage to get an afternoon off. I went to the Old Bailey to meet him. Abrahams had warned me that, as a defence witness, I couldn't watch the trial from the visitors' gallery, so I waited in the gloomy entrance hall. I paced up and down, worried in case I wasn't even meant to be in the building, keeping an eye on everyone who passed through.

A woman came out of the courtroom. I was standing inconspicuously in an embrasure and shrank even further back, so that she didn't see me as she left. I recognised her. It was Joan Mainwaring. What was she doing at the trial? I tried to calm down and told myself not to be stupid. She was his aunt, after all. It wasn't surprising she should come to the trial. And probably I'd got it all wrong – she hadn't come out of the court at all. She must have been in the gallery.

There was movement. People were leaving the court. I joined the trickle of men and women and waited by the visitors' gallery entrance for Alan.

His face was stony.

'How did it go?'

'Wait – I must have a fag.' When it was lit, he gripped my arm and propelled us along towards Holborn.

'Well, tell me – how did it go?' I was frightened now.

'Disaster.' Through gritted teeth. We were almost running. He was dragging me along, as if he couldn't get away from the Old Bailey fast enough.

'I saw his aunt. She must have been watching the trial.'

He stopped abruptly, then, still holding my arm, walked on more slowly. 'Watching! She was giving evidence. She made him sound like Stalin's right-hand man. It all started to unravel when the waiter from the Café Royal took the stand. He gave all this evidence about the row between Titus and Colin – the evening when Titus accused Colin of being a spy. He made it sound as though Colin really did threaten Titus. He didn't say how drunk Titus was. And he got it all wrong. He said it was Colin who talked about liquidating Titus. But it was Titus who said that, wasn't it? I can't remember any more. Oh God, the whole thing's so ridiculous, no one took it seriously at the time. Abrahams should call someone – Stan, anyone – to say it wasn't like that. But then this old scarecrow appeared and it got worse. She said she saw Colin. That evening. She said Colin was round at the house and she heard noises from next door. She saw him leave. She was rock solid. Couldn't be shifted. I thought our man's cross-examination was quite weak, anyway. And then somehow she smuggled in all these hints about what he did in the war.'

'But I thought Mavor didn't do anything in the war.'

'Colin! What *Colin* did in the war.' He shouted above the traffic noise. 'The judge stopped it, of course, but it was too late by then. All kind of implying that Colin was a pretty shady character and had a strong motive for shutting Titus up. It was a disaster.'

Alan was in a rotten mood all evening, sunk in an angry gloom, a kind of impotent rage. I tried to cheer him up, but I felt as bad as he did.

'You know this makes your evidence even more important. Absolutely vital. It's all up to you now, Dinah.'

. . . .

The prosecution case came to an end, and the defence case began. It would soon be my turn in the witness box. If there really was a doubt about the time of death, the prosecution would be out to destroy me. I had to be strong.

I wore my grey flannel suit. Now that the New Look had caught on in a big way, I felt it looked terribly dowdy. The papers that day were full of Princess Elizabeth's New Look trousseau for her impending marriage (she'd saved enough clothing coupons!). I couldn't decide whether I should try to look young and innocent, or confident and sophisticated. In the end I fell between the two stools and, I felt, looked too bohemian, messy, in spite of my suit, and even a bit tarty with too much dark red lipstick to keep my spirits up.

I was called after lunch. I had a horrible hollow feeling inside. A faint fog hung over the panelled courtroom. There was a continual scraping of papers and small sounds, like mice behind the wainscot. The proceedings were slow and tedious. There were unnerving pauses and silences. It was difficult to believe a man was on trial for his life. I looked at Colin, hoping he'd look back at me, but he didn't, just stared ahead, looking quite pale and calm.

It was all right at first. Colin's barrister took me through my statement. He did ask me about the Café Royal quarrel, and obviously my account was different from the waiter's. I thought I did quite well on that. Then we came on to the evening Titus died.

I said I had gone round to see the artist because I was thinking of buying a painting. The front door was ajar, so that although there was no response to my knock, I was able to enter the premises. I found Titus upstairs. I thought he was asleep and I left. However, afterwards I became uneasy. He'd looked odd. Had he been breathing? I was so anxious that at Notting Hill underground station I'd phoned 999. The next day I returned to Mecklenburgh Square with my husband and we found that Mavor was indeed dead. We immediately reported this to the police. Some time later I was still worried, and came to realise that Mavor had been dead when I first found him.

The prosecuting barrister rose to cross-examine me. He was tall, large, exquisitely polite. He even smiled in a friendly fashion.

'You say you telephoned the emergency services, yet there seems to be no record of this call.'

I swallowed. 'I don't understand why, because I did phone them,' I said firmly – and of course it was true. What I couldn't explain was why the call hadn't been logged – because I'd hung up in a panic. My palms were sweating. I felt slightly sick.

'The next day you and your husband found the victim dead. Yet when you reported this fact to the police, you said nothing about your visit the previous evening. Why was that?'

'It – it didn't seem relevant.'

'It didn't seem relevant.' He smiled. 'Perhaps you can tell the court when you sought a further interview with the police and gave them this additional information.'

I swallowed and told him the date.

'By that time it seemed relevant after all?'

'Yes. I'd thought about it a lot. I became increasingly worried.'

'Let me refresh your memory. You gave a further statement to Inspector Bannister on the day after the defendant was charged with murder. I put it to you, Mrs Wentworth, that this alleged earlier visit of yours only came to seem relevant when you were anxious to get your friend off the hook.'

I stared at him, genuinely indignant. 'That's not true.'

'I suggest that you never went round to see Mr Mavor that evening at all. The whole story is a complete fabrication in order to suggest that the victim was already dead before the time at which the defendant was seen at the house.'

'No.'

'You seriously expect the court to believe that although you thought you had found a dead body you did nothing about it until the following day?'

'I wasn't sure.' My voice sounded unconvincing, but I stuck my chin up. I just had to endure, I had to stick to my guns. 'I know it sounds odd, but the whole situation was – strange and the house was so dark and creepy. At first I thought – I assumed he was alive. Afterwards I began to wonder – and then I thought I was probably being silly, that I was being morbid, not thinking straight.'

'You weren't thinking straight! And perhaps your thinking became a little more twisted still when your friend was arrested. And you suddenly remembered that on the very evening when the crime was committed of which your friend stands accused, you had been to the scene of that crime and had found a dead body, which you failed to report to the police! I suggest that your story is a complete fabrication, Mrs Wentworth.'

'No!'

It went on and on. The more I stuck to my story the less plausible it sounded. By the time the ordeal was over, I even doubted it myself. I hung on doggedly but the KC annihilated me. That evening I sat at the kitchen table and cried and cried. Alan tried to be optimistic, but I knew he was worried – desperately worried.

Now that I'd given evidence, I could have attended the trial alongside Alan, but I never wanted to go near Number One Court at the Old Bailey again. I preferred to go to the office, where Stanley and I went over the trial reports obsessively, discussing it from every angle.

Subtly my relationship with him had changed. At one point he had half-heartedly offered to take the stand, to back up my story; but that was when we still thought we had an alibi witness. By the time that fell through, he'd changed his mind. He'd discussed it with Julius Abrahams – all Abrahams said to us afterwards was that he didn't think Stan would be a very strong witness. 'Just open another can of worms.'

I still liked Stan – he'd been very good to me – but I began to nurture an irrational resentment towards him – for backing the film, for marrying Gwendolen, for not doing more to help, when really there was nothing he could do. My resentment should actually have been directed at Radu and Hugh, but they had deserted the sinking ship, so there was no one to be angry with but Stan.

· · · · · · · · · ·

In his summing up the judge referred to me as 'naïve' and 'confused'. I suppose he was trying to be kind, and not to go too heavily for the idea that I'd deliberately lied. But of course he had to say it in the end – had to mention the prosecution's suggestion that I'd made the whole story up on purpose, in an effort to protect a friend.

The jury retired. At the end of the day there was no decision. They continued the next day, without a result.

On the third day they reached a verdict. Everyone hustled back into the court. Colin came out between two uniformed warders.

Alan and I sat at the front of the packed gallery. The atmosphere was thick with expectation and excitement. They were in at the kill. I hated them. They craned forward, their eyes gleaming with malice, licking their lips in anticipation. To them all this was just a gruesome thrill. One or two of them noticed me, nudged and stared. My face went hot, but I ignored them.

The jury filed in. The judge asked if they'd reached a verdict. A split second's silence: 'Guilty.' The guillotine clanged down, hope decapitated.

A murmur rustled round the gallery. Alan gripped my hand.

Colin made a single, stifled movement. The warder held his arm. Colin stared straight ahead. The judge placed his black cap on his head and spoke the frightful words. Hanged: Colin would be hanged.

I looked and looked at Colin. He looked stunned. Then he looked up towards us in the gallery. I wasn't sure he saw us. He must have felt so alone.

The crowd bulged forward, eager to see. The smell of their bodies seemed like the miasma of their satisfaction. They'd been fed. They'd got what they'd come for.

I was numb as we pushed through the crowd of spectators and out into the London dusk. We made for the kerb, hoping for a taxi. A man stepped forward. It was Inspector Bannister.

'You'll be hearing from me again, Mrs Wentworth. We'll be considering charges.'

I stared at him in bewilderment, but just then a taxi halted in response to Alan's gesture of command, and Bannister was swept aside as a few onlookers ran forward to see who we were. Alan and I clung together as the cab bore us away through the busy streets and back to anonymity.

· · · · · · · · ·

The days and weeks that followed were dreadful. The strain made me ill. Alan raged. There were more visits to Julius Abrahams and frantic phone calls as we tried to find character witnesses.

With Bannister's threat hanging over my head I went down to Alton in the hope of some help from my father. The reports of the trial and my part in it had enraged him. He shouted at me: what the hell had I been thinking of? 'And now that dismal little policeman is going to have you up for perverting the course of justice or accessory after the fact. Serves you damn well right.' As he raged, my mother twisted her hankie and looked unhappy. Afterwards she tried to comfort me, but it was just fussing about my health.

That evening was the worst of all. When I told Alan what had happened – the row, the accusations – I started to cry again. Instead of being sympathetic, this seemed to enrage Alan and he started to shout at me too. 'For God's sake, stop snivelling, you stupid little bitch,' he yelled.

I sobbed harder. Suddenly he sprang up, lunged across the table and slapped my face. There was a moment's silence. Shock – pain – disbelief. I stumbled backwards, making for the bedroom. I was shouting incoherently, shouting at him to leave me alone, shouting that it was all his fault.

I flung myself on the bed, still sobbing, great gasps, I couldn't catch my breath. The kitchen door banged. 'Leave me alone,' I shouted, but he came after me, and now he was hitting and punching me as I lay defenceless on the bed, unable to get away. Until finally I started to scream and he reeled back, staggered away, stumbled out of the room, slammed the front door.

I don't know what time he came back. Next morning we stared at each other in white-faced horror across the breakfast table.

'Dinah ... please ...'

I refused to speak to him. It was only later that day that I started to bleed. It was terrifying. Luckily the doctor agreed to pay a home visit. He told me I was having a miscarriage.

I hadn't even known I was pregnant. We'd never stopped taking precautions and one missed period when I was so worried meant nothing – or that's what I'd thought.

Alan didn't realise, but the tears I wept were of relief. I couldn't have coped with a baby. My mother would have been thrilled, but that would only have made things worse. The last thing I wanted was to be pulled back into her orbit – good God, I was barely twenty-one! My life would be over if I had a child now. Alan couldn't have coped either. It would have been the last straw for him.

We didn't discuss it, but I knew he felt dreadfully guilty; guilty because his violence had probably brought on the miscarriage; guiltier still because he hadn't wanted a child, and was thankful to have been let off the hook; guiltiest of all because he assumed I *did* want the baby. Women naturally wanted babies, of course!

I was glad, so glad I wasn't pregnant. Such mixed

emotions – the relief – the dread for Colin – the fear at the back of my mind that Alan would hit me again, the dark cloud of fear.

twenty-three

■□■■□□■□

'WE'VE BEEN GIVEN LEAVE TO APPEAL.'

I stared numbly at Julius. A faint smile flickered across the lawyer's narrow features. 'It's good news! But we haven't got long.'

Not long – not long: how long? I burst into tears. I couldn't help it. I sobbed and sobbed. After a while Julius passed me a big, white, clean handkerchief. 'Sorry ... sorry,' I blubbed.

'One of the few times tears haven't been called for lately,' he commented drily. He gave me time to recover and then said quietly, 'There's some other good news. Nothing official, but I've heard on the grapevine that they're not going to charge you. Bannister's been knocked back there. Looks as if your father may have had a word in high places.'

That made me feel tearful again. My father had been so angry – he'd certainly not even hinted to me that he was going to do anything to help. He disapproved of pulling strings to get what he wanted.

'You don't seem very pleased.'

'It's an enormous relief, of course it is,' I said miserably, 'but I didn't want to be treated differently because of who my father is.'

'There will have been other reasons,' said Abrahams soothingly. 'No one really believes you lied deliberately.'

The door opened violently. 'Look at this.' Naomi Abrahams was holding the *Evening News*. 'The Party's taken power in Prague.' She passed the paper to her brother.

'They've ousted the reactionaries,' he read out. '"Pledged to defend republican democratic regime against the forces of international reaction." That's excellent news.'

From where I was seated I could see that the headlines announced it as a disaster – but as I'd discovered from knowing Colin, the Communists always saw things like a photographic negative: the opposite way from everyone else.

Naomi Abrahams looked at her brother. 'It says there it's a coup.'

'Well, they're bound to take that line.'

'It hasn't exactly happened the way we'd have wanted it, though.'

'There was a democratic election. Now the so-called People's Party has walked out of the government. That's their affair. What did they represent, anyway, Naomi? They were the party of right-wing peasants, rural fascists.'

There was a silence, but the silence was still full of an unspoken argument they probably didn't want to have in front of me. 'Colin will be pleased at the news,' I said.

Julius looked amused. 'I should think the appeal will be uppermost in his mind, won't it?'

Just then there was a knock and the door opened again. 'Sorry I'm late,' said Alan.

When he heard the good news about the appeal he seemed stunned rather than glad – just as I'd been. He sat looking at the floor for a bit. Then he looked up. 'Couldn't they have told us that before Christmas?'

Christmas had certainly been miserable, locked in hostile imprisonment in Hampshire with my parents and thinking all the time of Colin in the death cell.

Abrahams ignored this. 'The appeal has been granted on the basis of new evidence,' he said, 'but it's going to be tricky. Anyway, let me explain.'

The conference over, we walked towards Holborn.

'Let's just take a look at the house,' said Alan suddenly.

I followed him reluctantly up the side street that led to Mecklenburgh Square. I'd walked through the darkness and the snow along this street as through a photographic negative, after I found the painter's body. Now it was freezing again and there were fears of another winter like the last one. And I was back in that dark, arctic winter and the ghostly house in the Square. As we passed the boarded-up house I had a strange feeling, as if Titus Mavor must still be lying there in the moonlight.

There was a dim light in the house next door. We walked quickly, almost furtively, past and then retraced our steps to the Lamb and Flag, where we'd arranged to meet Noel Valentine.

This evening he wore an ancient Harris tweed coat over his crumpled suit. He'd always pass unnoticed in a crowd, but there was nothing anonymous or indecisive about him. Although, for example, Alan and I would have been glad to stay in the warmth of the saloon bar, no sooner had we arrived than Noel proposed a meal in Soho; and what Noel proposed happened.

'I actually booked at L'Escargot – it's not as noisy as somewhere like Fava's.'

So he'd planned it in advance. I was glad I was wearing my new New Look suit. I was so sick of my old grey flannel that I'd splashed out in the sales at Marshall and Snelgrove, spending almost all my coupons on it. Dark red barathea with a full, pleated skirt; tight jacket with nipped-in waist, and curving lapels edged with black velvet to match the collar: it gave me a lovely figure. Out of doors in this cold weather my old coat concealed it. I'd had the coat altered with three bands of tweed from another, even older coat inserted in the skirt to lengthen it, but the effect was lumpy, and with its big shoulders and tie waist, it didn't have that New Look look at all. But when I removed it, the suit was revealed in all its glory and I caught admiring looks from nearby tables.

Noel was a notorious gossip, which was partly why Alan put up with him, ever hopeful of some piece of information that might help with Colin's trial – or now, with the appeal. Of course, with Noel it was two-way traffic; he expected juicy titbits in return for those he offered. He unfurled his napkin with a snap and wasted no time. 'Any idea why Enescu shot off to Hollywood like that? I know it was before Christmas, but lately all these rumours have started flying around again. I thought your friend Hugh Palmer-Green might have given you the lowdown. He sailed off into the sunset too, didn't he?'

'What rumours?' Alan was bristling at the implication that Hugh was somehow involved in whatever the rumours were.

I said: 'We didn't see so much of Hugh in the autumn – with the trial and everything.'

'Any news on that front?'

'He's been given leave to appeal.'

'Oh, that's very good news.' Noel's eyes gleamed behind his glasses. 'I wanted to talk to you about Titus Mavor as a matter of fact. I've made absolutely no headway in tracking down his collection of Surrealists. Possibly it doesn't exist. But his ex-cronies think it does.'

I stared at the menu and thought about Stanley's trip to

Paris – it seemed such a long time ago now.

'Enescu was cultivating Mavor like mad, wasn't he, until he got bumped off. And now, well, people are putting two and two together. Admittedly it adds up to considerably more than five. They say that property dealer friend of yours was backing his film – but maybe the money came from somewhere else. Didn't they go off to Paris together on several occasions?'

I remembered all Stan's suspicions of Radu and his Paris friends. 'Once,' I said firmly. 'I'm quite sure Stan wasn't involved in whatever it is you're suggesting. And I should know. I work for him after all.' I wasn't quite sure why I was defending him so valiantly.

'I know that.' Noel Valentine was looking me over. 'That's why I thought you might have picked up a few hints.'

'But he wasn't the only backer.' I recalled the meeting at Ormiston Court, when Radu had been so pleased with himself. Something he'd said … 'I can't remember, exactly, but I'm sure there was money from somewhere else as well. Anyway, Stanley regretted financing the film,' I said.

'That's nonsense, Di.' Alan was frowning. 'He's a shrewd businessman. Even if he had mixed feelings about Enescu, he knew it was a winner commercially.'

'And he'll be laughing if it does well in America,' added Noel. 'But that's something else I wanted to talk to *you* about, Dinah. Why are you working for a spiv like that? You're too good for him, my dear. Men like him, making a fortune out of post-war misery, you don't want anything to do with it. And as for marrying Enescu's discarded mistress – well, really!'

I couldn't see what was so terrible about that, except that it made Stan look slightly pathetic, Gwendolen's adoring spaniel. 'I don't think she's in love with him,' I said, 'so it's rather sad for him.'

'Di! That's so sentimental,' cried Alan, 'it's a business

proposition, surely you can see that.'

'Well, I've got another business proposition,' said Noel briskly, 'I want you to come and work for me, Dinah. My gallery will be opening soon. Come and see it next Wednesday. Lunchtime – you can get away then, can't you, Wentworth?'

. . . .

The gallery was located in the hushed precincts of St James's. The discreet wealth of the district offered an oasis from austerity and the menacing world situation. The people, mostly men, who passed along the pavement, had a well-dressed sleekness about them, wearing bowler hats and carrying umbrellas as narrow as sword sticks. I was glad I was wearing my dark red costume.

Noel Valentine met us outside Fortnum and Mason and led us down a side passage off Jermyn Street. The gallery stood between the bomb crater of a completely destroyed building and a boarded-up house. Unlike the galleries we'd passed, with their old-master displays of eighteenth-century paintings in elaborate gilt frames, it was modern.

A glamorous young woman in a black dress – more like a fashion model than a shop assistant – was seated behind a shiny black desk. She brought us coffee and we sat with Noel on a black sofa next to a tall plant with fleshy leaves sticking out from its single central stem. There was a white carpet on the black stained floor and an orange vase on the reception desk. It was all light years away from the Persian rugs and Louis Quinze gilt I'd expected. It was like something out of the 'Britain Can Make It' exhibition!

He showed us the little rooms upstairs, all offices, and even led us out onto the roof with its giddy-making fire escape. 'So – why don't you come and work for me? Art is more interesting than property. My gallery exists to encourage and market new art. I'm not interested in second-rate old masters – Salvator Rosa and all that rubbish, eighteenth-century genre scenes – *Christ* no. I'm here to promote the new stuff. Surrealism, for example. It's not fashionable in the way it was before the war, but I'm going to change all that. If things go well, the secretarial job would expand – advertising, publicity, that sort of thing.'

'It sounds interesting,' I said. I still clung to my dream of acting, but – especially with Radu in Hollywood – I'd almost – *almost* – accepted that that was off the agenda now.

'And Alan, I *seriously* want to interest you in a programme about the British Surrealist group.' There was no end to Noel's energy; he outlined his idea in impassioned tones. I couldn't decide if it was pure love of the art, or an eye to the main chance of commercial opportunity.

'I think you should take up his offer,' said Alan as we walked together back towards Piccadilly. 'He's right about Stan Colman. And if he can dig up some stuff about Mavor's paintings – '

'That's why you want me to take up the offer, isn't it? Because it might help Colin.'

'Not just that. It also helps you. You were keen on having a proper job. Now you've got one.'

He was right. 'And what about the programme he wants you to do?'

Alan shrugged. 'It's another good idea. But the appeal's the thing at present, isn't it.' He stomped along looking particularly thundery. 'I can't forgive myself, I simply can't. So keen to get involved in that ghastly film, I didn't see what was going on.'

'You couldn't have known.'

'Of course I could have known. Stan's trip to Paris – we

knew all about it. We just shut our eyes to it, we were blind, we didn't want to know.'

'We did talk it over with Julius Abrahams. He didn't want it brought up.'

'He's a lawyer, Di. They're always too cautious by half.'

. . . .

I was sorry to say goodbye to Stan, and I think he was sorry to lose me too, but we both knew the time had come. He was talking of basing his operations in Brighton. He could see I needed to move on. A new phase in my life was about to begin.

I did indeed now have a real job, but it was very different from my work in the War Office, where we'd all been working together for victory. Evidently a good secretary was loyal not to a common purpose, but to her boss. With Stan it had all been relaxed and casual, but with Noel, in spite of our social relationship outside the office, I was expected to work hard. Sometimes I stayed late at the gallery. Sometimes, I accompanied Noel to private views and cocktail parties. Alan had taken to drinking in the BBC pubs with his new friends after work and didn't mind, or even notice if I was late, because he was so often out in the evenings himself.

At first I'd thought Kay, the receptionist, might be Noel's girlfriend, but I soon discovered she was just another decorative item in the gallery, sitting around looking glamorous, while I did the work. Then I began to wonder if he was – well, like Colin, but by the third week I'd decided he was simply what he'd always seemed, a self-sufficient, self-absorbed bachelor, blithely unaware of how other people felt and indifferent to the crises that raged outside in the world, exclusively dedicated to his great passion, modern art. I was learning a lot from him, and I began to think of doing an art history course myself, but what really brought us together was our common purpose (though for very different reasons) in unearthing the truth about Mecklenburgh Square. There wasn't much time. The date for Colin's appeal had been set.

Over coffee I said to Noel: 'What are you doing about Mavor's paintings?'

'I'm going round to see the old girl.'

'Joan Mainwaring?'

'I thought you might come with me,' he continued. 'You've met her after all.'

'I can't do that, not with the appeal. It would look very bad if I went to see her while the appeal's pending. Might make her suspicious – or as if I was nobbling a witness.'

'I don't see why,' he said petulantly.

'You can go, though. But it's over a year since the murder. Won't his family have sorted his stuff out by now?'

'I somehow don't think so. Gerry Blackstone says they live in the country, not interested, never come to London, loathed all Mavor's arty friends. Got stuck with his bastard.'

'Gwendolen never ever mentioned the child, you know. Not once. Not ever.'

'Should I write to the old girl first? Or go round on the off chance?'

'Go round,' I said.

When he came back his glasses gleamed more than ever and a sly smile revealed his protruding teeth. 'She was really quite accommodating – actually let me into Mavor's place, you know, the house next door. It's more or less derelict. I'm surprised it hasn't been requisitioned and pulled down. I was petrified going up the stairs, thought the whole thing might collapse. But when we got to his room – his paintings are still *there*!'

The paintings: again I was back in that moonlit room, the

frozen winter darkness, the canvases flung about. I remembered them roughly stacked or pushed over in the room while Titus lay greenish in the moonlight, his limbs flung out, abandoned in the childish peacefulness of death.

'She said the family couldn't care less – told her to chuck 'em out. So far as she's concerned I can have them! Would you believe it! *But* – ' and he paused dramatically, '*no sign* of anything more important. I looked fairly carefully. The old scarecrow lay on the sofa smoking and watched me go through the canvases.'

'He died on that sofa, you know!'

'Did he? Well, she didn't care. Then, when we went back next door, there was an André Masson hanging in her front room. Made me wonder if she'd taken the lot. I thought I'd try the direct approach, you know – I said I'd heard Titus owned some rather *valuable* paintings by other artists. She gave me a funny look. "Oh, really?" she said, "well I wouldn't know about that, but the night before he died there was a bit of a commotion next door as if he was having a row with someone."'

'She said *what*?'

'Someone came to see him the night before he died and they had a row. And I thought – if it was about his paintings, not *his* paintings, but the ones he owned, well, he owed an awful lot of people a lot of money and I just wondered ...'

'That's not what she said.'

'Yes! It is!' He looked at me, baffled.

'It's not what she said at the *trial*. She said it was the *same* night. She said the row was the night Titus was killed.'

This took even Noel's mind off his own obsessions. 'Oh my goodness, that's really important. Could she really have made a mistake like that?' He thought about it. 'But it's only hearsay – I think. I don't think me saying she said it – I don't think that counts.'

'I must get on to the lawyer. I must tell him about this.'

I rang immediately, but Julius was out. However, as Noel and I chewed over it, we began to develop a plan. Noel would try to get her round to the gallery and somehow lure her into saying it again. And this time it would be recorded on his Dictaphone.

'Yes, that's what we'll do. I'll offer to pay her for Mavor's stuff. She didn't seem to give a hoot, but I daresay she wouldn't turn down the money if offered.'

'It'll have to be soon.'

'Mavor knew Dalí, you know. He was his disciple.' Noel was still brooding over the missing masterpieces. 'He certainly gave the impression he owned one – some, and a Max Ernst, and God knows what. But nothing's turned up in any auction rooms, so where are they?'

'Are you sure they exist?'

He smiled. 'Good point, Dinah. The famous Mavor boastfulness. What a disappointment that would be.' He picked a minute piece of fluff off his sleeve. 'Against that, Marius Smith certainly believed him; claimed to have *seen* them.' He jumped up. 'You know – we could go and see Marius! All three of us – Alan could interview him for the programme about the Surrealists; I could offer to represent him and pick his brains about the Dalí, etcetera, and you could buy yourself some pretty clothes! A week in Spain; how about it. Please say you'll come. And you must persuade Alan.'

. . . .

What a trip! It was complicated to arrange, with passports and the tiny foreign exchange allowance, and we couldn't have done it if Alan hadn't got the BBC to pay his expenses, so for him it counted as a work trip. Alan, of course, didn't approve of our going to Franco's Spain, and nor did I, but he squared our common conscience because he hoped it might help Colin. Time was so short. That made the trip even more urgent, and we rushed frantically here and there to get it organised.

It was the first time I'd ever been abroad. The journey lasted almost two days: first, the boat train to Newhaven; then the boat to Dieppe (it was quite rough); then another train to Paris and a mad dash across Paris to the Gare de Lyon to catch the overnight train to Madrid. We sat up all night, for hours and hours, in a carriage crammed with travellers, none of them English. But it was a wonderful moment when dawn broke over the south of France and I looked out of the window and found myself in a different world: vineyards and cypress trees in the pearly dawn!

The visit only lasted three days and it was all a blur – or rather, the opposite of a blur. Everything was so bright and hard-edged. Although it wasn't very warm, the sun shone, but what amazed me was that there was no austerity in Madrid. The moment we crossed the border we saw fruit and chocolate and biscuits on sale at every station and on our first day in the capital I could hardly believe my eyes. The women were gorgeously dressed, in furs and lovely clothes and jewellery. And the shoes! The shops were crammed with goods and the restaurants with food. We ate so much I was nearly sick. And then in the cafés afterwards, late at night, Madrid society preened itself, so sleek and glamorous.

Marius Smith was living just outside Madrid and as soon as we'd left the centre there was a completely different picture. The contrast was astonishing, the poverty unbeliev-able; crumbling tenements and then shacks and hovels alongside broken roads housed a population of beggars, children in rags, old women bent double, thin, knotty men carrying loads that would have befitted a donkey, women whose faces were blank with weariness and suspicion.

Marius Smith was sharing a two-room cottage with a sullen young woman who disappeared as soon as we arrived. I suppose I should have expected the squalor – but at least he'd been working; several finished canvases were stacked against the walls.

He plied us with olives and cheap wine. It was only midday, but he must have been drinking all morning. Still, he was reasonably coherent. He told us confidently that he knew Titus had owned three important paintings, one by Salvador Dalí, one by Max Ernst and a third by Miró. Titus, he said, had hinted that he had a buyer for two of them, but intended to keep the Dalí. Marius Smith was vague about the exact dates, but was sure it wasn't long before the painter's death.

Later, Alan interviewed him for the Third Programme. Afterwards, as we jolted back in a decrepit taxi Alan asked: 'Was it worth coming all this way just for that?'

Noel was cheerful. 'Yes.' He was emphatic. 'We've something definite to go on now. Not to mention the programme.'

Alan was angry with himself – with all of us. 'We should have thought of all this long ago.'

But at least we'd had a taste of the Mediterranean. The promise of a sun-drenched culture had burst into view and I couldn't wait to explore the sunny south.

Yet at the same time it made me more appreciative of austerity Britain. It put Churchill's notorious remark about the socialist Gestapo in perspective. It made nonsense of the endless newspaper grumbles about rules and regulations. In Britain you didn't see policemen armed to the teeth on every corner. Nor did you see beggars or children with legs like sticks. In the train going home I felt quite patriotic.

twenty-four

⬜⬛⬛⬛⬛⬛⬛⬛⬜

ALAN RIPPED OPEN THE AIRMAIL LETTER that was waiting
for us when we reached home. 'It's from Hugh.' He frowned at
the flimsy sheet. 'Good God! He's coming back, docking next
week … he's raving about Hollywood … just a flying visit …
he must be in the money, sailing to and fro across the
Atlantic … he says the studio's thrilled with *Be Still My Heart*,
and *House of Shadows* was a box-office sellout, now they want
more like that … new projects … ' He folded the letter up
slowly. 'Rather sickening in a way, these opportunities coming
up just when I've settled down at the BBC.'

'But you love the Third Programme, Alan! Don't you?' I
looked at him anxiously. I so wanted him to be happy, to be a
success. 'And is Hugh suggesting anything about you working
with them again? Is that why he's coming? Is it to talk to
you?'

'He's coming with Radu – he doesn't really say what it's
for.'

'And Stan's Brighton thing wasn't serious, really, was it.
You're much better off where you are,' I said brightly.

. . . .

Naomi Abrahams asked me to go to the Van Gogh exhibition at the Tate Gallery with her. Alan said she must be trying to recruit me to the Party. He was miffed not to be included. We both suspected it had to do with Colin's appeal, but in that case why didn't we just go to the Abrahams' office? An atmosphere of secrecy was creeping in, hole-and-corner meetings, as if we ourselves were involved in some kind of spy network, clandestine operations.

Most of the Tate was still closed because of bomb damage, but the exhibition was a kind of sign that things were getting back to normal. We had to queue for ages, but it was worth it. Another Mediterranean blaze of colour as we walked slowly through the crowded rooms, craning our necks to see over the shoulders of this art-starved public. It was so exciting, exhilarating. There'd been nothing like this in London for so long, they said, or ever as far as I was concerned.

'Let's find a quiet corner for a chat,' said Naomi when we'd gorged ourselves on the Van Goghs. We wandered away and found an almost empty gallery, where we sat on a bench facing a huge Scottish landscape.

'I've got something for you,' she said and took a brown envelope out of her bag. 'You could have collected it from the office, or we could have posted it, but it seemed better to hand it over direct – and then I thought why not do something nice for a change – you've had such a difficult time.'

I took hold of the envelope gingerly. 'What is it?'

'It's from Colin. We got it out at a legal visit, though I think the warder might have turned a blind eye. I mean, they check him all the time, now he's in the condemned cell.'

'Have you read it?'

She nodded. 'Go on – read it.'

I took out the sheets and unfolded them. 'It's for Alan.'

'Yes, but it's for you as well, and we thought – it'll upset

Alan and this way you can sort of break it to him in advance.'
She uncrossed and recrossed her legs.

> *Dear Alan*
>
> *A letter seems the only way to tell you how things are with
> me. There's so little time during visits and we're not alone then.
> I've dragged you into a lot of trouble and I owe it to you to explain,
> in so far as I can, of course. You may not understand, but I can
> only try.*
>
> *After the Italians surrendered there wasn't a lot to do. It
> seemed like my war was more or less over. For a short time it was
> almost like a holiday, but soon I was pretty bored. I tried to make
> contact with Italian comrades, with the partisans, but then I got to
> know another British comrade who turned up, Boris Anderson, and
> he suggested we go on up into the Balkans, where the Soviet army
> was gathering. Said it would be an opportunity to make contact.
> The Party wouldn't have approved, but we were just twiddling our
> thumbs and I thought, why not! We had some leave; we got hold of
> a jeep and off we went. Johnny was with us as well. I'd known him
> for a while. It was all pretty crazy, a wild idea. But somehow we
> made it all the way up to Romania and Bucharest. And that was
> very exciting. The Red Army had recently arrived! Imagine – the
> legendary Red Army. Boris's mother was Russian, he could speak
> the language, so soon we were hanging out with the officers at the
> Athenée Palace Hotel, where everyone gathered. Place was full of
> fascists and opportunists as well, either trying to get away or doing
> deals with the Russians. That's where I thought I saw Enescu, by
> the way. I got talking to one of their intelligence guys. He told me
> the British secret service had agents all around the Balkans before
> the war and withdrew them when the Nazis came. But now they
> were trying to re-establish bases, which was going to be pretty
> difficult in places like Romania that were about to become part of
> the Soviet sphere of influence. We got really pally and after a while*

he suggested I might see what I could find out about any British secret service types that might be hanging around. That seemed like a good idea to me. I was entirely in favour, and still am, of the expansion of communist democracy.

I thought it'd be difficult to gain the confidence of the British, I thought they'd have seen me fraternising with the Russians at the Athenée Palace. But there was a chap who'd just arrived and hadn't seen me there with them. He was a bit young and silly and not as careful as he should have been. It was easy to get him drinking and then he told me various things he should have kept quiet about.

Unfortunately, it didn't last. I used to meet with the Soviet guy in a little bar in a back street, nowhere near the Athenée, but Bucharest's a small place and my English contact caught me out. He came to see me the next day, said we needed to talk properly, so I suggested we meet somewhere out in the countryside, outside the capital. I said I couldn't be seen with him in Bucharest. I tried to give the impression I really wanted to work for him, that I was on the anti-communist side.

I'm amazed he fell for it – but he did. We went out in the jeep, Boris, Johnny and I, and he was all on his own. He was rattled when he saw there were three of us, but he threatened me just the same. He'd told his boss all about me, he said, I was going to be in a lot of trouble when I got back home. I didn't believe him, he was all on his own so far as I knew, communications were pretty bad, and even if he'd managed to contact London I'd given him a false name.

I thought it was all pretty silly. Here we were, somewhere on the edge of town in this dismal region of concrete blocks and wasteland with no one about. I thought we'd just turn around and drive back to the centre and forget all about it. Unfortunately, Johnny was very jittery and as we turned to go the English bloke made a move and Johnny misinterpreted it, thought he was going to shoot us up, so Johnny whipped out his revolver and shot the poor sod in the head.

After that I can tell you we got out of Bucharest pretty fast. Johnny's nerves were all to pieces and Boris was horrible to him, said he was a bloody fool who'd get us all into trouble. The journey back down into Italy was pretty hairy too, but we made it. Obviously, or I wouldn't be writing this.

This may explain why Joan Mainwaring has it in for me. She worked in intelligence during the war and must have guessed something. I know the British were becoming suspicious of me. And I'm the enemy, after all, so far as people like her are concerned. Before I left Bucharest I saw the Russians again. I was keen to help them. I am, after all, a socialist and a revolutionary.

What I can't forgive myself for is Johnny. It preyed on his mind. And you see he didn't know I was a Communist, not until we started to see each other again. It sounds absurd, but in some ways he wasn't all that bright, or he was just too naïve, but although he knew I was a socialist, he didn't connect it with communism. It was a big shock when I told him. I think it may even have been partly why he committed suicide. In retrospect, he felt he'd been a traitor, killing a British agent. He couldn't understand my point of view.

That's my greatest regret – Johnny's death. I'm angry that I'm to be hanged for a crime I didn't commit, but any Communist must be prepared for anything, even death, and I do feel that, however indirectly, this trial has been the result of my actions in Romania. And of those actions I'm proud.

I send you and Dinah all my love. You could not have been a better friend. You've supported me all the way. Please don't mourn for me – just carry on the struggle for socialism. That'll be my memorial.

Colin

I stared at the landscape opposite which we were sitting. Through my tears I gazed at its mountainous crags towering over a glen with dark rolling clouds above and a crofter and his dog shrunk to the size of Lilliputians by the immensity of nature.

We made our way back to the crowded foyer, and then we walked out into the cold light from the river and down the steps to the embankment.

'It's a pity Colin wasn't frank with us,' said Naomi.

'He didn't want Johnny's name brought into it.'

'But he's dead. He killed himself, didn't he?'

'Colin didn't know that for a while. We didn't tell him at first. We thought it'd just be too much for him to bear. But we should have, shouldn't we. Or perhaps it wouldn't have made much difference. Could you have used all this to discredit Joan Mainwaring's evidence? On the basis she was full of ill-will towards Colin, wanted some kind of revenge?'

'I don't know,' said Naomi. 'And I don't know if we can do anything with it now.'

We walked towards Westminster and Parliament Square.

'Does it mean the British secret service wanted him out of the way?' It seemed so melodramatic. Then an even wilder idea occurred to me. 'Or could Joan Mainwaring have murdered Titus and then got the blame shifted onto Colin?'

'I suppose she could have murdered him more easily than anyone else, but to do so in order for someone else to be blamed is just too far-fetched, isn't it? There might be someone in British intelligence who wanted revenge – or a group of Romanians wanted him out of the way, I suppose, but in either case they would have just killed Colin. No one in their right mind would rig up such a complicated scenario.'

'Colin was very suspicious of Radu Enescu,' I said bleakly. 'Perhaps there was something more he never told us.' All the old suspicions of Radu crowded back. 'But he's coming over here next week. Would he risk that if he'd had anything to do with the murder?'

'Someone else has been convicted of the murder,' Naomi pointed out. 'But again, he – or other Romanian anti-communists – would simply have liquidated Colin. The idea of anyone killing Titus in order to implicate Colin simply doesn't stand up.'

She was walking more quickly, almost as if she wanted to leave me behind, but I quickened pace to keep up with her. 'We *know* more,' she said, 'but I don't think it helps much. But we'll do all we can for Colin, you do believe that, don't you.' Then, as we crossed Parliament Square: 'I hate the Cold War,' she cried. 'Why are we all supposed to be against the Soviet Union now? Of course, I know it isn't all as it should be. I mean, Julius and I don't always see eye to eye about Stalin. And it's what we can do here in Britain that's important, we shouldn't defer to the Soviet Union as much as we do. We have two MPs and a hundred thousand people voted for us at the general election. We ought to be working for them. Well – we are, but ... and then – what's happening in Czechoslovakia? What do you think about that? I don't believe Jan Masaryk threw himself out of that window. I think he was pushed. They liquidated him.'

I hardly knew who Jan Masaryk was, but his suicide had been splashed all over the headlines. Attlee had said it was a tragedy; that Masaryk was a democrat who couldn't bear to live in a totalitarian state.

'You don't think there'll be another war, do you?' I said. 'My father's all for bombing the Russians before they get a nuclear bomb of their own. He quotes some book someone's written saying something like that. Get rid of Russia before they get rid of us.'

It was a grim thought. The permafrost of the Cold War had penetrated to the heart of life. The deadly cold was still in the wind from Siberia, but now it was the wind of war. The ice had got into our hearts, our souls were eaten up with it as we shivered under the sallow sky. It was always coldest winter, a political ice age.

twenty-five

WE WERE TO MEET HUGH AND RADU FOR DINNER. The table was booked for seven-thirty. It was not worth going home to Notting Hill, so I stayed late at the gallery. Noel had gone to Suffolk to see the Mavor family about the paintings: 'Just to make sure – I don't trust that old Mainwaring woman. I have to be sure it's all legal.' Glamorous Kay always left on the dot of five.

Alone, I sat at Kay's desk and stared at my reflection in the plate-glass front window. It was an odd sensation to be seated in this glass box, seeing only my reflected self, yet visible to any passer-by, as much on view as the two paintings on the white walls. Not that anyone passed down the side street. Daylight was fading – *l'heure bleue*, the twilight hour. It was very quiet, almost eerily so. I could hear the sound of traffic from Piccadilly, but it was a distant murmur, more like the sea sighing on Brighton beach than a busy roar.

I had nothing to do downstairs so I went up to my little office and busied myself with some filing. There was also a call to make – an appointment with an artist – but he was out, or didn't answer his phone.

The peal of the bell was so unexpected I almost tripped as

I scurried down the narrow flight of stairs. The door must not have been locked, for Radu stood in the middle of the room. He held a large bouquet.

'Dinah!' His smile assaulted me. He held out the flowers. 'For you – a beautiful woman must have flowers. So wonderful to see you.'

He looked very rich. The soft sheen of his camelhair coat spoke of that utopia beyond the ocean: America, the land of plenty. His air of wealth made the smart little gallery look almost tawdry.

I gazed at the blooms: wonderful, scented out-of-season lilac, tulips, yellow roses. I brought them to my face and drank in the scent.

'Lovelier than ever, Dinah.' He took a step towards me.

I moved away from him towards the stairs, but I knew I could end up backed into a corner. I laughed. It was intended as a disavowal of his compliment, but it sounded simply nervous. 'Radu! Why are you here?' It sounded stupid.

'How did I know *you* were *here*?' He moved still closer, looked me up and down, stripping me naked of the red suit I couldn't help being so glad I was wearing. And, as unwelcome as it was powerful, the old sensation surged up. My entrails melted. I was quite accustomed to men pouncing, to their clumsy and sometimes crude attentions. I could cope with all that. This was different: a man I distrusted, but to whom I was madly attracted.

I stood poised for his embrace, but instead he moved away. 'May I – ?' He gestured to the sofa and then sat down without waiting for my permission.

Now I felt humiliated. I'd betrayed myself. He *knew*.

'We are meeting with Hugh and your husband, *n'est-ce pas?*' he said, as though nothing had happened. (And nothing *had* happened.) 'I suggest to collect you. Sit down,' and he patted the sofa beside him. 'There is so much we have to talk about. So many things have happened. Gwendolen and Stan are married! You know, I long to hear about that.'

I couldn't bear it, I couldn't bear to stay alone with him in the empty gallery, wedged as it was between the bomb-damaged building on one side and the bomb crater on the other. 'Why don't we go for a drink,' I cried brightly. 'There's a nice little pub near here.'

I collected my coat and we stepped outside. He stopped by the bombed-out shell next door. 'Look – that is beautiful, I think.'

Between two steep houses there was a gaping cavity where a bomb had fallen and now the stagnant black pool of an emergency water tank filled the space. Radu peered down at it; then his gaze moved upwards to the walls where a patchwork of papers, paint and panelling survived as ghosts of the rooms that had been destroyed. There was even part of a staircase still attached to the walls and you could see the gallery fire escape hanging jaggedly in mid-air where it had been broken and twisted.

'Can you imagine,' he murmured, 'that would make a wonderful scene for a film ... if only my next film could be here.'

He held my arm rather too tightly as we walked along Jermyn Street. I was weak at the knees. I tottered along. But I was safe now. Yet I wanted to cry.

We reached the pub. It had only just opened and only a couple of lonely drinkers sat in odd corners. Radu didn't ask me what I wanted, but fetched me a sherry. 'This was always your favourite drink, I believe.'

I was touched he remembered, and now we were in the safety of the pub I did want to hear his news. I wanted to know why he'd come back. He swirled his whisky around in its glass, watching it as he did so.

'So Gwendolen is married to Stan.' He drank and stared moodily at the floor. 'I turn my back for five minutes – ' He turned to me with his false, flashing smile. 'But that is the way with you women. The treacherous sex.'

'For goodness' sake, Radu, she thought you'd gone for good.' I almost mentioned the suicide attempt, but thought better of it.

'I am glad for her, it is for the best. For me it is not so good; for my work. But to be truthful,' (Are you ever? I thought) 'perhaps it is true, that I wanted to get away. Gwendolen, you know, she is ... such a strange woman. You, Dinah, you are open, you are lovely, you are generous, you love men, I know that, but she ...' He shook his head. 'She is like a clenched fist.' He clenched his own hand into a tight ball, but not before I'd noticed the manicured nails. Effeminate – but *he* wasn't. 'Tight like this. I sometimes think she has a heart of stone. But what am I to do, Dinah?' He moved closer to me, always that little bit too close. 'I have the perfect film for her. *House of Shadows* has done so well in America, *Be Still My Heart* will be a huge success too. First they say they do not want Gwendolen, they have to have a big star, Rita Hayworth, perhaps, but now they see my films are such success – I can do *anything*. I can have my own star. I have the studio in the palm of my hand. For now. I have to seize the moment. Americans are impatient, they always want the newest thing. So tell me, Dinah, how can I persuade her? Or perhaps I should say, how can I persuade *him*? The good Stanley. He won't let her out of his sight, I think.'

Surely Radu was wrong there, for if Gwendolen wanted to go to Hollywood, Stanley would be powerless. His plan for Brighton studios would be a candle in the sun compared to Hollywood. 'He can't leave his business interests for any length of time, but if she wanted to go, how could he stop her? He'd do anything for her.'

Radu smiled. 'Is that so? Poor Stanley. So – I have to try to think of some way,' he said softly. 'Why did she have to marry? In Hollywood they are very virtuous, very moral. A peculiar morality. You can divorce, you can divorce and be married ten times, but a married woman, or an unmarried woman living openly with a man – that will never do. Marriage is the thing. Even a homosexual must be married.' He drank off his whisky, sprang up and waved a large, white five pound note across the bar. A fiver was such a grand gesture. And how opulent he looked in the shabby little lounge. One or two drinkers had trickled in by now and they looked so seedy by comparison; grey and stringy with austerity, while he was rosy with steaks and Californian sunshine.

Two sherries! I'd better be careful; it would never do to get tipsy, I didn't trust myself not to say or do something foolish if it went to my head. Radu took out a cardboard box of oval Turkish cigarettes. Intrigued, I took one. We both lit up. I liked the taste. 'So if I am to have her in my film,' he continued, 'it is better if Stanley comes too. But then perhaps they will think we are *ménage à trois* and that will not do either.' He smiled. 'The only way would be for her to divorce Stan and marry me. And after all,' he murmured, 'I do not want to marry her. Even to live with her again, no, never. Is it terrible I say this? But Gwendolen, she is an ice queen, you know.' He shrugged. Now he seemed weary. 'Who knows? But what am I to do? I feel I need her for my movie, and she has brought me good fortune, but still I think she is bad luck. She is – well, you know my country is the land of vampires, Transylvania. I think Gwendolen is somehow a vampire in a way.' He shrugged. 'Life is impossible sometimes.'

What could I say? There was a little silence, but I felt quite comfortable with him now. 'And what of Pauline?' he said abruptly. 'How has she taken to this marriage?'

'Pauline?' I hadn't thought about her for weeks – months. Only now did I recall that we hadn't seen her at Embassy Court. 'We went to see them – they live in Brighton now, you know. Pauline wasn't there – she must have been out.'

He was gazing at me again, and in order to move on to safer ground, out of the erotic zone, and also because I'd known ever since he'd materialised in the gallery that I'd have to ask him, I said: 'Did you ever see Colin in Bucharest?'

'Colin?' I'd startled him. 'It is terrible what has happened to him.'

'He was in Bucharest briefly at the end of the war.'

'Is that so? There were a few Englishmen there before I left, there were several in fact. We believed them to be British intelligence. I seem to remember one of them disappeared. Rumours were flying around. It was the Russians, it was some remnant of the Iron Guard, it was – who knew who it was. It was a very volatile time.'

'I wish we'd talked to you about this earlier.' But we'd been too distrustful of Radu to question him. Anyway, until I'd read Colin's letter, we'd had no questions to ask.

The letter had upset Alan. It had upset him so much.

Radu placed his hand over mine. 'I think this is difficult time for you.'

I nodded, close to tears.

'I think Colin thought – thinks I am some kind of swastika-brandishing Nazi. But believe me, Dinah, this was never true. It is true I went to Berlin, that I was still there after Hitler came to power, but it quickly became too difficult. Very soon I left. They were only making kitsch – saccharine romance, stupid comedies.'

That was what Colin thought *House of Shadows* was, of course.

Neither of us said anything for a while. Finally he looked at his watch: 'I think it's time we go to the restaurant.'

It was a peculiar evening. Hugh dazzled us with descriptions of Hollywood, of eternal sunshine, azure swimming pools, tufted palm trees like elephants' tails, giant cocktails and outsize sandwiches; but Radu protested. 'LA is not a city, it is just a vast, empty suburb with a million eerie winding roads with no pavements! No cafés – no street life – no *streets*! And their peculiar social customs! They are unbelievably provincial. They eat at five in the evening – four sometimes – and get to the office at eight in the morning. And then everything is new and nothing is original.'

'That's hardly the way to encourage Alan and Dinah!' joked Hugh. He was looking particularly pale and elegant. His cigarette at an angle, his pin-stripe suit immaculate (no more old sweaters and tweed jackets), he looked very much the Englishman in Beverly Hills, Michael Wilding, only with straight hair. Yet he seemed a little shifty and uncomfortable.

They were trying to persuade Alan to join them, but I wasn't sure if it was serious. They held their cards close to the chest, hinting and bluffing. Hugh seemed almost to be teasing, tantalising Alan. Alan fidgeted and frowned. He hated to be played with, yet I could see the lure of Hollywood had grabbed him.

The thought of suddenly moving to *California* – it was a dream, it was unimaginable, I couldn't believe in it for a second. And yet … wouldn't it be rather heavenly?

But Alan said brusquely: 'It's impossible for me to make any commitments until Colin's appeal has gone through. I'm the only friend he's got.' He looked darkly at Hugh – Hugh, who'd abandoned Colin without a second thought.

A nerve flickered beneath Hugh's left eye and his glance shifted about all over the room, anywhere away from Alan. 'At least he got leave to appeal. That's good news, isn't it.'

'The lawyers aren't too hopeful it'll succeed.'

'God! But surely they aren't going to hang an innocent man.'

'I wish I shared your optimism.'

Radu said: 'What would happen if this appeal succeeds? They will look for someone else, I think, another suspect.'

Alan frowned. In the uneasy silence I wondered why Radu had said that. He'd left the country as soon as he could, as soon as he'd finished the film. Why should he be bothered about another suspect?

Alan said: 'I don't really care as long as Colin gets off.'

But he did care. We were desperate, after all, for precisely that: for an explanation that would free Colin.

And maybe we almost had it. But tantalisingly, it wasn't quite within our grasp.

twenty-six

□■■■■■□■□

STAR SLAIN IN FRENZIED ATTACK

Actress Gwendolen Grey, star of box office hit, *House of Shadows*, was found battered to death yesterday in her Brighton flat. The actress retired from the screen at the end of last year to marry businessman Stanley Colman, who is helping the police with their enquiries.

. . . .

I was eating a sandwich lunch in the office and had bought a copy of *The Times* to read while I ate. The paper's front page, filled with the small print of columns announcing births, deaths and marriages (but not deaths like *this*) hadn't prepared me for the shock inside. The words didn't sink in. I reread them.

Gwendolen was – *dead*. And not just dead: murdered.

I thought of Radu in the gallery downstairs; how he'd wanted and hadn't wanted Gwendolen. Then I thought of Stan helping police with their enquiries – that meant they thought *he'd* done it. I put my head in my hands, simply unable to grasp it, to react at all.

'What on earth's the matter, Dinah?' Noel stood in the

doorway.

I showed him the paper, folded at the page. 'Good heavens. How frightful.' He sat down rather suddenly. 'How *extraordinary*.'

I rang Stan's office, but there was no answer, not that I'd expected there would be. I rang Alan, but couldn't reach him either. When I got home I listened to every news bulletin, but because of the Czech situation Gwendolen's death was less of a major item than it would normally have been. When I heard Alan's footsteps on the stairs I rushed to open the front door. 'Something terrible – ' I was incoherent. 'Have you heard about Gwendolen?' He stopped on the landing. 'Gwendolen?'

'Look!' I'd bought the *Evening Star* on the way home and thrust it towards him. Their coverage was lurid, compared with *The Times*. 'They've arrested Stan! And look what they say about Titus. See? "Macabre link to slain artist" – they've reproduced that portrait of her again.'

Alan took the paper and let the satchel he used as a briefcase drop to the floor. He sat down at the kitchen table. 'Any chance of a cup of tea?'

I'd already made a pot. He drew his cup towards him. 'They have to interview the husband, don't they. I don't suppose they think he did it.'

I was slightly hysterical. 'Suppose it's the same person.'

'As killed Titus? God! But ... we must get on to Abrahams. First thing in the morning.' As usual, he was mad with impatience, boiling with suppressed rage because he couldn't speak to the lawyer right away. I made supper. It was our treat for the week: our meat ration, consisting of two little chops, but it was wasted. We could have been eating cardboard.

'How was she murdered?'

'It doesn't say.'

'Radu comes back and the next minute – '

'But *why*, Alan? Why should he kill her? Why?'

. . . .

'They won't let me into the flat.' Stan's voice came hoarse down the line. 'They questioned me for hours. And I had – ' His voice broke. After a moment he continued: 'I had to identify her. It was – ' He choked again. 'She was suffocated, Dinah, so she didn't look so bad – but that made it worse almost, as if she weren't really dead. It was horrible. Horrible. They made me do it. I think they hoped I'd break down, confess or something.' He was almost sobbing down the phone.

'You say she was suffocated? Like Titus!'

'Well ... yes ... I hadn't thought ...'

'Where are you now, Stan?'

'At the office. They've released me on bail. Can you get round here? I need to talk to someone.'

'I've got masses of work. I don't think I can get away before five.'

Noel was standing in the doorway. 'Is that her husband? He's been released then? Are you going to see him? Is that wise? He must be a suspect. Will you be safe?'

I laughed. 'Stan wouldn't hurt a fly – and he adored Gwendolen. It couldn't possibly be him.'

'Adored her!' Noel advanced into the room. 'You can't possibly know that. Anyway, adoration usually leads to disaster in my experience. Wasn't there some suggestion she was going to leave him? Go back to Hollywood with the film director?'

I was truly surprised. 'I don't think so – I've heard nothing about that. That's not true.' But perhaps it was. Still: 'I just don't believe it's Stan.'

'If you think you're safe – if you think it's safe to see him, you might as well go now. That stuff can wait till tomorrow.'

'Thanks.' As I pulled on my coat, I said: 'Have you done anything more about trying to get the Mainwaring woman round to the gallery? You haven't forgotten. We were going to get her to say what she said to you about – '

'Yes, yes,' he interrupted. 'I haven't forgotten. I'm going to offer her a deal on Mavor's own stuff.'

'You said she didn't seem to care tuppence, she was ready to throw the whole lot out.'

'I've never met anyone yet who refused money for something they'd thought was worthless. But seriously, are you really going round to comfort the grieving widower? Are you absolutely sure it's safe?' But his eyes gleamed with curiosity. 'Be interesting anyway.'

By the time I got round to Stan's office, he'd calmed down, but he looked pasty and deflated, not the Stan I knew.

'When they let me into the flat – God knows when that'll be – I want you to come down with me, Dinah.'

'What's happened to Pauline?'

He looked bewildered for a moment, as if he'd never heard of Pauline. After a moment he said blankly, 'Oh – didn't you know? I told her to go after we moved down there. I mean, I gave her a month, she didn't have to disappear pronto, and in fact I found her a nice little billet as well, but – I was fed up with her, she gave me the creeps.' He looked down rather sheepishly.

'I just thought she was out that day we came down.'

He shook his head. 'She'd gone.'

'Did Gwen mind you doing that?'

Stan moved around the office, then leaned against a filing cabinet. 'D'you know, I haven't a clue. She didn't seem too bothered, one way or the other, to be honest. I didn't think I'd have the bottle. I *thought* she'd kick up, but then I got so sick of Pauline's miserable long face all the time, she really gave me the pip, I thought to hell with it, I'm going to put my foot down. I'm her husband, ain't I? And Gwendolen – you know that shrug of hers, and the way she just looks at you as though you weren't there. All she said was: "Aren't you being rather unreasonable?" Maybe she'd have sabotaged it later, sneaked her gradually back in again, but like I say, she didn't seem bothered.'

'How did Pauline take it? Where is she now?'

'That woman's a cold fish if ever there was one. She exploited Gwen, I reckon, there was no love lost there. I made her a reasonable offer – she didn't kick up a fuss. Said she wanted to stay in Brighton, didn't care for London anyway. So I found her a little flat in Hove and that was that.'

'Didn't Gwendolen feel lonely on her own?'

'I was there most nights. That's one reason the police think I might have had something to do with it. They say it happened on Monday and that was the one night last week I stayed in town. I *did* stay in town. Had a business meeting in the late afternoon and another engagement in the evening.'

'So you've got an alibi.'

In spite of his misery a crafty half-smile spread across Stan's face. 'Thing is, this geezer – can't drop him in it. You see – you know that country house I bought – well, the fact is, he's trying to find a way of getting round some government regulations, it's such a blooming nightmare getting raw materials, and the repairs it needs, I want – wanted – to get it sorted out quick ... for her, but now – ' His voice broke again. He blew his nose. 'I can't explain that to the coppers, they'll be sticking their nose in all my business affairs as it is if I'm not careful.'

'What about the evening, then? If you were in London you could hardly get down to Brighton and back up here in time, could you.'

He shook his head. '*That's* awkward too. Fact is, I was wining and dining a junior minister. Took him to Kettners. Waiter might remember me, I s'pose. But then his being there might come up, the minister I mean. And that could drop him in it too. The only good thing is the police admitted the porter said I left in the morning – I spoke to him, said I was going to London and wouldn't be back that night. Of course, they're saying I could have done that deliberately, to throw everyone off the scent, but the porter said neither he nor the night porter saw me come back and there was a parcel left for me which I didn't collect. They've got nothing on me, they've released me on police bail at the moment, but – ' He shrugged miserably. 'The papers have brought up the whole Titus thing again, haven't they. Do *you* think there's any connection? They're certainly trying to make one. Will that help Colin at all?'

'We don't know. But did you know Radu's come back?'

At first Stan looked stunned. Then a slow, cold anger seemed to build and hardened his face to a granite caricature. 'She never said.' The words were whispered, but hissed with venom. 'It was Radu, wasn't it. Has to be. He's back – she doesn't want to go with him, he – I'll *kill* him for all he's done to her.'

'He didn't go down there – well, I don't know if he did – she probably didn't know herself.' I was babbling, panicking at what I'd implied, afraid I'd said too much – and yet it was all so plausible: Radu a murderer.

'The police ought to know this,' he said. He squared his shoulders. 'I didn't kill her, Dinah, you know that, don't you. You don't for a moment think I – I mean I *loved* her. And I can't believe – even now ... and what makes it worse is I wasn't there. If I'd stayed down in Brighton ... She wanted me to move there altogether, you know. And I could have done. I could have done my business from there – *and* kept a toehold in London. I thought about it, I was thinking of having a suite at the Dorchester. And now it's too late.'

We were talking through the shrouded dusk of the room. I got up and turned on the light. Stan blinked in the sudden glare. 'It's getting late,' he said, 'what's the time? I – ' and then he must have suddenly remembered he didn't have to get back to Brighton, *couldn't* go back to Brighton, and slumped back in his chair. He worried me; he'd no one to look after him.

'You need to eat,' I said. 'Why don't you come back to the flat and I'll make something.'

He protested at first, but seemed too tired to argue for long. So I got a taxi ride home, which was nice. I made a dried egg omelette, pretty leathery, but he didn't seem to notice and for once there was a whole loaf of bread. As we drank coffee (the coffee Stan had always been able to get for us) his mood changed. 'It's rich, isn't it. That tinpot little policeman trying to pin it on me. Poor comment on the state of marriage, the way they always go for the victim's husband – or wife, as the case may be. Like *Brighton Rock*. You seen it yet? Doesn't do Brighton justice – it's a travesty, all gangsters and trollops. The boy in that, he hates his wife like poison, inveigles her into a suicide pact – ' He broke off, a look almost of horror on his face. 'Jesus, Dinah, I saw that film with her. Just last week. Oh God.' He put his head in his hands, almost knocking over his cup. After a bit he pulled himself together. 'They've sealed the flat,' he said, 'but that can't last forever. And the moment they let me back – it would help if you came down with me. Can't face it on my own.'

· · · · · · · · ·

Our arrival at Embassy Court was pretty grim. The flat had been unsealed, and there were few signs of the police search, but I think that made it even worse for Stan. He just stood and looked as if it wasn't his any more.

The doorbell rang. Stan didn't move from where he was staring out of the window at the sea, so I went to see who it was.

She towered over me, parcelled up in purple tweed and a multicoloured crochet shawl. Turquoise, amber, jet and coral beads were festooned over her bosom and amethysts dangled from her earlobes. Her face was like uncooked pastry, its pallor garishly emphasised with a jammy slash of lipstick.

'Beatrice Lomas. Forgive my intrusion. The porter told me Mr Colman has returned.' Her eyes gazed soulfully into mine. 'I *found her*, you know.'

'He's rather upset. We've only just got here.'

But Stanley had followed me into the hall. 'It's all right. Come in, Mrs Lomas.'

She took both his hands in hers: 'Mr Colman – my deepest sympathy.' He still just stood there. She released him and settled herself on the Knole sofa and looked round. 'They didn't make too much mess then, the police.'

Stanley looked grim. He said: 'Could you rustle up some coffee, Dinah?'

I assumed he felt he had to hear the gruesome details, but when I returned, they were sitting there in glum silence. 'There isn't any milk.' I set the coffee tray on the nest of tables. Beatrice Lomas rose to her feet. 'I have some. I'll fetch it – won't take a moment.'

I looked at Stan. 'Are you all right? What did she say?'

'A man called.'

The neighbour glided back into the room holding a dainty jug. She placed it on the table and returned to the sofa, where she sat with her knees slightly apart.

'This man who called – ' Stan could hardly get the words out. He'd been more like his usual self in the train, but the reality of the flat had knocked the stuffing out of him.

'Miss Grey's – I'm sorry, Mrs Colman, but I always thought of her in that film role, you know – her Romanian friend perhaps?'

Stanley flinched. 'He came here?'

Beatrice Lomas sipped her coffee. Her hands flashed with huge rings, topaz, amethyst and an emerald. 'It was some days before … she passed away. After her visitor had gone, Mrs Colman – Gwendolen – asked me to give her a reading – the cards, you know,' she added, seeing Stan's puzzlement. 'I believe she will have told you I'm a clairvoyant. She said she was thinking of going back to acting. I read the tarot for her. She didn't like what she saw.'

'Why? What did they say?' I cried. Alan would have scoffed at the very idea of fortune telling, and of course I didn't believe in it either, but it would be spine-chillingly horrible if this ridiculous woman had foreseen poor Gwendolen's death.

'That isn't how the tarot works,' she said repressively. 'Dark strangers – a journey – that's a very ignorant idea of what to expect. I'm not some vulgar Gypsy Petulengro on the pier, you know. But it was a disturbing spread.' Her accent was more Bromley than Romany. 'After that I didn't see her again until … well … '

Stan hung his head. He seemed more and more dejected. 'I know she missed that life,' he muttered. 'At first she said she wanted to get away from it all, but then … she sort of languished without it.' He sighed, a sigh so deep it was more of a shudder. 'I was hoping to start something here. Brighton's full of stars – I thought we'd meet a few important people in the industry – I thought if I got the Brighton studios going again, it'd all be hunky-dory. And now – without Gwendolen ... what am I going to do?' He buried his head in his hands.

'I know you're devastated, Mr Colman. But she wasn't destined to act again. Let's step downstairs to my flat. The aura here, the atmosphere – it's upsetting. Things will be clearer in a neutral environment. We'll have a reading. You'll find it helpful.'

Stan followed her like a lamb. They seemed to have forgotten about me. My indignation didn't last long, though, because this – I suddenly saw it, with a stomach lurch of nervous excitement – was an extraordinary opportunity. I had the run of the flat. Before all this happened I'd never have dreamt of snooping about and prying into other people's possessions. Now I had no scruples. I looked round the room. The framed poster on the wall had 'Gwendolen Grey' and *House of Shadows* drifting in spectral smoke across a murky night sky. In the foreground a lake glimmered darkly, and a wraith-like woman fled towards a wood; a sliver of moon hung high up and cast its ghostly light on the house in the distance.

There was a modern oak bureau in the space by the window. I pulled down the flap, excited and apprehensive. I riffled through the pigeonholes, but they contained nothing but unused envelopes and a ball of string. I had no idea what I was looking for. In any case, Stanley, or possibly the murderer, would have removed anything suspicious. And of course the police must have searched the place too. Anyway, what was there that *could* be suspicious? But this was too good a chance to miss, I had to carry on. There just might be something. A letter from Radu, perhaps, something incriminating. But there was nothing of interest in the desk drawers either, apart from a foolscap envelope containing newspaper cuttings about

Titus Mavor's death and Colin's trial; it wasn't surprising Gwendolen should have kept them. Whatever Gwendolen's relationship to Titus, she must have been interested – even she, who seemed so little interested in anything. But it reminded me of the way the newspapers had linked the two murders. Suffocation was the link; and the fact that the two victims had once been lovers.

Suffocation; to suffocate someone you had to be strong, Alan said. It wasn't as easy as it sounded. Unless you drugged them first – and that wasn't necessarily easy either. Titus had been drugged, but Bannister had never explained how Colin had managed to dose him with chloroform.

I moved on to the bookshelf. Gwendolen hadn't had many books. I don't think she was ever much of a reader. Some copies of *Reader's Digest* and some romances – Ethel M Dell and Baroness Orczy's *The Scarlet Pimpernel*. And an old notebook with a marbled card cover, rubbed away at the edges. I opened it and began to read the childish copperplate handwriting.

May 7, 1940
I shall write about things as they happen. But first he said I should write about childhood. Writers always write about childhood, he said. But that was so long ago.

My first memory. A seashell curled on the sand, indecent flesh-coloured, hard and shiny, like my private place, only spiky. He liked it when I said that. You're a true surrealist, he said.

We lived up and down the south coast, moving from furnished rooms to furnished rooms, all different, all the same. The landladies made Mamma cry. We always lived in the back streets, never had a view of the sea. We walked to the beach, down hilly streets, along cliffs, or followed the curve of a promenade as it made a long tongue round the bay. A hurdy-gurdy played. Donkeys plodded along the sands.

There were children playing on the beach, but I was always on my own.

Mamma wore pink and red voile, a pattern of flowers, and her red Japanese parasol, under cloudy skies. 'If we could only go back to the Riviera. Shan't we one day, Freddy?' But Papa in his armchair screened himself behind a copy of the *Racing Times* and didn't reply.

We moved again. 'Furnished rooms! Can we never have a place of our own?' 'Don't be so bloody middle class, Matilda. Who wants to be tied down? Where's your spirit of adventure?'

Papa had fought in the war. He coughed all the time. 'Wished I'd copped it in the trenches instead of dying by inches with this bloody gassed lung.' 'Oh, don't say that, Freddy!'

It frightened me too.

At first I liked Gordon. 'You're a free spirit, ain't you, Gwenny. Come and sit on Gordon's knee.'

I didn't want to do what Gordon wanted, but he made me in the end and when Mamma found out, she blamed me. 'It wasn't his fault, you led him on, you wretched child, you *disgusting* little trollop – '

I met Gordon on the turn of the stairs. He muttered something and fumbled some notes into my hand. I ran away. I took the train. The King had just died.

My room in Chelsea had no furniture, but it had yellow walls, I was living in a daffodil. I rolled up in an eiderdown the girl in the next room gave me and slept on the floor. It was more important to have some clothes. In my red dress with a skirt like a peasant and a black velvet choker I walked about in the King's Road and hoped I'd meet some artists. Quite soon I did, they wanted to paint me.

I was walking on air, living on air. Literally. Hardly anything to eat, but I had an air about me, someone said … putting on airs.

One evening I was swept up with a crowd and into a party in a seedy part of Camden Town. It seemed strange to me that there should be a town in the middle of London, which itself was a town, London Town.

He was there – in his blue overalls and white shirt and a red and white spotted scarf round his neck. And the red curls, like an angel, around his fresh, rosy, cherub's face. He was drunk, he was shouting a poem through cupped hands across the roar of the party until he saw me and made a path of silence between us like the parting of the Red Sea. We walked towards each other along the corridor of silence and the party ebbed away on either side. 'You're the most beautiful girl I've ever seen. Where have you come from? I have to paint you.'

When he saw my body and the ugly puckered scar, he said how beautiful it was, he liked the imperfection. What is flawless is never truly beautiful, he said.

He helped organise the Surrealist exhibition in London. Famous French artists and writers came specially. His own paintings would also be shown. The English Surrealists were small minnows beside the continental whales; it was their big moment.

The most famous of the foreigners gave a talk: Salvador Dalí. He had a curling moustache and very black eyes. He dressed in a deep sea diver's suit to give his lecture. He stomped onto the platform, but then something happened. He began to struggle with the helmet. Something was wrong. Titus and one of the Frenchmen rushed forward and wrenched off the helmet. There was no air inside and he'd nearly suffocated.

Dalí said he had to paint me. Titus was jealous – of Dalí, not of me. He wanted Dalí to be interested in him, in his painting, his painting of me if he wanted, but not in me myself. Dalí's wife didn't like it either.

He painted me anyway. The painting was very strange.

And then things went wrong. But I can't write about that.

I don't know why I thought I should write a diary. Nothing happens to me any more.

Something *has* happened now. I found her! She says I'm depressed, she's going to take me out of myself, she said. She said I must pull myself together. It's time I got a job. Firm but kind, she said. She'll look after me now.

I should never have guessed Gwendolen could write so poetically. Well, it was a bit fey. Such crushed pathos – was that the shrinking creature sheltering within the brittle shell of the Gwendolen I'd known?

I left the drawing room and opened the doors off the hall until I found the main bedroom. I pushed open the door, but this *did* seem an invasion of privacy, for after all it had been Stanley's bedroom too.

The room reminded me of Ormiston Court. The brocade curtains were pulled back, letting the cruel light in off the sea to expose the gilt and tapestry chairs, the pink satin counterpane, the kidney-shaped dressing table with triple looking glass and the built-in wardrobe.

I stood by the dressing table and picked up a heavy silver hand mirror. I touched the matching hairbrush with its elaborate raised pattern. There was a dusty fluff of black hairs caught in the bristles: Gwendolen's. I put it down hurriedly, with a shiver. There were trinket boxes and a cut-glass scent bottle with a round, crochet-covered pump, looking more like a slightly obscene medical accessory than an aid to beauty.

I looked in all the drawers, but I didn't find anything except clothes and make-up. It was ridiculous, when I thought about it, to expect to find anything important, and even if I did, I might not recognise it.

I pushed open the sliding wardrobe door for no other reason, really, than to inspect Gwendolen's wonderful clothes. The rail was stuffed with garments, crammed in so tightly I had difficulty pulling them apart. Her leopardskin coat was crushed against a blue-grey evening dress. I remembered that dress; it was the one Gwendolen had shown me. Next to it red taffeta was bursting to free itself from the packed rows of black astrakhan and pale mink, flowery dresses, garnet red tweed, bottle green wool. I inspected the textures and feel of the silks, the alpaca, the broadcloth and cashmere, and looked at the labels. A stiff black coat was by Dior. There was a lovely blue tweed suit by Hardy Amies, a *feuille morte* silk Jacques Fath cocktail dress, and the black-and-white cotton she'd worn on our day into the country. This was far more intimate, somehow, than letters would have been. The dresses were dead things, the husk, the shed skin of Gwendolen. Their presence, her absence, brought home to me she was really dead.

And how clothes stored memories! I stroked the blue-grey gown, pulled it forward, remembering Gwendolen's discomfort when Dr Carstairs had recognised her at the dance. I could see her now, in my memory, sliding away from him, trying to avoid recognition.

The blue-grey taffeta made a slight creaking sound. I pulled it right out and held it against myself, as I'd done in Gwendolen's other bedroom. It felt different now. Something had happened to the lining. It stuck right out. It must have come loose. I unzipped the bodice. I'd read about the canvas and buckram lining that shaped the New Look dresses –

there'd been a disapproving article in *Picture Post*, suggesting that the new fashions were very *old*-fashioned – as if a dress could drive women back to the home.

But this – as the inner surface of the bodice was revealed I could see there really was something wrong. There was something inside the lining. I pulled at the intricate stitching. There was a crackling sound.

'What the hell are you doing?'

Stanley stood in the doorway, a look of horror on his face. 'Stop it!' He stepped forward as though to prevent me physically.

'There's something inside it, Stan – that crackling, it isn't the lining ... '

'You'll hurt it,' he said piteously, as though it were Gwendolen herself I was tearing apart.

'Please – wait a minute, Stan. I'm doing my best. Let me just get it out.'

This made him angrier. 'Stop it! Stop it, Dinah!' he cried. He grabbed hold of my arm, but I wrestled away. He gave up and collapsed onto the bed, his head in his hands.

I had an intuition of what it might be as I struggled with the inside of the dress at the waist, pulling apart the outer skirt and inner layers of material. I tugged and tugged, but couldn't get at whatever it was. Then I remembered the nail scissors in the bedside table. I sat on the bed and, sawing into the stitching, I managed to separate the inner padding of the skirt and create a slit from which I slowly pulled out a roll of some other, stiff stuff. With a deep intake of breath I unrolled the canvas.

'Stan! Look!'

It was a painting.

Objects, some obscene, some unpleasantly indeterminate, littered the sand of a desert that receded to a distant point in eerie sunlight. The foreground morphed into a shadowed interior, divorced from the light of the vacant desert, where a girl with black hair stared at her reflection in an oval floor-length mirror on a stand. At her feet lay a hard, pink shell, its vulva-like interior facing outwards, exposed. The mirror seemed to float just above the viscous mauve ground, reflecting the girl's narrow, naked body, the mossy black pubic hair and nipples like mulberries; her buttocks, the cleft accentuated, glimmered in the slimily painted room. The girl in the painting was Gwendolen.

'It's Gwenny.' Stan's voice was stricken. 'Oh, my God.' I thought he was going to burst into tears.

'It's the Dalí!' I stared at the painting. The canvas had cracked a bit where it had been badly rolled. 'Titus's Dalí.' I couldn't believe it. 'We must show it to Noel Valentine,' I said. 'He'll authenticate it. He was certain that Titus Mavor had a Dalí painting. Titus must have given it to Gwendolen. It is a painting of her, after all.'

'But why did she hide it like that?' muttered Stanley. 'Ruined that beautiful dress. I'll tell you something. I wanted her to wear it, New Year's Eve. There was a dance at the Aquarium Ballroom. She looked better than Rita Hayworth in that dress, more of a star than any of them. She wouldn't have it. I couldn't understand why, thought it must be female cussedness, but it must have been ... we had a row over it. In the end she wore the red and she looked stunning in that too, out of this world. And now ...'

And now, I thought, she really was out of this world. I was assailed by a terrible sadness for a moment, although I'd never felt close to her. But now she was dead: like Titus. Titus and Gwen: was there a connection? What was it? 'Stan – why did you give Titus that money? The hundred and fifty pounds? Was it something to do with Gwendolen?'

He looked at me blankly. 'What? Oh ... that. Well, yes, it was, as a matter of fact. But what made you think of that now?'

'I don't know.'

'Mavor was a swine, you know. He was blackmailing her on account of the child. She was desperate to keep that from Enescu. Couldn't afford for it to come out once she was a film star.'

'There must have been quite a few people who knew, though; the Mavor family, people around Soho.'

'It was only Mavor who was threatening to leak it to the press. And to Enescu.'

Perhaps Radu found out, I thought, and made her pay for it.

twenty-seven

❏❏■❏■❏■❏❏

NOEL PLACED THE CANVAS ON HIS DESK. The four corners were held down by a paperweight, the inkstand and two books.

'Hasn't done it any good being rolled up like that. Damaged, I'm afraid. Still … ' He was too blasé to express his excitement in words, but his enthusiasm electrified the room. 'Will Colman want to part with it?' He took a turn up and down the little office. 'Why did she hide it? If Mavor gave it to her …'

'Perhaps she'd always had it,' I said, 'since before the war, since the time she was his mistress. Perhaps Titus was just boasting when he said he had a Dalí.'

'Yes, but then why hide it?'

'Perhaps Radu was jealous.' As soon as I said it, I knew that was absurd – Radu so clearly hadn't been jealous. On the contrary, he'd wanted to work with Titus.

'She was afraid he'd sell it, to get money for the film?'

'Joan Mainwaring's agreed to come here to talk about Mavor's own work. She might shed some light on it, d'you think? She'll be here any minute.'

Indeed, we heard voices downstairs and Kay came up to

say that she'd arrived.

'Are we going to try to record what she says?'

But we decided we'd confront her together. Kay would be there too. We'd all be downstairs in the gallery.

Joan Mainwaring had smartened up for the occasion and was dressed in a pre-New Look tweed suit and a maroon felt hat with a single feather at the side like a quill pen. She gave me a sharp look, but if my presence was a surprise, she didn't comment on it directly. Yet she must have suspected something, for she said: 'Have you really invited me here just to talk about Titus's daubs?'

Noel sat her down on the black sofa and drew up chairs for himself and me. Kay brought us coffee and then resumed her place behind the black desk.

'I've asked you here because I want to make a serious offer. I don't know if you know, but I've spoken to his immediate family, and they have no objection to my making an offer for them. There is one other thing, though. Titus used to put it about that he owned several paintings by very well-known modern artists, other Surrealists, and I wondered if you knew anything about them. There wasn't any sign of them when you generously allowed me to look round the other day ... '

'He'd sold them, of course.'

Neither of us had expected such a direct answer. The news must have knocked Noel back a bit, for there was complete silence.

'He was on his uppers, wasn't he.' A barking sound seemed to express her amusement at what must have been Noel's dismay. She lit a cigarette.

Noel recovered himself. 'Was it a private sale? None of them appeared at any auction.'

'His film director friend got rid of them for him. The *quid pro quo* was part of the proceeds would go to some trashy film he was making, the one with Titus's ex-mistress in it. At first I thought it might be because he was still a bit sweet on her. But he disabused me of that.'

'When did this happen?' My voice sounded much too loud. I was shaking.

'Oh ...' She looked at me. She still seemed to find our disarray amusing, the old cat. 'I don't really remember. The film director chap – he was Romanian, wasn't he – came round to see him. I was quite interested in him, I popped round when I saw him coming, Titus introduced us. After he'd gone Titus was quite elated, there was talk of him doing some designs for the film. Titus probably thought he was making an investment, revitalising his own career, salvaging his reputation, some tripe like that, because he was always so pickled he couldn't paint any more. The Romanian would have realised that in the end, so just as well for him Titus went to meet his maker. But the main thing presumably was the paintings. And he definitely got those, because Titus told me. Just to spite me. Think he thought I was hoping to get my hands on them. Which actually I was.' She was still smiling, but her voice was like shards being scraped off a rusting vessel. Her vocal cords must be giving out.

Radu had got what he wanted – the paintings. So he had no motive to murder Titus. I couldn't stop myself. My words tumbled out. 'Are you sticking to your story about Colin Harris? You got the day wrong, you know that, don't you.'

Her flinty stare gave no quarter. 'Your friend was working for the Russians. I don't expect you know that, but he was. And what makes you think I got the day wrong?'

Noel put a hand up to stop me telling her.

'You've got a lot to learn, my dear.' She turned back to Noel. 'So what sort of price are you going to give me for the daubs?'

'I need a drink,' said Noel after she'd left. 'There's some gin upstairs. And we can have another look at the Dalí. At least I've got that.'

We looked at the painting pinned down on his desk. I'd showed the notebook I'd found to Noel as well as Alan, and now we clearly saw the appendix scar. Dalí had even exaggerated it; it was lying along her flat belly like a detached object akin to the other enigmatic objects scattered in the foreground.

'That's funny.' I was back in her warm, softly-lit pink bedroom at Ormiston Court ... my embarrassment as she'd stripped off and pulled herself into the fabulous airforce blue dress ... with me pulling the hooks and eyes together at the back ... she'd pulled off the cami-knickers over her head ... 'She didn't have a scar.'

. . . .

Alan had got home before me.

'We have to see Pauline, we have to get hold of her somehow. We have to find out what it means.'

'But does it help Colin?' he said. 'It's all becoming so confusing now. Julius says they probably will be able to introduce the fact that Gwen was murdered in the same way, even though the Brighton police are sticking to the idea that her murderer copied the idea. Then there's Joan Mainwaring and whether she lied. And now – this. I just don't understand what it means.'

'That's why we need to talk to Pauline.'

'And then there's Colin's letter.'

We were lying in bed. Alan had been very low since the letter, and now he didn't want to make love, but lay stoically with one arm round my shoulder, holding me curled up against him. Colin hadn't been straight with him, hadn't told him the truth. It should have made him feel less guilty for having cut his friend out of the film contract, but somehow it didn't. He just felt bitter. 'If he thought that was the right thing to do,' he said over and over, 'I'd have understood, I wouldn't have told a soul. After all, the Russians were our allies.' But the truth was, he didn't understand. 'It's one thing to be a socialist, but it's quite another to go along with Soviet foreign policy.'

'Don't let's talk about that any more,' I whispered. 'You just have to accept that's what happened. You still want to get him off, don't you – so we have to see Pauline. There has to be something more we don't know about.'

· · · · · · · · ·

Stan gave me her address, and a telephone number too, which was better. It was odd to hear that unattractive, twangy voice again. Alan told me not to risk going to her flat, so we arranged to meet by the Brighton clock tower. I had to go alone; Alan had had so much time off work, he simply couldn't risk taking any more.

Brighton was chilly and misty that day. Pauline was late and I'd almost decided she wasn't coming, when I saw her making her way towards me, head down, her face half hidden by the peaked cap of one of those military-style hats that had been fashionable in the war.

'We'll go to Hanningtons,' she said. 'They have a nice restaurant.' And we walked down the road side by side in awkward silence. Pauline seemed to have aged, to be different from the Pauline I remembered. We reached the department store and she led me to the tearoom. She looked round furtively as she sat down, taking in the solitary man at the next table, eating baked beans on toast, and the two young women eating iced cakes further along.

'So what is it you want to know? What have you got all excited about? Still trying to get your Bolshie friend out of trouble?'

She didn't like it when I told her I'd found the Dalí. She seemed to freeze and sat in silence, smoking and smoking. I noticed how nicotine-stained her fingers were. I didn't remember her smoking that much. Eventually: 'You've got the painting. I could kill Beatrice Lomas. She wouldn't let me back in the flat. She had a spare key and I told her I'd left some things there, but she wouldn't. She never liked me. It was to get the painting. I knew where Gwen had hidden it. There were always different places she'd hide it. There was a special cupboard at Ormiston Court. I thought the dress was a rotten idea. And I told her often enough she ought to get rid of it altogether. Destroy it. It brought bad luck to everyone. And it'll bring bad luck to you.' She put her face close to mine. 'Have you just come down here to taunt me?' She smelled of clothes that had been lying in drawers for too long, a musty smell.

I flinched back from her. 'Taunt you? Why should I? I'd no idea it meant so much to you. I just wanted to know about the scar. I've no idea if it'll help Colin or not, but we do have to know what it means. Did Gwendolen have plastic surgery or something?'

'You don't *have* to know anything, do you. I don't have to tell you anything.'

'*Please*. Whatever it is, it can't hurt Gwendolen now.'

She still had said nothing when the waitress came to take our order. It wasn't until I was pouring tea that she said abruptly: 'If you let me have the painting. If you promise me that.'

'*I* haven't got it. It's in an art gallery, Valentines. I work there now.' Then, seeing her bleak, closed-up face, I said desperately: 'But I can get it for you somehow. I'll – I'll tell Noel Gwen left a will, that it was her bequest to you. I'll think of something. You can get it tomorrow. I promise. Come there tomorrow and I'll make sure you get it.'

'Promises! So easily broken, aren't they.' But I could see she was cracking. She *wanted* to tell me. I knew she did. 'As you say, Gwen's gone now. So it doesn't really matter.'

She leaned forward, too close to me again. 'It's quite a story, is Gwen's. When I first met her I was working in a hospital on the south coast. 1940. I was a staff nurse. She was an orderly. Strange girl, so cold and unfriendly. Yet so strikingly beautiful. It made such an odd impression. No one liked her, specially not the women. The men all tried it on, but she wasn't interested. Cold as a fish. I was intrigued; I sensed that underneath she was different. Tremendous repressed anger underneath the exterior somewhere ... rage. She took no more notice of me than of anyone else, but I was determined to *make* her like me. And little by little I wormed my way in and she told me all about her family.

'They ran a boarding house in Broadstairs – which was where we were, the hospital, that is. She hated them, her mother specially. She was a cold, hard woman, Gwendolen said, she got no love, she was more or less just a skivvy. Kept off school half the time, beaten if she didn't do as she was told. But then the war came, and she was called up for war work. At last she could escape! She said she was leaving home. Her mother flew into a rage and among all the insults she turned around and told her she wasn't their daughter at all.

'The story was that sometime not long after the end of the First World War this feckless, rackety couple had come to stay. The woman was expecting. Well, when she came back from the hospital, she had twins. She'd had not the faintest idea. They'd pulled one out and then the midwife said, my God, I think there's another one!

'Two babies were simply more than they could cope with. The landlady had no children of her own and she offered to foster one of them. Or was persuaded to, more likely. There was supposed to be some financial arrangement, but the couple moved on with the other little girl, said they'd come back. Of course, they didn't. Never paid her a penny.

'So you see, Gwendolen felt she'd been cheated. At least her real parents had had a bit of class. She was determined to track them down. She got this job in the hospital, long hours, hard work, rotten pay – joining the forces, going up to London, all that was out of the question, because every bit of her free time had to be spent trying to track down her parents. No luck. Then, just when she'd more or less given up hope, the other twin contacted *her*.

'I've called her Gwendolen, but she wasn't called Gwendolen then, in the hospital. Her name was Hilda. It was the twin whose name was Gwendolen.

'Gwendolen was in a bad way. She'd had a child very young – possibly even under age. She was still only twenty when she turned up; well, so was Hilda, of course. The father of the child – that was Titus Mavor – had deserted Gwen. Her parents were dead, but before she'd died her mother had told her she had a twin, and given her the address of the boarding house, so she went there and they knew where Hilda was working.

'Gwendolen's little girl had gone away to the country – evacuated out of London to stay with Titus's family. But somehow or other Gwendolen still had her ration book, don't ask me how, I expect she said she'd lost it and got a replacement, people got up to all sorts of dodges like that during the war, didn't they. She was still the mother of a child under five years old, so she was exempt from the call-up. Not that it did her any good. She was sinking into drink, hanging out with a few scruffy types around Chelsea and Soho.

'Hilda promised to help her. But then, just when they were going to start a new life together, Gwendolen was killed in an air raid. Direct hit on her lodgings. So Hilda took over her sister's identity.'

Pauline glanced at me. I think she wanted to gauge the dramatic effect of her tale.

'Seems pretty cold-blooded,' I said. Actually I could hardly take it all in.

Pauline grimaced. 'You have to understand; she'd led this terrible life. And it wasn't as difficult as you might think. People went missing in the war all the time, didn't they, unidentified bodies, all sorts of things. You could hardly blame her. Because you see, now Hilda was not only Gwendolen, but she was officially a mother. She didn't have to work as an orderly any more. She had a way into a different world, the artistic types Gwendolen had known. She hung around Soho, made a few contacts, eventually managed to get a job as a film extra ... She always said she couldn't act, but she must have been a good actress to pull the wool over so many people's eyes, being such a different sort of person, so different from the real Gwendolen, who was a pathetic little thing.

'You'd have thought she'd want to get rid of me, as well, wouldn't you. I was all part of that past life she'd hated. But I hung on; and actually she needed me. I was the only real thing in her life. I was the link to the past, the one person with whom she could still be herself, could still be Hilda. We knew too much about each other too. You could call it parity of terror, I suppose,' Pauline sneered. 'She knew I did abortions. I knew about her past. I knew what she'd done – but then, it wasn't so terrible. It wasn't as if ... I mean,

Gwendolen, the real Gwendolen was dead anyway. What did it matter?

'It was only when Titus Mavor appeared on the scene that things got awkward. He wasn't so far gone he didn't guess the truth. He saw her at a party, and of course she didn't recognise him, had no idea who he was. He knew about the twin, though. He must have done. You can see from the painting that Dalí knew, otherwise why paint her in the mirror.'

'Yes,' I said, 'Mirrors – doubles – twins. The Surrealists loved that sort of thing.'

'Titus started to blackmail her. She got Stanley to pay him off. She was terrified Radu would get to know, but what terrified her most of all was that it would come out she had a child, an illegitimate baby. Kiss of death, a scandal like that for an actress. And the funny thing was, it wasn't even her child. Ironic, in a way.

'It began to prey on her mind more and more. She became obsessed with the idea that Titus would in the end tell Radu. There was the plan of them working together; Titus was always so drunk – look how he spilled the beans about Colin. Gwendolen knew it would be bound to come out. And she knew Titus had the proof, or almost proof. He had the painting, and in the painting Gwendolen has an appendicitis scar. That scar was Gwendolen's. Hilda didn't have one. But Hilda knew about the painting. The real Gwendolen had told her, when they first met. She was so upset because Titus just took it, when rightfully it belonged to her. Dalí had given it to her.'

'Hang on,' I interrupted. 'A painting can't really prove anything. She could have said he just put it there, artistic licence.'

'Gwendolen – Hilda that was – wasn't bright enough to think of anything like that. Anyway she *felt* it revealed what she'd done. She was more and more obsessed with the painting. More and more frightened of Titus. She went round to Mecklenburgh Square to get the painting from him. She was determined to make him give it to her, you see. There was a quarrel and ... well ... '

'The chloroform – it must have been premeditated.'

Pauline's sallow cheeks reddened. She even looked slightly uncomfortable.

I was incredulous – so incredulous I could hardly feel angry. 'You can actually sit here and tell me Gwendolen did *that*, and you and she just *kept quiet* all through the trial. That's incredible.'

'It wasn't as if Titus suffered. I had chloroform from the hospital, you see. I used it sometimes myself, when girls were in a lot of pain. And once Gwen got the painting back she felt safe.'

'But you'd let Colin *hang*!'

Her gaze did falter then. 'I didn't care,' she muttered at last. 'I really didn't care. So many people had died in the war. What did one more matter? The only thing that mattered to me was that Gwendolen should be safe. I thought she had to be looked after. I didn't give a fig what happened to your friend. I couldn't have cared less. What mattered was Hilda – Gwendolen. And her, well, I don't think she quite realised what she'd done. She had such a capacity for cutting off from things. She sort of forgot she'd done it. She put it away, out of sight.'

I clenched my hands under the table. 'Why are you telling me this now? You'll have to give a statement. You have to go to the solicitors tomorrow.'

Pauline just smiled. 'I don't have to do anything.'

'You do. You do! Otherwise why tell us now?' But I knew why. She was *enjoying* it.

'I was jealous, you know. Gwendolen liked *you*. Always giving you things. That day you went down to the country with Stan – it was she who insisted on taking you along. Not me! I wanted to go, but she had to take you. She didn't really care about Radu. A woman has to have a man, but – '

'But when he left she tried to kill herself!'

'Oh, that was all an act,' said Pauline. 'To make sure Stanley came up to the mark.'

I was desperate; and angry. 'Pauline – I'll see you get the painting, but only if you give a proper statement to the lawyers. You have to tell them. Before it's too late.'

Her face was distorted with spite. 'You're changing the rules. You said you'd get me the portrait if I told you the truth. Now you're saying I have to tell some sodding lawyer.'

'Well, that's how it is, Pauline. You make a statement and I'll get you the portrait. Do it tomorrow. Go to London. Go to Abrahams. I'll tell them to expect you.'

I couldn't bear to be near her any longer. I rushed from the tearoom, forgetting I hadn't paid, and coming out into the street I didn't know which way to go to get back to the station. In a few moments I was on the Front. I stopped by the pier, shaking, and gazed out to sea, trying to calm down. The tide was out. The foam licked the shore with a faint hush and sigh as the waves expired along the beach.

Had I done the right thing? Would she make a statement? The whole story was so unbelievable – something that could only have happened during the war. Did I even believe any of it? Had Pauline herself killed Titus, perhaps? There were things that didn't make sense. How had 'Hilda' known, for example, that her twin would be killed in an air raid? How had she got hold of her documents, from a house that had been blown to smithereens? And who had killed Gwen? The chloroform – suffocation – the same method: Gwendolen couldn't have suffocated herself.

It was cold. I shivered. I had to get back to London. I hurried back into the town and found the right road and as I almost ran up the street to the station, I had an unmistakable feeling of being in danger, that danger was very close at hand.

twenty-eight

■■■■■■■■

ALAN WENT STRAIGHT ROUND to Julius Abrahams the next day. We assumed Pauline would go there. I'd given her the address. We didn't think it through. There was an awful possibility we managed to block out. We just believed that in the end she couldn't let an innocent man be hanged for a crime he hadn't committed when she knew the truth and could name the guilty person.

Noel was out of London and Kay was off sick with flu, so I had to be at the gallery. Again, we didn't think. The sense of danger I'd had the evening before had faded. I was anxious only about Colin now.

It was hard to concentrate on my work, but I did my best and one or two visitors turned up at the gallery, which took my mind off things. I was on tenterhooks all the time in the hope of Alan telephoning with good news. The phone did ring, but it was never him.

I became more and more tense. The silence of the office became oppressive. I sat downstairs at Kay's desk and tried to read a book, but I was restless and fidgety. I thought of locking up for the day and going home, but I stayed, because by now Pauline must have seen Julius. Alan would soon ring me, or perhaps even come to the gallery.

· · · · · · · · ·

But it was Pauline who came. She stood in the middle of the room and glanced round at the white walls with their two modern paintings. 'Where's the portrait?'

'Upstairs,' I said, automatically, 'but what happened at the lawyers?'

She gazed at me blankly as if she didn't know what I was talking about.

'Have you been to the lawyers, Pauline?'

She shook her head. 'I need to have the portrait.'

'You must go, Pauline. There's so little time. Please. The appeal's next week. I'll go with you. We'll take a taxi.'

'I've come for the portrait. I have to have it back. You shouldn't have stolen it.'

'I didn't *steal* it. And it's quite safe here. It's more important to –'

'I made a mistake. I shouldn't have told you anything. You shouldn't have come to see me.'

'You did the right thing. It was the right thing to do.'

I was pinned behind the desk. She stood between me and the door. I could telephone Alan, but I didn't know where he was. I could telephone Julius. But Pauline was talking.

'Why don't you understand? I don't care about that Communist, Colin Harris. I don't give a fig. I didn't want to see you. I was in two minds about that. But then when I did see you, I decided I wanted *someone* to know the truth about Gwen. I wanted you to know how I stood by her, I held her hand, I kept all her secrets. I kept her going. She wouldn't have survived without me. But was she grateful? It turned out in the end she didn't give a damn about me. Once she got Stanley, she thought she could get rid of me like a worn-out garment. She didn't lift a finger when Stan kicked me out. She could have stopped him, but she didn't. She thought she was safe once Colin was convicted. So I went back to see her. We had a row. She laughed at me.'

I stood up. I spoke as calmly as I could. 'If you tell the lawyers she murdered Titus, you'll have your revenge, won't you. Everyone will know her for what she was.'

'I just want the portrait.'

I said: 'If you have it, will you make a statement to the lawyers then?'

Pauline stared at me. I thought she was wavering. She was looking round frantically, her hands squeezing her bag. 'Where is it? You haven't got it. You're lying aren't you?' She was agitated now.

'It's in Noel's office. I'll bring it down for you.' I started up the stairs. But how stupid not to think she'd follow me. I looked back and there she was. 'Wait downstairs.' I was really frightened now. She kept on coming up behind me. I climbed faster. I stopped on the landing. Noel's door was shut. 'It's in here. Wait here while I fetch it.' I opened the door. For some reason she did as I said, stood twitching and fidgeting at the turn of the stairs.

The canvas was no longer where I'd last seen it, spread out on Noel's desk. I would be surprised if he'd rolled it up again, thus damaging it further, so where could he have put it? He *must* have rolled it up. I looked in the filing cabinet, the cupboard. It wasn't there. It wasn't anywhere.

She was in the doorway. 'It's not here, is it? You've lied to me.'

'It must be here somewhere.' My voice sounded trembly. She must know I was frightened. That wouldn't do.

I heard the door open downstairs. 'Dinah!' It was Alan. Thank God.

'I'm up here,' I shouted, 'with Pauline.' As I spoke I was wrenching open the door of a second cupboard, and there the canvas was. I brought it out. 'Here,' I said, 'take it.'

Alan's footsteps on the stairs; she looked round and at that point she must have panicked, for instead of trying to get past him, down to the gallery and out of the door, she started up the stairs to the second floor.

'There's no way out up there,' I cried. I heard her running on up. Alan rushed past me to follow her and I followed him.

She went right to the top of the house and out onto the roof. She made for the fire escape.

'It's not safe,' I shouted, but she was going too fast to see how it ended in nothingness, threw up her arms, releasing the painting. There was an astonished scream as she plunged downwards. The canvas twisted after her. She hit the stagnant black lagoon at the bottom of the bomb-site. We stared down.

· · · · · · · · ·

Alan phoned for the police. They took a long time to come, and when they came they questioned us for hours. They left at last and Alan put his arm round me. 'I'm proud of you. You were really brave.'

He told me he'd waited at Abrahams's office. Julius, he said, had been certain Pauline wouldn't turn up. He'd been in communication with the Brighton police again, who'd suspected her for a while and were about to charge her with Gwendolen's murder. 'We were afraid that if Pauline came to London at all, she'd go to the gallery. We should have called you – come round sooner – but he had a lot to tell me. And then Radu phoned him as well.'

'Radu?'

'I'm meeting him. You might as well come too. He wants to explain things. That's why he telephoned Julius. He wanted to make it quite clear he had nothing to do with the murder – either of the murders.'

Radu's hotel was not far from the gallery, a quiet, small, grand hotel in Mayfair. We sat in the hush of the lounge and once Radu started talking, I thought he would never stop. He told us about his country with its beautiful lakes and mountains. He described the pre-war sophistication of Bucharest, and how that had been destroyed first by its fascist factions, then by the arrival of the Red Army. He didn't remember ever seeing Colin in the capital, but he'd heard that the British secret services began to try to re-establish a foothold there after Romania was out of the war. For his part he was quite simply afraid of the Russians, he just wanted to get away.

'I want you to know – please believe me – I knew nothing of what was between Gwendolen and Titus.'

He had realised Gwendolen didn't want Titus involved in the film. But he needed Titus. 'It was not just for his contribution. I soon realised he was too far gone for that. But I heard he had these valuable works of art,' said Radu. 'My friend Mercier in Paris, he begged me to persuade Titus to part with them. He said if that happened, he'd part-finance the film, he'd give me some backing. So I more or less bullied Titus into parting with the Ernst and the Miró. He insisted he didn't have the Dalí any more, although he did. I suppose he dimly realised it wasn't a good idea to let me see it – as it was Gwendolen's portrait. But I got the others. Just in time – he was murdered soon after, but I was still able of course to make the deal with Mercier. So the film went on – I worked on it all those months, and all the time Gwendolen behaved stranger and stranger. After it was finished, I knew I had to get away.'

I watched him. Yes, he was vivacious and charming, but his lips were too full and his hair too wavy and his eyes too large. His animal magnetism no longer worked on me. He was just another continental Romeo. How could I have fallen for it! I liked him well enough, but ... that was all.

'I am sad Gwendolen has died in this horrible way. But they were *mad*, the two of them, those two women. And it almost drove me mad to be living with them all that time.'

He smiled, laughed, opened his arms. 'Now – is it bad to say this? – I am free. I have so much opportunity in Hollywood – perhaps you join me. What about it, Alan? You know I have said California is such a terrible place. But it is also beautiful, in its own way. Such a strangely unreal landscape, it's a kind of sweet surrealist nightmare, and yet it fascinates me in a way. Besides, it is the land of the future. Europe is finished, you know. And it is the land of film.'

I thought of our whole life changing. No more dark winters, only the land of sunshine; no more scruffy socialist bohemians, only the blank-faced hedonists of the Pacific coast; it was a mad, seductive dream.

I smiled foolishly and looked at Alan. He shook his head. 'The land of dreams,' he said, 'sounds wonderful, but I think we'll stick to reality.'

twenty-nine

□□□□□□□□□

THE DAY BEFORE COLIN'S APPEAL we were back at the Abrahams office. I hoped this would be our last visit. Julius and Naomi were both there.

'I'll just go through it with you,' said Julius, 'so that you're completely in the picture. Dinah – your going to see Pauline was very important, it's put a different slant on everything. But let's deal with Joan Mainwaring's evidence first. I think she was being perfectly truthful when she says she saw Colin. She may be confused as to which evening it was, but the police are ultimately responsible for that confusion too. Dinah – the night you went round and discovered the body, it had stopped snowing.' I nodded. 'The previous night there'd been a blizzard. Mainwaring says it was snowing, so it was the evening *before*. But the police were convinced Mavor died the evening you found him, Dinah. Owing to their own bungling they weren't willing to consider an earlier time of death. But, if you think about it, he was cold when you found him. He must have been killed earlier that day – even perhaps the evening before. You understand what I'm saying?

'What is more – but this is only, absolutely *entre nous* and you can be sure it's not part of the appeal case – Colin has now admitted that she was right. *She actually saw him because he was there.* At the last conference we had with him in private he finally told us he did go round to Mecklenburgh Square. He wanted to have it out with Titus – not kill him, of course, just have it out. No one answered when he knocked, but he gained access to the house the same way you did; the door didn't shut properly. Titus wasn't there. Must have been out in spite of the weather, or more likely staying with some girl and never came home. God knows what prompted Colin out on such a terrible night, but he said he'd worked himself up into a state about it. It had become an obsession.

'So Joan Mainwaring's evidence isn't a lie; it's just part of the confusion around the time of death. And we're going to go for that. We're going to argue that the police were completely incompetent and had no real idea when he'd died, or anyway, he couldn't have been killed at the time they thought he was. And then your evidence, Dinah, backs that up.

'Your account of what Pauline told you – Gwendolen Grey's confession at second-hand, as it were – isn't admissible evidence. On the other hand Gwendolen was murdered in the same way as Titus – and the very *fact* of Gwendolen's death muddies the waters because Colin can't possibly have murdered *her*. Finally, you told me, Dinah, about Dr Carstairs.'

'Did I?' I said. 'I'd quite forgotten.'

'I told you,' said Alan.

'Naomi went to see him, and he's made a statement.' Naomi leaned forward and turned over the papers on the desk. 'He seemed a kindly sort of man,' she said, 'but he blamed himself ...' She hesitated. 'This is more background than anything, but it all adds to the picture.' She began to read.

'"It is the case that both Hilda Howard and Pauline

Goodman were at St Swithins Asylum, Broadstairs, when I was appointed consultant there in 1940. It was my first consultant's post. However, neither of them was employed there. Hilda Howard was a patient, not an orderly. She was there because she'd tried to kill her mother. She was brought up by a foster mother, but was not told this until shortly before the attack. The foster mother felt that might have been the reason for the antagonism. Hilda had attacked her with a knife. The foster mother was lucky to survive.

'"Pauline Goodman had been a nurse, but she had suffered a mental breakdown. She, too, was a patient, which she found very difficult. She was always trying to act as though she were still a nurse. She would take fellow patients under her wing and try to develop a quasi-professional relationship. But it went further with Hilda than anyone else. Hilda had been in a locked ward to begin with, but she responded well to the regime. She calmed down and was moved to an open ward, gained some privileges, seemed to be making great strides. We organised occasional games of tennis and she even played in one or two of those.

'"But Pauline Goodman tried to gain an ascendancy over her, just as she had with several patients before. She became possessive; we had to separate them. Looking back, I can see it was a kind of *folie à deux* – that is, when a sane person becomes fatally involved in the delusions of someone deranged. Although that's not really the right term, since in this case neither of them was really sane.

'"They went missing, the two of them. We were very short-staffed – with hundreds of patients and soon matters were chaotic with Dunkirk and then the Blitz, so we can perhaps be forgiven for their having managed to abscond. If it hadn't been for the war, we would have made every effort to trace them. As it was, we reported matters to the police, and after that they got more or less forgotten. That was a dereliction of duty. When I saw Gwendolen Grey – Hilda Howard, as I thought, I assumed Gwendolen Grey was her stage name – at the dance, I again pondered what I should do. But after worrying about it for some time I decided that after so long, it was acceptable to leave things as they were."' Naomi stopped reading and looked at us. 'That's all,' she said, 'but it does make things clearer.'

'The last piece of the jigsaw,' I murmured. Yet nothing in life was as simple as a jigsaw, with one right answer for everything and everything slotting into place.

· · · · · · · · ·

Flashlights exploding – the journalists jostling at the foot of the steps – the statement Naomi read out: a flickering newsreel scene to be plastered all over the headlines the following day. Colin's conviction was quashed. The appeal was a sensation. Our grey austerity world created an audience ravenous for scandal, and the crowd that would have rushed the prison gates for the notice of Colin's hanging was now ready to cheer the Houdini who'd escaped a wrongful conviction.

Colin was free; justice had been done. It wasn't only that Julius had cast more doubt on the police assessment of the time of death. Whatever the legal niceties, he'd managed cunningly to bring Gwendolen and Pauline to the centre of the picture in such a way as to undermine the evidence against Colin. In the appeal court there were no smears about Colin's politics. The entire police case against him looked shakier and shakier until at last it collapsed under the weight of its own contradictions. In a way I too was exonerated – but the most important thing was Colin was free.

Yet in fact he was not quite free. The following day the

papers were full of barbed innuendoes. Somehow it wasn't enough that he'd been wrongfully convicted, some even queried whether justice in the wider sense *had* been done. They dragged up all the political stuff from the original trial again, hinting at what he might have been up to in the war, suggesting that at best he'd been a confused fellow traveller, at worst a fifth columnist or stooge of the Soviets and diehard Red. That was the trouble, I rapidly learned, some of the mud always sticks.

I'd believed you were innocent until proved guilty. To be acquitted on appeal was to have your name cleared. Now these illusions were shattered. How naïve I was. Still, I'd rather be naïve than cynical. World-weariness was the biggest bore. And I – we – Alan and I – still believed in him.

We'd expected him to come with us right after his release for a first celebratory drink, but he said he needed some time on his own. There was to be a celebration the following evening in any case.

We gathered in a rather anonymous hotel in Bloomsbury. Alan and I got there first and loitered at the bar with the next arrival, Naomi. The euphoria of the day before had evaporated and we felt rather flat.

We waited a little anxiously for more friends to turn up: Noel; Alan's BBC friends; some of the old Wheatsheaf crowd – they'd all promised to be there; Hugh and Radu – maybe; possibly a few of Colin's CP comrades. And of course the man of the hour himself: Colin. He should have been there from the start.

The first guest startled us: Colin's mother. None of us had ever met this stalwart elderly woman who wore a once-smart black coat, as though she were in mourning – although of course no one wore mourning any more. Alan valiantly bought her an orange squash and tried to make conversation.

Actually, she was quite talkative. Impossible, she explained, to come to London during the trial, as she'd been nursing her eighty-year-old mother. Alan's face assumed a mournful expression in anticipation of the old lady's death, but in fact she'd recovered.

Jock Bunnage, Colin's branch secretary, turned up, looking uncomfortable, then a few Charlotte Street regulars; Noel and a friend from the Courtauld Institute came along.

Finally, Colin arrived with Julius, plus a reporter from the *Daily Worker*. We all had a drink and raised our glasses to Colin.

Yet everyone was ill at ease. There was a peculiar absence of rejoicing. Alan bustled around Colin trying to get a smile out of him, but after the months in prison he looked haggard rather than elated.

I watched the entrance in case Hugh and Radu turned up. Eventually Hugh peered self-consciously round the door and sidled in.

Alan made a speech. Somehow he came across as overbearing as he clumsily tried to inject some vitality into the proceedings.

I watched him. I'd hardly known him when we married. Passion had blinded me to our differences in temperament, but now I saw his faults so clearly. And now too there was the ever-present shadow of his anger. He hadn't hit me again, but I feared his temper. I hadn't forgotten; it hadn't gone away. And although he thought I'd been plucky and smart over Pauline, at heart he had such old-fashioned ideas about women.

Still, we were married now for better or worse and I was determined to carve out an independent place for myself within that marriage. It would be difficult to resist as he tried to push me into a narrower role as His Wife. Now he was settled at the BBC he was edging away from our bohemian existence and wanted something more orderly. Soon, I knew, he'd decide it was time to have children. I wanted children too, but however difficult it might be, I refused to turn into my mother. I had to have some separate life as well.

So I watched him rather critically as he lurched red-faced through his speech. Yet as he stumbled on, my heart softened. For there was also his honesty. He was more honest, more honourable than the others. Hugh, Dr Carstairs, Radu, Noel, even Stan – had temporised and done what was easiest; Alan had stood by Colin, never wavered.

I too, after all, had been foolish. I saw that, now that I'd given up the silly Hollywood dream Radu had indulged me in. As if every girl didn't want to be an actress! It was a clichéd adolescent dream. Noel had nurtured in me a new and more realistic interest in art. Before Alan had squashed the frail beginnings of conviviality with his clodhopper speech, Noel's Courtauld Institute friend had been telling me about the courses you could do there. You should enrol, he'd said, the director, Anthony Blunt, is inspirational. If I trained there I wouldn't be just a secretary; I'd be a specialist. I'd work my way up from being Noel's assistant. One day I might even manage a gallery myself; or publish art books, or a magazine.

Alan ground to a halt. There was an awkward silence. Everyone looked at Colin, expecting him to reply. He was standing near Hugh. Both were scowling. Then Hugh said – lightly, but it was so venomous – 'A few words, don't you think, Colin? Aren't you going to thank British justice, even if you work for a system that doesn't have any?'

That was uncalled for! Why had he had to say *that*! There was a horrid silence. The audience, like clusters of statues, stared in mute embarrassment. The tableau was a momentary caricature of some religious painting with Colin at the centre, his mother on one side in supplication, like the Virgin Mary, an awkward band of disciples – Jock Bunnage, Julius, the *Daily Worker* reporter – huddled on the other, while Naomi stood apart like the Angel Gabriel. And Hugh – well, Judas Iscariot or Saint Peter, he was accuser and betrayer all in one.

Then Colin stepped forward, out of the picture. His face looked bonier than ever. He said quietly: 'I do indeed owe thanks to my legal team. Naomi and Julius have done more for me than I could ever have possibly asked or imagined. My friend Alan Wentworth has done even more. They all kept me hoping when there wasn't any. What I've been through this last year I can't begin to describe and I don't even want to. And yes, British justice has been vindicated – just about. But remember that British justice will only ever be as good as this rotten system we live under lets it be. Whatever the gutter press says about me and however many fair-weather fellow travellers find it all too much of an effort, the important thing for me is to go on struggling for international socialism. And that's what I intend to do.' And he turned and walked out of the bar.

Alan ran after him, but he soon came back, out of breath and dishevelled. Hugh made himself scarce. Noel escorted Colin's mother to a taxi. The guests dribbled away. Soon there were just the four of us; Alan, Julius, Naomi and me.

'Venomous chap, your friend Palmer-Green,' said Julius. 'Just as well he's going back to Hollywood.'

'He probably didn't even mean any harm.' Alan was deeply dejected. 'It's just gossip to him, that's all.'

'But it isn't gossip, is it?' Julius looked at Alan. His expression hardly changed, yet it conveyed his immense appreciation of human folly. 'You do see why the Party couldn't support him – certainly not openly.'

Involuntarily I put my hand to my mouth. What was he

saying? That Colin was ... what? That he was really working for the Russians? Now? Still?

I looked at Alan's stonily downcast face. 'He never said anything to me. I don't mind what he does. I just wish he'd told me.'

'A friend of mine came across Colin in Spain,' said Naomi. 'He said he thought the war suited Colin rather too well. Colin was in his element out there. That's what he said, anyway. And you know I think there are some chaps who just find normality too dull. Like those French resistance types, some of them haven't been able to cope with peacetime, or so you hear – turned to revenge attacks on collaborators, even got into gangsterism and crime.'

'I think it's more he felt guilty,' said Alan slowly, 'guilty for being what he is, for being a queer, that he might not be quite a man and so he had to be braver, take more risks, in order to prove that he is.'

The four of us sat there in silence. Alan was holding my hand very hard. 'Let's drink to him anyway,' he said. 'I'll always think of him as my friend.'

epilogue

□■■■■■■■□

AFTERWARDS YOU RETCHED WITH LAUGHTER. The sound ripped through the stagnant air. Then silence seeped back, stifling. Solitude; a moment before, there'd been two of you, but now you were alone.

It had been more difficult than you'd expected. It had been so intimate. You'd had to *embrace* the unconscious body, the body that was so like yours. You'd had to lean over your spitting image, you'd had to touch, to *minister* to it as though you were saving, not ending a life. The chloroform first; you came round behind her and took her by surprise. Then you pressed and pressed until you thought your arms would give way and the breath would burst from your lungs. *You* were the one gasping for air. It was hand-to-hand combat with a primitive force, a blind, unthinking will to live, distinct from the shell that housed it, a force that fought and struggled and clung to that body as you crushed the life out of it.

At last it gave up the ghost and left its inert and cloddish house of flesh just lying there stupidly. You staggered back. Who was it laughing and laughing? You'd killed yourself too, that was what was so *great*. You were *reborn*. With a different name and a different destiny. You weren't a working-class skivvy any more; you were a *lady*.

Who was it standing there, turned to stone?

But you had to get on. There was still so much to do. You shook yourself back into life. You rearranged the body so that it looked less peculiar, more *natural*. You found a half-empty bottle of brandy on the floor and poured it around in the hope of disguising the smell of chloroform. All the while you hurried, because you had to find what you'd come for, the things you needed so desperately, the documents and the painting, above all the painting. You wished now you'd talked more beforehand. There was so much you didn't know.

Too late for talk now. You searched everywhere, in cupboards, in boxes and cases and drawers. You hadn't expected so much *stuff*, it took much longer than you'd thought. And you hadn't expected to be so clumsy, and as you dropped things and tripped on the rubbish you were terrified someone would hear. The place was empty, but you kept stopping to listen for the sound of a key in the lock, for voices, a footstep on the stair.

Finally when you'd almost given up hope, you found what you were looking for – but only part of it. The identity card and the ration book and the rest of it were all in a box at the back of the cupboard. So that was all right. You took hers and left yours. But one thing was missing, the most important thing of all: the painting *wasn't there*. And then you remembered. Of course it wasn't there. She'd told you. The painter had taken it, the faithless lover, he'd taken the painting as well.

You dare not look any longer. You had to get away. You clicked the door shut, crept down the stairs and stepped out into the freezing afternoon. It would soon be getting dark. You pulled your hat down and hurried away, but not walking too quickly, trying to look casual and ordinary.

From now on, you'd listen to the wireless and buy a paper every day. Of course, it might not make the national news. Not that it mattered; there were corpses everywhere in wartime. There was nothing to worry about anyway, nothing to connect you to that room and its sightless body, nothing, that is, but the very thing that gave you perfect protection: that you were her double.

Then you had a huge piece of luck, your first real lucky break – after all those years of being the unlucky one. It was in the news all right, the very next morning, but for a very different reason. Another air raid; there were raids every night, bombs all over London. The Blitz and the blackout had obliterated what you'd done. It was as if it had never happened. You laughed and laughed again as the irony of it sank in. It must have been *meant*. She'd have died anyway. The whole house was flattened. So now there was only the future. Your new life, your *real* life, the one you'd so nearly been cheated of, could begin.

You walked on as twilight fell.

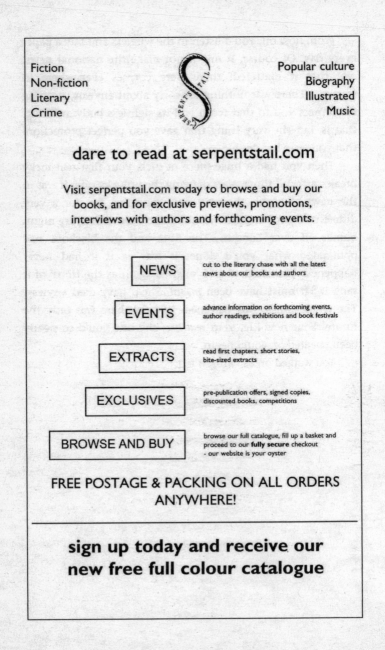